BETTER MOUSETRAPS

BETTER MOUSETRAPS

THE BEST MYSTERY
STORIES OF JOHN LUTZ

MOUSETRAPS

JOHN
LUTZ

EDITED BY
FRANCIS M. NEVINS, JR.

ST. MARTIN'S PRESS
New York

THE OTHER RUNNER (*Ellery Queen's Mystery Magazine,* October 1978); THE WOUNDED TIGER (*Signature,* November 1967); THE REAL SHAPE OF THE COAST (*Ellery Queen's Mystery Magazine,* June 1971); HIGH STAKES (*The Saint Mystery Magazine,* June 1984); BURIED TREASURE (*Alfred Hitchcock's Mystery Magazine,* August 1982); THE EXPLOSIVES EXPERT (*Alfred Hitchcock's Mystery Magazine,* September 1967); BIG GAME (*Signature,* August 1967); IN MEMORY OF . . . (*Alfred Hitchcock's Mystery Magazine,* January 1972); HAND OF FATE (*Alfred Hitchcock's Mystery Magazine,* July 1969); THE SECOND SHOT (*Ellery Queen's Mystery Magazine,* September 1984); THE SHOOTING OF CURLY DAN (*Ellery Queen's Mystery Magazine,* August 1973); THE DAY OF THE PICNIC (*Alfred Hitchcock's Mystery Magazine,* October 1971); MORTAL COMBAT (*Ellery Queen's Mystery Magazine,* January 1981); SOMETHING FOR THE DARK (*Alfred Hitchcock's Mystery Magazine,* November 1977); THE INSOMNIACS CLUB (*Ellery Queen's Mystery Magazine,* September 1968); THE MUSIC FROM DOWNSTAIRS (*Alfred Hitchcock's Mystery Magazine,* March 1979); THE LANDSCAPE OF DREAMS (*Ellery Queen's Mystery Magazine,* March 1982); UNTIL YOU ARE DEAD (*Alfred Hitchcock's Mystery Magazine,* January 1980); SOMETHING LIKE MURDER (*Ellery Queen's Mystery Magazine,* January 1978); TRICKLE DOWN (*Alfred Hitchcock's Mystery Magazine,* October 1985); DEAR DORIE (*Alfred Hitchcock's*

(Credits continued on page 347.)

Design by Jaya Dayal

Library of Congress Cataloging-in-Publication Data

Lutz, John, 1939–
   Better mousetraps: the best mystery stories of John Lutz / by John Lutz; edited by Francis M. Nevins, Jr.
     p. cm.
   "A Thomas Dunne book."
   ISBN 0-312-01389-2 : $18.95
   1. Detective and mystery stories, American. I. Nevins, Francis M. II. Title.
   PS3562.U854A6 1988
   813'.54--dc19   87-29930
                                                     CIP

First Edition
10 9 8 7 6 5 4 3 2 1

For Emma

CONTENTS

vii

INTRODUCTION

by FRANCIS M. NEVINS, JR.

F unny thing about the publishing business. Dozens of
Americans have started out in mystery fiction by
writing short stories of crime and suspense for maga-
zines. The prolific may turn out hundreds, the painstak-
ing a couple of dozen. The most talented of these writers
develop huge reputations as tale-spinners and see their
work reprinted regularly in mystery anthologies. But
until and unless they also become known as the authors
of mystery novels, the probability that any publishing
house will be interested in a collection of their short stories is about as high as the probability that it will start
handing out free copies of its best-sellers in Grand Central Station at rush hour. Who has seen a collection of
the best stories of Jack Ritchie, one of the finest writers
of short mysteries (and I do mean short) that ever
breathed? Poor man; he died without having published a
novel. Why is there no collection of the best crime stories
of Avram Davidson, or Clark Howard, or James Powell?
Simple; they have no reputations as crime novelists. Simple, and silly. Think of Hammett, Chandler, Woolrich,
John D. MacDonald, Stanley Ellin, Donald E. Westlake,
Bill Pronzini, Lawrence Block, and all the other giants

who could never have sold their mystery story collections if they had not first scored with mystery novels.

Which brings us to a friend and neighbor and colleague of mine named John Lutz.

In the early sixties he worked variously as a civilian switchboard operator for the St. Louis Police Department, a forklift operator, and a warehouseman for a grocery chain—mostly night shifts. By daylight he'd read voraciously—among his favorites at the time were John D. MacDonald, Ross Macdonald, John Collier, Gerald Kersh, and Roald Dahl—and pound out dozens of his own short stories at breakneck speed, sometimes not even bothering to make a carbon. I'm not certain when (or if) he slept. "It looked easy," he said, "so I tried it and found out it wasn't." None of his stories sold. That, he says today, was "part of the learning process." Dozens of rejection slips in a row have aborted thousands of potential literary careers, but Lutz refused to become discouraged. "I saw I could improve, so I kept at it." After a while the editors who turned down his material began to write supportive comments in their sorry-we-can't-use-this letters. "That's a good sign," Lutz says. "I'd know I was close to a sale then." Most of his stories were mysteries, because he liked to read them and thought they were relatively easy to sell. And one frabjous day in early 1966, he opened his mail and—presto!—a contract.

He was still working the night shift at a grocery warehouse when his first story came out—"Thieves' Honor" (*Alfred Hitchcock's Mystery Magazine,* December 1966). It opened the door for him, and acceptances soon poured in. Six of his tales appeared in 1967, ten in 1968, five more in 1969. Within a few years of his unheralded entry into the genre he was being published in *Ellery Queen's Mystery Magazine, Mike Shayne Mystery Magazine,* the science-fiction periodical *Galaxy,* the Diners Club magazine *Signature,* men's mags like *Knight* and *Swank* and *Cava-*

lier, even a long-forgotten supermarket giveaway called *TV Fact.* But the majority of his stories, a total of sixty-four from "Thieves' Honor" to the present, sold to *Alfred Hitchcock's Mystery Magazine,* and many of these are among his best. In 1975, his tenth year in the field, eighteen new Lutz tales were published, including five (under his own name and four pseudonyms) in a single issue of a single magazine. Now that's productivity!

In 1973, after being laid off from his job, John decided to take a crack at writing full-time. Two years later he and his wife Barbara and their three children and their dog Blondie, "of indeterminate breed and unpredictable temperament," migrated across St. Louis County to a roomy stucco house on a wooded corner lot in the affluent suburb of Webster Groves. John and Barbara and their younger daughter and the dog (who has mellowed) still live there today.

So much for the shape of his life. What about the shape of the world he put on the page?

There are no series characters in most of the Lutz short stories, but there are what one might call series elements. The two that readers tend to identify most closely with him are husbands seeking a method of wife-disposal and off-the-wall business organizations. Each of these will be found abundantly in the tales collected here. Occasionally, like the creator of two different series detectives who has his sleuths work together on a particular case, Lutz uses both of these signature elements in a single story, for example "Fractions" (*Alfred Hitchcock's Mystery Magazine,* June 1972), which is about a company that manipulates unwanted spouses into committing adultery.

Lutz can create a new business as easily as a rabbit can create another rabbit, but almost all of his imaginary entities have this in common: beneath the impressive facade, beneath the smiles and handshakes, they are out to take us. He has never been fond of the self-congratulatory social Darwinism that is known as the "free enter-prise" system, and even when dealing with real-world businesses rather than the self-invented kind, he has com-bined a healthy cynicism with imaginative bizarrerie and come up with dandy items like "Mail Order" (*Alfred Hitchcock's Mystery Magazine,* April 1975) and "Under-standing Electricity" (*Alfred Hitchcock's Mystery Maga-zine,* August 1975), which read as if Kafka had come back from the grave to collaborate on fiction with Ralph Nader. Of course, not all of the Lutz stories are of this sort, but the best of them do tend to stem from wildly distinctive premises, like "The Real Shape of the Coast" (*Ellery Queen's Mystery Magazine,* June 1971), with its lu-natic detective trying to solve a murder in the asylum, or "Dead Man" (*Alfred Hitchcock's Mystery Magazine,* March 1974), where we share the last hours of a tycoon locked into a walk-in vault with a few hours' air supply as he gropes desperately for a clue to the identity of his own murderer. Even before Lutz became well known as a mystery novelist, a sizable collection of his short stories could and should have been put together. Funny thing about the publishing business.

Lutz' two earliest novels came out during his first dec-ade as a writer. *The Truth of the Matter* (1971) is an orig-inal paperback thriller about a fugitive couple, a man and woman on the run, stalked across the Midwest by the police but mainly by their own lies and self-deceptions and fears. In his first hardcover book, *Buyer Beware* (1976), Lutz introduced St. Louis private eye Alo Nudger, whose trademark is a nervous stomach and whose specialty is the legal kidnapping of children spir-ited out of state during custody battles between divorced parents.

His next four novels were the breakthrough books that established Lutz as a writer to contend with. *Bonegrinder* (1977) deals with a Bigfoot-like monster terrorizing a

small town in the Ozarks, and even though it's crime
fiction only at the edges, it contains some of the best cha-
racterizations and atmospheric writing in the Lutz
canon—and almost none of the gore that most writers
would have slathered on by the bucketful. *Lazarus Man*
(1979) is a political thriller of the Watergate era based
on a fascinating what-if premise: the G. Gordon Liddy
figure, having served a long term in prison for following
the code and keeping his mouth shut, sets out to kill one-
by-one the Nixon figure and his cronies, who in turn send
their own hitman after the outraged avenger. In *Jericho
Man* (1980) Lutz mines the Lawrence Sanders vein of
urban violence, with a tough NYPD captain and a young
architect battling the madman who planted dynamite in
the foundations of several high-rises when they were
under construction and is now demanding one million
dollars' ransom. Finally, in *The Shadow Man* (1981) a
U.S. Senator is stalked through the Manhattan night-
scape by what seems to be a psychotic political assassin
with the power to be in several places at once.

Lutz never stopped writing short stories even when he
was turning out novels fast and furious, but his magazine appearances became rarer. A few of his tales of the
late seventies and early eighties feature series characters—Nudger, for example, made his short-story debut in
"The Man in the Morgue" (*Alfred Hitchcock's Mystery
Magazine,* February 1978), and *Bonegrinder*'s Sheriff
Billy Wintone in "That Kind of World" (*Alfred Hitchcock's Mystery Magazine,* July 16, 1980)—and an occasional non-series story of the period furnishes raw
material for a later novel. ("The Other Runner," *Ellery
Queen's Mystery Magazine,* October 1978, is the source for
one of the scariest of the murders in 1979's *Lazarus
Man.*) But stories like "Pure Rotten" (*Mike Shayne Mys-
tery Magazine,* August 1977) and "Dear Dorie" (*Alfred
Hitchcock's Mystery Magazine,* September 16, 1981) are as

crazy as any Lutz dreamed up in his early days, and "High Stakes" (*The Saint Mystery Magazine,* June 1984) is one of the most terrifying short suspensers since the death of Cornell Woolrich. The Edgar that the Mystery Writers of America awarded Lutz for one of the later Nudger tales, "Ride the Lightning" (*Alfred Hitchcock's Mystery Magazine,* January 1985), was an honor well deserved and long overdue. I'd bet money that there are more Edgars in his future.

After taking time out to write a pseudonymous paperback adventure novel for a book packager (*Exiled!,* as Steven Greene, 1982), Lutz began to concentrate on series mystery novels. In *The Eye* (1984), co-authored with Bill Pronzini, he revisted Lawrence Sanders country, pitting another decent New York cop with a troubled personal life against a psychotic perpetrator of random butchery. It's one of the most powerful *noir* thrillers of recent years, and Lutz is presently at work on a sequel.

Nightlines (1984) marked the return of St. Louis private detective Alo Nudger, but with modifications. His ill-advised first name is almost never mentioned, he no longer specializes in the legal kidnapping of children (or anything else), the narration has shifted from first to third person, and the protagonist's symbiotic relationship with his city has become almost as strong as Spenser's with Boston or Philip Marlowe's with L.A. More important, the new Nudger is one of the most memorable series characters in current crime fiction. He comes close to being a total loser, plagued by overdue bills and deadbeat clients and a bloodsucking ex-wife and shoddy consumer goods and his nervous stomach and most of all by his near-paralyzing unaggressiveness and compassion. His office is above a doughnut shop in a dreary suburb of St. Louis. He lunches at the nearby McDonald's but only when he has a discount coupon. He drives a dented old Volkswagen Beetle that he has trouble finding whenever he parks in a shopping-center lot and which tends to die on him for lack of adequate maintenance when he uses it to chase or shadow someone. He is the most Chaplinesque of PIs: whatever can go wrong on him, will. In *Night-lines,* perhaps Lutz' finest novel so far, Nudger encounters a suicidal woman whose life is even more messed up than his own while hunting the psychotic slasher who's been using the telephone company's private equipment-testing lines to make blind dates with his female victims. *The Right to Sing the Blues* (1986) takes Nudger to New Orleans, and the book throbs with the sounds of jazz, "the music of the lost." The most recent entry in the series is the excellent *Ride the Lightning* (1987), expanded from Lutz' Edgar-winning short story, with Nudger in a hopeless race against the clock to save a petty criminal from being electrocuted for one crime he may not have committed. More Nudgers will be published before and after this collection. On the day a new one comes in my mail, I drop whatever I'm doing and make a beeline for my reading chair.

For those who like their PIs concerned and compassionate but a bit less passive than Nudger, Lutz has begun a new series, set in central Florida and featuring Fred Carver, a fortyish and balding ex-cop whose police career ended and whose career as a private investigator began when he was kneecapped by a Latino street punk. In *Tropical Heat* (1986) he's hired by a lovely real-estate saleswoman to find her lover, who in the middle of a solitary continental breakfast on her terrace either walked out on her for no reason, or jumped off a cliff into the ocean, or was pushed off. The second Carver, *Scorcher,* will be published later in 1987, and more will surely follow.

John Lutz is in his late forties now. Soft-spoken and solidly built, with a salt-and-pepper mustache and beard to match, he sits at the word processor in the study of his

Webster Groves home, filling the little screen with the doings of lovers and losers, butchers and victims, fools and clowns, hunters and their prey. He has arrived. He is firmly established in the only job he's ever liked: building better mousetraps.

And now that his large economy-sized products have caused the reading and publishing world to beat the proverbial path to his door, here are some of the best of his miniature mousetraps, collected in a single package at last.

BETTER MOUSETRAPS

BETTER MOUSETRAPS

The Other Runner

I jog. Like people all over this mechanized world who have discovered the benefits of jogging, of what really is old-fashioned running.

I'm tired now, in my third mile this evening. I feel that I can't make it the mile and a half back to my cabin, but a part of me deep down knows that I will.

What I'm running on is an old bridle path. It once was cinder, but the mountain thunderstorms and melting snows have worn it to the hard gray surface on which I now struggle. The path is approximately two and a half miles long, meandering in a roughly circular route around Mirror Lake. For an instant I can glimpse through the trees and see the cedar shake roof of my small cabin, and as always the sight strengthens my determination to reach that point of triumph.

Around and above me the woods are green and shadowed, and occasionally I hear birds twitter in alarm at my approach, or a squirrel or rabbit bolt unseen for cover. I negotiate a slight rise, one of the most grueling stretches of my morning runs, and my thighs suddenly ache under the uphill strain, my breath rasping in louder quicker rhythm.

Then the high path levels out, sweeps in a sloping crescent to the south. A steep drop on my left, rising bare mountain face on my right. At my feet Mirror Lake suddenly glitters blue-green, a jewel nestled deep in a rough green setting.

I draw breath and resolution as I turn onto the final leg of my run, a series of small rises, then a long gentle grade to my cabin. That final downgrade is the best of the run, the very sweetest. Lovely gravity.

Half an hour later I've showered, and I sit now on the wooden porch of my cabin, my feet propped up on the porch rail, a cold can of low-calorie beer on the wicker table beside me. Totally relaxed, I wait for darkness.

I've been jogging for six weeks, since my divorce became final. When Marsha left me I took stock of myself, decided I needed to lose ten to fifteen pounds, strengthen my heart and lungs for the coming lonely battle with encroaching age. I was forty-three in March.

Of course age and weight weren't my only reasons for taking up jogging. Tension. Jogging is one of the greatest tension relievers there is, and I was under more tension during the divorce, the unexpected bitterness, than I would ever have guessed I could bear.

And perhaps I couldn't have borne it without the escape and spiritual experience of running, and the isolation of this tiny cabin near Mirror Lake. I've been here two weeks now, and each day I'm gladder I came. Oh, the tension remains, but now I easily hold it at bay.

Seclusion heals. And there is only one other occupied house on the lake, a large flat-roofed modern structure that juts from the side of the east hill like the imbedded prow of a ship. The Mulhaneys are staying there, Dan and Iris. Dan looks to be a few years older than my forty-three, a beefy graying man with a sad-pug, brutal face. Iris I've seen once, as she stood staring into the lake, a lithe long-waisted woman with long brown hair and graceful neck. One of those women who somehow by their silent presence will be able to exercise an attraction

4

for men even into old age, a woman not just alive but aflame—coldly aflame.

I've not yet spoken to either of the Mulhaneys; it was from the talkative shopkeeper at the one-pump gas station-grocery store near Daleville that I learned their identities. Though Dan Mulhaney I see almost every day. He's a morning jogger. Always a few minutes either side of nine o'clock he pads wearily past my kitchen window as I'm drinking my coffee. We wave to each other. He's never stopped; he can't break stride.

But one morning he does stop.

Mulhaney simply ceases exerting effort and his bulky white-clad form decelerates to a walk with machine-like inevitability. I stand up from the table and take half a dozen steps out onto the porch.

"Morning," Mulhaney says. "Thought I oughta introduce myself." He holds out a perspiring hand. "Dan Mulhaney."

"Earl Crydon." I shake the hand.

"Wife and I are staying in the house up on the hill. Here to get away from things."

"That's why I'm here myself."

"Vacation?"

"No, I'm a freelance writer, so my office can pretty well travel with me."

Mulhaney rubs large hairy hands on his shapeless T-shirt, stands silently, expectantly.

"Been jogging long?" I ask.

"About three months. I'm up to six miles. How about you?"

"I can do a bit over five, which is quite an improvement over my first outing. I run in the evenings, after things have cooled."

Mulhaney suddenly seems ill at ease. I offer him coffee.

"Better not, but thanks." He begins jogging easily in place to keep up his circulation. "I better get moving before I get stiff." He fades backward, graceful for a big man, waves, then turns and strikes a practiced, moderate pace. He jogs in the opposite direction from myself—clockwise. There is about him an air of mild confusion.

Next morning, as I sit sipping coffee in my crude pine-paneled kitchen, I hear Mulhaney's approach at exactly two minutes to nine. When he comes into view I raise my hand to wave, but he doesn't look in my direction. His pace is faster than usual, and on his perspiring flushed face is an expression of perplexity, of muted fright. Almost as if he is running *from* something.

"Morning!" I call through the window.

His head jerks in my direction and he smiles mechanically, gives a tentative wave. The rhythmic beat of his footsteps recedes.

That evening, as I jog through long shadows past the precariously balanced Mulhaney house, I can hear shouting coming from inside, a man and a woman, abrupt heated words that are only desperate, indecipherable sounds by the time they reach my ears. I jog on.

The next several mornings I watch Mulhaney jog past my cabin window and each time his beefy face wears that same quizzical, fearful expression. Then, on Friday morning, I hear the broken, slowing rhythm of his footsteps, and even before he comes into view I know that he's stopping to talk. I finish my coffee and rise to walk onto the porch to greet him.

Mulhaney invites me to join him and his wife that evening for cocktails and some outdoor-grilled steaks—after I've returned from jogging, of course. I accept, some side of me faintly resenting this intrusion on my self-imposed isolation, and tell him I'll run earlier this evening so I can be there at dinnertime. We decide on eight o'clock.

I get to the Mulhaney house at five minutes to eight, feeling fresh and relaxed after my early run and cool shower. Dan Mulhaney is waiting for me by a redwood gate at the top of a long winding flight of mossy stone steps that leads to the side of the jutting, angled house. We shake hands as he works a pitted metal latch and opens the gate.

"My wife Iris," he says, pride of possession in his voice.

Iris is standing near a white steel table on a brick veranda bordered by thick twisted ivy. She's wearing white shorts and a violet-colored blouse that brings out the violet of her eyes. She smiles. "A drink, Mr. Crydon? Scotch, martini, beer?"

"Beer. And it's Earl, Mrs. Mulhaney."

"Then it's Iris." As she walks toward an open door, she says, "I understand you're a compulsive exerciser like my husband."

"I like to run."

I walk with Mulhaney to a no-frills barbecue pit and examine three still-raw steaks.

"Extra lean," he assures me, as Iris returns with my beer in a glass and with her own martini glass replenished. We drift to the center of the veranda and sit at the white metal table. There is a hole in the center of the table for an umbrella, and round plastic coasters for our glasses.

"Beautiful place," I say, looking around me at glass and squared redwood. A red Porsche convertible squats in the gravel drive.

Iris shrugs. "I hate it."

I raise my glass and look at her, noticing the sheen of her eyes and the faint flush on her cheeks. The results of more than one or two martinis. "But you're staying here," I say.

"Daniel's idea." Her fingertips brush a faded purplish splotch on the side of her neck.

"Both of us had the idea, actually," Mulhaney says quickly. He swivels in his chair to check the wink of

7

flame above the rim of the barbecue pit. "Hey, I better keep an eye on those steaks." He stands and moves away.

"The salad's tossed," Iris says after him. She fixes a violet stare on me. "Daniel sort of twisted my arm to get me to come up here, Earl." A sip of martini. "Marital difficulties. Private matter."

I shift in my hard white chair, slightly embarrassed. "No need to tell me about it, Iris. I'm not qualified to give advice." I wonder how "sort of" was the arm twisting.

"You're not married?"

"Divorced."

Even her smile is violet. There is an unmistakable intensity there.

"I've had enough woman trouble to hold me for a while," I say, and truthfully.

"Well done?" Dan Mulhaney calls to me, probing the largest steak with a long-tined fork.

"Sure," I tell him, "go ahead and burn it."

Iris smiles at me and rises to get the salad.

Again that expression on Mulhaney's face, as if someone—or something—is chasing him.

I sit by my kitchen window, sipping coffee, and glance at my watch. He's early this morning.

The next morning he stops to talk.

"Hot for morning," he says, wiping his glistening face with his T-shirt.

I lean on a cedar porch post. "It is if you're jogging." I can see that Mulhaney is bothered by something more than the heat.

"Any large wild animals around here?" he asks. "I mean, have you ever seen any foxes, bobcats, or—anything?"

"Never anything bigger than a rabbit. There used to be bears and cougars in this area, but not for years."

He nods, his broad red face grotesque with a frown in the harsh morning light. "Have you ever been around hunting dogs, Crydon?"

"Not often."

"You can walk where there are a dozen of them lying in the sun, watching you and not watching you. Nothing happens. But if you run they'll sometimes chase you as if you were game."

"Instinct."

Mulhaney seems hesitant to speak further, but he does. "In the evenings, when you're running, do you ever get the feeling that something's—well, behind you?"

"I never have."

"There's an old Gaelic saying to the effect that if you run fast enough long enough, something is bound to give chase."

"Like the hunting dogs. And you think something's chasing you?"

"I don't think it—it's a feeling. Imagination, I guess. But I'm not the imaginative sort." He snorts an embarrassed laugh. "If I were you, I'd think Dan Mulhaney was due for a psychiatric checkup."

"Have you ever considered turning around?" I ask him. "Running back toward whatever you think is behind you?"

I'm surprised by the fear in his eyes. "No, no, I couldn't do that."

As he stands talking to me, helpless in all his aging bulk, I feel a wash of deep pity for Mulhaney, of comradeship. I tell him to wait and I go into the cabin. When I return I hand him my revolver. Perhaps this seems extreme, but it is only a small-caliber target pistol. And what if Mulhaney is right? What if something is running behind him, stalking him? This is still reasonably wild country.

"Carry this tucked in your belt if you'd like," I say. "If nothing else, it should make you feel more secure."

He holds the small pistol before him in gratitude and surprise. "You don't have to do this."

"Why shouldn't I? I haven't fired that gun in over a year, so I won't miss it."

"I'll pay you for it."

"Give it back to me when you leave here, or when you feel you haven't any more use for it."

Mulhaney grins, tucks the pistol into the waistband of his shorts beneath his baggy T-shirt. He really is grateful. We shake hands and he jogs up the path, his footsteps somehow more confident on the hard earth.

I go inside, pour another cup of coffee, and wonder if I've made a mistake.

But the pistol has nothing to do with Thursday's tragedy.

At ten o'clock in the morning a horn honks outside my cabin, a series of abrupt, frantic blasts. I walk to the door and see Iris sitting behind the wheel of the red Porsche. Her hair is tangled, wild. Her eyes are wild.

"I need your help, Earl! Something's happened to Dan!"

I shut the cabin door and trot to the car. "Where is he?"

"On the path. He went jogging this morning as he always does, but he didn't return. I went looking for him, found him lying on the ground. He—he doesn't seem to be breathing."

I move around and get in on the passenger side of the car. Iris rotates the wheel expertly, turns around in the front yard of my cabin, and the Porsche roars back up the path.

Dan Mulhaney is on the highest part of the path, where the hill drops abruptly toward the lake on one side

and to the smooth rock that rises steeply to a wooded
crest on the other. He is lying on his stomach, his body
curiously hunched, his head twisted as if he's straining to
get air. We get out of the Porsche almost before it stops
rocking, and I know immediately Daniel Mulhaney is
dead.

As I'm feeling automatically and hopelessly for vital
signs, my hand touches the cool steel of my revolver still
tucked in Mulhaney's waistband. He is lying on the gun,
concealing it.

"Does your cabin have a phone?" I ask Iris.

She nods, staring at her husband. "He's so still, so
waxlike. He's dead. . . ."

"We can't be sure. Go to your cabin and call a doctor,
Iris. I'll stay here."

She nods once, gets into the Porsche, and backs some
distance to a wide space at the base of the rise, where she
can turn the car around. When she is out of sight I reach
beneath Mulhaney's body and remove the gun. It hasn't
been fired. I tuck it inside my belt, beneath my shirt. I
didn't count on this happening; I don't even have a permit for the gun.

"It looks like a heart attack," the doctor says, forty-
five minutes later, as Iris and I look on. The doctor sighs
and slowly stands. He's a middle-aged but somehow
older-appearing man from nearby Daleville, a general
practitioner. "You say he jogged regularly?"

"Faithfully," Iris says. She seems to be in mild shock.

The doctor shakes his graying head. "It's a pattern.
Overweight, middle-aged, probably high blood pressure.
Trying to run like a man of twenty-five and his heart
gave out, would be my guess. Thousands of them die like
this across the country every year. It's a pattern."

"He was so . . . so healthy," Iris says.

"Maybe he just thought he was," the doctor answers
softly. "An ambulance is on the way. We'll take him to

11

Mathers' Funeral Home in Daleville if that's agreeable with you, Mrs. Mulhaney."

Iris nods.

"Why don't you take Mrs. Mulhaney home, give her this with a glass of water." He hands me a small white pill and glances at Iris. "A sedative. Nothing strong."

I get into the car beside Iris and she backs down the road, turns the car, and drives slowly toward her jutting redwood cabin. There is little I can say to her that will help, so I stare straight ahead in silence.

At the cabin she thanks me, assures me that she'll be all right, and with the small white pill clenched in her hand goes inside.

Half an hour later, from my cabin window, I see the ambulance carrying Dan Mulhaney's body carefully negotiating the narrow path. No need for speed, flashing lights, or siren. For the first time since the divorce I take a strong drink, sour mash bourbon on the rocks. I feel a sadness out of proportion to my mere familiarity with Dan Mulhaney.

It's impossible for me to work the rest of the afternoon. Clouds have moved into the area, casting even more gloom, and each hour brings a stronger threat of rain.

At five o'clock, much earlier than usual, I decide that I should run to beat the rain. It takes me only a few minutes to get into my jogging shoes, gray shorts, and faded red T-shirt. The gun I lent Mulhaney is still loaded, and rather than take time to unload it, or leave it in the cabin while I'm gone, I transfer it to the waistband of my shorts. Jogging is what I need to shake off my depression, to obscure the impressions of this morning.

I'm breathing hard by the time I reach the scene of Mulhaney's death. For an instant I feel a shuddering dread, then reassure myself by remembering that Mulhaney was older than my forty-three years, as well as overweight. I jog past the death site, instinctively avoid-

12

ing the exact spot where the body was found. I find myself running between the tire tracks of the Porsche, tracks that must have been left when Iris drove along the path and discovered the body, and when she drove us back to try to help Mulhaney.

And I wonder, why would she come back this way, the long way, instead of continuing past my cabin, the way the car was pointed? That way we could have reached Mulhaney in less than a minute. As my feet pound along the path, I see in the gray dust this morning's footprints from Mulhaney's shoes, exactly like my own footprints, only reversed. But his footprints don't describe a straight line; rather they move from one side of the path to the other, with varying spaces between them. He must have staggered in considerable pain before falling.

As I continue to run I keep staring down at the footprints pointing in the opposite direction from the way I'm jogging. Mulhaney staggered an incredible distance, almost all the way up the steepening hill. Why would a man in that much pain continue to run, to push himself? I know what that takes, even without the agonizing spasms of a heart attack.

I stop running.

Still breathing hard, I walk slowly back the way I came.

Now I can see the more subtle veerings of one set of tire tracks, hardly noticeable unless under close scrutiny. The zigzag, irregular patterns of Mulhaney's footprints are paralleled and bounded by the snaking set of tire tracks.

I stop walking where Mulhaney's body was found and backhand the sweat from my forehead.

It's a cold sweat.

She killed him. Dogged him up the hill with the car, at a point where he was already exhausted from over an hour of jogging. On one side of the path the bare face of the mountain rising steep and smooth, and on the other side the long drop to the lake. He had to keep running until he collapsed. If Mulhaney hadn't been dead on the path, Iris probably would have pushed his body over the edge to fall toward the lake. An accident, it would seem. Iris knew her husband was dead when she came to me for help.

Thunder suddenly crashes, echoing about me, but still it doesn't rain. I jog on toward my cabin, through air charged by the imminent storm.

Then a tingling of alarm through my body, and I hear the car's strangely atavistic roar.

The Porsche rounds the curve near my cabin and speeds toward me. I know it will reach the base of the hill before I can. *I will be in the same position Mulhaney was in!*

Iris works it artfully, varying her speed, always a split second from running me down, keeping me gasping, struggling to gain precious inches of life-sustaining ground.

As I glance back, I see her behind the wheel, her hair flowing beautifully, a fixed dreamy expression on her face. I know why Mulhaney didn't use the gun, know how much, in his possessive, brutish fashion, he must have loved her. I've no such compunctions, only chilling fear.

Unlike Mulhaney, I've had my brief respite while examining the tire tracks and footprints, enough to regain some of my stamina. I put on a burst of speed, draw the gun from my waistband, and twist my body to fire as accurately as possible. The gun kicks in my hand and I see astonishment on Iris' face.

It takes three shots to stop her. The Porsche stalls and nestles against the rocky side of the hill, one rear wheel off the ground. The windshield is starred and Iris is slumped sobbing over the steering wheel. I walk back and see no blood. She isn't hit.

"I was afraid you'd jog early," she says from the cradle of her arms on the steering wheel. "Was watching your cabin, hoping you wouldn't leave." Her head flies back and she stares madly at the sky. "It was supposed to rain!" She begins pounding the steering wheel with her fist. "It was supposed to rain early this afternoon and wash away the tracks!"

I help her out of the car and we walk toward her cabin to phone the county sheriff. Iris sobs, cursing almost with every step. Right now I'm sure she hates the weather forecaster even more than she hated her husband.

I live year-round in the city now. And I still jog. As my feet pound the hard earth I sometimes wonder about Daniel Mulhaney, if he really thought he was being pursued, stalked, or if he had some sort of premonition of his death, sensed some manifestation of his wife's hate.

An uneasiness comes over me at times as I run through lengthening evening shadows, and I remember what the prematurely aged doctor at Mirror Lake said. *It's a pattern . . .* And I remember what Dan Mulhaney said about how if you run fast enough long enough, something is bound to give chase.

And now and then I glance behind me.

The Wounded Tiger

It was a modern motel on the very edge of the city. Raynard Holcombe sat in the small room and listened to a flock of birds chattering in the huge tree outside the screened window. Holcombe was a tall man, slender but with weight in the right places. His features were regular except for the scar where the leopard in India had clawed him. The scar was a striking white line across his tanned forehead that made one eyebrow appear perpetually arched. And, like the leopard, Holcombe's occupation had left its mark on him; he was a professional hunter, every inch of him.

Something frightened the chattering birds, and they took to the air noisily as the wooden door to the cabin opened and a lean blond man of about thirty-five entered. "Von Eisle," he said by way of introduction, and sat down opposite Holcombe.

As he handed the blond man a white business card, Holcombe sized him up carefully: rather washed-out-looking, round-shouldered, painfully esthetic face with a pasty complexion and sad gray eyes. Yet, like his physical opposite Holcombe, there was a self-contained deadliness about Von Eisle.

"I was sent this card through the mail," Holcombe said, "accompanied by a note saying a friend had recommended me to you: Which friend?"

Von Eisle flicked a sad smile. "He prefers to remain anonymous."

Holcombe shrugged. "And just what is this company, Quest and Quarry, which you represent? You're connected with hunting, I presume."

"You presume correctly," Von Eisle said without emotion. There was a disturbing quality about the man's pathetic eyes.

"I drove a hell of a long way out here," Holcombe said irritably, "because I kept getting those cards of yours. I don't know why I'm here, but you'd better make it worth my while."

"You're here because of curiosity," Von Eisle said, opening a black attaché case he'd brought into the cabin with him. He took out a yellow file folder and absently thumbed through it. "You are Raynard Holcombe, age thirty-eight, unmarried, have been drinking a bit too much lately, and you've successfully hunted every worthwhile type of game in the world."

"So I have," Holcombe said flatly.

"You are a man who constantly seeks new challenges," Von Eisle went on, "and of late you can find none. It disturbs you."

"How do you know that?" Holcombe looked coldly at Von Eisle with his blue hunter's eyes, shooter's eyes backed by steady hands and calm nerves.

"Because," Von Eisle said, returning the stare, "it is our business."

"I thought your business was hunting, arranging safaris."

"So it is." Von Eisle smiled and folded his pale hands on top of the yellow folder. "You have hunted almost everything, Mr. Holcombe. You have experienced the charge of the Cape buffalo, the nerve-racking wile of the tiger, the swift and vicious bulk of the rogue elephant." The smile widened. "The only thing you haven't hunted is man."

17

"They're illegal, you know," Holcombe said. "A limit of none."

Now that the subject had been broached, Von Eisle again assumed his lackluster expression. He raised his blond eyebrows as if absently considering Holcombe's last remarks. "The business of Quest and Quarry," he said evenly, "is to afford you the opportunity to poach with a maximum of safety so that you may hunt this animal."

Holcombe was silent for a moment, then grinned incredulously. "I really think you're serious, Von Eisle, but I'm a hunter, not a murderer."

"Yes, yes," Von Eisle said with a mild but rather surprising show of impatience. "We don't propose you *murder* anyone. Your quarry consents to the game, even pays to play. Your quarry will be a man like yourself."

"Armed?"

"As you will be."

"Good Lord," Holcombe said, but he looked thoughtful, interested despite himself.

"If you'll permit me to say so," Von Eisle continued, "you are the kind of man who rarely turns down such a challenge. The company has made a thorough study of your background, a hunter's background in the true sense of the word."

"Yes," Holcombe said quietly, knowing that Von Eisle was right, searching within himself, not too surprised to find that he had no real compunctions about killing a man. "What will the weapons be?" he asked, careful to keep his tone of voice noncommittal.

"Before that, perhaps we should discuss the price. As we both know, you are a man of means. Our standard rate for clients in your income bracket is five thousand dollars."

Holcombe wasn't in a bargaining position. "Agreed." He waved the matter away with a flick of his sun-brown hand. "And the weapons?"

"Handguns. Thirty-eight automatics with silencers. Everything will be provided by the company, and everything will be untraceable. You will hunt for a two-day period in an area unfamiliar to both of you. It will be an area that affords plenty of cover; the company will see to that."

Von Eisle again thumbed through the contents of the attaché case. "How about New Orleans?" he asked.

"Good enough," Holcombe said.

"We'll provide you with a street map, of course. You'll take no identification, and you'll check into a hotel under an assumed name. You will have both a photograph and description of your quarry and the name of his hotel."

"And he'll have the same information on me?"

"Oh yes," Von Eisle said. "As you have no doubt gathered, we strive for an equal match." A strangely savage look came over his pallid features. "I compare it with stalking a wounded tiger that you know might double back on its spoor and stalk *you.*" He closed the attaché case with a loud snap and looked again at Holcombe.

"Now then, sir," he said gravely, "there are a few limitations, important limitations: You are not to hunt past the two-day deadline; you are not to hunt outside the city limits; and you are not allowed to enter your quarry's hotel. These same rules, of course, apply to your quarry."

"That's understood," Holcombe said. "When do I start?"

Von Eisle stood. "When we get the five thousand dollars." He reached into his pocket and handed Holcombe a slip of paper with a post-office box number typed on it. "When we receive cash payment through the mail, the company will send you in return a weapon, a detailed map of the area, further instructions, and, most important, a starting date. You will study the map and then send to that same box number the name of the hotel in which you intend to stay." He made an ineffectual gesture. "Of course the company has no headquarters, so if you are caught or linked with the crime you'll be completely on your own." He opened the door and paused. "Good luck to you, Mr. Holcombe."

Holcombe found that his heart was beating very fast. "This will require more skill than luck," he said, with something of his old enthusiasm.

Von Eisle smiled his sad smile. "Just remember, Mr. Holcombe, somewhere your quarry is discussing you as *his* quarry." He stepped out into the bright sunlight. "The thrill of the hunt," he said as he shut the door.

Holcombe drove the rented sedan swiftly but within the legal limit over the Huey P. Long Bridge across the Mississippi, listening to the tires hum on the hot pavement. The idea of actually hunting another intelligent, reasoning human being had grown on him. In fact, he wondered why he hadn't thought of it before, why dozens of hunters hadn't thought of it before. But then, he reasoned, how would one approach another and suggest such a thing? It took a company like Quest and Quarry to bring two such people together, and there was the added advantage of not knowing one another.

Of course there was the price, but as Von Eisle had later informed him, the victor of the hunt always had his money refunded, leaving the company with a neat five thousand dollar profit. The purpose of this monetary trophy, Holcombe assumed, was so the survivor could afford to play the game again, thus assuring Quest and Quarry of an abundance of game.

As Holcombe entered New Orleans, he felt his senses quicken. It was already the afternoon of the first day. The hunt was on.

He drove for a while through the uptown area, then turned left on Canal Street, toward the hotel where he had reservations under an assumed name, the same name under which he'd rented the sedan. He made a detour and drove carefully but unobtrusively around the hotel of his prey, taking in every detail of the old building and its surroundings. After making mental notes, he got back on Canal Street.

Leaving the car in a public garage, Holcombe walked the remaining six blocks down Canal, turned left onto a side street, and proceeded to the Bordeaux Hotel, a not-too-prosperous-looking establishment where he'd reserved a third-floor corner room.

After checking in and getting settled, Holcombe had room service send up a bottle. He took only one drink, then he got out the photograph of his quarry and studied it intently. The man was younger than Holcombe, rather pleasant-looking, with dark eyes and a very straight nose. He didn't appear to be an outdoorsman, but according to the company he'd played the game before, and this would offset Holcombe's greater experience. The company always tried to match their opponents evenly, Von Eisle had said, which was why many hunts ended unsatisfactorily, without a kill. Unsatisfactorily for the hunters, that is, because in such a case the company profited ten thousand dollars instead of five.

As Holcombe studied the features of his quarry, he decided he would call the man William Able, after a mulatto game warden he'd known and hated in Kenya. It would help to work up some animosity toward the man. Besides, there was an undeniable resemblance between his quarry and the real William Able.

Holcombe started to look at his wrist, then looked instead at the clock on the bureau. According to instructions he wore no jewelry and carried no identification of any kind, not even a wallet. He rose, walked to his open suitcase on the bed, and got out his powerful binoculars. Leaving the venetian blinds open just a little, he scanned the late afternoon street. By now, he reasoned, his quarry should be getting restless.

There were several people below: a shoeshine boy with a stand across the street where there were several outdoor chairs, a woman coming out of a shop, two men waiting for someone on the corner. Holcombe searched the men's faces carefully, making sure that neither was Able, then prepared to wait. He had a hunter's patience.

Two hours later, after checking at both windows at fifteen-minute intervals, Holcombe saw him. He was sitting across the street from the hotel entrance on a small wrought-iron bench outside a Spanish-looking florist shop. He was wearing a light-colored suit and there was a magazine in his lap that he was making no pretense of reading.

As Holcombe peered through the binoculars, he realized suddenly that Able was calmly scanning the hotel windows, and too late he saw the close-up dark eyes focus on the widened crack in the blinds and stare right back at him for an instant. Then, without a change of expression, the eyes were averted, but Holcombe knew he'd been seen. He stepped back from the window cursing and didn't look outside again for five minutes. When he did, he saw that Able was still sitting casually, staring right at his window.

Now Holcombe smiled. Swiftly, he checked the automatic with the silencer and put it in his shoulder holster. If Able expected to gain an advantage by watching the hotel from a safe, busy street, he was mistaken. Holcombe took an elevator to the ground floor and slipped out through a back service entrance.

By the time he got to Able's hotel it was dark. Holcombe waited until the street was momentarily deserted and, looking around carefully but casually, walked to a dark spot between two streetlights and slipped behind some bushes growing in an alcove of a large faded-green stucco building. Holcombe had noticed this place of perfect concealment across from Able's hotel earlier that day and was now prepared to use it. Hitching up his trouser legs, he sat on the hard ground and leaned back against the wall. He was wearing a dark sport jacket and slacks, making him all but invisible in the darkness behind the foliage, and he had a perfect shot across the street at the well-lit hotel steps against which Able would be silhouetted perfectly.

Holcombe had been there for over an hour, rubbing his legs to keep them from cramping, when suddenly there was a rustling of the bushes near him and something cracked into the brick-backed stucco. This was quickly followed by another crack, and bits of stucco struck Holcombe in the face. By that time he realized what was happening. Rolling quickly away, in the direction of the first two points of impact, he broke through the bushes and ran parallel to the building wall toward the corner. A bullet slammed into the wall behind him as he half fell, skidding, around the corner.

He ran three blocks and then entered a fairly large department store. After waiting out of sight inside one of the many exits, he dashed out and caught a bus just as the last of a crowd of shoppers was boarding.

In the bus he assessed what had happened. Able had outwitted him. Knowing that Holcombe would go to his hotel and wait for him, Able had figured the most likely spot where Holcombe would conceal himself and then had raked it with gunfire. From where? Across the street? His hotel window? Wherever Able had fired from, Holcombe was grateful that it was far enough from the bushes to prevent good accuracy with a handgun.

It was with anger and the bitterness of having been outsmarted that Holcombe lay on his bed at the Bordeaux Hotel that night. Though it did not for a minute occur to him that Able might win the deadly game, he had to admit to himself that he'd underestimated his younger and less experienced quarry. But, he told himself, now that he knew he was up against an opponent worthy of his mettle, things would be different. He slept that night, but his dreams were filled with tigers.

The second day of the hunt dawned hot and humid. Holcombe dressed and stationed himself outside Able's hotel, but there was no sign of the man. After lunch at a safe and crowded restaurant, Holcombe returned to the area of his own hotel and, from a discreet distance, kept an eye on the street and in particular the bench outside the florist shop. But Able didn't show.

Holcombe had supper in his room, and then, just as dusk was closing in, he looked out of his window and saw Able sitting calmly on the bench. Slow anger began to simmer in Holcombe. No matter what he did, it seemed that the younger and less experienced Able somehow seized the initiative.

In quick, decisive movements, Holcombe checked his handgun, slipped on his jacket, and left the room. Any kind of action was better than this barren game of wits that he always seemed to lose. If Able wanted to follow him, he'd get his chance.

Holcombe walked briskly out of the hotel, down the cement steps, and stopped suddenly when he reached the sidewalk. The bench was empty. He caught a glimpse of Able's striding figure about a half a block away and, grinning tightly, began to follow.

They walked for hours. The casual figure in the light-tan suit ahead of Holcombe never glanced back, but he was sure Able knew he was following. Holcombe never had even the remotest chance to get off a shot. He was led in a winding knowledgeable way down main streets and side streets that were always thronged with people taking in the pleasantness of the cooling summer night. Then, as they were walking down a narrow street lined with bars and loud strip joints, it began to rain.

It was just a cool mist, but it was enough to clear the street of people. They began to walk hurriedly in all directions, seemingly to the disjointed rhythm of the mingling music of half a dozen Dixie and blues bands that wafted out to the street from open club doors. For the first time Able glanced over his shoulder, then he entered a door under a neon sign that blinked "Red Lounge."

With extreme caution, Holcombe followed.

The inside of the Red Lounge was bigger than he'd imagined from the street. There was a wide area of tables and a long glass-fronted bar. At the moment the only source of illumination was a red light that bathed the raised curving runway among the crowded tables. On the runway was a slender brunette, singing and stripping to the improbable tune of "When the Saints Go Marching In." The background music, heavy with drums, was almost drowning out her voice, and Holcombe could see at a glance that she was very near the end of her act.

As his eyes adjusted to the diffused light, Holcombe spotted Able sitting at the very end of the bar. Elbowing through the milling, talking customers, Holcombe stood at the other end of the bar and ordered a whisky. Able was sipping a beer, staring at him quite coolly. Holcombe almost smiled at his quarry. Able hadn't counted on the rain.

The music was getting louder now, and Holcombe's temples throbbed in rhythm to the drums as the drink and the close atmosphere made him flush. The stripper's voice had built to a frantic crescendo to keep time with the madly building tempo. Behind him hands clapped in quickening rhythm and there were yells and whistles as the girl danced closer to the overhead microphone for her finale.

"Oh, when those saints go ma-ar-chin' in!"

Despite himself, Holcombe averted his eyes to look. His glance clung for a moment to the girl's shimmering red-hued flesh, and when he looked back Able was gone. Holcombe took a deep breath. He saw the back door near the other end of the bar and he knew that Able was probably waiting outside for him to follow. Tossing a five-dollar-bill on the bar, he made his way toward the front door. "Hey, Jack!" he heard the red-uniformed bartender call after him. "Your change, man, your change!" But Holcombe was already out the door.

It was much quieter outside and the mist was cool on his face. He began to jog easily toward the end of the block so that he could double around on Able and catch him by surprise.

And then something, a feeling that he'd experienced only a few times in his life, made him stop and turn.

Able was standing outside the *front* entrance of the Red Lounge. Even as Holcombe saw him in the wink of the red neon light, Able was reaching inside his tan jacket for his automatic and was deftly moving into position.

Holcombe ran madly, zigzagging for the nearest corner. He rounded it without knowing if Able had gotten off a shot or not, and he found himself running down an empty narrow side street of tall apartment buildings. There were footfalls behind him and he knew he had to find cover fast. Stopping and turning abruptly, he drew his automatic from its shoulder holster and fired three quick shots at the figure behind him. Then he ducked into a gangway between two buildings.

Standing with his back pressed to the rain-wet bricks, Holcombe realized the dangerous position in which he'd put himself. He was learning too late that in this game the pursuer had every advantage. Now he was trapped. Able either had run through a gangway himself and was training his gun on the back exit, or he'd found cover up the street and was waiting for Holcombe to emerge that way.

Holcombe had to make his break, one way or the other. It was a fifty-fifty choice, and even in the cool rain Holcombe was sweating trying to make it.

Then suddenly, in the echoing quiet, he heard the sound of a motor and saw the street brighten with the whiteness of headlight beams. It was a car, coming so slowly that Holcombe thought it might be a police cruiser, but as it passed the gangway he saw that it was a taxi. He heard it stop only a short distance down the street, and within a few seconds one of its doors opened and slammed.

Holcombe's choice was made for him. Steeling himself against the possible impact of silent bullets, he ran from the gangway toward the stopped cab that had just deposited a passenger. He waved his arms frantically as it began to pull away, and the driver spotted him in the rearview mirror and braked to a quick stop. In one smooth motion, Holcombe flung open a rear door and plunged inside.

"Kinda wet out there," the cabby said, grinning.

"Get the hell out of here fast!" Holcombe yelled. Only when he felt the acceleration, did he allow himself to sink back against the seat and close his eyes.

It wasn't until after they'd driven for about five minutes that Holcombe finally opened his eyes. His gaze fell on the watch on the cabby's right wrist. It was three minutes past midnight. The hunt was over.

Holcombe sat in the back of the cab and reflected bitterly. Never in all his hunting career had he wanted a kill so badly, and never had he been so frustrated. Regardless of what moves he'd made, Able had always managed to become the aggressor, the hunter. And hunting, Holcombe had found, was quite a different matter from being hunted.

He stopped at a reputable-looking place and had a few drinks before returning to his hotel, and this helped soothe the anger and frustration in him. But it all erupted again when he opened the door to his hotel room. There, in the only chair, sat Able.

"How did you get in here?" Holcombe's voice was edgy.

"With this." Able held up a small strip of celluloid. "Better than a key anytime. . . . Thought I'd drop by to congratulate you on a fine chase," the younger man continued affably as he stood. "That was a bit of luck with the taxicab, though. Usually—"

Holcombe brought him down neatly with a shot through the heart.

The bullet didn't exit from Able's back, so there wasn't too much blood. Holcombe walked quickly over and tucked his handkerchief under Able's shirt and into the wound to hold down what bleeding there was. Disposing of the body would be quite simple but a bit risky. Holcombe carried Able's corpse a few feet down the deserted hall to the self-service elevator. He pressed the button marked "B" and prayed that no one was waiting for an elevator on the floors below. No one was, and within five minutes the body was well concealed behind some wooden cases in a corner of the hotel basement.

It would take a few days before Able was found, and even then there would be some confusion as to the cause of death. For Holcombe had removed his handkerchief from the wound and placed the untraceable automatic, wiped clean of his own fingerprints, in Able's stiffening grasp. Then he'd removed Able's gun from its holster and had taken it upstairs with him. Probable suicide, he was sure the official police report would read.

Holcombe slept well that night, as he hadn't slept in

months, and the next morning he ate a hearty breakfast in the hotel dining room before returning home.

Nearly two weeks passed before Holcombe heard from the Quest and Quarry Company. That was when he'd received the phone call that had directed him here, to sit across a tiny desk from Von Eisle in another obscure motel.

"I presume I was called here to collect my five thousand dollars," Holcombe said. "And let me add that your company performs a unique and useful service. The hunt was very gratifying."

Von Eisle smiled his thanks pleasantly and his pale hands snapped open the black attaché case resting on the desk. He kept one hand inside the case and Holcombe suddenly suspected that he was aiming a gun at him through the upraised leather lid. Holcombe felt no real alarm at this, for it seemed to him more a protective than a threatening gesture.

"You did violate the rules of the hunt," Von Eisle said in his calm voice. "According to the newspapers, a bartender at a place called the Red Lounge remembered serving your quarry a drink at just ten minutes to midnight. He remembered the exact time because a stripper named Lollie Popp was just finishing her act. That means that your quarry couldn't have reached your hotel until at least twelve-twenty. At any rate, while the hunt was in progress he would hardly have entered your hotel."

Holcombe shrugged. He felt confident now, for there was nothing to link him with Able's death, and the Quest and Quarry Company stood to lose much more than he would if they went to the authorities. And Von Eisle posed no threat to him now, for the blond man couldn't be sure whether or not anyone knew Holcombe had come to the motel.

"What's twenty minutes, more or less?" Holcombe asked.

Von Eisle's sad eyes regarded him steadily. "Perhaps nothing," he said, with what might have been a trace of resignation.

"My five thousand dollars?" Holcombe's question was a command.

With his free hand, the blond man reached into the attaché case and tossed him a bulky white envelope.

Holcombe glanced inside the envelope at the green bills and smiled. "Is this the only reason you contacted me, or were you going to suggest another hunt? I'm ready anytime."

"As a matter of fact," Von Eisle said, "the company is holding a convention in this city for all of our past clientele. We hold them every so often—whenever it becomes necessary. The highlight of the convention will be an open season."

"Open season?" Holcombe's blue hunter's eyes were cold.

Von Eisle didn't answer but lowered his gaze and pretended to occupy himself with the contents of the black attaché case. Finally, wearily, he rose to leave.

"Yes, open season," he said sadly. "Good-bye, Mr. Holcombe."

The Real Shape
of the Coast

W here the slender peninsula crooks like a beckoning
finger in the warm water, where the ocean waves
crash in umbrellas of foam over the low-lying rocks to
roll and ebb on the narrow white-sand beaches, there
squats in a series of low rectangular buildings and
patterns of high fences the State Institution for the
Criminal Incurably Insane. There are twenty of the
sharp-angled buildings, each rising bricked and hard out
of sandy soil like an undeniable fact. Around each building is a ten-foot redwood fence topped by barbed wire,
and these fences run to the sea's edge to continue as gos-
samer networks of barbed wire that stretch out to the
rocks.

In each of the rectangular buildings live six men, and
on days when the ocean is suitable for swimming it is
part of their daily habit—indeed, part of their therapy—
to go down to the beach and let the waves roll over them,
or simply to lie in the purging sun and grow beautifully
tan. Sometimes, just out of the grasping reach of the
waves, the men might build things in the damp sand, but
by evening those things would be gone. However, some
very interesting things had been built in the sand.

The men in the rectangular buildings were not just marking time until their real death. In fact, the "Incurably Insane" in the institution's name was something of a misnomer; it was just that there was an absolute minimum of hope for these men. They lived in clusters of six not only for security's sake, but so that they might form a more or less permanent sensitivity group—day-in, day-out group therapy, with occasional informal gatherings supervised by young Dr. Montaign. Here, under the subtle and skillful probings of Dr. Montaign, the men bared their lost souls—at least, some of them did.

Cottage D was soon to be the subject of Dr. Montaign's acute interest. In fact, he was to study the occurrences there for the next year and write a series of articles that would be published in influential scientific journals.

The first sign that there was something wrong at Cottage D was when one of the patients, a Mr. Rolt, was found dead on the beach one evening. He was lying on his back near the water's edge, wearing only a pair of khaki trousers. At first glance it would seem that he'd had a drowning accident, only his mouth and much of his throat turned out to be stuffed with sand and with a myriad of tiny colorful shells.

Roger Logan, who had lived in Cottage D since being found guilty of murdering his wife three years before, sat quietly watching Dr. Montaign pace the room.

"This simply won't do," the doctor was saying. "One of you has done away with Mr. Rolt, and that is exactly the sort of thing we are in here to stop."

"But it won't be investigated too thoroughly, will it?" Logan said softly. "Like when a convicted murderer is killed in a prison."

"May I remind you," a patient named Kneehoff said in his clipped voice, "that Mr. Rolt was not a murderer." Kneehoff had been a successful businessman before his confinement, and now he made excellent leather wallets and sold them by mail order. He sat now at a small table with some old letters spread before him, as if he were a chairman of the board presiding over a meeting. "I might add," he said haughtily, "that it's difficult to conduct business in an atmosphere such as this."

"I didn't say Rolt was a murderer," Logan said, "but he is—was—supposed to be in here for the rest of his life. That fact is bound to impede justice."

Kneehoff shrugged and shuffled through his letters. "He was a man of little consequence—that is, compared to the heads of giant corporations."

It was true that Mr. Rolt had been a butcher rather than a captain of industry, a butcher who had put things in the meat—some of them unmentionable. But then Kneehoff had merely run a chain of three dry-cleaning establishments.

"Perhaps you thought him inconsequential enough to murder," William Sloan, who was in for pushing his young daughter out of a fortieth-story window, said to Kneehoff. "You never did like Mr. Rolt."

Kneehoff began to splutter. "You're the killer here, Sloan! You and Logan!"

"I killed no one," Logan said quickly.

Kneehoff grinned. "You were proved guilty in a court of law—of killing your wife."

"They didn't prove it to me. I should know whether or not I'm guilty!"

"I know your case," Kneehoff said, gazing dispassionately at his old letters. "You hit your wife over the head with a bottle of French Chablis wine, killing her immediately."

"I warn you," Logan said heatedly, "implying that I struck my wife with a wine bottle—and French Chablis at that—is inviting a libel suit!"

Noticeably shaken, Kneehoff became quiet and seemed to lose himself in studying the papers before him. Logan

had learned long ago how to deal with him; he knew that
Kneehoff's "company" could not stand a lawsuit.

"Justice must be done," Logan went on. "Mr. Rolt's
murderer, a real murderer, must be caught and executed."

"Isn't that a job for the police?" Dr. Montaign asked
gently.

"The police!" Logan laughed. "Look how they botched
my case! No, this is a job for *us*. Living the rest of our
lives with a murderer would be intolerable."

"But what about Mr. Sloan?" Dr. Montaign asked.
"You're living with him."

"His is a different case," Logan snapped. "Because
they found him guilty doesn't mean he is guilty. He says
he doesn't remember anything about it, doesn't he?"

"What's your angle?" Brandon, the unsuccessful mystery bomber, asked. "You people have always got an
angle, something in mind for yourselves. The only people
you can really trust are the poor people."

"My angle is justice," Logan said firmly. "We must
have justice!"

"Justice for all the people!" Brandon suddenly
shouted, rising to his feet. He glanced about angrily and
then sat down again.

"Justice," said old Mr. Heimer, who had been to other
worlds and could listen to and hear metal, "will take care
of itself. It always does, no matter where."

"They've been waiting a long time," Brandon said, his
jaw jutting out beneath his dark mustache. "The poor
people, I mean."

"Have the police any clues?" Logan asked Dr. Montaign.

"They know what you know," the doctor said calmly.
"Mr. Rolt was killed on the beach between nine-fifteen
and ten—when he shouldn't have been out of Cottage D."

Mr. Heimer raised a thin speckled hand to his lips and chuckled feebly. "Now, maybe that's justice."

"You know the penalty for leaving the building during unauthorized hours," Kneehoff said sternly to Mr. Heimer. "Not death, but confinement to your room for two days. We must have the punishment fit the crime and we must obey the rules. Any operation must have rules in order to be successful."

"That's exactly what I'm saying," Logan said. "The man who killed poor Mr. Rolt must be caught and put to death."

"The authorities are investigating," Dr. Montaign said soothingly.

"Like they investigated my case?" Logan said in a raised and angry voice. "They won't bring the criminal to justice! And I tell you we must not have a murderer here in Compound D!"

"Cottage D," Dr. Montaign corrected him.

"Perhaps Mr. Rolt was killed by something from the sea," William Sloan said thoughtfully.

"No," Brandon said, "I heard the police say there was only a single set of footprints near the body and it led from and to the cottage. It's obviously the work of an inside subversive."

"But what size footprints?" Logan asked.

"They weren't clear enough to determine the size," Dr. Montaign said. "They led to and from near the wooden stairs that come up to the rear yard, then the ground was too hard for footprints."

"Perhaps they were Mr. Rolt's own footprints," Sloan said.

Kneehoff grunted. "Stupid! Mr. Rolt went to the beach, but he did not come back."

"Well—" Dr. Montaign rose slowly and walked to the door. "I must be going to some of the other cottages now." He smiled at Logan. "It's interesting that you're so concerned with justice," he said. A gull screamed as the doctor went out.

The five remaining patients of Cottage D sat quietly after Dr. Montaign's exit. Logan watched Kneehoff gather up his letters and give their edges a neat sharp tap on the tabletop before slipping them into his shirt pocket. Brandon and Mr. Heimer seemed to be in deep thought, while Sloan was peering over Kneehoff's shoulder through the open window out to the rolling sea.

"It could be that none of us is safe," Logan said suddenly. "We must get to the bottom of this ourselves."

"But we are at the bottom," Mr. Heimer said pleasantly, "all of us."

Kneehoff snorted. "Speak for yourself, old man."

"It's the crime against the poor people that should be investigated," Brandon said. "If my bomb in the Statue of Liberty had gone off— And I used my whole week's vacation that year going to New York."

"We'll conduct our own investigation," Logan insisted, "and we might as well start now. Everyone tell me what he knows about Mr. Rolt's murder."

"Who put you in charge?" Kneehoff asked. "And why should we investigate Rolt's murder?"

"Mr. Rolt was our friend," Sloan said.

"Anyway," Logan said, "we must have an orderly investigation. Somebody has to be in charge."

"I suppose you're right," Kneehoff said. "Yes, an orderly investigation."

Information was exchanged, and it was determined that Mr. Rolt had said he was going to bed at 9:15, saying good night to Ollie, the attendant, in the TV lounge. Sloan and Brandon, the two other men in the lounge, remembered the time because the halfway commercial for "Monsters of Main Street" was on, the one where the box of detergent soars through the air and snatches everyone's shirt. Then at ten o'clock, just when the news was coming on, Ollie had gone to check the beach and discovered Mr. Rolt's body.

"So," Logan said, "the approximate time of death has been established. And I was in my room with the door open. I doubt if Mr. Rolt could have passed in the hall to go outdoors without my noticing him, so we must hypothesize that he did go to his room at nine-fifteen, and sometime between nine-fifteen and ten he left through his window."

"He knew the rules," Kneehoff said. "He wouldn't have just walked outside for everyone to see him."

"True," Logan conceded, "but it's best not to take anything for granted."

"True, true." Mr. Heimer chuckled. "Take nothing for granted."

"And where were *you* between nine and ten?" Logan asked.

"I was in Dr. Montaign's office," Mr. Heimer said with a grin, "talking to the doctor about something I'd heard in the steel utility pole. I almost made him understand that all things metal are receivers, tuned to different frequencies, different worlds and vibrations."

Kneehoff, who had once held two of his accountants prisoner for five days without food, laughed.

"And where were *you?*" Logan asked.

"In my office, going over my leather-goods vouchers," Kneehoff said. Kneehoff's "office" was his room, toward the opposite end of the hall from Logan's room.

"Now," Logan said, "we get to the matter of motive. Which of us had reason to kill Mr. Rolt?"

"I don't know," Sloan said distantly. "Who'd do such a thing—fill Mr. Rolt's mouth with sand?"

"You were his closest acquaintance," Brandon said to Logan. "You always played chess with him. Who knows what you and he were plotting?"

37

"What about you?" Kneehoff said to Brandon. "You tried to choke Mr. Rolt just last week."

Brandon stood up angrily, his mustache bristling. "That was the week *before* last!" He turned to Logan. "And Rolt always beat Logan at chess—that's why Logan hated him."

"He didn't *always* beat me at chess," Logan said. "And I didn't hate him. The only reason he beat me at chess sometimes was because he'd upset the board if he was losing."

"You don't like to get beat at anything," Brandon said, sitting down again. "That's why you killed your wife, because she beat you at things. How middle-class, to kill someone because of that."

"I didn't kill my wife," Logan said patiently. "And she didn't beat me at things. Though she was a pretty good businesswoman," he added slowly, "and a good tennis player."

"What about Kneehoff?" Sloan asked. "He was always threatening to kill Mr. Rolt."

"Because he laughed at me!" Kneehoff spat out. "Rolt was a braggart and a fool, always laughing at me because I have ambition and he didn't. He thought he was better at everything than anybody else—and you, Sloan—Rolt used to ridicule you and Heimer. There isn't one of us who didn't have motive to eliminate a piece of scum like Rolt."

Logan was on his feet, almost screaming. "I won't have you talk about the dead like that!"

"All I was saying," Kneehoff said, smiling his superior smile at having upset Logan, "was that it won't be easy for you to discover Rolt's murderer. He was a clever man, that murderer, cleverer than you."

Logan refused to be baited. "We'll see about that when I check the alibis," he muttered, and he left the room to walk barefoot in the surf.

On the beach the next day Sloan asked the question they had all been wondering.

"What are we going to do with the murderer if we do catch him?" he asked, his eyes fixed on a distant ship that was just an irregularity on the horizon.

"We'll extract justice," Logan said. "We'll convict and execute him—eliminate him from our society!"

"Do you think we should?" Sloan asked.

"Of course we should!" Logan snapped. "The authorities don't care who killed Mr. Rolt. The authorities are probably glad he's dead."

"I don't agree that it's a sound move," Kneehoff said, "to execute the man. I move that we don't do that."

"I don't hear anyone seconding you," Logan said. "It has to be the way I say if we are to maintain order here."

Kneehoff thought a moment, then smiled. "I agree we must maintain order at all costs," he said. "I withdraw my motion."

"Motion, hell!" Brandon said. He spat into the sand. "We ought to just find out who the killer is and liquidate him. No time for a motion—time for action!"

"Mr. Rolt would approve of that," Sloan said, letting a handful of sand run through his fingers.

Ollie the attendant came down to the beach and stood there smiling, the sea breeze rippling his white uniform. The group on the beach broke up slowly and casually, each man idling away in a different direction.

Kicking the sun-warmed sand with his bare toes, Logan approached Ollie.

"Game of chess, Mr. Logan?" Ollie asked.

"Thanks, no," Logan said. "You found Mr. Rolt's body, didn't you, Ollie?"

"Right, Mr. Logan."

"Mr. Rolt was probably killed while you and Sloan and Brandon were watching TV."

"Probably," Ollie agreed, his big face impassive.

39

"How come you left at ten o'clock to go down to the beach?"

Ollie turned to stare blankly at Logan with his flat eyes. "You know I always check the beach at night, Mr. Logan. Sometimes the patients lose things."

"Mr. Rolt sure lost something," Logan said. "Did the police ask you if Brandon and Sloan were in the TV room with you the whole time before the murder?"

"They did and I told them yes." Ollie lit a cigarette with one of those transparent lighters that had a fishing fly in the fluid. "You studying to be a detective, Mr. Logan?"

"No, no." Logan laughed. "I'm just interested in how the police work, after the way they messed up my case. Once they thought I was guilty I didn't have a chance."

But Ollie was no longer listening. He had turned to look out at the ocean. "Don't go out too far, Mr. Knee-hoff!" he called, but Kneehoff pretended not to hear and began moving in the water parallel with the beach.

Logan walked away to join Mr. Heimer, who was standing in the surf with his pants rolled above his knees.

"Find out anything from Ollie?" Mr. Heimer asked, his body balancing slightly as the retreating sea pulled the sand and shells from beneath him.

"Some things," Logan said, crossing his arms and enjoying the play of the cool surf about his legs. The two men—rather than the ocean—seemed to be moving as the tide swept in and out and shifted the sand beneath the sensitive soles of their bare feet. "It's like the ocean," Logan said, "finding out who killed Mr. Rolt. The ocean works and works on the shore, washing in and out until only the sand and rock remain—the real shape of the coast. Wash the soil away and you have bare rock; wash the lies away and you have bare truth."

"Not many can endure the truth," Mr. Heimer said,

stooping to let his hand drag in an incoming wave, "even in other worlds."

Logan raised his shoulders. "Not many ever learn the truth," he said, turning and walking through the wet sand toward the beach. Amid the onwash of the wide shallow wave he seemed to be moving backward, out to sea. . . .

Two days later Logan talked to Dr. Montaign, catching him alone in the TV lounge when the doctor dropped by for one of his midday visits. The room was very quiet; even the ticking of the clock seemed slow, lazy, and out of rhythm.

"I was wondering, Doctor," Logan said, "about the night of Mr. Rolt's murder. Did Mr. Heimer stay very late in your office?"

"The police asked me that," Dr. Montaign said with a smile. "Mr. Heimer was in my office until ten o'clock, then I saw him come into this room and join Brandon and Sloan to watch the news."

"Was Kneehoff with them?"

"Yes, Kneehoff was in his room."

"I was in my room," Logan said, "with my door open to the hall, and I didn't see Mr. Rolt pass to go outdoors. So he must have gone out through his window. Maybe the police would like to know that."

"I'll tell them for you," Dr. Montaign said, "but they know Mr. Rolt went out through his window because his only door was locked from the inside." The doctor cocked his head at Logan, as was his habit. "I wouldn't try to be a detective," he said gently. He placed a smoothly manicured hand on Logan's shoulder. "My advice is to forget about Mr. Rolt."

"Like the police?" Logan said.

The hand patted Logan's shoulder soothingly.

After the doctor had left, Logan sat on the cool vinyl

sofa and thought. Brandon, Sloan, and Heimer were accounted for, and Kneehoff couldn't have left the building without Logan seeing him pass in the hall. The two men, murderer and victim, might have left together through Mr. Rolt's window—only that wouldn't explain the single set of fresh footprints to and from the body. And the police had found Mr. Rolt's footprints where he'd gone down to the beach farther from the cottage and then apparently walked up the beach through the surf to where his path and the path of the murderer crossed.

And then Logan saw the only remaining possibility— the only possible answer.

Ollie, the man who had discovered the body—Ollie alone had had the opportunity to kill! And after doing away with Mr. Rolt he must have noticed his footprints leading to and from the body; so at the wooden stairs he simply turned and walked back to the sea in another direction, then walked up the beach to make his "discovery" and alert the doctor.

Motive? Logan smiled. Anyone could have had motive enough to kill the bragging and offensive Mr. Rolt. He had been an easy man to hate.

Logan left the TV room to join the other patients on the beach, careful not to glance at the distant white-uniformed figure of Ollie painting some deck chairs at the other end of the building.

"Tonight," Logan told them dramatically, "we'll meet in the conference room after Dr. Montaign leaves and I promise to tell you who the murderer is. Then we'll decide how best to remove him from our midst."

"Only if he's guilty," Kneehoff said. "You must present convincing, positive evidence."

"I have proof," Logan said.

"Power to the people!" Brandon cried, leaping to his feet.

42

Laughing and shouting, they all ran like schoolboys into the waves.

The patients sat through their evening session with Dr. Montaign, answering questions mechanically and chattering irrelevantly, and Dr. Montaign sensed a certain tenseness and expectancy in them. Why were they anxious? Was it fear? Had Logan been harping to them about the murder? Why was Kneehoff not looking at his letters and Sloan not gazing out the window?

"I told the police," Dr. Montaign mentioned, "that I didn't expect to walk up on any more bodies on the beach."

"You?" Logan stiffened in his chair. "I thought it was Ollie who found Mr. Rolt."

"He did, really," Dr. Montaign said, cocking his head. "After Mr. Heimer left me I accompanied Ollie to check the beach so I could talk to him about some things. He was the one who saw the body first and ran ahead to find out what it was."

"And it was Mr. Rolt, his mouth stuffed with sand," Sloan murmured.

Logan's head seemed to be whirling. He had been so sure! Process of elimination. It had to be Ollie! Or were the two men, Ollie and Dr. Montaign, in it together? They had to be! But that was impossible! There had been only one set of footprints.

Kneehoff! It must have been Kneehoff all along! He must have made a secret appointment with Rolt on the beach and killed him. But Rolt had been walking alone until he met the killer, who was also alone! And *someone* had left the fresh footprints, the single set of footprints, to and from the body.

Kneehoff must have seen Rolt, slipped out through his window, intercepted him, and killed him. But Kneehoff's

43

room didn't have a window! Only the two end rooms had windows, Rolt's room and Logan's room!

A single set of footprints—they could only be his own! *His own!*

Through a haze Logan saw Dr. Montaign glance at his watch, smile, say his good-byes, and leave. The night breeze wafted through the wide open windows of the conference room with the hushing of the surf, the surf wearing away the land to bare rock.

"Now," Kneehoff said to Logan, and the moon seemed to light his eyes, "who exactly is our man? Who killed Mr. Rolt? And what is your evidence?"

Ollie found Logan's body the next morning, face down on the beach, the gentle lapping surf trying to claim him. Logan's head was turned and half buried and his broken limbs were twisted at strange angles, and around him the damp sand was beaten with, in addition to his own, four different sets of footprints.

High Stakes

E rnie followed the bellhop into the crummy room at the Hayes Hotel, was shown the decrepit bathroom with its cracked porcelain, the black-and-white TV with its rolling picture. The bellhop, who was a teenager with a pimply complexion, smiled and waited. Ernie tipped him a dollar, which, considering that Ernie had no luggage other than the overnight bag he carried himself, seemed adequate. The bellhop sneered at him and left.

After the click of the door latch, there was thick silence in the room. Ernie sat on the edge of the bed, his ears gradually separating the faint sounds outside from the room's quietude—the thrumming rush of city traffic, a very distant siren or occasional honking horn, the metallic thumping and strumming of elevator cables from the bowels of the building. Someone dropped something heavy in the room upstairs. A maid pushed a linen cart with a squeaky wheel along the hall outside Ernie's door. Ernie bowed his head, cupped his face in his hands, and stared at the worn pale-blue carpet. Then he closed his eyes and sought the temporary anonymity of interior darkness.

Ernie's luck was down. Almost as low as Ernie himself, who stood a shade over five-foot-four, even in his boots with the built-up heels. Usually a natty dresser, to-

45

night he'd disgraced his slender frame with a cheap off-the-rack brown suit, a soiled white shirt, and a ridiculous red clip-on bow tie. He'd had to abandon his regular wardrobe at his previous hotel in lieu of settling the bill. Ernie had a face like a conniving ferret's, with watery pinkish eyes and a long bent nose. His appearance wasn't at all deceptive. Ernie ferreted and connived.

He had spent most of his forty years in the starkly poor neighborhood of his birth; and if he wasn't the smartest guy around, he did possess a kind of gritty cunning that had enabled him to make his own erratic way in the world. And he had instinct, hunches, that led to backing the right horse sometimes, or playing the right card sometimes. Sometimes. He got by, anyway. Getting by was Ernie's game, and he just about broke even. He was not so much a winner as a survivor. There were people who resented even that.

One of those people was Carl Atwater. Ernie thought about Carl, opened his eyes, and stood up from the sagging bed. He got the half-pint of rye out of his overnight bag and went into the bathroom for the glass he'd seen on the basin. He tried not to think about Carl and the thousand dollars he owed Carl from that card game the last time he'd been here in his hometown. He poured himself a drink, sat at the nicked and scarred plastic-topped desk, and glanced around again at the tiny room.

Even for Ernie this was a dump. He was used to better things; he didn't always slip into town on the sly and sign into a fleabag hotel. If he hadn't needed to see his sister Eunice to borrow some money—not the thousand he owed Carl, just a couple of hundred to see him down to Miami—he wouldn't be here now, contemplating on how he would bet on the roaches climbing the wall behind the bed if someone else were here to lay down some money on which one they thought would be first to reach the ceiling.

He smiled. What would Eunice think of him betting on
cockroaches? She wouldn't be surprised; she'd told him
for years that gambling was a sickness, and he had it
bad. Maybe she was right, harping at him all the time to
quit betting. But then she'd never hit the big one at Pim-
lico. She'd never turned up a corner of a hole card and
seen a lovely third queen peeking out. She'd never . . .

The hell with it. Ernie got two decks of cards from a
suitcoat pocket. He squinted at the decks, then slipped
the marked one back into the pocket. Ernie always made
it a point to carry a marked deck. A slickster in Reno had
shown him how to doctor the cards so that only an expert
could tell, and then only by looking closely. He broke the
seal on the straight deck and dealt himself a hand of soli-
taire. He always played fair with himself. Two minutes
after he'd switched on the desk lamp, tilting the yellowed
shade to take the glare off the cards, he was lost in that
intensity of concentration that only a devout gambler can
achieve.

After losing three games in a row, he pushed the cards
away and rubbed his tired eyes.

That was when someone knocked on the door.

Ernie sat paralyzed, not only by fear of Carl Atwater
but by fear of what all gamblers regard as their enemy—
the unexpected. The unexpected was what gave the dice a
final unlikely tumble, what caused the favorite horse to
stumble on the far turn, what filled inside straights for
novice poker players. This time what the unexpected did
was the worst it had ever done to Ernie; it delivered two
very large business-like individuals to his hotel room.
They had a key, and when their knock wasn't answered
they had opened the door and walked right in.

They were big men, all right, but in the tiny room—
and contrasted with Ernie's frailness—they appeared gigantic. The larger of the two, a lantern-jawed ex-pug
type with a pushed-in nose and cold blue eyes, smiled

down at Ernie. It wasn't the sort of smile that would melt hearts. His partner, a handsome dark-haired man with what looked like a knife scar down one cheek, stood wooden-faced. It was the smiling man who spoke.

"I guess you know that Carl Atwater sent us," he said. He had a deep voice that suited his immensity.

Ernie swallowed a throatful of marbles. His heart ran wild. "But . . . how could anyone know I was here? I just checked in."

"Carl knows lots of desk clerks in hotels all over the city," the smiler said. "Soon as you checked in, we heard about it and Carl thought you rated a visit." He grinned wider and lazily cracked his knuckles. The sound in the small room was like a string of exploding firecrackers. "Don't dummy up on us, Ernie. You know what kind of visit this is."

Ernie stood up without thinking about it, knocking his chair over backward. "Hey, wait a minute! I mean, Carl and I are old buddies, and all I owe him is an even thousand bucks. I mean, you got the wrong guy! Check with Carl—just do me that favor!"

"It's precisely because you only owe a thousand dollars that we're here," the dark-haired one said. "Too many people owe Carl small sums, welshers like yourself. You're going to be an example for the rest of the petty four-flushers, Ernie. It will be a bad example. They won't want to follow it. They'll pay their debts instead, and that will add up to a lot of money."

"There ain't no good ways to die," the smiler said, "but some ways is worse than others."

Both men moved toward Ernie, slowly, as if wanting him to fully experience his dread. Ernie glanced at the door. Too far away. "Just check with Carl! Please!" he pleaded mindlessly, backpeddling on numbed legs. He was trembling. The bonecrushers kept advancing. The window was behind Ernie, but he was twelve stories above the street. The fleabag room wasn't air-conditioned, so the window was open about six inches. Corner a rat and watch it instinctively choose the less immediate danger. Ernie whirled and flung himself at the window. He snagged a fingernail in the faded lace curtain, felt the nail rip as he hurled the window all the way open. The smiler grunted and lunged at him, but Ernie scampered outside onto the ledge with speed that amazed.

A gargantuan hand emerged from the open window. Ernie shuffled sideways to avoid it. He pressed his quaking body back against the brick wall and stared upward at the black night sky, the stiff summer breeze whipping at his unbuttoned suitcoat.

The smiler stuck his huge head out the window. He studied the narrowness of the ledge on which Ernie was balanced, stared down at the street twelve stories below. He exposed a mouthful of crooked teeth and laughed a rolling, phlegmy rumble. The laugh was vibrant with emotion, but not humor.

"I told you some ways to die was worse than others," he said. "You're part worm, not part bird." He pulled his head back inside and shut the window. Ernie got a glimpse of sausage-sized fingers turning the lock.

Be calm, he told himself, be *calm!* He was trapped on the ledge, but his situation was much improved over what it had been a few minutes ago.

Then he really began to analyze his predicament. The concrete ledge he was poised on was only about six inches wide—not the place to go for a walk in his dress boots with their built-up slick leather heels. And just to his right, the ledge ended four feet away where the side of the building jutted out, and there were no other windows Ernie might be able to enter. To his left, beyond the locked window to his room, was a window to a room that did have an air conditioner. The old rusted unit extended from the window about three feet. Not only would that

49

window be firmly fastened closed against the top of the unit, but there was no way to get around or over the bulky sloping steel squareness of the air conditioner to reach the next window.

Ernie glanced upward. There was no escape in that direction, either.

Then he looked down.

Vertigo hit him with hammer force. Twelve stories seemed like twelve miles. He could see the tops of foreshortened streetlights, a few toylike cars turning at the intersection. His mind whirled, his head swam with terror. The ledge he was on seemed only a few inches wide and was barely visible, almost behind him, from his precarious point of view. His legs quivered weakly; his boots seemed to become detached from them, seemed to be stiff, awkward creatures with their own will that might betray him and send him plunging to his death. He could see so far—as if he were flying. Ernie clenched his eyes shut. He didn't let himself imagine what happened to flesh and bone when it met the pavement after a twelve-story drop.

He shoved himself backward against the security of the wall with what strength he had left, his hands at his sides, his fingernails clawing into the mortar. That rough brick wall was his mother and his lover and every high card he had ever held. It was all he had. He was hypocrite enough to pray.

But the terror seeped into his pores, into his brain and soul, became one with him. A thousand bucks, a lousy thousand bucks! He could have gone to a loan shark, could have stolen something and pawned it, could have begged. He could have . . .

But he had to do something now. *Now!* He had to survive.

Not looking down, staring straight ahead with fear-bulged eyes, he chanced a hesitant, shuffling sideways step to his left, back toward his window. He dug his fingertips into the bricks as he moved, wishing the wall were soft so he could sink his fingers deep into it. Then he was assailed by an image of the wall coming apart like modeling clay in his hands, affording no support at all, sending him in a horrifyingly breathless arc into the night. He tried not to think about the wall, tried not to think about anything. It was a time for the primal raw judgment of fear.

Ernie made himself take another tentative step. Another. He winced each time his hard leather heels scraped loudly on the concrete. The material of his cheap suit kept snagging on the rough wall at his seat and shoulders, the backs of his legs. Once, the sole of his left boot slid on something small and rounded—a pebble, perhaps—with a rollerlike action that almost caused him to fall. The panic that washed over him was a cold dark thing that he never wanted to feel again.

Finally, he was at the window. He contorted his body carefully, afraid that the night breeze might snatch it at any second, craned his neck till it hurt, and peered into his room.

It was empty. The bonecrushers had left. The threadbare furniture, the bed, the hard, worn carpet, had never looked so sweet. One of Ernie's hands curled around the window frame, came in contact with the smooth glass. He could see the tarnished brass latch at the top of the lower frame, firmly lodged in the locked position.

He struck at the window experimentally. The backward force of the blow separated him from the brick wall. Air shrieked into his lungs in a shrill gasp, and he straightened his body and slammed it backward, cracking his head on the wall, making him dizzy and nauseated. He stood frozen that way for a full minute.

Gradually, he became aware of a coolness on his cheeks—the high breeze drying his tears. He knew he couldn't strike the glass hard enough to break it without

51

sending himself in an unbalanced tilt out over the street to death waiting below.

Carl's bonecrushers were probably already having a beer somewhere, counting Ernie as dead. They were right. They were professionals who knew about such things, who recognized death when they saw it. Ernie's lower lip began to tremble. He wasn't an evil person; he'd never deliberately done anything to harm anyone. He didn't deserve this. *No one deserved this!*

He decided to scream. Maybe somebody—one of the other guests, a maid, the disdainful bellhop—would hear him.

"Help! Help!"

He almost laughed maniacally at the hopelessness of it. His choked screams were so feeble, lost on the wind, absorbed by the vast night. He could barely hear them himself.

As far back as he could remember, desperation had been with him as a dull ache in the pit of his stomach, like an inflamed appendix threatening to burst. If it wasn't a friend, it was surely a close acquaintance. He should be able to deal with it if anyone could.

Yet he couldn't. Not this time. Maybe it inevitably had to come to this, to the swift screaming plunge that had so often awoken him from dark dreams. But tonight there would be no awakening, because he wasn't dreaming.

Ernie cursed himself and all his ancestry that had brought him to this point. He cursed his luck. But he would not let himself give up; his gameness was all he had. There was always, for the man with a feel for the angles, some sort of edge against the odds.

His pockets! What was in his pockets that he might use to break the window?

The first object he drew out was a greasy comb. He fumbled it, almost instinctively lunged for it as it slipped from his fingers and dropped. He started to bow his head to watch the comb fall, then remembered the last time he'd looked down. He again pressed the back of his head against the bricks. The world rocked crazily.

Here was his wallet. He withdrew it from his hip pocket carefully, squeezing it as if it were a bird that might try to take flight. He opened it, and his fingers groped through its contents. He explored the wallet entirely by feel, afraid to look down at it. A few bills, a credit card, a driver's license, a couple of old IOUs that he let flutter into the darkness. He kept the stiff plastic credit card and decided to drop the wallet deliberately. Maybe someone below would see it fall and look up and spot him. The odds were against it, he knew. This was a bad neighborhood; there were few people on the sidewalks. What would happen is that somebody would find the wallet, stick it in his pocket, and walk away. Ernie started to work the bills, a ten and two ones, out of the wallet, then decided it wasn't worth the effort and let the wallet drop. Money wouldn't help him where he was.

There was a slight crack between the upper and lower window frames. Ernie tried to insert the credit card, praying that it would fit.

It did! A break! He'd gotten a break! Maybe it would be all he'd need!

He craned his neck sideways to watch as he slid the credit card along the frame and shoved it against the window latch. He could feel warmer air from the room rising from the crack and caressing his knuckles. He was so close, so close to being on the other side of that thin pane of glass and safe!

The latch moved slightly—he was sure of it! He pressed harder with the plastic card, feeling its edge dig into his fingers. He could feel or see no movement now. Desperately, he began to work the card back and forth. His hands were slick with perspiration.

The latch moved again!

Ernie almost shouted with joy. He would beat this! In a minute or five minutes the window would be unlocked and he would raise it and fall into the room and hug and kiss the worn carpet. He actually grinned as he manipulated his weakened fingers to get a firmer grip on the card.

And suddenly the card wasn't there. He gasped and snatched frantically, barely feeling the card's plastic corner as it slipped all the way through the crack into the room. He saw it slide to the bottom of the window pane, bounce off the inside wooden frame, and drop to the floor. From where he stood, he could see it lying on the carpet. Lying where it could no longer help him.

Ernie sobbed. His body began to tremble so violently that he thought it might shake itself off the ledge. He tried to calm himself when he realized that might actually happen. With more effort than he'd ever mustered for anything, he controlled himself and stood motionless.

He had to think, think, think! . . .

What else did he have in his pockets?

His room key!

He got it out and grasped it in the palm of his hand. It was affixed to no tag or chain, simply a brass key. He tried to fit it into the narrow crack between the upper and lower window frames, but it was far wider than the credit card; he couldn't even insert the tip.

Then he got an idea. The putty holding the glass in its frame was old and chipped, dried hard from too many years and too many faded layers of paint.

Ernie began to chip at the putty with the tip of the key. Some of it came loose and crumbled, dropping to the ledge. He dug with the key again and more of the dried putty broke away from the frame. He would have to work all the way around the pane, and that would take time. It would take concentration. But Ernie would do it, because there was no other way off the ledge, because for the first time he realized how much he loved life. He flexed his knees slightly, his back still pressed to the hard bricks, and continued to chip away at the hardened putty.

After what seemed like an hour, a new problem developed. He'd worked more than halfway around the edges of the window pane when his legs began to cramp painfully. And his knees began trembling, not so much from fear now as from fatigue. Ernie stood up straight, tried to relax his calf muscles.

When he bent to begin work again, he found that within a few minutes the muscles cramped even more painfully. He straightened once more, felt the pain ease slightly. He would work this way, in short shifts, until the pain became unbearable and his trembling legs threatened to lose all strength and sensation. He would endure the pain because there was no other way. He didn't let himself consider what would happen if his legs gave out before he managed to chip away all the putty. Cautiously he flexed his knees, scooted lower against the wall, and began wielding the key with a frantic kind of economy of motion.

Finally, the putty was all chipped away, lying in triangular fragments on the ledge or on the sidewalk below.

Ernie ran his hand along the area where the glass met the wood frame. He felt a biting pain as the sharp edge of the glass sliced into his finger. He jerked the hand back, stared at his dark blood. The finger began to throb in quick rhythm with his heart, a persistent reminder of mortality.

His problem now was that the pane wouldn't come out. It was slightly larger than the perimeter of the window frame opening, set in a groove in the wood, so it couldn't be pushed inward. It would have to be pulled out toward the street.

Ernie tried fitting the key between the wood and the

glass so he could lever the top of the pane outward. The key was too wide.

He pressed his back against the bricks and began to cry again. His legs were rubbery; his entire body ached and was racked by occasional cramps and spasms. He was getting weaker, he knew; too weak to maintain his precarious perch on the narrow ledge. If only he still had the credit card, he thought, he would be able to pry the glass loose, let it fall to the sidewalk, and he could easily get back inside. But then if he'd held onto the card he might have been able to force the latch. The wind picked up, whipped at his clothes, threatened to fill his suitcoat like a sail and pluck him from the ledge.

Then Ernie remembered. His suitcoat pocket! In the coat's inside pocket was his deck of marked cards! His edge against the odds!

He got the cards out, drew them from their box, and let the box arc down and away in the breeze. He thumbed the top card from the deck and inserted it between the glass and the wooden frame. He gave it a slight twist and pulled. The glass seemed to move outward.

Then the card tore almost in half and lost all usefulness.

Ernie let it sail out into the night. He thumbed off the next card, bent it slightly so that it formed a subtle hook when he inserted it. This time the glass almost edged out of its frame before the card was torn. Ernie discarded that one and worked patiently, almost confidently. He had fifty more chances. The odds were with him now.

The tenth card, the king of diamonds, did the trick. The pane fell outward top first, scraped on the ledge, and then plummeted to shatter on the street below.

On uncontrollably shaking legs, Ernie took three shuffling sideways steps, gripped the window frame, and leaned backward in a stooped position, toward the room's interior.

Then he lost his grip.

His left leg shot out and his shoulder hit the wooden frame. Gravity on both sides of the window fought over him for a moment while his heart blocked the scream in his throat.

He fell into the room, bumping his head on the top of the window frame as he dropped, hitting the floor hard. A loud sob of relief escaped his lips as he continued his drop, whirling into unconsciousness.

He awoke terrified. Then he realized he was still lying on his back on the scratchy, worn carpet, on the motionless, firm floor of his hotel room, and the terror left him.

But only for a moment.

Staring down at him was Carl Atwater, flanked by his two bonecrushers.

Ernie started to get up, then fell back, supporting himself on his elbows. He searched the faces of the three men looming over him and was surprised to see a relaxed smile on Carl's shrewd features, deadpan indifference on those of his henchmen. "Look, about that thousand dollars . . ." he said, trying to ride the feeble ray of sunshine in Carl's smile.

"Don't worry about that, Ernie, old buddy," Carl said. He bent forward, offering his hand.

Ernie gripped the strong, well-manicured hand, and Carl helped him to his feet. He was still weak, so he moved over to lean on the desk. The eyes of the three men followed him.

"You don't owe me the thousand anymore," Carl said.

Ernie was astounded. He knew Carl; they lived by the same unbreakable code. "You mean you're going to cancel the debt?"

"I never cancel a debt," Carl said in an icy voice. He crossed his arms, still smiling. "Let's say you worked it off. When we heard you checked in at the Hayes, we got right down here. We were in the building across the street ten minutes after you were shown to this room."

"You mean the three of you . . .?"

"Four of us," Carl corrected.

That was when Ernie understood. The two bonecrushers were pros; they would never have allowed him to escape, even temporarily, out the window. They had let him get away, boxed him in so that there was no place to go but out onto the ledge. The whole thing had been a set-up. After locking the window, the two bonecrushers had gone across the street to join their boss. Ernie knew who the fourth man must be.

"You're off the hook," Carl told him, "because I bet a thousand dollars that you'd find a way off that ledge without getting killed." There was a sudden genuine flash of admiration in his smile, curiously mixed with contempt. "I had faith in you, Ernie, because I know you and guys like you. You're a survivor, no matter what. You're the rat that finds its way off the sinking ship. Or off a high ledge."

Ernie began to shake again, this time with rage. "You were watching me from across the street. The three of you and whoever you placed the bet with. . . . All the time I was out there you were watching, waiting to see if I'd fall."

"I never doubted you, Ernie," Carl told him.

Ernie's legs threatened to give out at last. He staggered a few steps and sat slumped on the edge of the mattress. He had come so close to dying; Carl had come so close to backing a loser. "I'll never place another bet," he mumbled. "Not on a horse, a football game, a roulette wheel, a political race . . . nothing! I'm cured, I swear it!"

Carl laughed. "I told you I know you, Ernie. Better than you think. I've heard guys like you talk that way hundreds of times. They always gamble again, because it's what keeps them alive. They have to believe that a turn of a card or a tumble of the dice or a flip of a coin might change things for them, because they can't stand things the way they are. You're like the rest of them, Ernie. I'll see you again sooner or later, and I'll see your money."

Carl walked toward the door. The bonecrusher with the knife scar was there ahead of him, holding the door open. Neither big man was paying the slightest attention to Ernie now. They were finished with him, and he was of no more importance than a piece of the room's worn-out furniture.

"Take care of yourself, Ernie," Carl said, and they went out.

Ernie sat for a long time staring at the floor. He remembered how it had been out on that ledge; it had changed him permanently, he was convinced. It had wised him up as nothing else could. Carl was wrong if he thought Ernie wasn't finished gambling. Ernie knew better. He was a new man and a better man. He wasn't all talk like those other guys. Carl was mistaken about him. Ernie was sure of it.

He would bet on it.

Buried Treasure

W hat is it that fascinates us about the past that lives within the memories of others yet is only wistful words, dry pages, and film to ourselves? Is it that we can't fully conceive of such a hazy yet achingly familiar world existing prior to our own? Or that we can?

I wondered about that as I signed the closing papers on our new-old home in Jade Point, Missouri. Jade Point was a small town, but within commuting distance of Saint Louis, and the house was a three-story Victorian monstrosity nearly a hundred years old. Exactly what Effie, my wife, had always wanted to own and renovate. I'd just received a substantial sum from the sale of my advertising agency back East; I could afford, barely, to be indulgent.

We'd bought the house from the estate of an old woman named Beatrice Logan, the last of a proud local family. As soon as we'd moved into the high-ceilinged deteriorated monster, my wife began to show me what she called the house's "buried treasure." I admit to being impressed. There were corners and alcoves in that house that probably hadn't been looked into in years. Effie came up with rare cut glass, solid brass fixtures buried beneath layers of faded paint, intricately scrolled woodwork now impossibly expensive to duplicate. But the most unexpected thing we found was the box in the basement.

It was a gray metal box, not large or exceptionally heavy, but obviously containing something that didn't rattle when shook.

"See if you can get it open, Warren," Effie said. "Anything might be inside."

I went to my toolbox and got a hammer. One sharp blow, and the box's steel lid sprang open.

Letters. Various papers. Curled and yellowed about the edges. Most of the postmarks were dated in the mid-thirties, the letters addressed to someone named Leonard Carvell. Effie and I read a few of the letters there at the base of the cellar steps. They were personal, at the time not very interesting, with frequent references to someone named Floyd. The handwriting was poor, with many misspelled words and malapropisms, and there was a curious, almost guarded obliqueness to the phrasing.

"These stamps might be worth something," Effie said.

"I think what I'd better do," I told her, replacing the letters and closing the metal lid, "is ask around and see if anyone knows the family. This Leonard Carvell might still be alive or have some survivors who'd want this box."

Effie agreed to the reasonableness of that idea, and the next day I drove in to Jade Point's tiny shopping area and asked in the A&P store and at the post office if anyone had heard of Leonard Carvell or his family. No one had. And no one had in the Drop-In Tavern next to the barber shop, though I sensed a surprised kind of reticence in some of the old-timers bent over the checkerboard near the end of the long mahogany bar.

"What now?" Effie asked, when I'd returned and

stretched out on the antique sofa she'd bought to match the decor of the living room.

"We'll put a classified ad in the Saint Louis papers," I said, shading the light from my eyes with my forearm. Some of the letters in the box had a Saint Louis postmark and were signed simply "Eddie." Strangely, none of the envelopes in the box had a return address.

"You word the ad and I'll phone it in for Sunday," Effie said, continuing to apply paint stripper to the curved oak banister.

The box's contents were probably worthless, of only personal interest, but we felt obligated.

For over a week there was no reply to our ad in the Saint Louis *Post Dispatch,* and I'd almost forgotten about the metal box, when late Tuesday morning the doorbell rang.

Effie was out combing the antique shops in nearby Greenville, so I answered the door to find an old man standing on the wooden porch, smiling nervously, wiping perspiration from his cheeks and forehead with a folded white handkerchief. "Did you place the ad about the Leonard Carvell letters?" he asked in a hesitant but hopeful voice.

I told him I had, told him my name was Warren Aikin, and invited him inside, out of the heat. He was a stooped man, probably in his early seventies, but still taller than my own six feet. His clothes were threadbare but once expensive, and he still moved well. He looked anxiously around as he entered and sat down in the wing chair near the cold fireplace. There was something fearless and rather desperate in his faded gray eyes. I waited for him to introduce himself. He didn't.

"I'd like to obtain those letters," he said gently.

"Are you a member of the Carvell family?"

He almost glared at me despite no alteration of his parchment-like features. "No, I'm not that."

I suspected then he might be an antique dealer or stamp collector trying to make a fast dollar or a valuable find. "Are you a dealer of some sort?" I asked.

He shook his head, saw that I didn't believe him, and said succinctly, "No."

"Then what claim have you to the letters?" I asked.

He wasn't a fool. "I could tell you, Mr. Aikin, but would you believe me?"

"Frankly, not unequivocally. I suspected my ad might attract some antique buffs or dealers, and to be honest with you, I had in mind only turning the box over to a family member. I'm no expert, but it seems to me there isn't any monetary worth there."

The old man seemed to think over what I'd said. He knew that whatever farfetched tale I heard, I would be skeptical and that I'd require some proof of any claim to Carvell family membership.

"I'll pay you a thousand dollars for the box and its contents," he said calmly.

I was stunned enough to have to sit down. "You know something I don't," I said.

"Do you accept?"

If the old man was willing to pay that much money for the contents of the box, they must be worth something to the Carvell family—if there was any family remaining. I would be selling someone's personal effects, and I began to wonder if that was even legal. I could just see some distraught Carvell materializing in a week or a month to sue me on some charge I couldn't imagine.

"I can't," I said. "I'm sure that eventually some member of the Carvell family will claim the box."

The old man nodded with an odd little smile. "Someone will," he said, and stood, nodded good-bye, and left.

I sat a while wondering who he was. For that matter, did *he* know? There was that cast to his eyes, and his strange manner, that suggested someone living in his own world, almost to the point of mental aberration. He had to be crazy to offer a thousand dollars for a batch of old letters and papers.

On the other hand, I'd have been crazy not to take a closer look at the contents of the metal box. I locked the front door and went down into the cellar.

Five minutes later, I had the box's contents spread over the dining room table. Mostly old letters; a guarantee on a wristwatch dated January 1934; a dozen blank title forms for automobiles licensed in the state of Illinois; even a yellowed operating manual for a vacuum cleaner. I began to read the letters, this time all of them, and thoroughly.

It didn't take long for me to discover that Leonard Carvell was also known as Blackie Carvell, and apparently had been an infamous Depression-era gangster. I was fascinated to conclude that the Floyd referred to in many of the letters was Charles "Pretty Boy" Floyd, the notorious bank robber and killer, who had hidden out in a Missouri roadhouse for many months and had even become an accepted part of the community. There was also, folded with a letter in a large envelope, a map of the state of Florida, and stapled to it a detailed map of a small area near central Florida. I held the penciled letter to the light streaming through the curtained windows and read,

> *Eddie,*
> *Keep the two pieces in seperet places. Betty L. is fine and will be ready to travel soon. See you in Chi. or St. Lu.*
>
> *Blackie*

I saw that the letter, addressed to a Mr. Eddie Pepp at a number on Oakland Avenue in Saint Louis, was stamped but not postmarked. It had never been mailed.

My curiosity was aroused. When Effie came home I told her something of what had happened and that I was going to drive into Saint Louis tomorrow. She said fine, she was going to Vandalia to see about a brass hall tree for the foyer. She also asked me who the old man was she kept seeing near the house. I told her I had a pretty good idea, but by then she was busy measuring the foyer.

It was easy to find Oakland Avenue in Saint Louis. It was an east-west avenue that ran past a sporting arena, office buildings, a TV station, and to the west some older apartment buildings and a hospital. I estimated that an office building sat at the former site of Carvell's letter to Eddie Pepp.

After parking my car in the lot of a small restaurant on a side street, I walked across the heat-scoured cement, went inside, and asked for a hamburger and information. I found that, in the thirties, the address on Oakland Avenue had been that of a large amusement park. Not an unreasonable hideout for a Depression-era desperado.

When I was finished with the greasy hamburger and a cup of coffee, I drove from the restaurant to the downtown library. I asked the librarian for microfilmed copies of the mid-thirties Saint Louis papers. Then I sat at one of the microfilm viewers and began to read.

It wasn't hard to piece together the violent career of Leonard "Blackie" Carvell. He'd appeared in the news first in June of 1932 as a murder suspect, avoided trial in that case, but not for the September 1932, slaying of a tavern owner during a holdup. He was sentenced to life imprisonment in the state penitentiary but escaped en route. In 1933 he went on a bank-robbing spree along with two partners, Vern Molako and Eddie Pepp. Molako was killed by police in a small Arkansas town in late 1933, but Pepp continued his partnership with Carvell for the next four years. They robbed several more banks and were suspects in a kidnapping case and a bombing.

In June of 1937 Carvell was shot to death after a Union, Missouri, bank robbery, surprised by federal agents in a farmhouse outside of Jade Point, Missouri. The June 14, 1937, paper contained a death photo of a lean-faced man with a shock of unruly dark hair. The paper also revealed that the thirty thousand dollars stolen in that robbery, which was committed by two armed men, hadn't been recovered.

I scanned the papers for the next several months of that year. I could find no record of the money's having been found.

When I got back to Jade Point late that afternoon, I kissed Effie hello and made directly for the desk where I'd placed the steel box. I got out the letter to Eddie Pepp and the Florida maps and examined them again.

The larger map was an old Florida roadmap with a red-penciled route to a town called Oleana; the smaller map was a carefully inked, detailed drawing of what looked to be three roads that formed an obtuse triangle, a number of small squares that no doubt designated houses, and smaller circles and odd shapes within the triangle. There was no scale and no revealing marks or lettering on the map. In the upper-left corner of the paper on which the smaller map was drawn, outside the lined boundaries of the map, was a small scrawled five-pointed star.

None of it meant anything to me.

But when I started to return the letter and maps to the envelope, something hindered me. I looked inside the envelope and found another sheet of folded paper, exactly like the sheet on which the smaller map was drawn. The sheet of paper was blank but for a scrawled star in one corner and an X to the right of center. The star was a replica of the one in the upper-left corner of the map paper.

It wasn't long before I caught on. I pressed the map against the inside of a window pane so the light shone through it, then placed the blank paper against it so the stars matched. That rested the X at a spot near the center of the triangle formed by the roads. I held the papers there and used a pin to pierce the center of the X and mark the map beneath.

I knew then that what I had in my hand might be a genuine treasure map, worth thirty thousand dollars. And I could figure out who the old man must have been, and why he kept up his constant watch on the house.

"Effie!" I shouted. "I'm going to Florida!"

She listened to what I had to say and told me I was crazy.

But I went.

Oleana was a small town off Highway 24 with a population of 2,966. I pulled my rental car into the lot of the Oleana Drowsy-Stop Motel and went into the office to register.

Darkness was falling, so after settling into my room, I had dinner at the motel restaurant. Then I went back to my room and tried to make time pass by watching a string of television shows.

The next morning, after a virtually sleepless night, I got in the car and followed Carvell's map to where the roads formed—or used to form—a triangle. The area had become part of central Florida's pattern of progress.

The three roads were still there, but one of them was now a four-lane highway. I was in orange-grove country. The medium-sized, almost uniformly shaped dark-green trees dotted with bright orange stretched nearly from horizon to horizon. Letting the car roll uphill at idle speed, I reached a relatively high spot and parked to survey the area of the small map.

Most of the houses on the map were gone, but I was excited to see in the approximate spot of the map's X a large and unusual rock formation whose shape matched precisely the shape of one of the figures on the map. The neat rows of orange trees had parted widely there to miss it and I also saw what appeared to be a thick tree trunk. I checked the map and found a circle drawn to designate a tree exactly where the stump rose angled from the ground. Even from where I sat it was simple to make out the area of the map's X, near the tapered end of the rock formation.

I'd had the foresight to bring a spade in the car's trunk, and I parked on the road shoulder and walked with the spade toward the rock formation. There was no one around; the nearest building was over a quarter of a mile away and appeared deserted. The only sound among the brightly sunlit orange trees was the occasional whir of unseen traffic on the nearby four-lane highway. I determined what I thought was the exact spot of the X and plunged the shovel into the soft, powdery earth to mark it. Then I rolled up my sleeves and began to dig.

Within ten minutes, I struck what appeared to be a pipe jutting upward to ground level. At first I thought it might be an irrigation pipe, but I saw that it was rusted and the end was stuffed with dirt. I began to dig harder.

What I discovered after an hour's hard digging was the lid of a rotted wooden box approximately two by five feet. From each end of the box a rusted pipe jutted toward the earth's surface; perhaps markers. There was a hasp and padlock on the box's lid, but rust and time had worked their deterioration and I easily sprung the black-pitted hasp from the moldering wood with one stroke of the shovel.

Grinning inanely, still struggling for breath, I bent and flung open the box's rotted lid.

There was no money in the box—it contained the bones of a child.

I felt my face contort stiffly as I drew back, scrambling up the sloping sandy side of the hole I'd dug. Standing numbly at the edge of the hole, I found that I couldn't avert my gaze from the horror.

Alongside the head of the skeleton were the moldering remains of what looked like a small battery-operated pump. I knew then that the two pipes were for air, and that the child had been buried alive. Near the colorless tattered clothing that still clung to the bones were a tarnished heart-shaped locket and some crumpled papers.

The sound behind me made me wheel so suddenly that I almost slipped and fell back into the hole I'd dug.

The old man I had talked to in Jade Point was standing there, pointing an ancient long-barreled revolver in my direction. But he was gazing past me, into the hole.

"You trailed me all the way down here. . . ." I said unbelievingly.

"I had to." The light of unreason I'd noticed in his eyes shone brighter now than before. On each side of his drawn lips the sagging flesh of his cheeks was twitching.

A car door slammed, and we both turned toward the sound.

"He followed me. . . ." I heard the old man say in a soft, tragic voice touched with fear.

A plain white sedan was parked nearby, and a short gray-haired man was striding toward us with a shotgun slung beneath his right arm. He was absurdly paunchy, walking with much effort, his legs pumping with rubbery uncertainty on the powdery earth.

I turned and found that the old man was gone. Then I saw him beyond the orange trees, hobbling with fear-born speed toward where his car must have been parked.

The dumpy gray-haired man had walked up beside me, and we both stood and watched the old man disappear beyond the trees.

"No point chasing him now," the man said, as we heard the racing whine of a car engine. There was a hint of strained control in his voice.

Dazed by the unfolding of events, I looked at the man. He was in his late sixties, with an open, deeply etched face and vivid blue eyes that had seen too much too long, eyes that contained a deep-set desperation.

"Sheriff Seth Davis," he said by way of introduction, "Oleana County. Who are you?"

I told him in a stammering voice. "What . . . what is all this?" I asked.

"It's the remains of the Bosner girl," he said. "Six-year-old Sissy Bosner was kidnapped from her wealthy family in Miami in 1937 and held for a hundred thousand dollars ransom. It was never paid. Two men named Carvell and Pepp were suspected, but nothing was ever proved for lack of evidence."

"Carvell and Pepp . . ." I said. "My God, they buried her alive, let her . . ." I turned and gazed at the spot where the old man had disappeared beyond the orange-dotted trees, driven by decades-old fear and guilt.

"You let me know where you're staying, Mr. Aikin, and go on back there. I'll need you later for a statement."

I nodded, gave him the information he requested, and drove back to the motel, trying not to think about the terror that must have passed through a six-year-old mind, buried alive in darkness, with each breath a searing agony. Whatever compassion I might have had for Eddie Pepp disappeared.

I expected Sheriff Davis to appear at my Oleana motel that afternoon, but he didn't. And he didn't show up that evening. Or the next morning.

In the motel restaurant, as I read the morning paper, I understood why.

Thick black lettering low on the front page told me that Owen Bosner, aged, wealthy, one-time king of the Florida citrus processing industry, had hanged himself in an Orlando hotel. Mr. Bosner had become almost a total recluse after personal tragedy in the mid-thirties. After his six-year-old daughter Sibyl Ann "Sissy"

70

Bosner was kidnapped, Owen Bosner decided that the kidnappers were bluffing and refused to pay the demanded ransom. Though Depression-era gangsters Edward Pepp and Leonard "Blackie" Carvell were suspected of the crime, charges were never brought because Sissy Bosner was never found and had supposedly been seen alive and well on a Chicago street corner by a distant relative. Only that reported sighting by what seemed to be a reliable witness prevented kidnapping and murder charges.

Intimates of Owen Bosner said that he was haunted by his decision for the rest of his life, living in seclusion and employing a full-time staff to scour daily copies of virtually every newspaper in the country for some clue to his lost daughter's fate. This quest apparently came to dominate his life and in his mind became the sole reason for his existence.

But what interested me most was the photograph of Owen Bosner, taken in 1976, a melancholy likeness marked by the tragic uncertainty and guilt that must have dogged him into the waning hours of his life.

Bosner and I had met at my house in Jade Point, Missouri. I knew he had found the truth he had so long feared and sought, that had been his obsession.

I used the telephone then to try to make connections with Sheriff Davis of Oleana County. There was no Sheriff Davis, I was informed. There was not even an Oleana County.

Immediately I left the motel and drove along sun-washed highways back to the orange grove where I had unearthed Sissy Bosner's remains. A heavy, guilty regret settled over me. My classified ad in the newspaper had set turning old and inexorable wheels.

I stood amid the wind-rustled orange trees with a lump in my throat. The hole had been refilled, the loose earth neatly leveled.

There was no statute of limitations on murder, but

"Sheriff" Eddie Pepp was no longer worried. It must have been Carvell who had buried Sissy Bosner alive, then for some reason, probably unexpected sudden pressure from the law, had been forced to flee abruptly from the state, and was the only one who knew her whereabouts. Pepp was to have handled things in Florida, including the collection of the ransom and release of Sissy Bosner. Both Pepp and Carvell were wanted in several states, so the Saint Louis address had been a mail drop, a forwarding service, so they couldn't be traced through the mails. Through it, Pepp was supposed to learn where Sissy Bosner was concealed.

But Pepp, waiting in Florida while Sissy Bosner waited underground for endless days and nights with only so much food, water, and sanity, never learned where Sissy was hidden. Because Blackie Carvell, apparently the lodger and secret lover of Beatrice Logan in the house I would later buy, had been killed in Jade Point by federal agents before he mailed Pepp the map and letter. The old-timers at the Drop-In Tavern in Jade Point had been reticent with me, a newcomer in town, because they wanted to protect the reputation of the recently deceased Logan woman.

Owen Bosner's maniacal determination to find his daughter had received a great deal of publicity, and he had the vast resources to indulge in such a search. Pepp, who never before had killed, could only protect himself from a murder charge by staying in Florida and observing Bosner, and moving in whatever fast and deadly fashion was necessary to reclaim and better conceal Sissy Bosner's body if ever it was located. It was easy to imagine any man in such circumstances becoming paranoid.

So through the years Pepp must have watched the reclusive and obsessive Owen Bosner ever more warily, as the part of central Florida where he knew the body must be became heavily developed with industry, highways, and tourist attractions, increasing daily the chances that someone would uncover Sissy Bosner's remains and thus prove that she had been kidnapped and murdered in Florida and never seen in Chicago.

Owen Bosner's obsession had created and nourished Eddie Pepp's. The two men were bound together in a pattern of apprehension. And as each of them aged, their obsessions became the mainsprings of their otherwise empty lives, the very purpose of those lives. All of the passing years had strengthened rather than diminished this strange adversity that had developed into need. Probably Pepp even had paid off one of Bosner's employees to keep him posted if Bosner interrupted his reclusiveness to travel.

Pepp must have followed Bosner to Saint Louis, then back to Florida even as Bosner followed me. Then he cleverly passed himself off as a sheriff when Bosner saw him and ran from him. How both men must have doubted and suffered through the years! One from the fear of a murder charge, the other from the guilt of not having paid a long-ago ransom. And both from the slow, insidious cancer of obsession.

But now it was ended. Pepp had reburied the incriminating, pathetic bones where he could be sure they wouldn't be discovered, in their final resting place, this time leaving no map except within the darkening confines of his own fear-wasted mind. And with them he had buried his reason for living.

Even in the blasting sunlight, I shivered sadly as I walked back to my car.

I hoped Eddie Pepp had treated the buried treasure gently. And that now it would be part of an undisturbed past, alive only in faded photographs and yellowed newspapers.

The Explosives Expert

B illy Edgemore, the afternoon bartender, stood behind
the long bar of the Last Stop Lounge and squinted
through the dimness at the sunlight beyond the front
window. He was a wiry man, taller than he appeared at
first, and he looked like he should be a bartender, with his
bald head, cheerfully seamed face, and his brilliant red
vest that was the bartender's uniform at the Last Stop.
Behind him long rows of glistening bottles picked up the
light on the mirrored backbar, the glinting clear gins and
vodkas, the beautiful amber bourbons and lighter Scot-
ches, the various hues of the assorted wines, brandies,
and liqueurs. The Last Stop's bar was well stocked.

Beyond the ferns that blocked the view out (and in)
the front window, Billy saw a figure cross the small
patch of light and turn to enter the stained-glass front
door, the first customer he was to serve that day.

It was Sam Daniels. Sam was an employee of the Hulton Plant up the street, as were most of the customers of
the Last Stop.

"Afternoon, Sam," Billy said, turning on his professional smile. "Kind of early today, aren't you?"

"Off work," Sam said, mounting a barstool as if it
were a horse. "Beer."

Billy drew a beer and set the wet schooner in front of

Sam on the mahogany bar. "Didn't expect a customer for another two hours, when the plant lets out," Billy said.

"Guess not," Sam said, sipping his beer. He was a short man with a swarthy face, a head of curly hair, and a stomach paunch too big for a man in his early thirties—a man who liked his drinking.

"Figured you didn't go to work when I saw you weren't wearing your badge," Billy said. The Hulton Plant manufactured some secret government thing, a component for the hydrogen bomb, and each employee had to wear his small plastic badge with his name, number, and photograph on it in order to enter or leave the plant.

"Regular Sherlock," Sam said, and jiggled the beer in his glass.

"You notice lots of things when you're a bartender," Billy said, wiping down the bar with a clean white towel. You notice things, Billy repeated to himself, and you get to know people, and when you get to know them, really get to know them, you've got to dislike them. "I guess I tended bar in the wrong places."

"What's that?" Sam Daniels asked.

"Just thinking out loud," Billy said, and hung the towel on its chrome rack. When Billy looked at his past he seemed to be peering down a long tunnel of empty bottles, drunks, and hollow laughter; of curt orders, see-through stares, and dreary conversations. He'd never liked his job, but it was all he'd known for the past thirty years.

"Wife's supposed to meet me here pretty soon," Sam said. "She's getting off work early." He winked at Billy. "Toothache."

Billy smiled his automatic smile and nodded. He never had liked Sam, who had a tendency to get loud and violent when he got drunk.

Within a few minutes, Rita Daniels entered. She was a tall pretty woman, somewhat younger than her husband.

She had a good figure, dark eyes, and expensively bleached blond hair that looked a bit stringy now from the heat outside.

"Coke and bourbon," she ordered, without looking at Billy. He served her the highball where she sat next to her husband at the bar.

No one spoke for a while as Rita sipped her drink. The faint sound of traffic, muffled through the thick door of the Last Stop, filled the silence. When a muted horn sounded, Rita said, "It's dead in here. Put a quarter in the jukebox."

Sam did as his wife said, and soft jazz immediately displaced the traffic sounds.

"You know I don't like jazz, Sam." Rita downed her drink quicker than she should have, then got down off the stool to go to the powder room.

"Saw Doug Baker last night," Billy said, picking up the empty glass. Doug Baker was a restaurant owner who lived on the other side of town, and it was no secret that he came to the Last Stop only to see Rita Daniels, though Rita was almost always with her husband.

"How 'bout that," Sam said. "Two more of the same."

Rita returned to her stool, and Billy put two highballs before her and her husband.

"I was drinking beer," Sam said in a loud voice.

"So you were," Billy answered, smiling his My Mistake smile. He shrugged and motioned toward the highballs. "On the house. Unless you'd rather have beer."

"No," Sam said, "think nothing of it."

That was how Billy thought Sam would answer. His cheapness was one of the things Billy disliked most about the man. It was one of the things he knew Rita disliked most in Sam Daniels, too.

"How'd it go with the hydrogen bombs today?" Rita asked her husband. "Didn't go in at all, huh?"

Billy could see she was aggravated and was trying to nag him.

"No," Sam said, "and I don't make hydrogen bombs."

"Ha!" Rita laughed. "You oughta think about it. That's about all you can make." She turned away before Sam could answer. "Hey, Billy, you know anything about hydrogen bombs?"

"Naw," Billy said. "Your husband knows more about that than me."

"Yeah," Rita said, "the union rates him an expert. Some expert! Splices a few wires together."

"Fifteen dollars an hour," Sam said, "and double time for overtime."

Rita whirled a braceleted arm above her head. "Wheee . . ."

Like many married couples, Sam and Rita never failed to bicker when they came into the Last Stop. Billy laughed. "The Friendly Daniels." Sam didn't laugh.

"Don't bug me today," Sam said to Rita. "I'm in a bad mood."

"Cheer up, Sam," Billy said. "It's a sign she loves you, or loves somebody, anyway."

Sam ignored Billy and finished his drink. "Where'd you go last night?" he asked his wife.

"You know I was at my sister's. I even stopped in here for about a half hour on the way. Billy can verify it."

"Right," Billy said.

"I thought you said Doug Baker was in here last night," Sam said to him, his eyes narrow.

"He was," Billy said. "He, uh, came in late." He turned to make more drinks, placing the glasses lip-to-lip and pouring bourbon into each in one deft stream without spilling a drop. He made them a little stronger this time, shooting in the soda expertly, jabbing swizzle sticks between the ice cubes and placing the glasses on the bar.

"You wouldn't be covering up or anything, would you, Billy?" Sam's voice had acquired a mean edge.

"Now *wait a minute!*" Rita said. "If you think I came in here last night to see Doug Baker, you're crazy!"

"Well." Sam stirred his drink viciously and took a sip. "Billy mentioned Baker was in here. . . ."

"I said he came in late," Billy said quickly.

"And he acted like he was covering up or something," Sam said, looking accusingly at Billy.

"Covering up?" Rita turned to Billy, her penciled eyebrows knitted in a frown. "Have you ever seen me with another man?"

"Naw," Billy said blandly, "of course not. You folks shouldn't fight."

Still indignant, Rita swiveled on her stool to face her husband. "Have I ever been unfaithful?"

"How the hell should I know?"

"Good point," Billy said with a forced laugh.

"It's not funny!" Rita snapped.

"Keep it light, folks," Billy said seriously. "You know we don't like trouble in here."

"Sorry," Rita said, but her voice was hurt. She swiveled back to face the bar and gulped angrily on her drink. Billy could see that the liquor was getting to her, was getting to them both.

There was silence for a while, then Rita said morosely "I *oughta* go out on you, Mr. Hydrogen-bomb expert! You think I do anyway, and at least Doug Baker's got money."

Sam grabbed her wrist, making the bracelets jingle. She tried to jerk away but he held her arm so tightly that his knuckles were white. "You ever see Baker behind my back and I'll kill you both!" He almost spit the words out.

"Hey, now," Billy said gently, "don't talk like that, folks!" He placed his hand on Sam Daniels' arm and felt the muscles relax as Sam released his wife. She bent over silently on her stool and held the wrist as if it were broken. "Have one on the house," Billy said, taking up their almost empty glasses. "One to make up by."

"Make mine straight," Sam said. He was breathing hard and his face was red.

"Damn you!" Rita moaned. She half fell off the stool and walked quickly but staggeringly to the powder room again.

Billy began to mix the drinks deftly, speedily, as if there were a dozen people at the bar and they all demanded service. In the faint red glow from the beer-ad electric clock he looked like an ancient alchemist before his rows of multicolored bottles. "You shouldn't be so hard on her," he said absently as he mixed. "Can't believe all the rumors you hear about a woman as pretty as Rita, and a harmless kiss in fun never hurt nobody."

"Rumors?" Sam leaned over the bar. "Kiss? What kiss? Did she kiss Baker last night?"

"Take it easy," Billy said. "I told you Baker came in late." The phone rang, as it always did during the fifteen minutes before the Hulton Plant let out, with wives leaving messages and asking for errant husbands. When Billy returned, Rita was back at the bar.

"Let's get out of here," she said. There were tear streaks in her makeup.

"Finish your drinks and go home happy, folks." Billy shot a glance at the door and set the glasses on the bar.

Rita drank hers slowly, but Sam tossed his drink down and stared straight ahead. Quietly, Billy put another full glass in front of him.

"I hear you *were* in here with Baker last night," Sam said in a low voice. "Somebody even saw you kissing him."

"You're *crazy!*" Rita's thickened voice was outraged.

Billy moved quickly toward them. "I didn't say that."

"I knew you were covering up!" Sam glared pure hate at him. "We'll see what Baker says, because I'm going to drive over to his place right now and bash his brains out!"

"But I didn't even see Baker last night!" Rita took a pull on her drink, trying to calm herself. Sam swung sharply around with his forearm, hitting Rita's chin and the highball glass at the same time. There was a clink as the glass hit her teeth and she fell backward off the stool.

Billy reached under the bar and his hand came up with a glinting chrome automatic that seemed to catch every ray of light in the place. It was a gentleman's gun, and standing there in his white shirt and red vest Billy looked like a gentlemen holding it.

"Now, don't move, folks." He aimed the gun directly at Sam's stomach. "You know we don't go for that kind of trouble in here." He looked down and saw blood seeping between Rita's fingers as she held her hand over her mouth. Billy wet a clean towel and tossed it to her, and she held it to her face and scooted backward to sit sobbing in the farthest booth.

Billy leaned close to Sam. "Listen," he said, his voice a sincere whisper, "I don't want to bring trouble on Baker, or on you for that matter, so I can't stand by and let you go over there and kill him and throw your own life away. It wasn't him she was in here with. He came in later."

"Wasn't him?" Sam asked in bewildered fury. "Who was it then?"

"I don't know," Billy said, still in a whisper so Rita couldn't hear. "He had a badge on, so he worked at the plant, but I don't know who he is and that's the truth."

"Oh, no!"

"Take it easy, Sam. She only kissed him in that booth there. And I'm not even sure I saw that. The booth was dark."

Sam tossed down the drink that was on the bar and

moaned. He was staring at the automatic and Billy could see he wanted desperately to move.

A warm silence filled the bar, and then the phone rang shrilly, turning the silence to icicles.

"Now take it easy," Billy said, backing slowly down the bar toward the phone hung on the wall. "A kiss isn't anything." As the phone rang again he could almost see the shrill sound grate through Sam's tense body. Billy placed the automatic on the bar and took the last five steps to the phone. He let it ring once more before answering it.

"Naw," Billy said into the receiver, standing with his back to Sam and Rita, "he's not here." He stood for a long moment instead of hanging up, as if someone were still on the other end of the line.

The shot was a sudden, angry bark.

Billy put the receiver on the hook and turned. Sam was standing slumped with a supporting hand on a barstool. Rita was crumpled on the floor beneath the table of the booth she'd been sitting in, her eyes open, her blond hair bright with blood.

His head still bowed, Sam began to shake.

Within minutes the police were there, led by a young plainclothes detective named Parks.

"You say they were arguing and he just up and shot her?" Parks was asking as his men led Sam outside.

"He accused her of running around," Billy said. "They were arguing, he hit her, and I was going to throw them out when the phone rang. I set the gun down for a moment when I went to answer the phone, and he grabbed it and shot."

"Uh-hm," Parks said efficiently, flashing a look toward where Rita's body had lain before they'd photographed it and taken it away. "Pretty simple, I guess. Daniels confessed as soon as we got here. In fact, we couldn't shut him up. Pretty broken."

"Who wouldn't be?" Billy said.

"Save some sympathy for the girl." Parks looked around. "Seems like a nice place. I don't know why there's so much trouble in here."

Billy shrugged. "In a dive, a class joint, or a place like this, people are mostly the same."

Parks grinned. "You're probably right," he said, and started toward the door. Before pushing it open, he paused and turned. "If you see anything like this developing again, give us a call, huh?"

"Sure," Billy said, polishing a glass and holding it up to the fading afternoon light. "You know we don't like trouble in here."

Big Game

Dr. Mindle was dead, and his files were missing. He'd been a discreet top-drawer psychiatrist, an immensely dignified doctor who numbered among his patients many of the city's upper strata of society. But he didn't appear very dignified now. Ironically, the spasmodic agony of death had shaped his features into a strangely contented smile. And lying there on his side on the soft carpet with his knees drawn up and his eyes closed, he appeared almost childlike. The neat hole in the center of his forehead looked decidedly out of place.

COMMISSIONER SAYS NO NEW CLUES IN SEARCH FOR PSYCHIATRIST'S MURDERER, the newspaper on Pendela's bed read. Pendela flicked the paper onto the floor and smiled. Resting on his pajama-clad chest was a thick stack of brown cardboard folders, which he was leafing through with enthusiasm. The patients were identified mostly by number, to be sure, but there were clues in the folders, and even an occasional name or phone number. Pendela allowed himself a small chuckle. Thirty-five of the wealthiest mental cases in the city, he decided, some of whose wealth was now to be channeled to Pendela.

He studied the files for another two hours, trying to make what he knew was an all-important choice. Soon the red cover of Pendela's over-sized bed was strewn with the folders. He cut an odd figure there in his huge bedroom, surrounded by his own garish paintings. For Pendela fancied himself an artist first, a blackmailer second. Years ago he'd tried to impress the city's wealthy art patrons with his beautiful oils, his dynamic color sense. They had either ignored him or actually laughed at him, but it was Pendela who would now laugh last—and best.

He chuckled again as he came across a particularly interesting case and set it aside for future reference. Blackmail had been profitable for Pendela, but it had been hard and time-consuming, leaving him little time to devote to his art. The endless hours of checking records, of waiting outside motels and taverns, had been a tragic squandering of a talent that should have been concentrating on something worthy of its immensity. Yet it did leave him *some* time to paint, and despite the derision of the so-called experts, Pendela lived in one of the most luxurious apartment buildings in the city. Though his spacious apartment somewhat resembled a madman's art gallery, the furnishings were nonetheless to his taste and expensive.

And now Pendela would blackmail as he painted, with the bold stroke and colorful simplicity of genius. The doctor's murder? Nothing; Pendela had actually enjoyed it. And of what importance was the death of an old man who stood in the path of Pendela's destiny?

Case number 333 was the patient Pendela decided on. A man incapable of violence, but a man nevertheless guilty of a horrendous crime four years ago in another part of the country. Number 333 had served his time, paid his debt to society, but Pendela knew society didn't forgive that easily. He would have to pay again.

After arranging the brown folders in a neat stack with 333 on top and locking them in his wall safe, Pendela returned to bed and switched off the light. He lay for a long time contemplating the foolproof simplicity of his plan.

It would serve well as the subject of a painting: a simple, four-colored, obviously airtight box against a backdrop of monetary green.

The idea so amused Pendela that as he dropped off to sleep there was a distinct smile on his lean, aesthetic face. He would sleep well tonight. He knew that elsewhere in the city there were those who would not.

In the morning, Pendela phoned 333 and arranged a rendezvous for that evening in a little-frequented restaurant he knew. Even over the phone Pendela knew he'd made the right choice. The man's voice was quivering with fear and shame.

Number 333 turned out to be small, balding, and forty-ish, an ugly innocuous little man with watery blue eyes. His name was Myron Coil, and as he sat across the table from Pendela now, his fingers dug like claws into the red-and-white-checked tablecloth.

His own well-manicured fingers toying with a coffee cup, Pendela fixed an icy stare on Myron Coil.

"You told me over the phone," Coil said nervously, "that you knew something about Dr. Mindle's missing files. . . ."

Pendela waited before answering. "That's precisely what I told you." He sipped his coffee. "May I call you Myron?"

"Of course," Coil said eagerly.

"I prefer to call you Mr. Coil."

The little man's eyes widened and he shrank back into his chair.

Pendela calmly continued. "Understand, Mr. Coil, what you did would revolt the soul and turn the stomach of any civilized man. And I am a civilized man."

Coil's head was bowed.

"There is no excuse," Pendela said, "nothing to justify your actions. Four years ago you lost your family, your friends, your job, and you served time in prison, and now you are alone. But you haven't paid enough."

Coil was almost crying. "My God, one mistake—"

"Was all that Benedict Arnold made. And I assure you that if your crime were as widely known, you'd be held in much greater scorn by your contemporaries than he was by his. Even if you live to be two hundred, you will not have paid enough for the atrocity you committed." Pendela leaned across the table. "You understand that, don't you, Mr. Coil?"

Coil's eyes were brimming, his voice desperate. "I understand," he said. "H-how much do you want?"

"Want?" Pendela feigned surprise. "But I don't want to blackmail you, Mr. Coil. I want to hire you."

Coil's mouth dropped open and his lower lip trembled with the sudden hope that shone in his eyes.

"I'll pay you five hundred dollars a week, tax free," Pendela said, "which is a sizable raise over your meager clerk's salary."

"But pay me for what?" Coil asked haltingly, wonderingly. "For what kind of work?"

"You might call it investigation," Pendela said with a smile. He tossed a dollar on the table for the coffee and stood up. "Come with me now and I'll show you."

There was a brief moment of indecision for Coil, but he really had no choice and he knew it. As he stood, Pendela rested a hand on his shoulder.

"Your secret will be safe with me, Mr. Coil."

In stunned confusion, Myron Coil followed the striding Pendela out of the restaurant.

They stepped out of the self-service elevator that went up to Pendela's apartment, walked down the short hall, and Pendela opened the door.

Coil seemed fascinated and a little baffled by the huge paintings that hung on the walls.

"I am an artist," Pendela explained. He watched closely for Coil's reaction to the paintings, but the little man merely blinked and crossed the room to sit uncomfortably in a modern white sling chair.

One of the tasteless ones, Pendela thought, and sat down across from Coil in a stuffed leather armchair of chrome yellow. He studied Coil thoughtfully. So far, the man seemed perfect for what Pendela had in mind. Dr. Mindle's files had revealed that Coil was one of the few patients who'd paid only a nominal fee for psychotherapy—mainly because the doctor was interested in his case from a clinical standpoint. Coil definitely was the nonviolent type, but still Pendela had taken precautions.

"In a safe-deposit box at Citizen's Bank," Pendela said, "are several letters explaining in detail your revolting conduct of four years ago. These letters are addressed to several of your key friends and associates in the city, and if you undertake any sort of violent or legal action against me they will be delivered—whether you succeed or not."

After watching Coil blanch at the thought of such letters, Pendela rose, opened the wall safe, and withdrew Dr. Mindle's files. He placed the files on a small cocktail table next to his chair and sat down again. "Your file," he said to Coil, "is also in the safety-deposit box at Citizen's." He lifted the top file and tossed it carelessly to Coil, who caught it as if it were about to burst into flame.

Pendela made a steeple with his long forefingers and leaned back. "Your job will be to find the people those file numbers represent," he said. "It shouldn't be difficult. There are plenty of leads in the files and the people are all prominent. When you find them, you will contact them and explain that you are working for a syndicate that knows their secret. Then you will multiply by ten the hourly fee that they were paying Dr. Mindle, and instruct them to send that amount each month in a plain white envelope to a post-office box number that I'll give you later. Then you will return the file to me and go on to your next case."

There was a beaten, resigned look on Coil's face now as he realized that Pendela's was the least dreadful of his alternatives.

Pendela smiled ecstatically at the ironic beauty of it. "In a sense," he said, "I am blackmailing you into becoming a blackmailer."

The emotional Mr. Coil pressed his eyes closed and took a deep breath, as if trying to control himself and keep from crying.

"Surely it's not as bad as all that," Pendela said with mock sincerity. "If you'd prefer, look upon yourself as my 'business manager.' " He got up and returned the remaining files to the wall safe. Then he turned again to Coil. "In exactly one week, you will meet me in the same restaurant at nine o'clock. You will return the file to me and receive your new one. Is that understood?"

Coil nodded and got up to leave. Without speaking, he found his own way out.

"You would do well to remember your own precarious position," Pendela said as the beaten little man closed the door gently.

It worked beautifully. Myron Coil appeared at the restaurant at the appointed time, small and sad-eyed. He handed the file across the table to Pendela.

"She agreed to pay," Coil said in his tremulous voice. "She lives on the west side of town, the widow of a famous architect, and she's afraid."

"Of course she's afraid," Pendela said with a pitying smile, "and of course she's wealthy. That's why these people were chosen, Mr. Coil. Now don't bore me with details about the personal life of a wealthy dowager. Details are your job; I'm only interested in money."

"She said to ask you—"

"Mr. Coil," Pendela interrupted him, "I don't care what she said, I don't care who she is. Let them remain as anonymous to me as I was to them."

Coil was silent, his eyes lowered. Pendela reached into the attaché case beside him on the table and handed Coil another file. "Until next week, Mr. Coil." Pendela downed the rest of his coffee and left, leaving Myron Coil to pay the bill.

And so it went, until only a few of the fifteen files Pendela had chosen remained. The money flowed to Pendela in a steady and bountiful stream. Soon they all would be paying, and the time would arrive when Myron Coil's usefulness would end. Implicated as he was, Coil posed no danger to Pendela, so when the time came Coil himself would be billed for his sins—nominally, of course. He would pay like the rest.

Never before had Pendela been able to spend so much time at his easel, and his art progressed marvelously. He was standing now appraising his latest painting, an oil of the Third Street Bridge—brilliant yellow touched with pink, but unmistakably the Third Street Bridge, spanning, instead of the river, an immense and seductive multicolored nude. *Pollution* he had named it, a title vague enough to provoke thought.

Then the doorbell rang. Pendela called out to enter, and there in the doorway stood Myron Coil. One of Dr. Mindle's files was tucked under his arm.

Pendela's eyes glinted with anger. "You would *dare* come *here?*"

Coil's voice was more desperate than usual as he closed the door softly behind him. "I had to!"

"The reason being?"

"The case I'm working on—Two hundred forty-two. I contacted him and he . . . he knows about what I did four years ago."

Pendela stalked toward Coil, his lips pursed in thought. "But how could he?"

"I don't know, but he said if whoever was my boss wouldn't see him, he'd expose me." Coil was searching Pendela's face with his watery blue stare. "Please . . ." he whined.

"Control yourself," Pendela said coldly. He was puzzled and annoyed by this new development and he needed time to think. "Leave the folder with me," he said. "I'll phone you when I've worked something out."

Coil handed the folder to Pendela and blushed with relief. "Thank you," he murmured.

Pendela watched him back out of the door, feeling only contempt for the sniveling fool. Then he mixed himself a drink and sat down to study 242's folder.

The things that Coil had found out were written in a neat clerk's hand on a separate piece of paper. Number 242's name was William Morgan, salary $50,000 a year, married, two children, upper middle-class neighborhood. Unfortunately, Mr. Morgan was a kleptomaniac. Dr. Mindle's hourly fee had been only $60, so Morgan's monthly payment would be only $600. Pendela raised his eyebrows. Surely that wasn't too much to ask of a man making Morgan's salary.

Pendela laid the file aside reasonably sure that Morgan wasn't the homicidal type and decided to see him. He couldn't have one patient upsetting his plan with an irrational act. Anyway, it would be almost pleasurable to watch the entwined sinner squirm in the net and beg for mercy. Still, he hoped Morgan wasn't as sickeningly emotional as Coil.

Pendela stood in the cool night drizzle and peered through the deserted restaurant's steamed window at Morgan, who was sitting at the designated corner table. A waiter came with a glass of beer, and Morgan began to drink it slowly and with obvious relish. He was a big man, with a hawk nose and ugly symmetrical eyes. For a man about to beg, he looked disturbingly calm.

Pendela entered the restaurant and walked up to the table. "Morgan?"

The man nodded, looking up with interest at Pendela.

Pendela asked the waiter for a cup of coffee and sat down. When the waiter had left, Pendela said, "I represent the syndicate."

"No you don't," Morgan said. "You represent you. Myron Coil told me."

"He *what?*"

The waiter came back with the coffee, and Pendela sat silently waiting for him to leave again. As he stared across the table at Morgan's stern, calm face, it struck him that he'd seen the man somewhere before.

"Now," Pendela said, "just what did Mr. Coil tell you?"

"Everything." Morgan took a sip of beer. Without blinking he said suddenly, "I have a gun aimed at you under the table."

Fear ran down Pendela's back like a trickle of ice water. "I suppose you know it makes no difference what happens to me," he said with a slight quaver in his voice. "The files are locked away in a bank vault, in a safety-deposit box, and I've seen to it that they'll fall into the right hands in the event of my untimely death."

"No," Morgan said calmly, "you keep the files in your wall safe. Only Myron Coil's file was in that bank vault, and the letters about him."

"*Was?* What do you mean *was?*"

For the first time Morgan smiled, but it was a curiously humorless smile. "One of Dr. Mindle's patients was a bank president."

Pendela's hand trembled and coffee sloshed out of his cup and into the white china saucer. He could feel the balance of power shifting with terrible suddenness. "You're lying!"

"I wouldn't lie," Morgan said. "My real name is William Monohan, Police Commissioner Monohan. That's why I can legally shoot you here in this restaurant if you don't come along with me now." He smiled again. "Resisting arrest."

"You *couldn't!* You *wouldn't!*"

"Oh, I wouldn't want to. I'm a gentle man. Most of Dr. Mindle's patients are gentle. But I've killed before in the line of duty, and you'd be a feather in my cap."

With fear rising bile-like in his throat, Pendela rose and walked out of the restaurant ahead of Police Commissioner Monohan.

"Your place," the commissioner said when they were outside, and they walked the six blocks to Pendela's apartment in silence.

When the doors of the self-service elevator closed and they were alone, Monohan spoke again. "As I said, we're all gentle people, really. That's why the twelve of us decided to solve our problem together. None of us wanted a murder on his own conscience, and this way, if we're all implicated, we can trust one another." He pressed the button and the elevator began to whine upward.

"Murder!" Fear hit Pendela in sickening waves.

The commissioner nodded grimly. "I can see to it that it won't be investigated too thoroughly."

"You're insane!"

"Of course. And so is the governor. If any one of us does have to shoulder the blame for this, there'll be a quick and convenient pardon."

"The governor! You don't mean . . .?"

"I do mean," the commissioner said. "Dr. Mindle was a very influential psychiatrist, with very influential patients." The elevator stopped, the doors slid open, and the gun came out of the commissioner's pocket. "You put the bite on some very important people, and it turned out to be more than you could chew."

They walked down the plush entrance hall, the commissioner's revolver lightly touching Pendela's back. A carpeted last mile, Pendela thought, and fear racked his body. He could picture them, all of them, waiting in his apartment, seated on his soft carpet, lounging in his fine furniture, making derisive remarks about his paintings.

They were at the door now, and Pendela's legs were trembling so violently that he could hardly stand. The commissioner whispered in his ear, "It will be quick, but I can't promise you it will be merciful." He jabbed the gun sharply into Pendela's back, knocked three times, and pushed in on the door.

The door swung open onto blackness, but Pendela knew they were there. He could smell the unfamiliar scent of cigarette smoke; he could see unfamiliar dark shadows; he could hear the faint rustle of their movements; *he could feel them!*

As Pendela's trembling hand flicked the light switch, they all stood up.

In Memory Of...

T he Langs stood quietly beside the small open grave. Florence Lang wore an expression of restrained grief on her fleshy, rather pretty rose-colored face; the proper expression for such an occasion, Hollis thought. Mr. Lang, a short, thin, and very erect man of about fifty, appeared impatient. His stern seamed features were set hard above the red ascot he favored instead of a tie. He shifted his slight weight from one foot to the other and stood with his slender hands folded in front of him.

"What are we waiting for?" he asked. He had a slight German accent.

Hollis started to answer just as the bells of Saint Michael's Church, four blocks away, began to peal the hour. Instead of speaking to Mr. Lang, he nodded in the general direction of the clear, wavering notes and stooped to pick up the small wooden box by the grave. The Langs had chosen to purchase a box rather than furnish their own.

Quickly but very carefully Hollis placed the box into the three-foot hole, seeing that it sat flat on the earth and no corners were caught on the narrowing sides of the grave. He brushed some dark bits of dirt from the tiny stone at the head of the grave and stood.

The small headstone read simply:

TAG
1959–1971
A LOYAL COMPANION

Hollis stepped back and walked away from the Langs then, to let them be alone by the new grave of their pet for a few minutes. Ten years ago, when he'd first bought the business, he used to say a few awkward words over the graves, but they had sounded hollow, mechanical, and embarrassingly ridiculous. He'd since decided to time the burials with the chiming of the church bells and let it go at that. Hard enough for him sometimes to share in the remorse over the death of a man, much less someone's pet—not that the grief wasn't just as real, the bond of affection sometimes greater. So now he stood waiting for the Langs, listening to the hum of traffic on the busy highway that bordered his kennel and pet cemetery.

"Come on," he heard Mr. Lang say, "we're going to be late at the Davidsons'."

Hollis saw no change of expression on Mrs. Lang's pleasant, middle-aged face as she stood gazing down at the grave. When Mr. Lang turned to walk toward Hollis, she followed, her gaze caught for a moment on the grave as if she regretted looking away. The bells had stopped pealing now and the vibrations of their clear tones hung, fading in the summer air.

"How much do I owe you exactly?" Mr. Lang asked Hollis.

Mrs. Lang looked imploringly at her husband. "Charles, he said he'd bill us."

"I can send you a statement," Hollis said.

Mr. Lang, holding himself erect, was at eye level with his wife, and he gave her a stern sideways glance. "We might as well settle now," he answered, his small hard features turned up to Hollis, "and get it over with."

Hollis nodded. "Whatever you say." He didn't look at Mrs. Lang. "Fifty dollars is the usual charge."

Mr. Lang drew a leather-covered checkbook from his suitcoat pocket and with a ball-point pen scrawled the amount and his signature on the check. He handed the check to Hollis and turned to go.

Mrs. Lang looked at Hollis then in somewhat the same way she'd looked at her husband earlier.

"You can visit the grave any time you want," Hollis said to her.

"Thank you." The lined corners of her pale lipsticked mouth turned up in a sad come-and-gone smile, and she followed her husband to their new red car, opening the door for herself and getting in with her knees primly together. As they drove slowly past the wire kennels the dogs put up their usual frantic and short-lived barks and howls.

Hollis watched the car move around the bend in the gravel drive and pass his small white frame house. Then he could no longer see the car, but he heard the crunching sound of a tire spinning on gravel as Mr. Lang turned onto the road and accelerated, and the dogs quieted.

In the silence Hollis stood for a while thinking about Mrs. Lang. He could almost feel the tension between her and her husband. Their relationship, a hundred things he couldn't identify but was aware of, reminded him of the relationships between some dog-owners and their dogs. He supposed a psychiatrist would call it a love-hate relationship. To some dog-owners it was obedience. The dogs were whipped, dominated, and made to live within certain—sometimes cruel—routines, and still with affection they regarded their owners as their masters. Perhaps some people were the same way.

Of course Mrs. Lang hadn't seemed that type. She had come to Hollis yesterday about the burial, and he had seen immediately that she'd been very fond of her Scottie, Tag. It wasn't the misguided gushy kind of affection usually associated with an elderly matron and her poodle; it seemed to Hollis to be the sensible, mature grief of an intelligent woman who had lost a long-time pet of which she was very fond. In a restrained, quiet way they had made arrangements to have Tag buried in the pet cemetery the next day, and she had given Hollis instructions to use the expensive cedar box rather than the pine. He had gotten the impression that she and her husband had money.

"How old was Tag?" Hollis had asked as he walked her to her car.

"Eleven," Florence Lang had answered, "but he didn't die of old age, I'm sure. It was something he ate."

The way she had said it made Hollis sure she suspected the dog had been poisoned. "Have you considered having a veterinarian perform an autopsy?" he'd asked.

She had shaken her head and smiled her strained smile. "It wouldn't help to find out if Tag was poisoned. It wouldn't change things."

When the Langs had brought the dog this morning, wrapped in a heavy towel, Hollis had looked at its distorted muscles and fixed, bare-toothed death grin and known at once it had died of strychnine poisoning, but he had said nothing.

The deep-throated barking of his own Alsatian, Luke, broke through his thoughts, and he remembered there was work to be done. He turned for a moment and looked at the mound of dirt by Tag's open grave, set among more than a hundred other graves marked by small plaques, stones, or simple wooden crosses. Then he walked toward the toolshed to get a shovel.

Florence Lang came the next weekend, with a small bouquet of daisies. She looked in much better spirits and there was genuine warmth in her smile as she greeted Hollis.

He was hosing down the cement dog runs, and he turned off the water and returned her smile, feeling the catch in his back as he stooped to twist the faucet handle. He wasn't getting younger; it was almost six years now since Margaret had died. Hollis wondered why he'd thought of Margaret as he saw Mrs. Lang walk toward him.

Now there was some embarrassment in her smile. "I . . . came to put these on Tag's grave," she said. "I know it seems foolish. . . ."

"Not to me," Hollis said. "Not if you were fond of the dog."

He watched her walk to the grave, stepping gracefully among the undersized markers and crosses, and stoop to place the daisies near the headstone. When she returned he asked her if she'd care for a cup of coffee, and she accepted.

They went into the tiny office where Hollis had an electric percolator set up, and he poured two cups. Mrs. Lang didn't request cream or sugar. She sat in a worn chair and began to sip her black coffee.

"Did you win all these?" she asked, looking at the trophies and awards on the wall behind Hollis' desk.

"We'll have to give credit to Luke," Hollis said with a smile. "That's his picture, winner of three national championships—but that's been a long time ago. My wife and I used to enter our dogs in a lot of shows, but she died six years ago and I guess I lost interest then."

"You have a nice place here," Mrs. Lang said, "quiet, peaceful. I suppose you must love animals."

Then Hollis didn't know why he said what he said, but suddenly there the words were, in the air between them as if they had spoken themselves. "I think Tag was poisoned. Your husband wasn't very fond of the dog, was he?"

For just an instant Mrs. Lang looked shocked. Then

with a steady hand she raised her cup to her lips and took a long sip of hot coffee.

"I'm . . . sorry," Hollis said, running a hand down his long sun-etched face as if he were weary.

"It's all right," Mrs. Lang said. "What you said is true—Charles wasn't very fond of Tag. He's not the kind of man to be overly fond of animals, or of most people for that matter. You're quite right. . . ." Then, obviously aware that she had said too much, she added, "He has his faults, like everybody else."

"Sure," Hollis said. He settled his lean body on the edge of the desk.

"I know what you're thinking," Mrs. Lang said in a pleasant, conversational voice. "You're thinking Charles couldn't be very fond of me." Her hand was still steady about the handle of her cup.

Hollis felt the sudden flush of blood to his face. "You're right," he admitted, "I was thinking that." He smiled a smile that wouldn't quite hold. "I'm the first to admit it's none of my business."

"My husband has his points, like everyone else," Mrs. Lang said with just an edge of defensiveness.

"You said that about his faults," Hollis reminded her.

"Well, I did, didn't I?" Mrs. Lang said. "I'll stand by both statements, Mr. Hollis." She looked at her wristwatch in alarm and stood. "Oh, it looks like I'm going to be late for my garden club."

"I didn't mean to keep you," Hollis said.

Mrs. Lang's smile was plainly meant to put him at his ease on that point. "I kept myself, Mr. Hollis, really. It was not your fault."

He took her empty cup and held open the screen door for her.

"Thank you for the coffee," she said politely as she picked up her purse and walked past him.

Hollis sat again on the desk and listened to her drive

99

away. She had left behind her, in the small office, the scent of a perfume that many women her age used. Lilac, he thought it was.

Mrs. Lang came often after that, sometimes to lay flowers on Tag's small grave, sometimes only to stand and look down at it for a while. She always stopped for a cup of coffee with Hollis, and they would talk.

Mrs. Lang never said anything else really detrimental about her husband, bound as she was by the loyalty of marriage, but Hollis could interpret the things she said. There developed a trust between them, and an understanding.

Then one day she came into the office and Hollis could see she'd been crying. Her eyes were moist and aggravated and her blue mascara had smudged slightly. At first Hollis thought she might have been crying over the dog, but her hand trembled when she took the steaming coffee cup from him and sat down.

"What is it?" he asked, squatting down beside her and resting his hand on hers to put her at ease.

"We argued," Mrs. Lang said quietly. "That's all."

"About what?"

"It doesn't matter now."

"What did he say to you?"

Mrs. Lang pulled her hand from beneath Hollis' and curled the fingers of both hands around the warm cup. "He wants to move," she said, "to Europe. I don't want to go. This is my home, this country, this city. My mother lives here, and I take care of her. He and I argue about it all the time. It's not a big thing, I suppose, but we argue about it."

"Did you ever think of letting him go alone?" Hollis asked.

"If I don't go with him he will go alone. If he leaves me I'll have nothing, nothing at all."

"Surely you'll have some money, support, alimony."

Mrs. Lang stared into her cup. "Yes, some money, I

suppose." As Hollis watched, she began to cry, only one small tear that trailed a pale mark on her made-up cheek. "He called me old," she said, "over and over, old, old, old . . ."

Hollis stood, feeling the pain in his back from stooping too long, and rested the back of his hand on her shoulder.

A horn honked, and he looked out the unwashed window to see a customer standing outside holding a Doberman pinscher on a leash. Hollis walked out and examined the dog's inoculation papers without going back into the office. After getting the Doberman settled in one of the dog runs, he returned and found that Mrs. Lang had stopped crying and was sitting calmly, sipping her coffee.

They talked for a long time then, as if nothing had happened, never touching on her argument with her husband. At last, when Mrs. Lang was leaving, she turned at the door and spoke very carefully to Hollis. "I've decided to get another dog," she said. "A big one, a Great Dane."

Hollis nodded. "If you want one, maybe that's a good idea."

Her quick little smile, the scent of her perfume, and she was gone. Hollis got to work on the registration papers for the litter of pups his Alsatian bitch had just delivered, and he forgot all about the Great Dane until Mrs. Lang's next visit, two weeks later.

Hollis was outside painting the corner post of the cemetery gate when she came. It was a warm summer day, but not too warm, with a soft breeze, so they stood outside and talked.

"I can't stay too long," Mrs. Lang said, looking at the wet half-painted post.

"As long as you like." Hollis set down the brush and placed the lid on the can of paint for emphasis.

Mrs. Lang smiled, looking at him rather steadily through her pale blue eyes. "It's about the Great Dane I bought—remember the one I told you about?"

Hollis leaned on a dry portion of the post and nodded.

Mrs. Lang looked away from his eyes then, staring at the ground. "He . . . died, I'm afraid."

Hollis looked at her carefully, saw how the merciless sun behind him brought out the fine lines in her face. "Poisoned?"

"I think so," she said, still looking down. Then she looked again directly at Hollis in a way that made him stop leaning on the post. "I'd like it if he could be buried here."

The summer breeze came up stronger than usual, turning the weather vane atop the toolshed in another direction. "He can be," Hollis said in a gentle measured voice.

Mrs. Lang smiled her quick smile and gave a sigh of gratitude. "I . . . we'll furnish the box this time. I have a large box, an old steamer trunk."

"All right," Hollis said. He placed his heel on the paint-can lid and pressed it on tighter. "Do you want a stone?"

"I think just a cross will do," Mrs. Lang said.

"Of course," Hollis said. "You hadn't had the dog very long. What was the name?"

"King," Mrs. Lang said thoughtfully. "His name was King."

"Early tomorrow morning?"

She nodded. "Thank you, Mr. Hollis."

Hollis watched her walk to her car, and before she opened the door she turned and looked back at him. He wiped his big hands on his paint-stained trousers and smiled at her. As she drove slowly past the kennels, the dogs began their begging, lonely howls.

Early the next morning she arrived alone in the red car, and Hollis was standing outside to greet her. The trunk was an old black one, with brass latches and thick leather straps. There were traces of paper and glue on the sides where travel stickers had either worn or been torn off. As Mrs. Lang watched, Hollis wrestled it from the trunk of the car and moved it through the cemetery gate to the open grave.

They said nothing for a moment, and Hollis listened to his heavy breathing in the cool morning air. Then the church bells began to chime loudly, some ancient simple hymn that Hollis didn't know. He lowered the trunk into the grave and stood looking down at its marred and faded lid.

Mrs. Lang walked away then, to wait in the office while Hollis filled in the grave. As he bent over the shovel he could feel her eyes on his back as she stood at the window, watching each rhythmic scoop of earth.

When Hollis was finished he joined Mrs. Lang in the office and they talked for a while before she left, about the weather and how pretty the geraniums were near the cemetery gate.

Mrs. Lang visited Hollis often after that, always taking time for a cup of coffee and a friendly chat. She seemed to Hollis to be happier, more contented, but perhaps that was only when she was in his presence. Sometimes she would bring a small bouquet of daisies and place them on Tag's grave, but Hollis never saw her place flowers on the Great Dane's grave.

Hand of Fate

Y OU MIGHT say Robert tripped over his own two feet. The stairway to the basement was long and very, very steep, and the steps themselves were bare gray-painted wood, without any rubber treads (the treads that Celia had often nagged him to tack down). Robert thought his heel had caught on the edge of one of the steps. He remembered thinking that as he was falling, bouncing, tumbling, dreading the intense pain he would feel from the sharp blows being inflicted upon him by the hard plaster wall and the unyielding steps, but as he lay sprawled on the gleaming tile floor at the bottom of the stairs he felt no pain.

For a few seconds there was blackness and a tingling sensation at the back of his head, but as he lay, fearing to move, mercifully there was no pain. Then, cautiously, he tried to move, and he discovered that he could not. His muscles simply would not respond to the messages sent by his brain. He could not, in fact, even feel the hard coolness of the floor beneath his back.

Robert lay looking up at the acoustic tile ceiling, fighting the panic and fear that was blossoming in his mind. He tried to call for help, but no sound came. Or was it possible that he was calling and couldn't hear himself? Closing his eyes, he listened for the other sounds of the house, the occasional soft crack of expanding or contracting wood, the muted hum of the refrigerator, and was that water dripping somewhere? A car door slammed outside, far away, and Robert opened his eyes. He could hear, anyway, and he could see.

Not that he could see much; only the white ceiling, the top of the paneled walls, just a glimpse of the mirror behind the bar at the other end of the basement, and, by rolling his eyes as far as possible to the top and the left side of their sockets, he could see the first three steps leading back upstairs.

No point in panicking, he told himself, until his rescuers could take stock and see how badly he was really hurt. At least they'd know he was alive. The paralysis might not be as serious as it appeared on the surface, maybe only a pinched nerve, a temporary condition, something along that line, something doctors would know about. But when would they find him?

Celia would find him first. She should be home from shopping within the next few hours. He'd hear her key in the door, the turning of the knob, the rustling of thick paper bags and the *tap, tap, tap* of her high heels along the entrance hall, then softer over the living room rug, sharper again into the bedroom, the kitchen, looking for Robert.

She'd call his name, but he couldn't answer, and she might not look in the basement.

Of course she'd look in the basement, if he wasn't anywhere else in the house—unless she'd think he'd gone golfing. Despair flooded in on him as he remembered that he'd told her that morning that he was going to play golf. She didn't know that Kramer had telephoned and the game was off.

Well, she'd look in the basement eventually. The bar was down here, and she probably would want to mix herself a drink after walking in and out of department stores in the hot afternoon sun. Robert wasn't in any pain. He could wait.

Hours passed . . . endlessly, endlessly. Robert had never realized that the basement was so quiet, so changeless. Then he heard a vague scratching, a slow rhythmic skittering on the tile floor near him. He rolled his eyes to the side and saw a gigantic cockroach approaching from not more than a foot or two away. Repugnance welled up in him, and he tried to jerk his head violently away from the disgusting insect, but of course his head didn't move. Damn! He'd meant to call the exterminator last week. Robert forced himself to be calm. If a cockroach crawling over him was his worst problem he was lucky.

The soft scratching stopped. The cockroach started off in another direction, away from Robert's face, then stopped again. Relieved, Robert turned his eyes back toward the ceiling. The bug must have come from the laundry room. He'd take care of that when he got a chance.

Robert tried again to move the various parts of his body, and a silent shout of joy lumped in his throat when he looked down and saw the tip of his left shoe moving from side to side. He could barely swivel the foot, with all his effort, but the feeling was returning, the paralysis was wearing off.

Within an hour Robert could move the fingers of his left hand. He could actually make a loose fist and feel the fingertips against his palm. Whether he was getting the tactile sensation from his fingertips or from the flesh of his palm, he couldn't tell.

There was a tremendously loud grating sound, and tears came to Robert's eyes. A key! Celia's key in the front door lock!

The door opened and he heard her footsteps, just as he'd imagined, across the living room carpet, into the other rooms, and he tried to call but couldn't. Then he noticed something else, other footsteps, softer, more widely spaced, a man's footsteps.

A neighbor, Robert decided; Mr. Gotham from next door, or Ned Pipps from across the street. She'd have help at least, someone to carry him upstairs. Strange, though, that they weren't saying anything.

Celia giggled. "Wait," she said. "He'll be gone all afternoon."

"How can you be sure?" Robert didn't recognize the man's voice.

"He will be . . . chasing his stupid golf ball."

"To each his own," the man said.

Then neither of them spoke for a moment.

Robert almost moaned in hurt and frustration. He knew a tear must be trickling down his cheek, but he couldn't feel it. He'd suspected. Of course the signs were there, but he hadn't actually *known*.

Celia giggled again.

"Fore!" the man yelled jokingly. *It was Pipps' voice, Ned Pipps!*

It all added up to Robert now, the beautiful wife, ten years younger than her husband, the Casanova neighbor. How many husbands, he wondered, had it all added up for suddenly like this?

They were saying more, in another room, and Robert couldn't quite understand them.

". . . A drink . . ." Celia was saying.

"Scotch?" Ned Pipps called, from very near the top of the stairs, in the kitchen.

"Some in the basement," Celia said loudly. "And hurry, darling."

Four footsteps, and the door to the basement stairs opened above Robert. The hum of the refrigerator was suddenly louder. Robert tried to roll his eyes far enough to see up the stairs, but three steps were all his vision could take in.

"Celia?" Pipps' voice was uncertain.

Robert heard her walk into the kitchen, not in high

heels anymore. There was a long silence at the top of the stairs before she spoke.

"Is he dead?"

"I don't know," Pipps said. "Suppose we go down and see."

The wooden stairs resounded with their footsteps and Robert heard the cockroach scurry away. Their legs came into view, Pipps' gray trousers and Celia's stockings and red house slippers. They stood on the second step.

"He isn't dead," Pipps said.

"I know," Celia said. "He's looking at us."

"He doesn't seem to be able to move," Pipps said. "Not a muscle."

"Now what do we do, Neddy?" Celia sounded exasperated, her first sign of emotion. "What do we do now?"

"Take a closer look," Pipps said.

They came down the rest of the way and bent over him dispassionately, like doctors over an operating table. Celia was wearing her red dress, with the circular sterling silver "love" pendant Robert had given her dangling from her neck on its long chain. Expensive, Robert thought, as the silver glinted in his eye. *Love was expensive.*

"Can you hear me, Robert?" Celia asked.

Robert flexed his fingers but they didn't notice.

"He can hear," Pipps said. "He heard us come down the stairs."

"He can see and hear," Celia said. "He knows about us now."

"So he does."

"We've got to do *something,* Neddy!" Celia's blue eyes were wide, her long blond hair hanging straight down like golden rain as she bent over Robert.

"Only one thing to do," Pipps said. "Call a doctor."

Celia straightened, and Robert looked up and saw the

jaw muscles tighten along the lower line of her chin. "We can't do that, Neddy. He *knows* about us!"

"But can't you see he's badly hurt?" There was genuine consternation on Pipps' lean handsome face, genuine pity.

"Of course I can!" Celia said quickly. "That's just it. He'll probably die anyway, even if we call a doctor."

"In heaven's name, Celia, he's your husband!"

"Exactly. And half of what he has is mine, but only half. Not even that if he chose not to grant me a divorce."

Pipps gazed down at Robert again, clinically. "He probably won't live a month."

"That's long enough to make out a will, Neddy. Besides, who knows how long they can keep him alive in a hospital, months, years, like a vegetable? People live like vegetables now. I wouldn't want that for him—or for us."

Robert lay looking up at them, listening to their breathing, deeper, harder, faster.

"Why don't you speak the words?" Ned Pipps said at last.

"All right," Celia said calmly. "I want you to kill him."

Pipps walked across the basement to the bar, out of Robert's range of vision. Robert heard him open the small refrigerator, drop two ice cubes into a glass. Liquor—Robert's most expensive Scotch, no doubt—splashed briefly over the ice cubes.

"How?" Pipps asked, frowning.

Now Celia walked out of Robert's vision. He rolled his eyes painfully, straining to see her, but it was useless.

"It will look like an accident," Celia said. "In fact he's already had the accident. All you have to do now is see that he's had a fatal one."

"Easier said than done," Pipps said into his glass.

"Maybe you could just lift his head and hit it against the bottom step," Celia said.

"The police aren't idiots, Celia! There are all sorts of things to consider, position of the body, angle of impact, blood smears. . . . They're regular research scientists."

They walked back and stood over Robert again, looking down at him with thoughtful frowns. Pipps glanced toward the top of the stairs, then back at Robert, then at Celia.

"There is one possibility," he said. "Suppose Robert had the same accident again?"

"I don't get it, Neddy."

Pipps flicked his lighter and lit one of those ultra thin cigars he always smoked. He had dash, Robert thought inanely. Celia had always had a weakness for men with dash.

"I can carry him back to the top of the stairs," Pipps said, "and let him fall again." He blew a thick cloud of smoke, pleased at his own ingenuity. Robert could see that the matter had become impersonal to Pipps now, merely a challenging problem to be solved.

"I don't know . . ." Celia said. "What if he's still alive?"

"It's sure to be fatal," Pipps argued. He gingerly nudged Robert's ribs with the toe of his shoe, bringing no response. "Look what the first fall did."

"We could burn the house down," Celia said. "It's insured. Something like that is what I had in mind."

"Fires don't just start, Celia! They investigate those things."

"Why don't we talk upstairs, Neddy?" Celia wrapped her arms about herself and looked down at Robert. "It's chilly down here, and besides, he makes me nervous."

"Whatever you say, dear," Pipps said. "We have time."

Without a backward glance they both stepped around Robert and climbed the stairs. Robert thought he would explode as he watched them tread the third step and pass out of sight. If only there were some way! Some way he could at least convey his terror, his panic! If only he could show them the horror of what they were doing to him!

Robert heard them talking in low tones upstairs, but he couldn't understand what they were saying. He made himself think. He was never one to give up on anything, least of all his life. But what could he do? How could he fight? He wasn't sure which plan they would eventually choose. Celia would submit to anything to get Pipps to kill him.

Robert's eyes darted from side to side, the only movement in the still basement. Then he stared upward toward the tiled ceiling. His heart was pounding with fright.

He could feel his heart now! That was something. He moved his left foot again, easier this time. The paralysis seemed to be wearing off on his left side, but not fast enough—not nearly fast enough. Then a glimmer, a very faint glimmer of hope shone in Robert's eyes. He began to flex the fingers of his left hand. They were getting easier to move, getting stronger. He lay like that for an endless time, listening to the drone of their voices from upstairs, flexing and unflexing his fingers.

The voices stopped. The door at the top of the stairs opened. Robert's hand was still.

Pipps came down the stairs first, then Celia.

"I don't want to watch, Neddy," Celia said in a distasteful voice.

"You're going to have to help me with him," Pipps said. "He's not exactly a feather."

Pipps stood over Robert, a freshly lit thin cigar jutting at a jaunty angle from the corner of his mouth. With a look of resolution on his face, he stooped to lift Robert by the shoulders.

"You manage his feet, pet."

Celia bent and gripped Robert's ankles.

"Together now," Pipps said.

"Always together, darling," Celia answered, and they lifted.

It was like somebody else being lifted, like watching the basement sway and whirl. Robert felt nothing. Then his head lolled forward on his chest as Pipps began to back up the stairs, half carrying, half dragging him. Robert could see Celia's arms about his ankles and the red of her dress as she strained to push him forward. He counted the stairs going up as Pipps took each labored, backward step. Eleven . . . twelve . . . thirteen. Odd how he hadn't noticed that unlucky number before.

"If this doesn't work, we can always use the alternate plan," Pipps said to Celia as he rested with Robert propped against his legs. He sounded slightly out of breath.

Celia walked around him into the kitchen. "Please, Neddy, get it over with."

Pipps let out a long sigh, then he lifted Robert by the shoulders and turned Robert's body so that they were facing each other, letting Robert drape halfway over his shoulder. Robert sagged against him, looking down Pipps' back toward the floor. He saw the floor move slightly toward him, then away, as Pipps bent his legs to fling his burden down the stairs. That was when Robert's left hand clutched the material of Pipps' trousers.

"Hey!" Pipps yelled in a startled voice.

The stairs, the ceiling, Pipps' surprised face, Celia looking horrified, all these whirled and revolved madly before Robert's eyes as he and Pipps tumbled down the steep stairway. Then about halfway down, Robert, still clutching the handful of material, wound up on top of Pipps. They slid the rest of the way to the basement like that, Robert partially cushioned from serious injury by Pipps' body, with Pipps' head and back bouncing cruelly on each step. All the way down Robert felt nothing, only heard the sickening impact of the blows on each body.

Robert lay on his back again at the bottom of the stairway, his left hand empty now. He could hear Pipps moaning in pain. Celia came down the stairs.

"My head's bleeding!" Pipps moaned. "And my arm, I think it's broken!"

"Poor Neddy!" Celia said. "And Robert's still alive! *Now* what on earth are we ever going to do?"

They were both silent for a long moment before Pipps spoke through pain-clenched teeth.

"We'll have to use our other plan."

"But how can we, Neddy? What about you?"

"I'll leave by the back door," Pipps said, "and cut through the yard and along the culvert. Then I'll make my way home and tell Evelyn I was jogging on the old creek road and tripped and fell down the embankment."

After a thoughtful pause Celia clapped her hands. "It should work, Neddy!"

"Help me up," Pipps said.

Robert knew Pipps could get out the back of the house unseen. Just two months before Celia had talked Robert into putting up a high redwood fence for privacy. He knew now what kind of privacy she wanted, a private route for Pipps to reach the back door.

With Celia's help, Pipps struggled to his feet and stood swaying.

"Help me up the stairs," he groaned. "Then after I leave, wait about ten minutes before you do anything. Evelyn and I should have left for the hospital by then."

Robert watched them move slowly up the steps and out of sight. Now what? What were they going to do to him now? There were so many ways. So many ways to kill a man who couldn't move, who couldn't even speak to beg.

He heard Pipps limp across the kitchen floor above him, the soft opening and closing of the back door. Celia walked about for a while, into the hall, the bedroom, pacing.

Robert heard her come back down the stairs. Then she was standing over him, gazing down into his eyes. There was an odd determination etched on her soft face. "I'm sorry it turned out like this, Robert."

Robert rolled his eyes and watched her as she walked across the basement. She stooped and extinguished the pilot light on the gas heater they'd had installed when they finished the basement. Then she turned the valves on high.

He felt a genuine surge of hope. The gas heater ran off a small bottled gas tank outside the house, and Robert knew that the tank was approximately half full. Even though he would be left lying on the floor, where the gas would settle, he didn't think that spread over the entire area of the basement there was enough compressed gas in the bottle to asphyxiate him.

"Of course there's only a bit more than half a tank," Celia said as if reading his mind, "but asphyxiation isn't what we had in mind, dear. Here, let me show you. . . ."

Robert saw her reach into the pocket of her dress and draw out his gold cigarette lighter, the one she'd given him for Christmas. Opening the cap of the lighter, she pinched the wick between thumb and forefinger and drew it higher. Then she stepped around Robert and flicked the lighter's lever, leaving the cap open so the flame wouldn't go out. Carefully, she set the lighter in the center of the second step.

"A time bomb," she said, stepping back and smiling down at Robert. "Neddy and I worked the idea out together. If the police do find the lighter when they investigate, they'll think you ignited the gas when you lit a cigarette."

Robert felt his heart racing in fear. It wouldn't take long for the gas to settle and spread across the basement floor, then rise slowly to the level of the second step. There might not be enough gas to suffocate him, but there was surely enough to touch off a tremendous explosion in the still basement.

"Good-bye, Robert," Celia said.

Frantically, Robert shaped his fingers as if he were grasping a pencil and tried to make writing motions. Celia stared down at the hand curiously, then smiled a wistful smile

"Last words, Robert?" She was absently toying with the silver "love" pendant he had given her. He saw the curiosity on her face. The drama of the situation appealed to her.

"Why not?" she said. She walked across the basement and returned with the bridge score pad and a pencil. "Make them brief," she said, placing the pencil between his fingers and sliding the paper beneath his hand.

She stood and watched while he scribbled on the small tablet. He let his hand fall across the paper palm up, over what he had written.

Celia bent down. "What does it say, Robert?" She moved his hand aside and reached for the writing tablet, squinting to read.

Robert tensed his hand and waited, patiently, patiently, until he was sure. Then, like a spider pouncing on its prey, his hand closed about the gently swinging, dangling pendant. His fingers worked madly, frantically, gathering in the heavy silver chain. Celia's eyes darted to Robert's face in surprise, then she tried to jerk away.

"Let go, Robert!" she screamed, but by the time she thought to try to slip her head through the chain it was too late. Robert's clenched fist was against her neck, squeezing the chain into the tender flesh of her throat. She began to gag.

Robert applied all the pressure of which he was capable as Celia's face turned a mottled red and she began to struggle furiously. Though Robert's arm was stiff from the tenseness of his hand, it revolved freely and without feeling at the shoulder, and except for the pain where the chain cut into his hand it was as if he were watching Celia being strangled rather then strangling her himself. Robert relished that pain in his hand, he loved it! A last bit of life for Robert as Celia was dying! A last bit of life before death!

Celia collapsed to the floor, pulling Robert's arm straight up behind his head. She'd kicked off her slippers and her bare heels began to beat on the tiles. She was beyond his range of vision now, and he didn't actually see her die. He only saw one pale hand flutter briefly in the air. Then Celia was still and Robert relaxed his grip.

The minutes began to pass, slowly and heavily in the still basement, and Robert stared with horrible fascination at the steady blue-red lighter flame and breathed the acrid odor of the leaking gas that was rising, rising inexorably to the level of the second step where the burning lighter waited to touch it off.

His bulging eyes trained unblinkingly on the even, tapering flame. Robert lay waiting, waiting . . . waiting.

The Second Shot

They drove from the funeral directly to the old sanitarium. Dr. Mindle sat in the back seat while his assistant, Dr. Raymond Xavier, and research director, Dr. Will Cleary, rode in front. Xavier was driving: it was his car, a five-year-old gray Plymouth with a small plastic skull dangling on a string from the rearview mirror. Dr. Xavier had a perverse sense of humor.

The funeral had been Dr. Carlson's—a psychiatrist who had served on the State Parole Advisory Board, of which Dr. Mindle was chairman. Carlson had drowned in his backyard swimming pool, leaving a wife and three teenaged children. The tragedy had rocked the staff of Beachwood Sanitarium profoundly. Even in the limited time of his biweekly consultations, the affable Dr. Carlson had become quite popular with everyone at Beachwood. As managing director of the sanitarium, Dr. Mindle had arranged schedules so that as many of the staff as possible could attend the funeral.

"Are you sure you have the key?" Dr. Mindle asked Xavier.

Dr. Xavier's muscular shoulders shifted beneath his dark suitcoat as he half turned to glance back at Dr. Mindle. "Yes, sir. The real-estate agent gave it to me yesterday in town."

117

Mindle nodded, removed his glasses, and polished them with a massive white handkerchief. He replaced the thick spectacles, adjusted them with a tap of his forefinger to the bridge of his nose, and sat back to watch the lush green countryside glide past.

It wasn't Beachwood Sanitarium that they were driving toward. A few miles ahead of them, in a secluded area on a bluff overlooking a bend in the Missouri River, sat the deserted Lanvale Sanitarium. Lanvale had been a small rest home that had failed two years ago. It was a converted Victorian mansion that had earlier served as a modest hotel. Space was becoming precious at Beachwood, so Dr. Mindle was considering recommending the purchase of Lanvale as an adjunct facility. Time was almost as precious as space at Beachwood, so he had decided to drive directly to Lanvale after the funeral with Xavier and Cleary so they could examine the building and grounds and be back at Beachwood by early afternoon for the repressed-rage symposium.

As the Plymouth bounced up the rutted side road leading to Lanvale, Dr. Mindle leaned forward to peer through the windshield. The deserted sanitarium loomed ahead of them, replete with Victorian dormers, wood scrollwork, and cupolas. Not in such poor condition as Dr. Mindle had anticipated. Nor as large.

Dr. Xavier drove up the circular driveway and parked in front of the gallery porch. The three men climbed out of the car and stood looking up at the tall double doors with brass lion's-head knockers. Xavier towered over the smallish Cleary and Mindle. He was built like a fullback, which indeed he had been in college. Dr. Cleary, though not much over five feet tall, was broad and strong. Dr. Mindle was neither tall nor broad, an almost dainty man in tweeds, who moved with a slow and certain precision. If Dr. Mindle *had* ever played football, he would never have been caught out of position. Dr. Mindle had been captain of his college debating team. Xavier should have scored so many points.

"I suggest we go our separate ways and look the place over," Dr. Mindle said. "Then on the drive back to Beachwood, we can discuss our impressions."

Dr. Cleary nodded agreement, the late-morning sun highlighting his bushy red hair. Xavier hefted the key in his beefy right hand and stepped up onto the porch beaming his perpetual disarming smile. His footfalls echoed on the enameled plank floor. "According to the agent," he said, unlocking the front door, "the electricity has been turned back on."

"Why don't you two look over the grounds while I give the interior a cursory examination," Dr. Mindle suggested.

He stepped inside, immediately found a toggle switch, and flipped it upward. The dim interior was abruptly exposed to the glare of the bright lights. There wasn't a stick of furniture in the place, but the condition of the floor and walls seemed sound. The boarded windows hadn't been tampered with by vandals and all of the fixtures that Dr. Mindle could see from where he stood were intact.

As Xavier and Cleary began a slow, appraising stroll around the front of the house he closed the door behind him and began walking from room to room, switching on lights as he went.

At the top of the wide stairway, he pushed open a door and entered the first of what had been patients' quarters. It was a small room, bare and in need of paint. Brilliant rays of sunlight lanced between the boards nailed to the outside frame of the only window. The light Mindle had switched on was a single low-wattage bulb inside a wire cage mounted in the center of the ceiling.

The room was minimal, Dr. Mindle decided, but it would do.

The click of the door latch made him turn. The door was closed and bolted. The man who had been concealed behind it when the doctor entered stood staring fixedly at him, cradling a double-barreled shotgun.

When Dr. Mindle's heart stopped racing, he concentrated on his observations. The man was medium-height and strong-looking. The impression of power he exuded was not so much the result of his size as it was of the tense, forward lean of his body. He was wearing a black T-shirt, faded jeans, and muddy boots. He might be a hunter, but it was the wrong time of year.

"Dr. Mindle," the man said, raising the twin barrels of the shotgun, "my name is Stanley Brandt."

The last name struck an ominous note in Dr. Mindle's mind. His dismay must have shown on his face.

"That's right," Brandt said, "I'm Marie Brandt's husband. The Marie Brandt who was brutalized and murdered in her bed by Arthur Taylor—tortured and killed by a vicious stranger who should still have been behind bars for the murder of his own sister, but who was on the loose because you set him free." Brandt's long drawn face became pale as bone, his haggard eyes burning and unblinking. "You and your board of so-called experts!" His voice caught with emotion. It was almost a sob.

Dr. Mindle had seen patients in Brandt's state of obsession. He knew that Brandt was capable of pulling the twin triggers. It was a twelve-gauge shotgun, holding two rounds. Two shots. Sure death from either barrel at this close range. The doctor had two sincere objectives: he wanted to help Stanley Brandt, and he wanted to survive.

He attempted to reason with Brandt, though he knew that was a contradiction in terms. Brandt was far beyond reason, in the shadowed primal depths of the mind, acting on his compulsion for vengeance. Dr. Mindle needed to play for time. Xavier and Cleary were outside. Help was nearby.

"How did you know I was coming here?" he asked.

Brandt grinned cadaverously, a caricature of a smile. "I've been watching you. I knew you were interested in buying this place and that your assistant picked up the key at the realtor's office yesterday. I pretended to be interested in the property and the agent told me you planned on returning the key this afternoon. It was logical that you'd come here after Dr. Carlson's funeral. So you see, killing him served two purposes. It exterminated him, and his funeral provided a time frame for your arrival here. I simply came here an hour ago, let myself in by forcing a basement window, made my way up here, and waited."

Dr. Mindle felt a cold weight drop through him. "You killed Dr. Carlson?"

"Of course. *And* Dr. Mathers *and* Dr. Eustice. All within the past three days. Mathers' and Eustice's bodies haven't been discovered yet. I planned it that way, so I'd have time to finish off everyone on the psychiatric board who recommended setting Taylor free. You're the last of them, Dr. Mindle, and after I use this shotgun to kill you, I'll use it on myself. I can put the barrel in my mouth and easily reach the trigger. It will be all over and no one will be able to touch me for what I've done. I'll be as free as Taylor." He laughed violently, but the twin barrels of the shotgun remained steady, aimed at Dr. Mindle's stomach. "Isn't that justice, Doctor?"

"No," Mindle said. "Justice was granting Arthur Taylor his parole."

Brandt was thrown. His eyes widened in surprise. "Why, you're as insane as Taylor!"

Dr. Mindle shook his head in disagreement. He

121

removed his glasses and polished them with his large handkerchief, the reflection of the sunlight through the cracks in the boarded-up window glinting off the thick lenses. A spot of brightness played like a whimsical spirit on the bare wall.

"Arthur Taylor murdered his sister thirty years ago," he said. "He had been a model prisoner. Every psychological test indicated that he would never kill again. The tests aren't perfect. We can be wrong. We were wrong in Taylor's case. But society can't storehouse people for decades without taking a chance on them eventually. It would be inhumane."

"What Taylor did to my wife was inhumane."

"I agree. It was tragic and reprehensible. You have my pity and deepest regret, Mr. Brandt, though I know it means nothing to you in your present state of mind. A terrible mistake in judgment was made. Your wife paid for it." Dr. Mindle replaced his glasses and returned the handkerchief to his pocket. "I can only be sorry."

"Wrong," Brandt said in a flat voice. "You can be dead."

"Carlson and Mathers and Eustice are dead," Dr. Mindle said. "And your wife is still dead. The men you killed had families that will grieve as painfully as you grieve the loss of your wife. You've only made a terrible thing worse, Mr. Brandt. Don't continue to do so by taking two more lives, no matter how much you yearn to kill, and to die."

Brandt bared yellowish teeth in a skeletal grin. "I do believe you're begging, Doctor."

"No, I'm imploring. For both of us."

"The way you implored the parole board to turn Taylor loose on society?"

"There is an element of self-destructiveness in most murderers," Dr. Mindle explained. "When they kill, they are, in a metaphorical sense, slaying a part of themselves.

That self-destructiveness which had been in Taylor's makeup seemed to have disappeared. Regardless of what you say and of what happened, Taylor deserved a second chance. No system is perfect."

"I'm unimpressed."

"Dr. Mindle?"

It was Xavier's voice, from outside in the hall. Brandt's wild eyes shifted to the door and back to his prey.

"Where are you, Dr. Mindle?"

"Don't answer!" Brandt cautioned.

Dr. Mindle removed his glasses again. He tilted the lenses and aimed the bright spot of reflected sunlight at Brandt, letting it rest just below his throat, and began once more to buff them with his handkerchief.

"Dr. Mindle?" Xavier's voice was closer, becoming concerned.

Theirs was the only closed door in the hall and so it must have drawn Xavier's attention. The doorknob twisted and turned and sudden loud knocking exploded the quiet of the small room.

Brandt's eyes darted toward the sound. At that moment Mindle aimed the bright reflection from his thick lenses directly into Brandt's eyes. When Brandt's gaze swung back toward the doctor, he was startled by the brilliance, temporarily blinded.

Dr. Mindle moved with surprising quickness. He stepped to the side and wrested the shotgun from the stunned Brandt. The roar was deafening, and Dr. Mindle felt the rush of the heavy buckshot flying past him on its way to embedding itself in the wall instead of in flesh and bone. The room hummed with the shot's reverberation.

"Dr. Mindle!"

Two voices now. Xavier and Cleary were flinging themselves at the door.

Dr. Mindle leveled the shotgun at Brandt.

Brandt only smiled. "I'm a much larger man than you are, Doctor. And I don't think you can bring yourself to pull the trigger. I'm going to take the shotgun away from you, and I'm going to kill you. It's you or me."

Dr. Mindle, appraiser of men, studied Brandt's narrowed eyes. "Yes," he said, "I believe it is."

The crashing at the door became louder. Time was running out. Brandt flexed his knees, coiled his body to pounce.

Then, to his astonishment, Dr. Mindle handed him the shotgun.

Mindle stepped back and stood with his hands at his sides. "You're right," he said softly, "I can't pull the trigger. There is one shot left and very little time. Now we'll see which you yearn for the most, Mr. Brandt. Vengeance? Or death? To which are you the most committed? In which direction will you swing the barrel of the gun?"

The crash of the splintered door flying open was simultaneous with the roar of the second shot.

The State Patrol arrived at Lanvale ten minutes after Dr. Cleary phoned them from a service station on the highway. When they got there, they found Dr. Xavier standing over Stanley Brandt, who was slumped in a corner with his head bowed, hugging his drawn-up knees.

"You took quite a chance," the patrol sergeant said to Dr. Mindle after he'd heard what happened.

"I felt sure that if forced to choose between revenge and escape into death, Brandt would decide on the latter," Dr. Mindle said. "I was surprised when his resolve broke, and he pulled the shotgun away from his head at the last moment and fired the final shot into the ceiling."

"You must have impressed him with the courage of your convictions," the sergeant observed wryly. "You were lucky."

"So was Stanley Brandt, if luck was a factor."

Dr. Mindle watched them lead Brandt away. Possibly Brandt could be helped, and might even eventually benefit from the same quality of mercy that had granted Arthur Taylor a second chance. Dr. Mindle hoped so. At least something might be salvaged from this tragedy of the system gone wrong.

He had fully expected Stanley Brandt to kill himself there in that tiny locked room. Though Dr. Mindle's decision to return the shotgun to Brandt had been correct, the result had been unforeseen. For the second time in six months, he had misjudged his man. But this time he was glad.

The Shooting of
Curly Dan

Ollie Robinson was my great-great-grandfather, and he didn't know himself how old he was or where he was born. He was a smart man, but he didn't have much education, and he kept to himself most of the time because of how the other kids would make fun of him. When I was younger I used to laugh at him myself, then all of a sudden one day I got to thinking, I was thirteen, and he was—what? One hundred and thirteen? But I had found out that when he told a story, it was worth listening to, because he was a man who'd done things and been places and met people.

One night when Mom and Dad weren't home he told me the story of Curly Dan's murder that happened when Grandpa Ollie—that's what I called him—was a gandy dancer for the Alton and Southern Railroad. That railroad is gone now, and so are gandy dancers, I expect. Grandpa Ollie didn't tell me how long ago it happened, but it had to be a long, long time. It didn't matter to him, though, because for Grandpa Ollie, sitting there half crippled in his cane chair, chin stuck out and skin loose and wrinkled like an old dollar bill, the past was sometimes right there all around him.

I was sitting near his chair, listening to the even in-and-out rhythm of his breathing and thinking he was asleep. Way off somebody was beating on something metal with a hammer, and maybe that's what kept him from dozing off like he usually did. But he wasn't asleep, and he began talking to me in a voice clearer than his usual voice—younger-sounding, like he was really back there living what he was telling me, living it all over again. . . .

All the railroads had crews of gandy dancers in them days (Grandpa Ollie began), eight or ten strong men to a crew and a caller. I was a gandy dancer for three years with the A and S, but I guess you don't know what a gandy dancer be. When trains go over and over a set of rails, them rails gets crooked and outa line with each other, and somebody's got to set 'em straight again. They got a machine does it now, but then it was done like most things, with sweat and muscle.

There was nine men on each Alton and Southern line crew, 'long with a line chief usually. The company engine would drop us off way out where the rails didn't have no care for a long time and we'd walk along carryin' our pry bars while the line chief kept his eye on the rails that needed work done on 'em. There was a flat cart with water and tools that we pushed along with us, 'cause we done other work besides just truin' the rails. Sometimes we'd have to take a hammer and drive loose spikes, or shovel earth under a section of roadbedding that had give way.

The day Curly Dan was killed we didn't have a line boss, like we didn't sometimes the day before payday, 'cause the foreman, he be workin' on the payroll and paperwork, and he figured ol' Ivy Joe was good enough to be caller and boss both. The line boss and his crew was over on a section of track the other side of a rise, close

enough so we could hear the ringin' of their steel and
sometimes their voices.

Ivy Joe, that wasn't his true name, but his initials was
I. V., so that's what we called him. Now we'd walk along
the track, carryin' our pry bars, till Joe spotted a place
needed work. Our pry bars was about five feet long and
tempered steel, kinda curved and flattened on one end.
When we wanted to line track we'd stand in a row 'long-
side it and put the flattened ends of the bars under the
rail. Then, like the big boss always told us, everything
depended on rhythm. Nine men had to move like one.
That's where Ivy Joe's callin' came in, and he was the
best caller the A and S ever had.

When we all had our pry bars 'neath the rail, ready to
use 'em like long levers, that's when Ivy Joe started callin' and we'd all tap the rail in rhythm. Then at the last
of his chant he'd raise his voice sudden and we'd all put
our backs in it together and there'd be a loud ring of steel
and we'd move that rail. Over and over we'd do it till the
rails was true, then we'd walk on downtrack to the next
bad spot.

It were a hot day when the murder happened, and we
hadn't had a water break since middle mornin' and the
sun was near high. Steel was ringin' and Ivy Joe was
callin' the rhythm:

> *"Tell me line boss eyes be blind*
> *How he gonna tell if the rails in line?"*

And we'd all pull back together and strike steel in
rhythm to inch the rail over. We stopped for a water
break after that bad section were trued and I can tell you
ain't none of us didn't need it.

Then we worked on ahead, leavin' the water and tool
cart sittin' behind as usual till we found another bad
place. We was workin' hard on a bend in the rails for

some time 'fore Ivy Joe noticed Curly Dan wasn't with
us.

"Where that Curly Dan?" he says, standin' with his
big fists on his hips. "You know, Slim?"

Slim Deacon was the one helped Curly Dan read letters
from Albany. His lean body kinda bent and he shook his
head.

"Chaney?"

Chaney were a big man, always grinnin', and he
grinned wider and shrugged his heavy shoulders.

"Ollie," Ivy Joe says to me, "you run on back to the
tool cart an' see if that lazy Curly Dan be layin' out on
us."

I took out runnin', listenin' to the ringin' rhythm of
the line crew across the rise while my feet hit the ties.

When I rounded the bend and ran a ways, there be
Curly Dan, layin' on his side, kinda curled up around the
water jug that was still sittin' on the ground. His blue
shirt back were covered with blood where he'd been shot,
the bullet goin' clear through, and when I got closer I
could see he'd been shot in the back of the head, too, like
someone wanted to make sure he be dead.

Everything seemed unnatural quiet and still there.
Even the water just below the top of the jug were as calm
and still as Curly Dan hisself.

I run back halfway round the bend, yellin' and wavin',
and the rest of the crew followed me back to Curly Dan's
body. For a while we all stood and stared, lookin' from
one to the other.

"How come we didn't hear no shot?" Arky said. He
was a short wide man from Arkansas that always had a
blade of grass in his teeth.

Ivy Joe looked round him towards the rise and a grove
of trees. " 'Cause the killer timed his shot with the
rhythm," he says. "Brogan's crew be workin' over the
rise when we was here, and when they hit steel hard is

when the killer pulled the trigger from the trees over there."

Then Ivy Joe walks over to the grove of trees and a while later comes back holdin' a pistol. "It be a small gun," he said, "and I found where the brush was flattened down where the killer was hidin'." Then he looked real close at the body, standin' there holdin' the pistol and thinkin'. "Load Curly Dan onto the tool cart," he said, and we did that and put up the tools and water jug that was still layin' there from our last work break. Kelly, a bowlegged man with a big mustache, and a man name of Tall Al slid Curly Dan well to the back so's he wouldn't get blood on any of the tools.

"What we gonna do now?" Chaney asked, standin' with his arms crossed.

"We gonna work," Ivy Joe told him. "We gonna work on." And we went on down the tracks.

"Who'd have any reason to shoot Curly Dan?" Ben Zebo said while we was walkin' back to where we'd left off workin'.

Nobody answered 'cause everybody know'd who. There was three men on the crew coulda done it for reason. Chaney was sweet on Curly's little gal, Molly Ann Parker, who'd been all his till Curly Dan took her over. And a man named Handy Billy Grover, he was awful sweet on her too, and he and Curly Dan'd had a fight about her just a few days ago. If any of 'em had any sense they'd just waited, 'cause Molly Ann woulda come round to 'em again. Then there was Arky, who Curly Dan owed fifty dollars to, and who'd been in a argument with him last week over Curly Dan not payin' up.

Ivy Joe know'd all these things, but he didn't say any of 'em as we kept on walkin' 'long the tracks, listenin' to Brogan's crew ringin' steel on the return line over the rise. Kelly with the big mustache was laggin' behind us, pushin' the cart along the tracks real slow and keepin' his distance from Curly Dan.

We got to where we was linin' track, took our places again along the outside rail, and slid our pry bars under the steel. Ivy Joe started to clink his bar in rhythm and sing like always.

"Work be hard but I ain' gonna moan
Work my han's 'til I see de bone!"

Steel rung and we moved that rail 'bout an inch. It were a song Ivy Joe'd sung lots before and we was all in rhythm, pullin' hard and together.

'Long the bend we was workin' was the worst section of track on the Alton and Southern but for the Gibsey Hill, and we could look ahead in the sun and see rail shimmerin' outa line for a long ways. We worked on and sweat was runnin' down us all.

"Somebody hide an' shoot Curly Dan
Shame to kill dat young good man!"

All the while Ivy Joe sang we was tappin' rhythm on the steel, all together and bendin' our backs to it at the last when he'd raise his fine voice. Movin' rail, we was, and then walkin' on to more rail. The sun be high and hot as I ever felt it, and we was all walkin'-weary soon, throats dry and eyes burnin' with sweat. I seen Arky in front of me, staggerin' some as we walk on down the line.

"When we gonna stop for water?" Chaney yelled, but Ivy Joe, he didn't hear and kept right on workin'.

"Somebody on de railroad crew
Know how to shoot when the rhythm do!"

And the steel clang together like one clang, all through the song, then loud like to make your head hurt.

131

We work on for must've been hours like that, in kind of a daze like you'd get when Ivy Joe was callin' rhythm. We was all tired and achin', and I remember how my back felt like it was blazin' and it pained me to lean. Still we kept the rhythm, 'cause the job, it be all rhythm.

> *"There be sorrow for Molly Ann*
> *Somebody done gone an' shoot her man!"*

I pulled up and back on my pry bar, feelin' a pain down my stomach, and the rail hardly move and I heard a little clink just a eyewink after the other men had pulled hard together.

"Water," Handy Billy called out, and we all called out for water. Billy's clothes was stickin' to him and his face be all swollen where he kept wipin' his sleeve to keep the sweat outa his eyes.

> *"Someone here he done hang back*
> *Kill Curly Dan when we move downtrack!"*

Much pain as there be, we still tried to keep up the rhythm. My mouth was dry as sand and the pain almost kept me from straightenin' as the steel rang, and again I heard that clang of a pry bar outta time.

> *"One man kill fo' a woman's all*
> *Now a rope gonna stop his fall!"*

"I got to have water!" Handy Billy yelled again with his voice all cracked when the steel ring, and I could hardly hear if there was a late ring that time.

The heat be risin' from the ground, and I know'd any time I was gonna fall flat on my face, but we worked on, gaspin' for breath and tryin' to ignore the achin'. Then again there was a late ring of steel, this time later than before, and there was a thuddin' sound too, and we

132

turned and seen the last man in the crew layin' out on the ties with his chest heavin'.

Ivy Joe walked on back and looked down at him. "You the one killed Curly Dan, Chaney," he said like he know'd for sure.

Chaney just looked up at him and kinda croaked.

Then Ivy Joe let us all have water, but not Chaney. Ivy Joe standed over him with the ladle full after everybody else drunk. He let a few drops fall down on Chaney's forehead.

"You killed him," Ivy Joe said again.

"I done it," Chaney said in a raw voice. "I done it to get Molly Ann, an' I used her gun. Danny, he had it comin' to him!" He raised up a hand what was all bloody and blistered like everybody else. "Now gimme some water!"

Ivy Joe let him drink then, and I didn't think Chaney was ever gonna stop drinkin'.

"How'd you know it were him?" Handy Billy asked, wonderin' on his luck at bein' Molly Ann's one and only again. "It didn't have to be a railroad man to time his shot with the rhythm."

"It be a railroad man," Ivy Joe said. "That's why he left the gun, so's we wouldn't find it on him. I know'd it was prob'ly one of three men at first: Arky, Chaney, or you, Handy Billy. I figured it wasn't Arky that shot a man who owed him money, 'cause it's day before payday. Least he'd do is wait a day or two."

Ivy Joe looked back towards where we come from. "Instead of linin' up for water, the killer hid in them trees during water break, seein' Curly Dan was last in line for a drink, then picked him off when the rest of us was walkin' away uptrack. Then he caught up with us 'fore we missed him and was there to help us move track."

"But it coulda been somebody else," Billy said. "It coulda been somebody from the crew over the rise."

"I know'd it were someone from our crew," Ivy Joe said, " 'cause of the way Curly Dan was layin' curled round the water jug where he'd been drinkin'. He musta been shot first in the back, then fell, 'cause the bullet come out the front and there were no hole in the jug, or the jug wouldn't be full like we found it.

"Now from that distance a shot in the head is a funny way to make sure you done finished a man off, but that's where Curly Dan was shot again while he were layin' there on the ground. Why in the head? Like I said, so's not to break the water jug and lose our water. So then I know'd the killer was on our crew and was the only one hadn't had a water break since early mornin'. In this heat, first man to drop from thirst would likely be Curly Dan's killer. And when it were Chaney that dropped first I *know'd*."

Ivy Joe sent a man on ahead, and we stayed where we was till a whistle blowed and smoke raised up and the big company engine come on down those straight true rails to take Chaney back to the company yards. To take him back where by and by the hangman be waitin' for him.

Then we started workin' again.

The Day of
the Picnic

"South into the hot barren country of Southern California, east all the way into Arizona, that's the range of the California condor."

"Those birds fascinate you, don't they?" Judith asks. It is another of her stupid questions that are beginning to annoy me more and more.

"They are magnificent," I tell her, bracing myself for a bump as the jeep speeds over the rocky land. Of course they are magnificent; with a wingspread of over ten feet that carries them up, up in spiraling circles over a mile high, then enables them to ride the air currents in sweeping arcs for up to a hundred miles in search of carrion. "There are only an estimated fifty or sixty of them left, you know," I say.

Judith says nothing. She *is* beautiful—except, perhaps, for her rather prominent nose. Despite the heat that has been withering us for over an hour, she still looks fresh in her tan safari jacket and gray slacks. Her blond hair is drawn back and tied with a black ribbon. Appropriate, I think.

The jeep bounces high into the air. There is a metallic sound and the horn rim drops into my lap, then onto the floor to rattle beneath the seat.

"For heaven's sake, Norton, watch where you're driving!"

She says nothing about the horn rim. Secretly she feels that I'm cheap; I know that. Perhaps that is one of the things about Rod Smathers that appeals to her, his undisciplined spending habits. She thought I should buy a newer jeep, from a registered dealer, but why should I when Harry Ace's Premium Motors had just the vehicle I needed. As I told her, I am an experienced naturalist, and I know just what type of transport is best for my purposes. She didn't know, of course, that I immediately had a new muffler put on the jeep, for it's against the law to drive in certain areas of the vast condor preserve, and today, especially, I didn't want to attract unwarranted attention.

It was I who suggested this little picnic outing. I waited a full three months after buying the jeep from Harry Ace, for I am by nature a cautious man. Also I am a possessive man, and I couldn't live with the fact that behind my back Judith was seeing the loud and freewheeling Rod Smathers. Let us call it the territorial imperative.

The steering wheel shimmies in my hands and I let up on the accelerator as the jeep lurches over some especially rocky terrain.

"It's terribly hot, Norton!" Judith complains. "Couldn't we have gone to the mountains for this picnic, where there are trees and some shade at least?"

"I suppose we could have," I say, watching her take a long drink from the canteen. "But I wanted you to see these birds. It's a sight I wouldn't want to share with just anyone." She offers me a drink, but I refuse with a curt wave of my backhand. "Be watching the sky," I say, and dutifully she turns her face to the sun.

"I'm hungry, Norton," Judith says in her protesting whine.

"We'll eat soon," I tell her, thinking of the dry sandwiches she's packed that are bouncing on the rear seat. "If you eat now, it will just make you thirstier in this sun." At the mention of water she takes another drink. Judith has always been the pawn of suggestion. I suppose Rod Smathers knew that instinctively.

"There!" I say, downshifting and braking the jeep to a halt.

Judith's eyes, the exact shade of blue as the cloudless sky, wander aimlessly as they search the airy void ahead of us. Then she sees the tiny black form off to the west. It has to be a condor!

Getting out my secondhand binoculars, I focus them on the dark form. Only one bird flies like that, huge wings outspread and curving gently upward, ending in five guiding feathers spread like the reaching fingers of a hand. The giant bird wheels to the east, giving the impression that it is somehow suspended from above, then turns gently and glides lower. I start the jeep and drive slowly forward, handing the binoculars to Judith. "You watch him," I say, and she fits the lenses to her searching eyes.

The condor has landed.

I stop the jeep and motion for Judith to speak quietly. "Bring the canteen," I say. "We'll walk from here."

She obeys, and we move forward over the sun-baked uneven ground. We stop behind a cluster of rock, and we have a perfect view.

"I wanted you to see one up close," I say. "We're in luck today."

"He's huge!"

I am strangely thrilled by her enthusiasm. It is a big condor, with a wingspread of perhaps eleven feet. It is feeding on a half-eaten pronghorn antelope, recognizable only by its horns, for the condor has turned the carcass inside out to reveal the gleaming skeleton and sun-dried meat.

"They always do that," I say. "They tear at the navel or rectum of their prey with their beak and pull the innards out before feeding."

"How terrible!" Judith says, her eyes riveted on the huge bird.

The condor knows we are here, I am sure, but as long as we keep our distance he will ignore us and not flap away in wily caution. As we watch, he lowers his bare orange head and neck and digs at the half-eaten carcass with his curved beak.

Then a dark shadow moves slowly over the terrain and we actually hear the whir of wind through the wing tips of the second huge condor that glides over us and lands near the carcass. Dark as its own shadow, dragging its massive wings, it walks in clumsy lurches toward the antelope and begins feeding.

"Sometimes," I tell Judith, "they gorge themselves so that they can't take off for hours. Though what's left of that antelope isn't enough for that to happen."

"It's disgusting," she says, but she is hypnotized.

We've had a hot walk, and I offer her the canteen. She takes a long drink, and I smile at her.

"What's funny?" she asks, blinking heavily at me.

"Perhaps the whole world," I say, watching her face closely. "I wanted especially for you to see these birds close up, to see the talons and the curved beak, and to know how they feed, using the unique sharp tools nature has given them to disembowel a carcass." I screw the cap on the half-empty canteen and lick my lips. Perhaps the sun is affecting me slightly.

The strapless binoculars drop from Judith's hand and she crouches there, making no attempt to pick them up, not realizing that she's dropped them.

"You see," I tell her, "I know about you and Rod

Smathers, about what you've been doing behind my back. So I pulled a little trick on you, Judith, and loaded the water in the canteen with enough barbiturates to stop the hearts of ten unfaithful women. But the little trick isn't over."

From a hundred yards beyond us comes the muffled flap of huge wings against the ground. Judith stares at me with sleepy eyes held wide by horror-arched brows. "Oh, no, Norton!" She slumps from her crouching position to sit with her back against a rock. Her jaw moves, and she tries feebly to raise both hands, but cannot.

When her eyes close, I undress her and carefully fold her clothes. Then I drag her body out from behind the rocks, listening to the flapping of kitelike wings as the condors take to the air behind me. I lay Judith on her back on the bare ground and press my ear to the still warm flesh beneath her breasts, listening for a heartbeat. There is none; she is quite dead. She is carrion. I have no feeling at all.

Leaving Judith there, where telescoping eyes can see her from miles up, I gather her clothes and walk back to the jeep. I get a drink from the other canteen and notice with satisfaction that my hand is not shaking. Then I drive some distance away and stop, training the binoculars on the two condors still circling above the scene I've left. Presently they are joined by a third condor, and at last the three of them glide downward in ever narrowing circles.

I cannot stop laughing for a long time as I put the jeep in gear and speed northward. Judith's bones might not be found for months, and then who will know how the bleached and nameless skeleton met its fate? The thing now, I realize, is to get clear of the area as quickly as possible, and I urge the bucking jeep on to higher speeds.

What's that?

Something dark, bouncing out in front of me, *a wheel!*

Suddenly the left front of the jeep digs into the earth and I am hurled forward and up. *Smash!* against the windshield frame. *Smash!* onto the hard ground and I slide, my legs bent grotesquely beneath me! There is the distant rending of metal and tinkling glass, and then with blinding pain my neck and shoulder slam into a rock and I am lying still on my back. Time seems to have ceased.

Above me the sky seems to shimmer like rising heat waves and hours and hours pass.

Finally, I roll onto my side and try to rise, but I cannot. My left shoulder is scraped to an ugly red and burning rawness but there is no pain in my legs, only a creeping numbness. I try to crawl but lack the strength to do even that. Waves of nausea assail me as I see again the bouncing, free-rolling loose wheel. *Harry Ace has done this to me!*

Or is it Judith's fault—and Rod Smathers'?

I try to control myself, lying there in the searing heat. It doesn't matter who is responsible. The front wheel of the jeep came off and here I am, and it is up to me, Norton Saltt, to get myself out of it. If only I could move!

There is blood running from a cut on my head into my eye, and I remove my torn shirt and dab at the painful wound, then wrap the shirt about my forehead. Again I try to crawl, but I drag my crippled body forward only a matter of inches before the pain and numbness overcome me. My heart begins to pound unreasonably fast, as if it possesses some secret knowledge.

I do not see it land, but I turn my head and it is there—a very large condor, about a hundred feet from me, with huge soot-black wings spread and resting partly against the ground as it balances awkwardly. It fixes a saucer eye on me that is not the eye of a warm-blooded animal like myself, but the eye of a bird. In weighty, clumsy lurches it moves toward me, its gnarled talons clacking on the hard ground, and I wave an arm weakly and scream as loudly as I can through my parched throat.

It stops.

When I lie still, my body vibrating with my pounding heart, the condor lurches forward again and rests not more than fifty feet from me, watching. I watch, too, the red-orange and wrinkled skin of its neck and head, the whitish curved beak, the unbelievably long and wicked talons. *I have never known such fear!*

I glimpse above me the spread of mammoth black wings with a flash of gray beneath, and a huge shadow moves across the land as another condor soars low, then glides upward to arc in slow and lazy circles.

Then I see that the circles are narrowing, *and that I am their focal point!*

Through my horror I try desperately to dredge up every bit of information I've ever learned about the giant condors, but as I lie there watching those narrowing, swooping circles, listening to that clacking feathered walking, one bit of information on which even the experts disagree burns in my mind like an agonizing, glowing coal. No one really knows if the great birds wait until their prey is completely dead before they begin to feed.

No one really knows.

Mortal Combat

It is said that in Mexico the only event that begins on time is the bullfight. Police Lieutenant Rafael Castillo knew this to be true, so it was ten minutes to four when he walked with the rest of a large crowd through the main gate of Plaza Mexico. Manolo Ruiz, the fast-rising matador from Merida, was to fight the first and fourth bulls that afternoon. Fortunately, this spectacle was to take place on Castillo's day off, so he was pleased to be among the more than 50,000 aficionados who would watch Ruiz practice his deadly art.

It took Castillo little time to find his seat halfway up on the sun-brightened side of the huge stadium. No sooner had he sat down and let his bulky five-foot-five frame relax in the pleasant warmth than the ceremony began. The horseman in black galloped his steed across the dirt ring and reined to a halt before the judge's box, sweeping off his plumed hat and sitting impatiently in the saddle while awaiting permission to begin the timeless sequence of events that would lead inexorably to death.

After receiving permission, he backed his horse across the ring and took up position at the head of the bullfighters waiting on the sunny side of the stadium. The paseo began, moving slowly across the ring. The three matadors, having made the sign of the cross, strutted in front

142

behind the black-coated horseman. They had visited the little chapel beside the ring and were prepared.

Each saluted the judge's box while walking calmly to the measured music of the band. Castillo watched Ruiz, a broad-shouldered slim-waisted man in a glittering suit of lights with pink stockings, as the procession disbanded. On Ruiz's vivid dark features was a tranquility that contrasted with the excitement now generated among the crowd.

The trumpet wailed above the sound of the band, signaling the running of the first bull. The toril doors opened immediately and the bull burst into the ring, the yellow pennants pinned to his hump flying as he lowered his head and charged the brave peones who antagonized him with their crimson and yellow capes. Ruiz watched carefully the reaction of the bull, learning what he could about its habits, discovering which horn it favored as it charged.

When he was ready, Ruiz stepped from the shelter of the burladero into the ring and made a series of passes, beautifully executed veronicas. The crowd cheered as he brought the bull to a confused standstill with a rebolera, swinging the cape gracefully around his lean body; then he turned his back on the bull and strutted away.

The overture was ended. The *tercio de varas,* the first stage of the bullfight proper, was about to begin. The picadors rode into the ring on their padded horses, wielding long lances tipped with steel spikes. Castillo watched as they placed the pics carefully to reduce the strength of the bull's hump muscle so that the great head hung lower.

The bull was drawn away from the horses, drums and trumpets sounded, and the banderillas were to be placed. A thunderous cheer rose from the circular stadium as Manolo Ruiz strutted out to place the banderillas himself in the bull's neck. He moved confidently toward the pawing bull, a solitary man who stood composed before the nightmarish thing with horns that was positioning itself to charge. Lieutenant Castillo felt the excitement stir in him, the primal thrill he'd felt even as a child when his father had brought him to the bullring.

In the quiet lull as the crowd waited for the bull's charge, Castillo's pager beeped relentlessly at him from his shirt pocket.

He cursed, watched Ruiz plant the pair of colorful banderillas perfectly, then left his seat to go down into the stadium's concrete tunnel and find a phone.

The precinct sergeant connected him immediately with Sergeant Corerra.

"I'm at Plaza Mexico," Castillo said, even before Corerra could say hello. "Ruiz is in the ring at this moment."

"And something else is going on at this moment, I'm afraid, sir. A man named Roberto Lopez has murdered his wife on Calle Planeta. He's barricaded himself in his house and is armed."

"With a gun?"

"A machete, sir. He used that on his wife."

Castillo got the exact address from Corerra and told him they would meet there as soon as possible.

"Ruiz has good days and bad," Corerra said before hanging up. "How does he look today?"

"This is one of his better days," Castillo grunted disconsolately, and slammed down the receiver. Perhaps this wouldn't take long, he told himself. Possibly the matter would be cleared up by the time he arrived. But probably not. Above him the crowd roared as he strode toward the gate.

Castillo drove along Insurgentes, then west on the Paseo de la Reforma, past the swank hotels and Sanborn's, then north on a side street and through the Zona Rosa with its exclusive shops and restaurants that catered to rich tourists. Soon he was into one of the poorer neighborhoods of Mexico City. He consulted his map, found that he was going in the correct direction, and within half a mile made a left turn onto Planeta.

He saw the crowd immediately. Over a hundred people were being held back by at least a dozen uniformed policemen who had cordoned off part of the block. Everyone in the crowd was looking at a tiny brick building, the bottom half of which had been a leather-goods shop but was now boarded up. Rickety wooden stairs led to a second-floor door on the near side of the building. Castillo saw several officers crouching against the brick wall beneath the landing.

Sergeant Corerra was waiting for Castillo. He was a small thin man with an upturned narrow mustache and thoughtful dark eyes. Like Castillo, he was wearing civilian clothes.

"He's upstairs," Corerra said, pointing toward the door at the top of the rickety wood steps.

The door was open or completely off its hinges. Only shadow was visible inside.

"What's happened?" Castillo asked.

"Roberto Lopez and his wife Mariana rent the upper floor. An hour ago Roberto's brother went up to see them and found Mariana dead with Roberto sitting near her holding a machete. Hector, the brother, ran from there and phoned us."

"Has anyone talked to Roberto?"

Corerra nodded. "I have. From the landing outside the door. He admits that he killed his wife. He says he is unemployed and poor and tired of struggling. They argued over the wife's infidelity. He lost his head and killed her. He told me that if I came inside he would kill me."

"Did he say where he expects all this to lead?" Castillo asked.

Corerra smiled totally without humor. "Roberto Lopez is not talking rationally. Nevertheless, I believed him when he said he would kill me."

"No doubt he said it convincingly." Castillo flicked a match to flame against the nearby lamppost and lit a half-smoked cigar he'd produced from his pocket. "Did you find out who Roberto Lopez is?"

"He has a history of mental illness manifesting itself in severe depression. Sometimes suicidal. A violent man."

"And a sad one. Has he a criminal record?"

"Three charges of assault. One conviction, five years ago. He is on parole." Again the humorless smile. "Obviously he has violated the terms of his parole."

"And just as obviously," Castillo said, "I must try to talk to Roberto Lopez."

He smoked the cigar to a half-inch stub, then ground it out on the pavement with his heel. The still smoldering remains he kicked into the gutter. Then he borrowed Corerra's revolver, tucked it beneath his shirt, and walked toward the wooden stairway leading to the open door and the shadows beyond.

The stairs creaked loudly as he climbed them. He did not try to conceal his presence. On the narrow landing he stood motionless to one side of the doorway. There was no sound from inside. A peculiar odor of sweat and blood and animal fear wafted out to compound Castillo's own fear. The sun seemed suddenly very bright and hot. Castillo found himself thinking of Manolo Ruiz standing beneath that same sun in the bullring at Plaza Mexico. Was the bull dead by now? Or was Ruiz?

"Roberto Lopez!" Castillo called. "This is Police Lieutenant Castillo! We need to talk!"

The silence inside was unbroken.

Castillo waited several moments, wondering if Roberto Lopez had used the machete on himself. He was ashamed to find himself hoping that was so. He glanced down and saw the crowd, the policemen, staring up at him, their faces blank yet expectant.

"I'm going to come in, Roberto," Castillo said loudly to the silence. "Alone, only to talk."

When it was apparent that he was again to go unanswered, Castillo moved into the open doorway, paused to let his eyes become accustomed to the dimness, then stepped inside.

His gaze riveted on what was left of the woman, and his courage shriveled as he imagined the rage that must have been behind such butchery. A faint sound to his left made him suck in his breath harshly and turn.

Roberto Lopez was standing beside the doorway to the kitchen. He was a huge man wearing dark shorts and an untucked white shirt patterned with blood. His arms hung at his sides limply, and from his right hand dangled a machete so long that its blade almost touched the floor.

He said, "You should not have come in here, Lieutenant Castillo."

For a moment no reply came from Castillo's fear-numbed tongue. "It is my job," he managed to say at last, in a voice whose calmness surprised him.

"I killed her," Roberto Lopez said, pointing with the machete to his dead wife.

"Yes," Castillo answered in the same quiet voice, "and now it's time to come with me, to sit down and talk about what has happened."

"You want to lock me up."

"No," Castillo said, "I don't want to. I can promise that you won't be harmed."

"Can you promise that I won't be locked up?"

"No."

"I've been locked up before. I won't be ever again. Mariana is better off than I am now."

"That doesn't have to be true," Castillo said, "if you'll come with me."

"No matter how many of you they send here for me," Roberto Lopez said in a quavering voice, "no matter how many lies you tell me, I'll never go with you."

"You must try to think reasonably for—"

Without the slightest change of expression on his broad face, Roberto Lopez raised the machete and charged Castillo.

Even as he ducked, Castillo was groping for the gun beneath his shirt, cursing himself for having decided to leave it concealed so as not to upset Lopez. He heard the machete slash the air above his head and felt the icy rush of its passing. He rolled to the right on the hard floor, his heels clattering. The machete thunked into the wood a few inches from his face. He scrambled into a corner, gun drawn.

The effort of pulling the machete from the floor had caused Roberto Lopez to stumble backward and half fall against a threadbare chair. He laughed an oddly melodic, empty laugh, stood up straight, and again charged Castillo.

Castillo squeezed the trigger over and over reflexively.

The bulk of Roberto Lopez struck the floor near him in a lifeless heap. Castillo heard thunderous footsteps on the stairs outside. His eyes darted to the left, to the broad machete blade embedded in the wall beside his head.

Shadows played across the scene as one after another the police poured into the room, guns at the ready.

"He's dead!" someone said. "They're all dead!"

"No," Castillo said, "not all of them, thank God."

And Corerra was helping him up.

By the time Castillo got back to Plaza Mexico, Ruiz had just finished killing his second bull. It must have been a grand performance. He had been awarded both ears and was parading around the arena, followed by his assistants who were tossing back the hats, coats, and various objects that the crowd was sailing into the ring in wild tribute. Again Manolo Ruiz had faced and defied death, with courage and grace.

The drag mules were hauling the dead bull from the ring by the chains fastened around its horns. They were dragging it very slowly out of respect for the fight it had made, while the crowd demonstrated its adulation for both toro and torero.

Standing in the midst of the cheering crowd, Castillo looked at the bull and wondered if perhaps Roberto Lopez, all his impoverished life goaded toward a final few minutes of rage-filled mortal combat, deserved at least such a tribute. True, he had murdered his wife, who also certainly deserved better, and yet he was a man and this was an animal.

But Roberto Lopez would be buried in a pauper's grave. And Rafael Castillo would continue to do his job without adulation. Without recognition. Without thanks.

Ruiz strutted past in the bullring, smiling handsomely and waving, and Castillo began to cheer with the rest of the crowd.

Something for the Dark

"It bothers me," the lieutenant said.

"It didn't bother the jury," I told him. "They found me guilty."

The scent of fear wafted across the waxed wood table where I sat in the prison visiting room. I understood the lieutenant's fear, felt sorry for him, but nothing could be done about that. He was a conscience case and always would be.

"Your wife had many enemies," he said in a voice dulled by the resonance of the words in his memory. My lawyer had reminded the jury of Miriam's enemies over a dozen times during the trial.

Of course I had pleaded not guilty, claiming my confession had been made under duress. But I had little doubt as to the trial's outcome. The smoking gun, the locked room . . . Justice was as blind as I was.

I heard the lieutenant shift his weight uncomfortably in his chair, caught the scent of his lime after-shave lotion as it mingled with the doubt that would never loose its hold on his conscience. He'd been the arresting officer, the one who'd forced my confession and whose testimony at the trial had destroyed my case. He had reason to doubt, but doubt was all he could do.

The lieutenant's breathing leveled out as he relaxed somewhat. On the left side of my face, I felt a subtle coolness as someone quietly opened the door. A soft-soled shoe whispered abruptly on the cork floor. I heard the lieutenant turn in his chair, felt faint vibrations along the wide table as he strained to see the visitor. "You have about ten more minutes, Lieutenant," the voice of Graves the guard said evenly, "then I have orders to take him back to his cell." I felt the movement of air as Graves left, heard the click of the door latch, the turn of the key, the sigh of the lieutenant as he leaned on the table and made it live with the tenseness of his frustration.

Miriam had stood by me in my blindness. That says all I need to know about her, all I need to remember. It proved her love for me.

It's true about Miriam having had many enemies, but what gossip columnist doesn't? I can vouch that everything in the Miriam Moore Tells All columns was true. And more importantly, there was much that was true that Miriam kept out of her columns. Probably only I know that. Miriam was too concerned with her image of quintessential bitch ever to tell anyone of the dirt she didn't write. She knew that image gave her a certain credibility with her readers and meant an uninterrupted flow of money into the bank.

My medical expenses after the accident were astronomical.

I honestly believe that if it weren't for the accident, for me surviving after all those dark months in the hospital, Miriam would have given up her column. It bothered her more than anybody knew, some of the things that happened as a result of her stories. I tried to tell her she wasn't responsible for what other people did when confronted with the truth. The agonizing part is that neither of us really believed that.

"She was shot exactly in the temple from a range of less than fourteen inches," the lieutenant said. "That's what won't go down with me, that a blind man could fire a revolver with that much accuracy."

He'd never be able to let it go. "I can see my lawyer should have subpoenaed you," I said.

"You've been sentenced to die, Edwards. You'll be the first under the new state law. But you don't seem concerned, and that bothers me almost as much as the accuracy of the death wound."

I shrugged. "There are few successful blind fugitives. I was dead when Miriam died. I knew that would be the case and decided to kill her anyway. I'm not happy with my predicament, but it's not unexpected."

"Suppose you told me the truth confidentially," the lieutenant suggested in a conspiratorial tone. "There's no way you can get another trial now, and you could deny this conversation if you wanted."

"The truth came out in court, the way it's supposed to happen."

He sighed again. I felt sorry for him and wanted him to leave. There was no other direction for our conversation to take. I had been found sitting in a room locked from the inside, the gun in my hand, Miriam on the floor dead of a bullet wound in her head. How could the lieutenant blame the jury for finding me guilty? How could he blame himself? He should never have become a policeman; he was a creature of the heart, doomed to suffer.

I heard chair legs scrape, felt the caress of air on my face as the lieutenant stood. His defeat permeated the room, a tangible question that would never be answered, that would thrive in dark places.

"This is your last chance, Edwards," he told me, knowing it was his last chance. "I'd like to know—I need to know—if you're really guilty."

I wanted to tell him everything, but I couldn't risk it. He started to say something else, then abruptly left the room, his footsteps fading on the other side of the thick door he closed behind him. Leaving me alone.

I sat quietly with my hands on the smooth tabletop, thinking despite myself of that day of the unexpected thunder in the tiny bedroom, of my wrenching fear as I crawled over the coarse carpet toward the source of the great crash that still hovered in the charged air. My hands had sought like separate, desperate animals before me, exploring every contour of the deep-woven rug. Then the sticky wetness, the well-like, sucking edge of the wound, the gun, the still flesh.

The gun was in my hand as I made my way to the closed door and locked it. Already I could hear and feel approaching footsteps in the hall outside. For a long time I ignored the knocking. Then the door was forced.

I'll never let them know the truth—that the haughty and wise Miriam Moore committed suicide. I owe her that and more. They never found the note she had written, the note I'd folded into a narrow, tight strip and wedged between the molding and the wall near the floor.

They found me seated on the carpet, my back against the wall and the murder weapon in my hand. A guilty man in any impartial court of law.

So now the lieutenant has to wonder, and I feel sorry for him. And as long as I keep my silence, I have to wonder along with him. Was I actually guilty in a way the jury couldn't imagine? Was I responsible for Miriam's death? I know I'll have to live and die with a question even more haunting than the lieutenant's, a question I'll do anything rather than face:

What was in Miriam's note?

The Insomniacs Club

Walter Thorn's rubber-soled shoes trod silently on the shadowed pavement. He looked about him, his slender face under the thinning brown hair its usual combination of intensity and frustration. There should be noise, he thought, as he gazed at the rows of tall brick buildings that towered into the darkness on either side of him. He was walking at the bottom of an immense stone canyon, a place of hollow echoes, but it was three A.M. and there simply was no noise to create echoes. The only thing stirring was Walter, and it seemed to him that his passage down North Street was like his passage through life—silent, unnoticed, meaningless.

He reached beneath his jacket and drew a pack of cigarettes from the breast pocket of his pajamas. Yes, he thought again—for he was prone to daydreams if not night dreams—if I were a motion picture director I'd have noise here, maybe a far-off police siren, an ashcan lid falling, hollow footsteps. . . . He flicked his lighter and slid it back into his pants pocket. He wasn't a motion picture director, of course; he was an accountant—had been for ten years, at the same firm, and for almost the same salary.

He drew on the cigarette and resumed his walk in the night. There was a dreamlike treadmill quality to walking through the Sterling Executive Apartment project, for all the buildings were alike, neat four-story brick moderns. And you could walk six blocks in any direction from Walter's building before seeing anything different. Walter had lived here for almost a year now, at his wife's insistence. Lately he did everything at Beulah's insistence.

Walter's step faltered for a moment when he first heard them—footsteps, hollow-sounding and echoing, as he would have directed them in a movie. He walked on as before, tossing his cigarette into a small puddle of water in the street and hearing it hiss minutely and angrily as it was extinguished. He wasn't too worried, for there was a marked absence of the hoodlum element here in the Executive Apartment area.

The man turned the corner half a block up and walked toward him. Walter felt a twinge of uneasiness. As the man passed one of the evenly spaced streetlights, Walter saw that he was well dressed, but like Walter his clothes seemed to have been hastily put on.

They closed in on each other, the hollow footfalls growing louder. Walter kept his eyes averted until he was a mere ten feet from the approaching figure; then he looked up and took in the man's appearance carefully—medium height, dark hair, a bit older than Walter's forty-five and better-looking, wearing a half-buttoned light raincoat against the threat of showers. Walter braced himself and got ready for anything.

"Evening," the man said, smiling pleasantly. "Can't sleep either, huh?"

That was all. He didn't even break stride and was past Walter before he could think of a reply.

Walter let out his breath in relief. Sure! In a big group of buildings like this there probably were plenty of people who couldn't sleep, maybe even a few insomniacs in each building. And probably a lot of them walked at night just like Walter. It was a common thing, and so it was not so uncommon that they should meet occasionally in the early morning hours. Habit, as well as good sense, would tend to make them confine their pacing to the perfectly squared well-lighted streets of the apartment area rather than stray out into one of the surrounding poorer neighborhoods. Walter didn't have a monopoly on insomnia.

Walter's deduction turned out to be right, for he happened to meet the same man the next night on East Street. This time Walter nodded pleasantly as they passed. Then the night came when the man asked Walter for a light, and they struck up a conversation and introduced each other.

The man's name was Alan Kirkland, and it turned out he lived three blocks from Walter in Executive 20. All the apartment buildings were numbered, from 1 through 60, and they all rented for the same exorbitant amount, with the exception of Executive 1, which rented for more. Prestige.

It turned out that this necessity for prestige had caused Kirland, like Walter, to begin living at the very limit of his means. But now there were unexpected bills to pay, and Kirkland couldn't sleep.

It seemed to Walter, as their acquaintance progressed, that Kirkland was leading up to something. And one cool night when they ceased their aimless walking and sat on a hard bus-stop bench, Walter got an inkling of what that something was.

"Have you ever wondered, Walter," Kirkland asked as he leisurely packed his briar pipe, "how many insomniacs like you and me there are in a big project like this?"

"Often," Walter said.

"And as you know, Walter, lots of us, when we can't sleep, *really* can't sleep—we almost *have* to get outside and walk. You know there are a lot of people out walking the streets in the early morning, more than most people think. You go stir crazy otherwise."

"Indeed you do," Walter said, watching Kirkland fire up the briar, noticing little flecks of gray shimmering in the dark hair on his temples.

Kirkland flicked the match away. "The fact is, Walter, a number of us early morning insomniacs have gotten together to form a sort of club."

"Club?" Walter asked. "What do you do?"

"Why, we meet, Walter. Like all clubs, we meet."

"That's interesting," Walter said. "The Insomniacs Club."

Kirkland sat quietly puffing on his pipe, volunteering nothing more. It was just like him to catch the conversational ball and tuck it in his pocket.

"How, uh, many are there in your club?" Walter asked.

"Counting me," Kirkland said, "nine. Six men and three women."

Women, Walter thought with a sudden flush. He had a wild notion of what Kirkland was driving at. Too wild a notion, he told himself, a little bit ashamed. He'd been faithful to Beulah for the eleven years of their marriage. Though from time to time he couldn't help asking himself why.

Kirkland swiveled his body on the bench to face Walter. "Have you considered," he asked in a confidential tone, "that there are certain advantages to friendships formed after midnight? Though we members of the club know one another, we know little *about* one another except for our common bond of insomnia. And more importantly, no one, none of the day people, connect us with one another—to them we are perfect strangers."

Walter swallowed. "You mentioned certain advantages?"

157

Kirkland smiled. "I named them, Walter, I named them. It's up to us to use them."

"But how?"

Kirkland placed a hand on Walter's shoulder, somehow making Walter feel uncomfortable. "Suppose you come along to our meeting tomorrow night?" Kirkland asked through teeth that clenched the pipestem. "It isn't anyone that we invite, you know. The membership is limited."

Walter considered asking why but thought better of it. He fought down his hesitancy and for once decided to act on impulse. "I'm honored," he said, and then in an attempt at a joke added, "After all, I haven't much else to do."

Kirkland's hand tightened on his shoulder. "You'd be surprised, Walter." He smiled broadly around the pipe and stood up. "I'll meet you here tomorrow night—say at three?"

"Fine," Walter said, getting to his feet.

They parted, both men trying to beat the dawn home.

The next night Kirkland took Walter to the meeting in an apartment of a bachelor member of the club, a very fat man named Leon Stubbs. By 3:15 A.M. they were all there, sitting as comfortably as possible on Stubbs' modern furniture and sipping his liquor. Walter had been given a particularly strong martini.

"I suppose we should get the meeting under way," Kirkland said, standing and walking to a part of the room where he was visible to everyone. He seemed to be the unofficial president of the club. Walter glanced nervously around at the club members, whom he'd been introduced to and half of whose names he'd already forgotten. For a fleeting moment he wondered if he could be home in bed dreaming.

"Now," Kirkland went on, his voice like a pinch to

Walter's idle thought, "we have a new candidate for membership in the person of Walter Thorn. I've known Walter fairly long and I've talked to him considerably of many personal matters. I think he's the man to make our final member."

Walter noticed that the members were paying rapt attention. The men, some of them with pajama cuffs showing beneath trousers or shirts, sat as if at a business meeting. The women wore the look that Beulah had when she was talking long distance to her sister in Washington. Walter had been disappointed to find that two of the women were quite average-looking, but the other, a Miss Morganford, was a somewhat more promising blonde. Miss Morganford, wearing dark slacks and bedroom slippers, was sitting next to Walter on the sofa.

"If you recommend him, Alan," Stubbs said, "I don't think we'll find much fault with him."

"That's right," a fortyish woman with horn-rimmed glasses said. "After all, it was Mr. Kirkland who brought us together."

Kirkland produced his briar pipe from a pocket and stood for a moment thoughtfully rolling it between thumb and forefinger. "I propose that we acquaint Walter with the purpose of our club and let him decide whether or not he wishes to join. Take my word that he's an honorable man, and if he chooses not to join us I'm sure he'll remain silent. Anyway, things should be got into operation as soon as possible. For some of us the need is quite pressing and further delay would be foolish."

Walter heard some of the members exhale loudly and a tall red-headed man shifted uncomfortably.

"Well?" Kirkland asked.

The members murmured assent.

Kirkland smiled and addressed himself to Walter. "The fact is, Walter, like all of us here you have an increasing need for money; you're bogged down, bored with your work, unhappy, not getting any younger. And if it isn't a need for money that's robbing you of your sleep, it's something that can be alleviated by money. Life has become nothing more than a monotonous struggle."

Walter bowed his head uneasily.

Miss Morganford touched his knee. "It doesn't hurt to admit it," she said in an understanding voice.

"All right," Walter said softly, "I admit it."

"So much I've learned from our conversations, Walter," Kirkland said, more to the members than to Walter. "And I want you to know that you're among friends here."

Walter forced a smile. "Then the purpose of the club is sort of—group therapy?"

Leon Stubbs chuckled, but Kirkland pursed his lips thoughtfully.

"In a way," Kirkland said, "only we intend to do something specific about our common problem."

"But what?"

"Eliminate it." Now Kirkland lit the briar and puffed miniature clouds of smoke into the room. "As I said before, Walter, there are certain advantages to after-midnight friendships." He waved the pipe to take in all the occupants of the room. "We know one another, trust one another, but to the daytime world there is nothing to connect any of us." His eyes narrowed behind the smoke. "Here is a fact that be used to our advantage." He focused his narrow eyes on Walter. "Tell me, does your wife know when you leave the apartment at night?"

"I've mentioned it sometimes," Walter said, "but usually she doesn't. She sleeps like a log."

"It's a curious fact," Kirkland said, "that the mates and family members of most insomniacs do sleep like logs. It reduces the risk of our plan to an absolute minimum."

160

"But just what is the plan?" Walter asked, noticing that the back of Miss Morganford's hand still rested against his leg.

Kirkland looked at him with a sardonic but respectful smile. "It's illegal—you should know that before we go further."

Walter put his hands on his knees as if to stand. "You'd better not go any further," he said nervously. "I don't want to be responsible for hurting anyone."

"Oh, wait," Miss Morganford said pleadingly. "At least hear us out. I'm sure you'll change your mind. I wouldn't hurt anyone either."

"No one will be hurt," Kirkland said reassuringly. "Only some big insurance companies, and for amounts that, while substantial to us, they'll hardly miss."

Walter sat back. "Then the crime is stealing."

Kirkland nodded.

"From who?"

"Why, from each other. That's why there's no risk; the victims will cooperate."

"I don't understand," Walter said as Stubbs poured him another ready-mix martini.

"Look," Kirkland said, brandishing the briar pipe, "suppose one of us here in this room burglarizes another's apartment at a set time when it's perfectly safe? Suppose every one of us here in this room burglarizes another's apartment? None of us are known to be acquainted. To the police it will simply look like ten unconnected crimes pulled off by the same thief, because we'll use the same *modus operandi* each time. They'll think a professional burglar is working this area."

"It makes sense," Walter said, sipping his drink. "And the insurance—"

"Exactly! Each of us has some heavily insured jewelry. When it's stolen we'll each collect the insurance money. I've arranged for the jewels to be sold to a reliable fence, and the proceeds will be evenly split among us." He grinned. "Pays better than an accountant's job, Walter, and it's just as safe—safer. Several insurance companies will be involved, so they'll pay off and will hardly bother to check. And you'll never have to worry about anyone here talking, because we'll all be equally guilty—and we'll all find it equally profitable."

Walter finished his drink slowly. "It *does* sound fool-proof—"

"You think about it, Walter," Kirkland said, still smiling. "I'm sure we can rely on your silence in the meantime. Heck, I'll bet you wouldn't want Beulah even to know you were here."

"No," Walter said shakily, "I wouldn't. Yes, I will think about it."

The club members, in a noticeably more relaxed mood, lapsed into amiable chatter as another round of drinks was served by Stubbs, and before the sun came up the meeting was adjourned.

Walter thought the matter over for a week. Each night while walking the streets he would just happen to run into Kirkland and his persuasiveness, and Miss Morganford even broke the rules of the club to telephone him and personally urge him to join. It was no wonder that at the next meeting of The Insomniacs Club, Walter became a member and was told the details of the plan.

He was shown how the lock on Stubbs' front door could easily be slipped with a piece of celluloid, and all Executive Apartment locks were of the same type. A piece of celluloid would be dropped at the scene of the first burglary to establish the method of entry, but from then on the doors would simply be left unlocked. On each robbery the same pair of ribbed gloves with a distinctive identifying mark on the forefinger would be used. The future burglars were all reminded to leave glove prints.

162

An irregular schedule covering five weeks was worked out, with the apartments of successive victims arranged in an unsymmetrical and unpredictable pattern. Walter's apartment was to be robbed last because he'd just increased his insurance and a five-week interval would be least suspicious. Each victim told the time of night or early morning most convenient for the crime to be safely committed and made sure his or her future burglar knew exactly where every member of the family slept and exactly where the jewels were kept. The victim was to mess things up a bit before retiring for the night, so the burglar could get in and out quietly and in a hurry.

As for the choice of burglar and victim, each member would be a burglar the crime before he himself would be victimized. Thus before any attention at all was cast on him he would have the previous crime's loot safely hidden away outside the apartment project. He would then leave the ribbed gloves in an agreed-on spot in *his* apartment for his burglar to slip on as soon as he wiped off the doorknob and entered. This way there was no chance of anyone being caught on the street before a burglary with the incriminating gloves, for they would be waiting conveniently at the scene of each crime.

And with the loot hidden in nine different spots—nine because it would be safer not to have the necessary first victim commit a later robbery—there would be no chance of anyone absconding with the jewels; so when they did sleep, the club members would rest easier. It would all be finished before the police had even a chance to get a whiff of anything suspicious. On a date a few weeks after the last burglary, The Insomniacs Club would meet again, the loot would be given to Kirkland and, on his insistence, two elected club members would go with him that morning to sell it and hold the money. At a meeting the next night the small fortune would be divided in equal shares.

Everyone made sure of his instructions, and until the future wave of jewel thefts that was to sweep over the Executive Apartments had ended, club meetings were postponed.

Things seemed to progress with incredible smoothness. Three days after the last club meeting Walter read on page eight of the newspaper how $10,000 worth of jewelry had been stolen from Miss Mary Gordon, a resident of the Sterling Executive Apartments. Walter smiled to himself as he sat across the table from Beulah and read this item. He knew that a tall redheaded man named Fenwick had committed that robbery, and he knew that in two nights Miss Morganford would walk into Fenwick's apartment, slip on the same gloves, and relieve the Fenwicks of their jewelry. Then, four nights later, it would be Miss Morganford's turn to be robbed. And eventually—here Walter did smile behind the paper—it would be his, Walter Thorn's, turn.

The plan seemed to be working so flawlessly that Walter actually looked forward to his turn with delicious anticipation. On September eleventh at 2:15 A.M. he was to walk into Alan Kirkland's apartment, slip on the gloves he'd find under the entrance hall throw rug, and walk to the door of the master bedroom—Walter knew where this was because his apartment was laid out the same way. Kirkland, who would already have displaced things in the apartment while his wife was sleeping, would be lying next to his soundly sleeping mate and actually watch as Walter walked to the top-left drawer of the triple dresser and quietly emptied Mrs. Kirkland's jewelry box. Then, a scant two minutes after he'd entered, Walter would make his exit, touching things here and there to leave the distinctive glove prints.

As Walter waited his turn, he watched the newspaper stories on the robberies move through editorials and lingerie advertisements toward the front page. And as more robberies occurred, police protection in the apartment project increased. This meant little or nothing, for the police were pathetically undermanned and the Executive Apartment area was large. Only once during a late night walk did Walter see a police car cruise by, and then it was two blocks away. Getting in and out of the apartment buildings unseen posed no problem. In fact, so helpless were the police that they had the newspapers explain the method of entry in the rash of jewel thefts and urged all citizens of the area to install special locks on their doors. And some citizens did—but not the citizens who counted.

As Walter knew it eventually would, the early morning of September eleventh came to pass, and he found himself walking silently down East Street on his rubber soles toward Kirkland's apartment in Executive 20. The warm night was quiet and the street was empty, but still Walter felt an indefinable qualm, an unexpected queasiness at what he was about to do.

He shook this feeling off as he stepped down from the curb and crossed a deserted side street. He made himself think of how things would be after the burglary, picturing himself on Stubbs' sofa sitting next to Miss Morganford, each of them drinking a martini and counting their part of the proceeds.

Then he was in the deep shadow of Kirkland's apartment building. Glancing up and down the dark street to make sure he was unobserved, he breathed deeply and casually entered, as if he lived there. He walked swiftly up the marble stairs and down the soundproofed hall, and before he knew it he was standing trembling in the Kirklands' entrance hall, just inside the front door.

Walter reopened the front door a crack and wiped the knob clean of his own prints with a handkerchief, closed the door again, then got out his small penlight, and found and put on the gloves. He moved across the deep carpet into the Kirklands' living room.

Walter flashed the penlight beam about as he moved silently toward the master bedroom. Kirkland had done his job, opening drawers, tilting picture frames, over-turning lamps. And he'd done it all with the telltale gloves, so even if by some wild quirk Walter was seen entering and leaving the building it would mean nothing, for the thief would have had to spend at least twenty minutes to search so thoroughly before finding the jewels. Walter would be gone in less than two minutes.

He entered the bedroom cautiously, seeing the two figures on the double bed. The drapes were partly open and there was enough light in the room to get the jewels without the aid of the penlight. Walter held his breath, moved to the correct open dresser drawer, and reached inside. His hand closed on the jewels in the open box and he began to stuff his pockets.

"What is it, dear?"

The woman's voice cut through Walter's body like a blade of ice.

"What the hell?" Kirkland's voice said.

There was a rustling movement on the bed behind Wal-ter, then an ear-shattering scream, long and loud. A string of pearls broke in his clenched hand and the pearls went bouncing about the room. "Oh, good Lord," Walter moaned aloud, and he was out of the bedroom and run-ning.

He hit the apartment door and fumbled it open, then he was dashing down the hall toward the stairs. There was light, and voices around him. A door opened down the hall and a small bald man stuck his head out, shut-ting the door partway and peering out curiously at Wal-ter as he flew past, like a man watching a mad dog, ready to slam the door if it veered in his direction. Walter stumbled down the marble stairs, crashed into the front door, and was out in the street.

Windows were now lit up and sirens were wailing as he ran down East Street.

"Stop him!" Kirkland shouted—and that's when Walter knew.

It became clearer to him with every jarring step, with every stab of pain in his ribs. He'd been chosen to make the pattern complete. The robberies wouldn't be investigated further by the police because the thief would already have been apprehended. Naturally the thief would concoct some fantastic story rather than say where he'd sold the jewels and hidden or spent the money; so the insurance companies would take their losses and decide the jewelry had vanished in the mysterious channels of the underworld. And to prove Walter's guilt beyond question, after his arrest the robberies would stop.

A siren screamed loudly and a police car suddenly screeched to a rocky halt directly in front of Walter. He tried to spin on his heel but he tripped and fell sobbing on the suddenly bright pavement. He heard two more cars squeal to a stop and headlight beams blinded him.

Iron-strong hands yanked Walter to his feet and he was leaned against the rough brick wall of Executive 16 and expertly searched. They collected the evidence—the stolen jewelry and the ribbed gloves. He could hear them asking him at the station, "Where were you on this night and that night?" "I go out walking," he'd answer; "I have insomnia." He could hear them laughing.

His arm was twisted behind him, and he was led back up the street toward a waiting patrol wagon. He could feel hundreds of eyes on him as he lowered his head in defeat and shame. "Alan—" he pleaded to Kirkland as he was led past the crowd of onlookers, but it was natural that the thief would case his future jobs and know his victims' names. The shame cut deeper as he was pushed up into the back of the patrol wagon.

But to Walter the worst part of all was when the door of the patrol wagon was slammed shut. Then for the first time he was plagued by the vision of endless future nights—nights when he would wake up perspiring in a ten-by-ten cell and there would be no place to go.

The Music
From Downstairs

W hoever he was, Lorna, he blew a beautiful trumpet. Like Gabriel.

I know what you and the people at the church must think of me, and, believe it or not, that's the worst part. I know most of all what *you* must think, and sometimes at night I just wish I could die and be rid of the shame.

But it mustn't be in God's plan for me to die yet.

The apartment over Nat's Club was all I could afford. I'd never have moved into a place like that unless I was sure I'd find a job, and that I'd be able to move before sending for you.

But there isn't much demand here in the city for a man who spent twenty years working in a coal mine. I guess, what with the mine being closed for six months now, Haleville is in pretty rough shape. We were wise to decide to move, but it was one of those things that didn't happen to work out, especially for you and the kids. Believe me, that's who I'm thinking of most.

Not being a drinker, I never set foot in Nat's Club. The entrance to my upstairs apartment was in back, and after a glance or two at the flashing red neon sign over the door, I never paid any attention to what went on there.

Except for late at night, when the trumpet player went into his solo.

Some people might have called the police and complained about the noise. But from the first the music soothed me. Those clear notes would come drifting up through the bare wood floors and fill the dark bedroom with a peacefulness I could almost touch. It was like the sad-sweet core of life, set to music. I'd lie there for hours thinking about you and the kids, and how it would be when I found a job and sent for you. I was glad then that the mine had closed. I always hated working underground.

Every night those gold rising notes would carry me off somewhere until I slept, making all the walking I'd done that day, all the useless job interviews and applications, seem not to matter.

After a while, the trumpet music somehow stayed with me through the days. It got so I could almost turn it off and on, like an imaginary radio that played the same lonely notes over and over.

Did I tell you the trumpet music was lonely? It wasn't a song you could name. It was the same every night but not the same. "Improvisation," I found out they call it. That's music that's supposed to come from the soul, and whoever played the trumpet must have had a soul like mine.

Lorna, I missed you. I swear that's what caused it. I was lonely, and one night there was this Doris Rollins at the bus stop, and we talked. It began innocently. It's important to me that you know that.

She never had what happened in mind any more than I did. She told me all about her family, and I told her all about you and Billy and Jill. I could sense she was lonely too, and we became friends.

About that time the trumpet music changed. Or maybe it was me that changed. The same full rich notes would drift up at night, but now there was something more forlorn in them. Not that the music wasn't more beautiful than before—more beautiful than we even heard in church, Lorna—but now it was sad and kind of yearning-like.

The music was playing when Doris phoned me. It was eleven o'clock at night and she was crying. Her husband had beat her, she said. She needed a friend, Lorna. She came to me, and I became more than a friend. I didn't dream you'd ever find out, much less that things would turn out this way.

She came to me often after that, in the early hours of the morning, before she went to work. That first night she'd gone back to her husband—she said she always did, that she had no choice, for the kids' sake. I guess that's what life's all about, Lorna, finding out we don't have the choices we thought we had. Now I'm down to no choices at all.

I was stretched out on my back on the bed with my eyes closed, listening to the music from downstairs, when I heard the door buzzer. It was past eleven-thirty, so I was surprised to see Doris at the door. She started to cry as soon as she looked at me.

Naturally I thought her husband had beat her up again, but that wasn't it. I helped her cross the room and sit down in the worn-out armchair. She told me she was pregnant.

I was stunned, Lorna. But even standing there with the wind almost knocked out of me by the news, I got to thinking. She was a married woman, and the odds were good that her husband was the father.

But she told me her husband couldn't be the father, that he'd had some sort of sickness that had left him sterile. And besides, he hadn't slept with her in months. It was his sickness that caused him to beat her.

She said she'd told him about us, that she'd had to. And that now I had to tell you.

It was strange what happened then. All I could think about was my loneliness for you, and I felt first a great sadness, then a hate and anger for Doris—a rage. I don't remember picking up the ashtray and hitting her on the head with it. They didn't believe that in court, but it's true.

They didn't believe much of what I said in court. Not after I told them about the trumpet music and they told me that Nat's Club had been closed for two months before Doris died.

Now I'll spend the rest of my life in a cell like this one, and I guess I deserve to. They say I'm a menace, even to myself. That's why they've taken everything away from me that might be used as a weapon. At least they think they have.

And if it was lonely in that apartment over the club, it's more lonely here. And monotonous. It's sameness that can drive a man really crazy. Like day after day in the mines.

The only thing to occupy my mind here is the drummer in the cell below. I figure he must be a professional drummer, because he has a perfect sense of rhythm.

He beats on the walls constantly. It helps.

I know you have to leave, Lorna, but before you go, will you move a little closer to the bars? So I can reach you.

The Landscape
of Dreams

E lectric-shock therapy does odd things to the memory.
It causes periods of forgetfulness, with total dis-
regard for the order in which events happened. And in
that same random order it causes periods of remem-
brance.

Memories are imbedded something like fossils in the
rock strata of our years. Dr. Melinger told me that once.
Or did he only agree when I suggested that analogy? The
thing is, mental therapy is like conducting an archeologi-
cal dig, only when you reach the fossils, sometimes they
seem to come to life. And there are plenty of interesting
memories buried in everyone's layers of years, even in
those of a forty-year-old Indianapolis housewife like me.

There's no point in telling you about what caused my
problems—about Jeff leaving me, or our son Billy dying
of a drug overdose. Maybe the misery of the present is
what makes me think more and more, awake and in
dreams, about my childhood on an Illinois farm less than
two hundred miles from here. About the willow tree that
grew outside my bedroom window.

Willows are the most beautiful of trees, the most
graceful. And the saddest, which is why they're known as

173

weeping willows. This one, which grew too near our two-story white-frame farmhouse, was one of the largest willows I've ever seen—unless I'm just remembering it through the eyes of a ten-year-old girl. It was higher than the roof, and its long drooping branches draped to the ground and waved gently in the flatland winds, reacting to every soft current as if it were some lonesome plant that grew on the bottom of the sea.

Its spreading branches formed a sort of shelter, a quiet still point of the universe that I could reach by climbing out my bedroom window onto a thick limb that paralleled the house. I could move inside the concealing branches of the huge tree, secretly observing the rest of the world through a soft green veil. I got into the habit of spending time in the tree on warm summer nights, embraced by its thick branches in the soft moonlight that filtered in through the dense foliage.

Sometimes I'd go into the tree during the daytime. Once, when I was lying unseen on one of the big limbs, I heard my bedroom window close. There was no way out of the tree. The branches that reached ground level were too slender to support even my ten-year-old body. I had to call for help. I remember my mother, beautiful then, pushing through the lower branches with her own arms like graceful limbs, looking up at me and smiling a tolerant, loving smile, reaching to help me down. It is one of those crystallized moments of childhood, precious ever after in my memory.

Mother believed I climbed into the tree from the ground, I'm sure. I never told her about how I often went there from my window when everyone thought I was asleep. She would have forbidden that, of course, and I would have obeyed. Now I know that if I had confessed that day, everything would be different.

The willow tree figures in my dream, but that's not

surprising. Willows are ideally suited to the landscape of dreams.

In the dream, which occurs about every third night, I see through the tree's delicate green veil two people moving in the moonlit yard. My mother and father, talking softly, unintelligibly, in some foreign language, perhaps. They enter the barn and leave the wide door open so they can see each other in the yellow moonlight. Their words become louder. Father yells something about a phone call. Then he is on the ground. *In* the ground! A hole, a grave, has been readied in the barn's dirt floor. Mother raises her right arm to her forehead. She turns and drops something long and silver and picks up a shovel. I can hear her sobbing as she fills in the grave.

Dr. Melinger was interested in the dream. My father, you see, ran away with my mother's sister, my Aunt Verna, when I was ten. Aunt Verna had been afraid to face Mother and had taken the train to Louisville, where Father later joined her. My mother never got over that. Religion and family were one and the same to her. Mother was a fourth-generation Corbet, a descendant of the town's founders. Family honor was her life.

We never mentioned Father or Aunt Verna after they ran away together. Not once. Not even when Mother was a frail gray woman in her sixties, still living on the farm.

I've been back to the farm a few times during the past ten years. It's the same, only most of the surrounding fields have been parceled off and sold to neighbors. And the willow tree was cut down long ago. It got diseased and had to be removed so it wouldn't rot and fall on the house. A tree that big could cause a lot of damage.

I had discussed the dream with Dr. Melinger the day before he introduced me to a swarthy man in a light gray suit, a Mr. Edwards.

Mr. Edwards smiled a nice smile and we shook hands. His hand was as dry as wheat chaff. I'd given Dr. Melinger permission to phone Mr. Edwards. I had loved my father, who was a tall man who thrived on hard work and listening to the radio.

"Mr. Edwards is the FBI agent I told you about, Doris," Dr. Melinger said to me. "He wants you to help him get to the truth. And getting to the truth is what would help you."

"It seems that your father and Verna Corbet weren't heard of after they left Homesville," Mr. Edwards said.

"Everybody knew they ran away together," I told him. "They were ashamed. Things were different thirty years ago. Maybe they even changed their names."

"That's possible. In fact, it's likely. Still, Dr. Melinger and I think we should check into the matter further. For the sake of everyone involved."

"You think what I dreamed really happened," I said.

"Not necessarily."

"I think it did," I told him. I saw him glance at Dr. Melinger. I didn't care. I loved my father. I loved both my parents, and still do. But I understood my mother. She couldn't bear the thought of Father running away with her own sister. That struck not only at her, but at her sense of family honor. She was a Corbet; Aunt Verna was a Corbet. Mother had lost her mind for a while and killed Father. I loved her, but I couldn't forgive her for that. And there was such a thing as justice.

"I've talked to the sheriff in Homesville," Mr. Edwards said. "I'd like you to make a phone call to your mother, a call that will be recorded. The tape might provide the justification for digging up the floor of the barn where you saw your father buried in your dream."

I agreed to do that, and watched while Mr. Edwards and a bureau technician set up the recorder near the phone. Then I dialed Mother's number at the farm. She'd be home, probably watching a TV soap opera.

The phone rang twice.

"Mother, this is Doris."

"Why, Dorie . . ." She sounded surprised. I only phoned on holidays, usually. "It's good to hear from you. Nothing's wrong, is it?"

"I don't know, Mother."

Long silence. "What do you mean, you don't know?"

I felt a funny lump in my throat. I could hear soap-opera theme music in the background. "Mother," I said, "I think Father is dead. I think you had something to do with it. In the barn. I think he's under the barn."

Her intake of breath was like a harsh wind. She didn't say anything. Mr. Edwards had earphones on and was staring sober-faced down at the desk.

"Can you tell me it isn't true, Mother?" I asked.

"The barn's been torn down for years," she said. "There's a new barn."

"Then he's under where the old barn was," I said. "Can you tell me it isn't true, Mother?"

"What's gotten into you, Dorie?"

"Can you tell me it isn't true, Mother?" I pleaded.

"Dorie . . ." She was crying.

"Please, Mother!" And I was crying, too. I hung up. I was afraid of what might happen if I didn't.

Mr. Edwards peeled off his earphones. "Thank you, Doris," he said. "I think this is what we needed. I can get the court order immediately. Do you want to drive to Homesville with us later today, to show us where the old barn was?"

Dr. Melinger nodded and smiled at me. A reassuring smile.

"I want to be with my mother," I said.

"Certainly," Mr. Edwards said. He shook hands with Dr. Melinger.

Mother was dead when we reached the farm. She had turned Father's old shotgun on herself. They wouldn't let me see her. Sheriff Hunicutt and Mr. Edwards held me on the porch.

Beside the body there had been a note in Mother's handwriting, a confession that she had murdered Father because she couldn't bear the thought of him living with her sister Verna. Their relationship would be a constant embarrassment, a permanent dishonor to the Corbet name. Mother was too proud to accept that, so she had killed him.

I showed Mr. Edwards where the old barn used to be, then a deputy took me back to town while the rest of the men started to dig. As the patrol car pulled from the driveway, I saw the wide flat stump of the willow tree. There were a few graceful shoots rising from it, swaying in the breeze. Young growth, the way I was in the dream.

Later that day they told me they found Father's bones four feet under the ground. The sternum still bore the mark of a long-ago knife thrust. The vision from the willow had been true.

Dr. Melinger explained to me back in Indianapolis that I had suppressed the dark knowledge of my mother's murder of my father because I didn't want to believe it had happened. It wasn't uncommon, he said, for his patients to have blocked such occurrences from their conscious minds. The shock treatments had jogged my memory and brought things to the surface, like the firing of a cannon over a deep lake. I would be better now, he assured me, despite the tragedy of my mother's suicide.

For a while I believed him. Until I had the second dream.

Time plays tricks. Memories aren't like a slide show, in sharp focus and neat chronological order.

I was in the willow tree again, on a warm summer night thirty years ago, watching two figures through the sad green veil of branches, and listening.

"You can't be pregnant!" Father said to Verna.

"Precautions don't always work, Carl," Verna said patiently, though a little fearfully. "I'm going to have a child. Your child. Nothing can change that."

Below me my father seemed to become smaller, as if Verna's words had released a weight that suddenly descended on him. A wind ruffled Verna's flower-print dress, which seemed strangely luminous in the moonlight and in the glare from the downstairs windows.

"My God!" Father said. "My God, what now?"

"We have to tell Myra when she comes back from town," Verna said. "There's nothing else to do."

"That's crazy!"

"There's nothing else to do, Carl!"

But Father thought of something else, and in his panic he couldn't stop himself from doing it. They were standing near the corner of the house, where several tools were leaning against the porch rail. One of the tools was a pitchfork that father had intended to equip with a new handle. He jabbed Verna in the stomach with the pitchfork, and she squatted down with one hand on the ground, kind of like she was going to shoot marbles. Either Father or Verna let out a soft, desperate whine.

The pitchfork moved again, a familiar motion I'd seen Father make with it a thousand times to gather hay. Verna said, "Carl," and fell over backward.

Father was still standing, leaning on the pitchfork and staring down at Verna, when Mother drove up in the car. She got out and walked toward him, moving slower as she got nearer.

179

"Verna's dead," Father told her, not looking away from the body.

"I can see that." I had never heard Mother so calm. Her voice made me think of lemonade and shelling peas, and the wheatfield on a clear, still day.

"She told me she was pregnant," Father said.

Mother seemed to straighten, even as she stared down at Verna. "I suspected, Carl."

"How could you?"

"I'm not the fool either of you thought I was."

"I lost my head, Myra. I don't know how it happened. I killed her." He dropped the pitchfork and took a heavy step toward the porch.

"Where are you going, Carl?" Mother asked curtly.

"To phone the sheriff."

"No, you're not."

"I have to, Myra. Do you understand that I killed Verna? I killed your sister. I killed her baby."

"Turning yourself in won't change that," Mother said.

"I *have* to, Myra!"

"Carry her to the barn, Carl. I'll bring the shovel."

"What?"

"We're going to bury Verna. We have to get her out of the way before Dorie wakes up tomorrow. Then you can think about things, and if you still want to phone the sheriff, he'll still be there to answer the phone."

Father stood for a while with his hands on his hips.

"Pick her up and bring her, Carl. Damn you, you owe me *that,* after what you've done! You owe the Corbets that!"

He shook his head, but he did what Mother said. He lifted Verna and carried her toward the barn.

Mother followed with the shovel.

All this must have happened on the same night that was in my first dream. But whether it did or not, I'll never

180

tell Dr. Melinger about the second willow-tree dream. Mr. Edwards will never go digging for another body beneath the old barn floor, where Aunt Verna had been with Father all these years, but not in the way she'd planned.

I understand what happened now, and I understand Mother's pride, the Corbet pride. She could endure even the public knowledge that her husband had gone away with her sister, but not that he had impregnated Verna, then murdered her. A Corbet might marry a philanderer, but not a killer of a woman and her unborn. Mother would never rest if people knew that about her.

That's why she became a murderess herself. And though anyone who might have been hurt by father's crime is now beyond all harm, no one will ever learn the truth from me. Despite what's happened, I owe Mother and the other Corbets that much. I loved her and still do. That's in the blood, Corbet blood, and there's no changing it, not ever.

And me? I'm willing to accept what remaining silent means for me. I know I'll continue to dream, to be trapped within the branches of the weeping willow tree. Until my mother helps me down.

Until You Are Dead

T he glass jars of enamel added to the colorful formless composition that was being created as one-by-one they exploded against the brick wall. Wilson Benton was smiling as he picked up each jar and hurled it with the conscienceless exuberance of a mischievous seven-year-old.

Mrs. Hefferman, whose hobby was the making of ceramic pots, mugs, praying-hand plaques, and the like, kept her brightly colored enamels on a dusty shelf in the garage. Usually the garage door was closed and locked. But not today, when Wilson happened by, spotted the neat row of jars, looked at the wide expanse of brick wall on the other side of the alley, and surrendered to the temptation.

"What do ya think you're doin'?"

The voice belonged to Randy Hefferman, Mrs. Hefferman's twelve-year-old nephew who lived with her. With Randy were Bob Rourke, a gangly boy of ten who was the best ballplayer in the neighborhood, and Frankie Toller, an overweight and overbearing eleven-year-old who nurtured a developing skill at instigating trouble among others while remaining outside the fray.

There wasn't much that Wilson could say to Randy's indignant question. Wilson had, almost literally, been caught red-handed. He stood silently, a frail dark-haired boy with wide and fearful brown eyes that took in the older and heftier Randy with morbid apprehension. The glass jar containing Chinese red dropped from his suddenly sweating hand to shatter at his feet and join the shards of broken glass in the cobblestoned alley.

"He broke the lock on the garage an' got that stuff an' smashed it," Frankie Toller said accusingly.

Wilson swallowed. "I didn't!" he choked.

Randy moved a menacing step closer to him. Wilson could smell his breath; he'd been eating the hot chili his aunt often made. "Didn't what?" Randy asked.

"Break into the garage!"

"Then how'd you get all my aunt's paint jars an' break 'em up?"

"The door was open! It was!"

"She always locks it," Frankie Toller remarked.

Bob Rourke stood silently staring at Wilson. He was only vaguely interested in what was going on, but he would go along with whatever Randy and Frankie decided to do to the trapped and unquestionably guilty Wilson.

Randy moved still nearer and Wilson's throat went dry. A coppery corruption of fear lined the sides of his tongue.

"Ain't no reason to break all that stuff just 'cause the door was open," Randy said. His hand pistoned out, pushing Wilson backward, broken glass crunching loudly beneath the soles of his tennis shoes.

"What we gonna do to him?" Frankie asked eagerly. "Can't let him get away with it."

"Tell your aunt," Bob Rourke suggested to Randy.

"Naw, she won't do nothin'," Frankie said. "Besides, we ain't snitches."

Randy's cool gray eyes flared with sudden inspiration. He placed his fists on his hips. "Take off your shoes," he said to Wilson.

Frankie grinned.

"He cuts up his feet through them socks and we'll get in trouble," Bob Rourke observed.

"He's the one in trouble," Randy said fiercely. "This'll teach him not to break into people's garages and bust up their stuff!"

"He'll cut himself," Bob Rourke repeated. "Anyway, he ain't gonna take off his shoes."

"If he don't, we'll make him!"

Wilson's hands were trembling. Frankie and Bob Rourke stepped closer to stand beside Randy. Wilson looked into Bob Rourke's narrowed eyes and knew he could expect no help from that direction.

"Now!" Randy demanded.

Wilson bent and removed his shoes.

"Now walk!" Randy demanded.

Wilson stared down at the glittering multicolored fragments of glass.

"You heard Randy!" Frankie said.

Wilson took a step. Another. He felt the uneven pressure of the glass on the soles of his feet, threatening to break through the dirty cotton of his socks and imbed itself in his flesh. Gingerly, fearfully, he took light, carefully aimed steps, almost wishing that the jagged glass would penetrate the bottoms of his feet and create a pain that might alleviate the overpowering sense of shame that was enveloping him.

But finally he reached a clear spot beyond the broken glass. His feet were undamaged; the cotton socks had been enough protection. He stood staring at the three boys on the other side of the expanse of glimmering danger.

"See," Frankie told Bob Rourke, "he didn't even get cut." He sounded disappointed.

Randy was looking at Wilson with something like startled recognition. "He's a coward," he said gravely. "The guy's a coward." It was as if he'd heard about cowards but had never really expected to see one. And now here was one, standing directly in front of him. Not only that—it was someone he knew.

"He's a coward all right," Frankie agreed.

For a moment Wilson felt totally alienated from his world, as if it had unexpectedly come to his and everyone's attention that he had webbed feet. With one abrupt stroke he was separated from the rest of humanity.

"I—"

But the rest of humanity was no longer interested in anything he had to say. Its three representatives turned and walked away toward the mouth of the alley. Frankie glanced over his shoulder for just an instant, but no one else looked back. As they rounded the corner and disappeared, Bob Rourke gracefully leaped to slap the bottom of a rusty Coca-Cola sign protruding from the brick building. The metal sign twanged and continued to vibrate loudly.

Wilson stood for a long time, still holding his shoes in his right hand, staring at the bright world beyond the mouth of the alley. Then he shivered. That world would never be the same. He had been, if not a close friend, an occasional companion of the three boys who had just left him. But he was no longer one of them. He could never be one of them again.

Pearl Harbor had been bombed six months ago. When war had been declared, Wilson Benton, now twenty-six years old, had, in a patriotic fervor, attempted to enlist in the Army. A perforated eardrum and weak eyesight had caused him to be turned down and classified 4-F. Not knowing what else to do, he'd returned to his art studies.

Wilson was considerably talented as a painter in oils. His ambition was to be an illustrator; once, the art director of *The Saturday Evening Post* had given him encouragement in a long friendly letter. Nature was Wilson's favorite milieu for his art, so with what savings he'd accumulated he leased a tiny clapboard cabin in a gently rolling lush green area of the Ozark Mountains. He intended to spend the summer and part of the fall at the cabin painting. Then, with what he'd created, he would again approach the world of magazine illustration and try to establish a beachhead.

The cabin was a one-room affair with a sharply peaked roof. Though it wasn't equipped with electricity, it did have a septic tank and indoor plumbing. Wilson slept in a comfortable feather bed, cooked his meals on an old iron wood stove, and sat up nights listening to the Silvertone radio he'd hooked up to two six-volt car batteries.

Once a week he would drive into Colver, the nearest town, in his dented gray '36 Chevy coupe and buy groceries to haul back in the trunk. Sometimes he would pull to the side of the narrow dirt road that led to the alternate highway and survey a particularly beautiful view, returning the next day to sketch or paint there. Primitive, yet with a deceptive, almost feminine loveliness that disguised nature's ongoing life-and-death struggle, the rolling green Ozark country was ideal for Wilson's purpose. He was content with what he was accomplishing.

The cabin had a large window that provided northern light, but often during the day Wilson would set up his easel on the side of the wooden front porch and work outside. It was on one of those days that he heard the racketing bang and clatter of a car approaching the cabin along the seldom traveled dirt road. As he stepped down from the porch, he saw a haze of dust among the high branches of maples near the road's sharp bend; the car was very near.

It was a Model A Ford, rusty, the top cut off, the engine exposed. One of the rear fenders was hanging half off and clanking against the car's body as the tall rubber tires bounced over the deep ruts.

When the driver saw Wilson he hit the brakes and the old Ford pulled to a squealing, rattling halt before the cabin. There were three men and a woman in the car, two of the men in the front seat. The man in the back was slouched sideways, his legs stretched across the woman's lap, his bare feet propped up on the glassless window frame. The cloud of dust raised by the car caught up with it and slowly settled in the brilliant sunlight.

"What you doin' at the Harris cabin?" the driver asked Wilson. He had blond hair and a scraggly beard that was more the result of neglecting to shave than a conscious attempt to grow chin whiskers. The other two men were dark-headed. The woman—or girl—was a brunette with a dirty face, freckles, large blue eyes, and lissome arms, one of which was flung carelessly across the back of the rear seat. None of them appeared to be more than twenty years old, and Wilson guessed the girl to be in her teens.

"I rented the cabin for the summer," Wilson said, moving closer to the car so he wouldn't have to shout. "My name's Wilson Benton."

The girl appeared puzzled. "What for would you rent a place like this?" she asked in a grating soprano voice.

"I paint. I like it here."

"Paint what?" the driver asked. He rubbed a hand across a long nose that had been broken many times. His pale gray eyes were set too close together and regarded Wilson with indifferent curiosity.

"Pictures. Some of them for magazine illustrations."

"Oh, that kinda paintin'," the girl said.

"Ain't that somethin'?" the man with her in the back seat spoke up. His lank hair was hanging in his eyes. He had a wide lantern jaw and was missing several front teeth. Wilson couldn't tell by the tone of his voice how he'd meant his remark.

The man on the front passenger's side, who would have

been darkly handsome if he were clean and well dressed, grinned. "Don't mind 'em, Wilson," he said. "I'm Josh Edwards." He pointed to the driver. "Zach Wheelright. Them in the back is Bandy McCane and Maybelle Sue Dover."

"Lotsa pretty things around here to paint, all right," Maybelle said.

Bandy McCane gave a jut-jawed broken-toothed sneer and peered at Wilson from beneath his unshorn hair.

"Ol' Bandy'd be jealous if you was to pose for Wilson, Maybelle," the driver, Zach, remarked.

"Don' matter," Maybelle said to Wilson with a perfect smile, and took in the other occupants of the car with a circular wave of her arm. "These'ns are all gonna be gone into the Army afore the end of summer."

"How come you ain't in?" Bandy asked. "You look to be of age."

"I tried," Wilson said. Unaccountably, he felt himself blushing. The change of his color wasn't lost on Bandy McCane.

"How hard you try?" he asked derisively.

"Hard enough," Wilson said. "They told me I was Four-F."

"Lotsa reasons you can be Four-F," Zach observed skeptically.

"Glad I ain't a reject," Josh said in a solemn voice. "Comes a time to fight, an' this is it."

Wilson nodded. "I agree."

"I'd like to see your pictures sometime," Maybelle said, blatantly changing the subject.

"No time now," Zach shouted, jamming the old Ford into gear and gunning protesting life into the clattering engine.

"No call for painters in this man's war!" Bandy shouted over his shoulder at Wilson as the Ford's big wheels dug into the earth without slipping and the car shot forward. Maybelle lifted an arm in a languid farewell that Wilson barely saw through the dust as the car disappeared beyond the rise where the road gently curved.

Wilson walked back up onto the porch, listening to the measured hollow thunder of his boots on the warped planks as he strode to his canvas. The conversation with the four native Ozarkians had disturbed him more than it should have.

Two days later he returned after painting a landscape from high on a nearby bluff to find that the cabin had been broken into and many of his paintings had been slashed.

He stood staring at the disruption of the cabin's interior, unable to see clearly for a moment as an aching helpless rage flared deep in his stomach, then gradually receded to a painful smoldering. So personal seemed the attack, it was as if the torn canvas were an extension of his own flesh.

After cleaning up and salvaging what he could of his materials, Wilson drove into Colver to see the local sheriff.

"Who knowed you was at the cabin?" Sheriff Bayne Haynes asked. He was a large man with a vast stomach paunch, beady intelligent black eyes in a fleshy mottled face, and a walnut-gripped .45 Colt revolver holstered to his hip. He was gazing at Wilson amiably from where he sat turned in his swivel chair facing away from the long rolltop desk against the office's far wall. His lean deputy, Rawly Krebs, slouched nearby against a dusty switchboard.

Wilson hesitated, then told the sheriff about his conversation with Josh, Zach, Bandy, and Maybelle.

"I don't know definitely that it was them," he added.

"They's good boys, but they do tend to act up," Sheriff Haynes said absently.

"Thass a fact," Krebs added.

"Anything exceptin' your paintin's broke up?" the sheriff asked.

Wilson thought about that. "No," he said finally. "A few things were knocked to the floor, furniture turned over, but nothing really broken."

Haynes rose from his chair with the ease and seeming lightness of an ascending hot-air balloon. There were wide, almost black perspiration stains beneath the arms of his tan uniform shirt. "Down the road a short piece from your cabin," he said, "is a cutoff to Ezekiel Ferber's place. Now, Ferber's got himself a phone. You have any more trouble you run on down there, use that phone to call here, an' me and Rawly'll be up to your place faster'n you can shout rabbit."

Krebs looked at Wilson and nodded his narrow pockmarked head. "Thass a fact."

"All right, fine," Wilson said. There didn't seem much else that could be done.

"If'n it was who we figure, they had their fun an' ain't likely to come back. Thass the way they is, those three boys. Not mean—jus' too full a vinegar."

"As I said," Wilson emphasized, "I don't really know who it was. But I thought you should know that it happened."

Sheriff Haynes' bushy graying eyebrows rose and fell like writhing caterpillars. "Oh, you did the right thing, an' no doubt about it." Deputy Krebs nodded silent agreement. Haynes licked his lips and squinted at Wilson. "You—uh—do anything to rile them boys? On accident, maybe?"

"I don't think so," Wilson said. And that was true. He hadn't done a thing. It wasn't his fault they were going into the Army and he was 4-F, or that Maybelle had seemed to take a shine to him. "I take it Maybelle is Bandy McCane's girlfriend," he said cautiously.

The sheriff raised his expansive chin and smiled

faintly. "You might say she's the girlfriend of all of 'em, from time to time. Thass how it is sometimes here away from the city, Mr. Benton."

Wilson swallowed and nodded, imagining despite himself Maybelle's pale languid arms and luminous blue eyes. Sheriff Haynes was staring hard at him.

Wilson thanked the sheriff and walked toward the screen door to the street.

"Things'll sure be quieter when them boys is gone to the Army," the sheriff remarked behind him.

"Thass a fact," Deputy Krebs said.

From the sheriff's office, Wilson walked directly across the street to Holfer's Service Center and General Store, a small frame structure with two gas pumps in front and a flat-roofed addition that stocked groceries and hardware. He noticed that the sheriff's '38 Dodge was at Holfer's, being worked on by a lanky grease-stained young boy. The car was dusty-black with large gold replicas of a sheriff's badge emblazoned on its doors. When Wilson entered the store he saw Zach Wheelright slouching at the counter paying for a package of chewing tobacco.

Zach turned, spotted Wilson, and grinned guiltily as he scratched at his sparse blond beard. He unwrapped the tobacco and slowly bit off a large plug. Then, chewing laboriously behind his wide grin, he walked past Wilson and out the door. Wilson saw that he had a slender broken paintbrush tucked behind his left ear.

For a moment Wilson wanted to return to the sheriff's office and inform Haynes of what he'd just seen. Then he decided against it. There was no point in further stirring up things if, as Haynes had predicted, the matter was over.

Wilson bought five dollars' worth of groceries to last him the week, loaded them in the trunk of the Chevy, and returned to the cabin.

* * *

That Friday, when he was working indoors near the cabin's north window, Wilson heard a scuffling sound on the front porch and felt his heart double-pump, then grow heavy with fear. He put down his brush and palette and walked softly to the door.

When he opened the door he found Maybelle standing on the porch alone.

"Tol' you I wanted to see your pictures," she said, smiling. She was wearing a low-cut gray blouse and a long skirt of material so thin that the outline of her compact body showed through. She was barefoot, and Wilson found himself involuntarily staring at the dusty neat squareness of her pale toes. "Ain't you gonna ask me in?" she said.

He raised his gaze to her eyes. *The girlfriend of all of 'em from time to time.* "Sure," he said brokenly. He gave her smile back to her, amplified. "Come on in."

She seemed to be genuinely enthralled by his work, giving awed girlish exclamations as she examined the pastel landscapes, crying that she recognized most of the views before her on the canvas. Wilson brought up the subject of the vandalism that had occurred two days before and Maybelle seemed horrified. But she didn't deny the probable identity of the culprits. "Zach, Josh, and Bandy, I 'spect," she said, shaking her head in disdain.

She offered then to show Wilson a spot he might want to paint, and they left the cabin. Maybelle led him up the hill on the other side of the road, then down along a path to a clearing dotted with wildflowers in the tall wind-stirred grass. It was an exceptionally pastoral spot, though too flat and indistinctive to paint. Wilson didn't tell Maybelle this. She teased him, moving up against him as if by accident as they walked, letting the backs of her fingers barely brush his hand.

"The view from between those big pines is sure pretty," she said, pointing with Michelangelesque grace toward a patch of cloud-marbled blue framed by green branches.

Wilson trudged up the slight rise to the high point between the pines, studied the unspectacular view, then turned to ask Maybelle where, specifically, she meant for him to look.

Maybelle was gone.

A hollowness in Wilson's stomach seemed to fill with something dark and bitter. He began to walk, then run back toward the cabin.

When Wilson flung open the door and saw the wreckage a sob expanded to form a lump in his throat, then erupted from him in a frustrated snarl. This time the damage was worse—almost every canvas slashed, furniture ripped open, food pulled from cupboards and smashed or scattered. But worst of all, Wilson knew that Maybelle had made a fool of him; she had used herself as a diversion while the three men returned to the empty cabin. On the wall near the sink was scrawled *4-F* in Wilson's yellow oils. The blood rushed to his face as he whirled, slammed the door, and stomped noisily from the buckled wood porch.

He got into the Chevy and started the engine. He would drive down the road to Ezekiel Ferber's place, as the sheriff had suggested, and phone for the law.

Wilson had pulled out onto the narrow road and traveled fifty feet before he knew something was wrong. The car was bouncing violently, swerving and pulling to the right. He braked, turned off the engine, and got out.

The right rear tire was flat. Wilson kicked the misshapen rubber and pounded on the gray rounded slope of the car's fender. He would have to walk to Ferber's.

Then, bending down, he saw the wide slit in the tire's sidewall. It had been slashed.

But why only that tire? Could it be that his antagonists wanted him to think it was only an ordinary flat so he would walk to Ferber's? So they could return and do even more damage? Wreck anything they'd missed? Scrawl more messages? Perhaps even burn down the cabin?

Wilson opened the trunk of the car and got out the spare tire, the jack, and the X-shaped iron lug wrench. He could quickly change the tire, drive to Ferber's, and maybe phone the sheriff in time for him to get back up and catch the vandals in the act.

He jacked up the back of the car, loosened the lug nuts with the wrench, and fumbled with them, removing them the rest of the way by hand. Sweat was trickling down his face and tiny insects circled him, buzzing about his eyes and flitting at his mouth and nostrils. He wrestled the airless tire off the car and turned toward the spare.

Then he heard the unmistakable roar and clatter of Zach Wheelright's decrepit car approaching. He remained crouched behind the Chevy and peered over the fender to see traces of raised dust beyond the road's bend. The engine noise was loud; the car was almost upon him. They must have thought he had taken the path through the woods to Ferber's on foot and the cabin was again deserted.

Then came the crash.

The surface of smooth metal before Wilson smashed into him as the Chevy was struck and bounced backward off the jack. There were startled cries, tinkling glass, and the hiss and trickling surrender of a broken radiator.

Wilson was on his hands and knees, fighting to catch his breath from the blow he'd received in the chest. Hazily he could see Zach, Bandy, Josh, and Maybelle tumble from the wrecked Ford. Zach sat down and held his head in both hands. Maybelle stood leaning dizzily against the side of the Chevy. Josh and Bandy were swaying, supporting each other. They had expected him to be gone, all right, Wilson realized. But they hadn't expected the crippled car to be jacked up in the middle of the road just beyond the bend.

"You wrecked my car!" Zach was saying, staring at Wilson from between splayed fingers vividly marked with blood. He cursed and struggled to his feet.

Josh and Bandy moved nearer to flank him, lending the threat of their presence to his words.

"*You* wrecked it!" Wilson managed to gasp.

"You come over here!" Zach screamed.

Wilson didn't move.

"Ain't you got ears?" Bandy asked. The initial shock of the accident had passed and although he was holding his injured left arm tight against his body, he was grinning. Josh still seemed woozy from his head striking the windshield. He was standing, swaying, with his fists on his hips.

Wilson sighed and began to rise.

"Not like that, you yellow coward scum!" Zach shouted. "Stay on your hands an' knees where you belong!"

Maybelle began to laugh.

Wilson stayed very still.

"We'll kill you if you don't," Josh said to Wilson. "Maybe we'll kill you if you do."

Wilson was paralyzed, breathing painfully as if each lungful of air were somehow thickened almost to a liquid consistency. Fear was a thing alive within him, pulling marionette strings despite his humiliation.

He began to crawl.

Maybelle laughed again. They were all laughing now except Zach, who was staring with a thin knowledgeable smile at Wilson.

Then Wilson's left hand was stung by one of the glass fragments from the shattered windshield and headlights. He paused.

"Keep comin'!" Zach warned.

Wilson's right hand came into contact with the lug wrench.

"You heard!" Bandy said, not laughing now. For emphasis he slapped his right hand hard against the loose fender of the Ford, causing the metal to twang and vibrate loudly.

Wilson didn't remember rising, but he had, still clutching the lug wrench. He surprised himself even more than the three men as he was suddenly before them, swinging the tire iron, hearing and feeling it smash the flesh and bone of Zach's skull. Arcs of bright blood glistened in the air. The injured Bandy tried to grab Wilson's arm. Wilson was too strong for that now—stronger than anyone had ever been. He brushed the clutching fingers aside, brought the wrench down behind Bandy's ear. Someone was clawing at Wilson's neck with sharp fingernails. Maybelle. He whirled, lashed out with the wrench that seemed weightless in his hand, then pursued Josh, who was trying to stagger around the rear of the Ford, and laid open his skull with one effortless swing. Then he returned to Bandy, who was sitting cross-legged on the ground before Maybelle's bloody body. Bandy started to beg with his eyes and distorted mouth. The shadow of the raised lug wrench fell upon him like a cross. The shadow grew. The wrench descended.

It was Ezekiel Ferber who came across the scene and fled home to phone the law. Sheriff Haynes and Deputy Krebs arrived within half an hour in the sheriff's dusty black car with the gold insignia on the doors. The doors slammed in unison as Haynes and Krebs left the car to swagger toward where Wilson was sitting slumped on the Chevy's running board, the heavy lug wrench on the ground between his feet. The sheriff and his deputy paused.

Somewhere in a far dark part of Wilson's mind he could

feel himself spinning, falling in intermittent, sweeping plunges toward an inevitable timelessness.

"Gawd, Gawd, Gawd," the sheriff was saying, "he killed 'em all." His face was white. "There weren't no reason whatsoever for this."

"Thass a fact," the deputy said in a soft, awed voice.

"Those are the facts," the prosecutor said.

"They're the plain facts," the jury foreman said.

"—Until you are dead," said the judge.

MAYHEM
WITH A WINK

Something Like Murder

I was leaning slightly from my fifteenth-floor window in the Norwood Arms, watering my geraniums, when Mrs. Vixton passed by wearing a pink flower-print kimono of shimmering silk. She passed by vertically, you understand, not horizontally, which would have been much more conducive to her health though not nearly so remarkable.

She saw me, I believe, though to her I was of only passing interest. Still, I'm sure I saw a slight inclination of her head in my direction. Whatever else might be said of Mrs. Vixton, she was never a snob. She was descending face down, her arms spread incredibly wide, a frozen, determined expression on her face, as if she might yet have time to catch the knack of flying. Startled, I overwatered the geraniums. I didn't look down; there was no doubt of the outcome.

My name, incidentally, is Cy Cryptic. Not my real name, of course. I'm a movie reviewer for one of the larger papers here in town, and Cy Cryptic sounds and looks more like show biz than Marvin Haupt.

I'd have forgotten completely about Mrs. Vixton's death, except that cinematically it might have been effective, when a week later in the lobby I overheard a chance remark between Mrs. Fattler of the third floor and Gates the doorman.

". . . from her window . . ." I heard Mrs. Fattler say, dragging out her vowels as women often do when discussing a tragedy.

I edged closer. "Mr. Cryptic," Mrs. Fattler said in greeting, and Gates gave his ridiculous little salute. I joined the conversation.

Mrs. Vixton had committed suicide, I was told, by leaping from the south window of her apartment while the horrified Mr. Vixton looked on. A typewritten signed note was found later, expressing Mrs. Vixton's despondency and her desire to leave this world. I did not mention that I had seen Mrs. Vixton resplendent in midair the morning of her death. I did not think it wise in light of the fact that the Vixtons lived on the fourteenth floor, in the apartment *below* mine.

The matter of Mrs. Vixton's gravity-assisted death kept creeping into my mind that afternoon as I sat through an advance showing of *Life's Slender Thread,* a French import about, believe it or not, a man who pushes his mistress from a high window rather than turn her over to a gangland czar. It was a happy-ending film of unlikely gimmickry, small consequence, and incoherent subtitles. Yet the movie did create a certain mood. When I left the theater I decided to call on Mr. Vixton before writing my copy.

Mr. Vixton was of medium-height, a pear-shaped man in his fifties, with a sleek set to his neck and shoulders that suggested that once he might have been lean and muscular. We shook hands and he invited me into his apartment, a twin to my own but for Vixton's tasteless and mismatched furniture on a riotous green-and-black carpet. The carpet alone might have driven Mrs. Vixton to suicide. But I knew that it wasn't suicide.

"Sit down, Cryptic," Mr. Vixton invited, waving a compact arm toward a low sofa with clear Lucite arms.

I sat, glancing at the south window. "I'm sorry about your wife," I said. "Are you?"

Vixton stood with his arms crossed; he cocked his head, then laughed. There was something froglike in his broad bespectacled features, his wide downturned mouth.

"I thought you might have seen me leaning out to water my geraniums," I said. "At any rate, I could never be sure you hadn't."

"And I could never be sure you didn't see my wife pass by you, Cryptic. Yours was the only window she had to pass above this fourteenth floor, after which it didn't matter. But as it happened, I did see your hand holding the watering can, some few seconds after Gloria's fall."

I leaned back in the gauche sofa and crossed my outstretched legs at the ankles. "I surmise that you pushed her from the roof."

"You surmise correctly. That way there would be no window frame for her to clamp onto, and no sign of a struggle in our apartment. I tricked her into signing the note I had typed, lured her onto the roof, then pushed her. None of it was difficult—certainly it was easier and more profitable for me than a divorce. What I'm curious about, Cryptic, is why you came down here and brought out in the open what both of us could only suspect—that you did see Gloria pass your window, and you knew that I was aware that you had."

"I could never be sure you wouldn't kill me," I said candidly, "and if I went to the police with my story, they might not have believed me and you might have killed me out of revenge or to protect yourself, or possibly even sued me for libel."

"Truthfully," Mr. Vixton said, "I was considering the first alternative—to kill you. It was that glimpse of the watering can . . ." He frowned slightly, a toadlike contraction of his features. "But how does this visit improve the situation?"

"The situation, as I see it, is that we can't trust one another. You'll always feel I might go to the authorities, and I'll always feel you might do something drastic to preclude that eventuality. Now, what needs to be done is for circumstances to be arranged so that we *can* trust one another. Suppose you had something on me?"

Vixton puffed his cheeks and seemed to deliberate. "Something like murder?"

"There is a young woman named Alicia whom I often escort."

"I've seen her," Vixton said. "A charmer."

"Suppose I do away with Alicia in your presence, even let you photograph the event? That would make us even, so to speak, and we could be confident of each other's silence."

"It would be a standoff," Vixton said slowly, brightening to the idea. "Better than a standoff, actually, as I'd have absolute proof of your guilt. But what do you have against Alicia?"

"Absolutely nothing. She's merely convenient for our purpose."

I watched Vixton consider this, then saw his eyes darken at the sudden thought behind them. "I'm even more convenient than Alicia, Cryptic. Wouldn't it solve your problem if you"—he laughed a flat croaking laugh—"murdered me?"

"You're *too* convenient," I told him. "One: you're in the apartment below me; the police are bound to question me and suspect. Two: however deeply buried, I do have a motive. On the other hand, I'm only one of Alicia's many escorts, and she and I get along splendidly and always have."

Vixton nodded slowly. "It's crazy but it makes sense— if that makes sense."

"It does," I assured him. "Alicia lives in a west-side penthouse apartment on the thirtieth floor. I'll arrange things so we can go there together tomorrow night, and she can meet the same fate as your late wife."

Vixton's broad face widened in a smile. He chuckled,

then laughed aloud and went to the bar in the corner and poured us each a drink. We toasted tall buildings.

The next night Vixton and I took the elevator to the thirtieth floor of Alicia's building and walked down the deep-carpeted hall to the door labeled with her apartment number. She must have heard us coming, for as I raised my hand to knock, the door opened.

"Cryptic," she said, "how good to see you!"

But it was better to see her. She was slender and tan in a long pink dress, with honey-blond hair cascading in carefully arranged wildness to below her shoulders. She wanted to be in films, and on looks alone she had a chance.

"This is Mr. Vixton," I told her, as Vixton and I stepped inside. "He's a film producer from Los Angeles here to consider some outdoor locales for a movie."

Alicia's eyes took on a special, harder light. "Which of the studios are you from?"

"I'm an independent producer," Vixton said smoothly. He regarded Alicia with what passed for professional interest. "According to Mr. Cryptic, you're a talented young woman."

"All she needs," I said with a smile, "is a little push."

Vixton coughed as Alicia led us out onto the balcony for drinks.

The balcony was large, bounded by a low iron rail on the east side and a four-foot-high stone wall on the north and south. Along the base of the iron rail ran a trough of rich earth from which grew a dense wall of exotic green foliage, including two small trees. Like many cliff dwellers, Alicia was addicted to what green she could squeeze into her steel-and-cement-dominated existence.

Vixton had a martini, as did I. Alicia, as usual, drank a whiskey sour. I hastened to mix the drinks, my plan being to drop several capsules of a depressant into each of Alicia's whiskey sours. "Dangerous when mixed with alcohol," I had said to Vixton earlier, showing him a handful of the tiny capsules. "Downers in the true sense of the word."

In the thin cool air of the balcony I heard Vixton's harsh voice rasp. ". . . going to be a great movie . . ." He actually seemed to be enjoying himself. Alicia was on him like wet clothes.

After the third whiskey sour Alicia's eyelids seemed unable to make it more than halfway over her beautiful blue orbs, and I nodded to Vixton. While he watched, I held Alicia by the waist and guided her toward the iron railing.

"Don' wanna dance," she protested.

Vixton readied his pocket camera as I positioned Alicia just so before the lush green wall of foliage beyond which was the star-speckled night sky. "Cryptic!" she said, suddenly alarmed.

"Sorry, love," I said, and pushed with my right hand. There was a quick sharp flash.

Alicia disappeared between the dense branches, tumbling backward. One high-heeled shoe flew off as her tanned ankles flicked through the green leaves and disappeared. I heard a trailing scream, punctuated by Vixton's, "Got it!"

I glanced through the branches and quickly turned my head. "Let's go!" I said to Vixton, but he was already at the door that led inside the apartment. We took our martini glasses with us and hastily wiped our fingerprints from whatever else we might have touched.

There was no one in the hall as we walked quickly along the spongy carpet to the elevator and punched the button. Within a few minutes we were descending to street level. Perspiration had boiled to beads on Vixton's flat forehead.

We left by the building's side exit, got in my car, and

quickly, but not too quickly, drove away. As we rounded the corner and passed the front of the building we saw a knot of people and a bare tanned foot protruding from a fold of pink material on the sidewalk. I drove faster.

Two days later I gave Vixton the details of Alicia's funeral.

And that's how we accomplished it—the perfect crime. I got the idea from *Life's Slender Thread,* that abominable French film. Only instead of a thin nylon rope, as was used in the movie, we used a net from which there was access to the open window of the vacant apartment below Alicia's. It's true that Alicia wants to break into movies, but as a stuntperson, as I suppose they're now called. As promised, I might be able to arrange something for her.

After being caught in the net, Alicia quickly climbed through the window below, then ran out into the hall where she took the service elevator to ground level with Vixton and me minutes behind her. She then faked a crowd-gathering fainting spell on the sidewalk directly below her balcony.

I no longer have anything to fear from Vixton, but just in case, I've moved out of the Norwood Arms and will be extremely difficult to locate. There was no way I could bear to kill Alicia, or even Vixton. Seeing that sort of thing done constantly on film is one thing, actually doing it another. I'm not a violent person; I like musicals.

My one concern is that Vixton will go to see *Life's Slender Thread.* But that isn't likely. Not after the review I gave it.

Trickle Down

Endicott said, "I steal for a living." He crossed his legs and relaxed in the soft leather chair before G. David Grobner's massive polished cherry-wood desk.

Grobner was Endicott's physical opposite. While Endicott was six feet tall, Grobner was barely over five feet. Endicott had a calm, almost lethargic air about him; Grobner was an intense hard charger who doubtless regarded himself as a visionary leader of inferior beings. But blond and handsome Endicott and swarthy and gargoyle-ugly Grobner had this in common: they were chasing the dollar. And catching it.

"I make a profit for a living," Grobner replied to Endicott. "Making a profit is my function as chairman of the board of Grobner Industries. I'm responsible to the people who pay my salary: the stockholders. The stockholders are the gods of the business world, Mr. Endicott. It is in the service of those gods that I've hired you."

"Are you saying that I'm a thief and you are not?" Endicott asked.

Grobner smiled a nasty smile. "Are you trying to justify either to me or to yourself what you do for a living?" he replied.

"I'm merely pointing out that I'm your agent. Nothing more. I'm not moralizing. My justification is the same as yours."

Grobner stood up, but he was still dwarfed by his magnificent desk. His expensive dark business suit was tailored perfectly on his stocky body, but Endicott noted that his own suit was no less expensive or well tailored. Boil all the theorizing and excuses away, and he and Grobner were in the same business, the one Grobner had so simply and aptly described as "making a profit." That was, literally, the bottom line.

Endicott stood up lazily; it even seemed for a moment that he might yawn and stretch. But he smiled and said, "I have my instructions. And my money." His work wasn't the sort of thing one did by contract. Trust based on discretion played a major role in his business.

For years Endicott had toiled in the dark anonymous foliage of the corporate jungle until he was approached by a company in competition with the one that employed him. If Endicott would only supply them with his own company's chemical formula for a new odorless pesticide, the rival company would pay him well in dollars and silence.

Endicott stole and sold the formula. And he didn't stop there. He approached the business of theft as he would have any other business. He became a professional, then he became the best of the professionals. Euphemisms such as "industrial espionage" were not for him. From the beginning he'd regarded himself, not without some perverse pride, as a thief. It was essential that one maintain a sense of reality in this business.

When an important client like Grobner Industries needed information from another company, the word would be dropped in the right places, and Endicott would hear. He didn't work cheap, but he was reliable, kept no written records, and, most important, his discretion could be relied upon. The Sphinx had nothing on Endicott when it came to keeping a secret.

He'd stolen some defense blueprints for General Armaments, and the chairman of that multinational company was a friend of G. David Grobner, to whom he had recommended Endicott. It hadn't taken Grobner long to act.

And once he'd received his commission, it didn't take Endicott long to make his own move. He'd already cased the Budman Building. It was an old twenty-story structure in a rundown part of the city, near the river. Budman Enterprises, makers of industrial couplers, had no security force and a building as old as theirs hardly provided a challenge for someone of Endicott's expertise.

At midnight, scarcely ten hours after he'd talked to Grobner, Endicott parked his inconspicuous Ford compact in the next block, changed into his jogging shoes and dark jacket, then walked back and easily scaled the chain-link fence surrounding the Budman Building's parking lot. He noted that there were no cars in the lot—no ambitious souls working late, probably not even a night janitor.

The alarm took only five minutes to bypass. Endicott picked the lock on a side door and was inside, a shadow moving among shadows. Blood raced and pulsed in his veins. He could hear his breath hissing in the building's heavy silence. The excitement, the almost sensual exhilaration, was part of the reason he was in this business; he admitted that to himself at times like this. Disdaining the elevator, he jogged soundlessly up the stairs to the third floor. The strain in his thighs felt grand.

Grobner's directions were precise, as might be expected. Endicott moved lightly down the hall to the fourth door on the right, Brad Budman's office. Budman's name, above the word "President," was lettered on frosted glass.

The door wasn't even locked. Endicott opened it and was in a large reception room. He didn't have to use his penlight; illumination from the lights of a nearby all-night parking garage filtered through the loosely woven material of drawn drapes.

Budman's office door was locked, but that delayed Endicott only a few minutes.

There was less light in the office. Endicott took off his jacket, draped it carefully over the shade of the desk lamp, and switched on the lamp. Perfect. Now the office was dim and shadowed, and there was hardly enough light to be noticeable from outside, yet he could see well enough to work.

There was the large file cabinet in the corner, just as Grobner had said. It would be locked. The file folder containing the specifications for the advanced pneumatic coupler would be in the bottom drawer. Things were going smoothly, professionally. Endicott smiled and stepped toward the cabinet's square-cornered dark hulk.

He stopped, turned his head, and froze when the office door opened and a woman stepped inside.

The woman was tall, almost as tall as Endicott. She was long-limbed, lean-waisted, and athletic looking. Her face was oval and ghostly pale, framed by straight dark hair parted down the middle of her scalp. Like Endicott, she wore a startled, frightened expression.

Then she noticed Endicott's dark clothing, much like her own dark jacket and jeans, and she thought about things for a moment and the alarm left her features: one night creature had recognized another. She was almost beautiful now that she wasn't afraid. "Well, a thief," she said to Endicott. "But not a dangerous one. If you had a weapon, you would have had it out by now."

"The same might be said of you," Endicott told the woman, admiring her quick and calm appraisal of the situation. "I suspect neither of us carries a weapon because we're both professionals. The term thief is one I accept; it's my occupation. As I expect it is yours."

The woman slowly shook her head, her long hair swaying. "I'm not a thief," she said. Endicott didn't like the way she said it. "My occupation is fire. I burn things down for a living." Her expression changed; the light of pure reason glittered like bright pinpoints in her dark eyes. "We might be able to work out a deal here."

"I only want a file out of that cabinet," Endicott said, not without contempt. He considered arsonists sick people. Psychopaths. "Then you can set your fire and make yourself and your employer happy. An insurance fraud, no doubt."

"No doubt," the attractive arsonist said. "And you might be surprised at the names of some of my previous clients."

"And you'd be surprised at the names of *my* previous clients," Endicott said. He was fast developing a strong dislike for this firebug, though there was much about her that intrigued him. It was almost as if Fate had something in mind for them.

"As a matter of fact," said the man who'd been hiding behind the file cabinet, "you have at least one previous client in common."

He was a lean, elegant man in a well-cut dark business suit. His features were regular and pleasant, and his hair was razor-groomed at precisely the right length. An Everyman with quiet class. He looked like a big-company mid-level executive, and maybe he was.

The flesh on the back of Endicott's neck began to crawl. The firebug's presence might be a coincidence, but this man's presence meant that Endicott, and probably the firebug, had been set up. And not by Fate. "Who is this client?" Endicott asked.

"General Armaments. They have to be discreet, I'm afraid, considering what they have at stake. They owe it to their stockholders."

And Endicott realized that General Armaments, with the help of G. David Grobner, had arranged this nighttime conference.

"I have to be discreet myself," the firebug said. "So General Armaments needn't worry." There was a little-girl tremor in her voice; her heart was learning what her mind already knew. "Really! Please! I'm in business just like they are. I burn things down for a living."

"And I steal for a living," Endicott said, as if to confirm what the firebug had said. But he realized it was hopeless, hopeless. What was about to happen was good business, and he knew it.

The pleasant well-groomed man by the file cabinet had drawn a silenced automatic from beneath his pinstriped suitcoat and was smiling the sort of smile that people in sales smile when the deal is closed.

"I believe both of you when you say you're discreet," he said reasonably. "I'm in business just like you two. Only I kill for a living. Because nobody's perfect."

He squeezed the trigger twice, effectively.

Dear Dorie

M y wife is Dear Dorie. Not to me, but to the millions of readers of her household-hints column that is syndicated to over a hundred major newspapers. You know the sort of column I mean, the one on page six of the Features section that tells you how to resole your own shoes or convert a common bathroom plunger into an attractive plant stand, or maybe tells you a hundred and one uses for eggshells. Dorie, at age thirty-five, writes the most popular of all these columns, and is herself a devotee of the economical clever shortcut or fresh approach. The trouble is that most of her household hints are more clever than they are practical, which is why Dorie is no longer dear to me.

A classic metamorphosis of love to hate, you might say. Within a year after our marriage I came to loathe eating sandwiches on day-old bargain bread, sleeping beneath a quilt one square of which I recognized as a pocket of my favorite old sportcoat, walking across a living room carpeted wall-to-wall with free sample squares of the discontinued products of various looms, watching snowbound television received through copper plumbing that had been utilized as a giant TV antenna. Her many fans would be pleased to know that Dorie lives what she writes. As for me, I long for the company of a free-

spending real blonde who doesn't bleach her hair with
lemon juice rather than the expensive brand-name stuff.

On the other hand, Dorie has made a pile of money.
Myself, I'm too practical to settle for a divorce and half
our assets. Dorie would understand that. So there seems
to be no way out of this torturous yet profitable marriage
other than over Dear Dorie's dead body. Maybe she
knows a way to make some tool or kitchen utensil into a
gun.

But I know better than to resort to that. No gun,
knife, blunt instrument, or radio in the bathtub will work
here. I'm going to have to come up with something that
looks like an accident and can't be proved otherwise if the
police suspect. They do always suspect the husband, so
I'm compelled to devise something clever. And soon. Because Dorie is driving me whacko.

"Look, Huey," she says, spinning her dumpy frame
like a model demonstrating the lines of a new dress. "My
latest. Isn't it the perfect solution for all those runny
noses and household spills?" What she's demonstrating is
a roll of toilet paper strung from her belt on a length of
yarn. "If you slosh milk over a glass rim or your kid's
nose is dripping," she proclaims, "all you have to do is
pull and tear and you have a towel at your disposal any
place, any time!"

Great, if you don't mind walking around all day with a
roll of toilet paper perched on your hip.

"Clever," I say, going back to the magazine I'm reading. I'm not fool enough to get on the bad side of Dorie.
She can be vengeful and devious. Like the time we had an
argument and she stuck the label from my roll-on deodor-
ant onto a similar bottle of some kind of super household
glue—the brand they show on television supporting the
weight of an automobile. I spent five uncomfortable
hours and uttered a dozen unreasonable promises before
she told me the simple kitchen-ingredient formula that

would dissolve the glue. I don't want to endure anything like that ever again.

"I'll think of something," I mutter, absently scratching beneath my left arm.

"What was that, Huey?" Dorie asks.

"Only talking to myself, dear," I tell her, turning another page of the gourmet magazine over which I'm salivating.

"You can break that habit by carrying a recorder, then playing it back at the end of each day to hear how ridiculous you sound," she assures me.

That afternoon, as we eat our lunch of leftovers combined to make tasteless and nourishing dishes, I wonder as I have many times why we must exist like underpaid scroungers. We have plenty of money. And we lease a convenient tenth-floor apartment in one of the safest areas of town. But everything inside that apartment is handmade, makeshift, secondhand, or bargain-basement.

Lunch is over. I start to clear the plastic-coated washable paper plates while Dorie yanks a few squares of paper from the roll at her waist and wipes off the table. As I place the dishes in the sink, I snag my thumbnail on one of the plates and curse. There is a nasty tear in the nail.

"Tsk, tsk," Dorie says, examining the nail. "But no problem."

Before I know it, she's placed a glob of her diabolically quick-drying plastic cement on the thumbnail. "That should hold until the nail grows out far enough to trim," she says cheerily.

True, but a glance at my hand gives the impression I'm Dr. Jekyll in the process of becoming Mr. Hyde.

Time to go shopping. I accompany Dorie to a local used-clothing store, where she spends four dollars on a Women's Marine Corps skirt for her and a threadbare oversized suit for me. She has a way to make the suit look like new, she says, altered to my size with nothing but cleverly concealed safety pins.

After a stop at a nearby bakery for half-price stale glazed doughnuts, we head for home. We are walking, naturally—a raincoated woman with what appears to be a malformed hip and a nervous-looking man with an ugly right thumb. Maybe I'm imagining the stares of passersby. I'm imagining a lot of things lately. Such as what it must be like to live alone.

"Simplicity," Dwayne, my venerable bartender, tells me that evening, "breeds success." I go regularly to Dwayne's Dungeon to escape Dorie. At Dwayne's the drinks are grossly overpriced. I like that.

"You mean," Lacey, the glamorous platinum blonde, asks from a barstool near mine, "like it's easy to fix a Model A Ford with a pliers and screwdriver, but these fancy new models you gotta take to a dealer when something goes wrong?"

"Like that," Dwayne confirms.

Lacey nods sagely and sips her beer. Herself undeniably simple, she is another feature of Dwayne's Dungeon that appeals to me. I suspect she is really a plain brunette who spends a fortune each week at the beauty parlor.

"So the car manufacturers lose business to the simpler, smaller foreign models," Dwayne says. "They get too clever and outsmart themselves is what happens. People do that all the time. Am I right?"

"Righter than you know," I tell him, wondering what it would be like to spend more time with Lacey. She truly is a beautiful girl—or manages to look like one. Dorie, under the best of circumstances, is not actually pretty. Pretty isn't economical or ingenious.

"What's that?" Lacey asks. I realize she is talking to me.

I'm sitting with my legs crossed and my pants legs

have worked up my calves. Lacey is pointing to the button sewn near the top of my left sock. "My wife sews buttons on all my black socks," I explain. "That way I don't confuse them with brown socks in the dark."

Lacey and Dwayne stare at me.

"That," Lacey says, "is stupid."

I feel myself flush. "Oh? How would you solve the problem?"

"If you were my husband, Huey, sometimes you'd wear one brown sock and one black sock."

I laugh so hard I spill some of my drink. Dwayne wipes the puddle from the bar with a real towel, grinning wonderingly at my outburst of mirth. Lacey is laughing along with me. She'll laugh at anything.

"What's funny?" Dwayne asks.

"I would love to wear one brown sock and one black sock," I tell him. "It's a nice, simple approach to the problem."

"Simplicity is the key to life," Dwayne reminds me.

And maybe to death, I tell myself. Living with Dorie has indeed affected my mind. I've been making complicated what really is a relatively simple problem to solve, the problem being Dorie's continued existence on planet earth. Dwayne has spoken wisely and provided me with heightened determination.

The next morning, I carry a yardstick to the window and look down at Second Avenue ten stories below. Then I open the window a crack, insert the yardstick so it protrudes outside a few feet beyond the sill, then close the window on it.

After making sure no one is in the hall, I climb the stairs two flights to the roof service-exit. I cross the graveled roof to the building's Second Avenue side.

I've always been afraid of heights, but I force myself to look down over the tiled edge of the roof until I can

218

see the yardstick two stories below; then I move with careful sideways steps until I'm directly above the yardstick and with a key I make a tiny scratch on the tile. With a last shuddering glance down at the sidewalk, I hurry back to the apartment.

No one's seen me, I'm sure. I remove the yardstick and replace it in its holder fashioned from a cardboard tube that once held wrapping paper. I've solved the problem of Dorie's physical strength and ferocity. It might be impossible for me to force her out a window. Certainly there would be at least some subtle sign of struggle or wrongdoing. Unless that emancipating action occurred elsewhere.

When Dorie returns from her morning meeting with an editor I treat her with my normal subservient amiability. While listening to her typewriter clattering in an adjoining room I sit blankly before a flickering TV soap opera, staring inward at my own private drama, summoning courage.

The mad typing stops. Dorie is revising what she's written. I inanely find myself wondering if ordinary toothpaste will remove blood. Was that in one of her columns? It doesn't matter, I tell myself, and I call, "Dorie!"

She enters the living room with a quizzical, annoyed expression on her shinily scrubbed face. Dorie hates to be disturbed while at work.

"I've made reservations for us for an hour from now at Rinaldi's," I tell her. Rinaldi's is the most expensive restaurant in the city, specializing in lobster, which Dorie despises.

Her lemon-lightened eyebrows meet above the bridge of her nose in an ominous scowl. "You *what?*"

I reach down and activate the concealed tape recorder by my chair as Dorie begins to rant. It goes very well.

I'm able to goad her into screaming at me for the next five minutes.

Supper that night consists of rice, lettuce salad, and an unusual dish incorporating beef cubes and Jello. I am chastised. Dorie and I have reached a truce. She informs me over her cup of generic coffee that she forgives me for my aberrant behavior. I do the dishes.

Two days later, as we're seated in the living room sharing the morning newspaper, I swallow hard and mention that I recently noticed something that might interest her professionally. "And what's that?" she asks dubiously, having never received an idea from me that she's used in her column.

"I was up on the roof yesterday," I begin.

"Doing what, for heaven's sake?"

My mind races, gears slipping cogs. "I'd never been up there before—never really examined it."

Dorie flashes me an astounded look.

"What I saw," I continue, "was a weather vane on the next roof. It seems to be homemade, mostly out of cleverly snipped and painted beer cans."

Dorie drops her section of newspaper and leans forward intently. "Beer cans?" No doubt she's thinking of the hundreds of uses she has found for drained beer cans—vases, pencil holders, gift containers, wind chimes —but so far no weather vanes.

I grin and put down my paper as if infected by her curiosity and enthusiasm. "Come on," I say. "I'll show you."

She stands immediately, thinking of nothing but a new column idea. As I get out of my chair to accompany her to the roof, I punch the play button of the concealed recorder, which is turned to top volume.

By the time we reach the roof the silent first two minutes of tape have run and the recording of our most recent argument is blasting through our apartment. At least one of the neighbors will hear us shouting.

I lead Dorie to the mark on the tile at the roof's edge directly above our apartment window.

"There," I say, pointing toward the jumble of duct-work and air-conditioning equipment on the roof across the street.

Dorie's eyes narrow as she strains to locate the weather vane. "I don't see anything, Huey."

"You have to move over here," I tell her, positioning her precisely before the mark on the tile. "You have to look between those two chimneys."

"I still don't—"

She never finishes what she's about to say. I've planted the palm of my right hand firmly against the small of her back and pushed her out into space twelve stories above the sidewalk. Even as I shove, I turn away, afraid of being made dizzy by the sight of her plummeting body.

I hurry back downstairs to the apartment, unseen, and let myself in. I've already opened the window over where Dorie's broken body now lies. The recording of our argument has run down and is silent. I bend and scoop up the recorder, and even as I phone the police with my tragic story the tape is being erased.

Within a few minutes the police are knocking on my door. I repeat my story to two uniformed officers, turning in what I consider to be a very believable performance. I'm definitely going to relish the role of grieving widower.

A lanky redheaded man who introduces himself as Lieutenant Gaston sits across from me in the living room and listens to my story. He has questions.

"So you had an argument," he says, "and you told your wife you wanted a divorce?"

"Correct, Lieutenant," I admit shakily. "No doubt some of the neighbors heard us shouting."

The lieutenant consults his notes. "She objected to a divorce, became distraught, told you she was going to commit suicide rather than lose you, then jumped out the window."

"Exactly," I tell him. "Of course, I didn't dream she was serious"—I manage a mournful sniffle—"until it was too late."

"That window?" Lieutenant Gaston asks, pointing.

I nod. The window is still open, the curtains hanging limp in the motionless summer air.

Gaston sighs and stands. "Would you accompany me downstairs, sir?"

I feel suddenly ill. My throat is dry. "To identify the—?"

"Not exactly," Lieutenant Gaston says. He holds the door to the hall open for me.

Neither of us speaks as the elevator descends, or as we walk through the lobby to the Second Avenue exit. The crowd that has gathered gapes at me. As we step from the air-conditioned lobby, my knees abruptly feel weak. Dorie's body is behind a roped-off area guarded by policemen. The rope is lifted and Lieutenant Gaston holds my elbow as we duck underneath. I cannot bring myself to look at Dorie.

"If your wife jumped from the tenth-floor window of your apartment," Lieutenant Gaston asks, "how do you explain that?"

Now I do look.

Dorie isn't as horrible a sight as I'd imagined. Strangely, there is very little blood, only an odd contortion to her broken limbs. The really horrible sight is the long white ribbon of toilet paper, gracefully extending from the now thin roll on her hip up, up, up, to where the other end of the paper is snagged on one of the roof tiles.

The paper is the barely perforated kind that's as difficult to tear as old rags. It must have caught on the roof as I pushed Dorie, then unfurled from the roll on her waist as she fell.

"I'm waiting for an explanation," Lieutenant Gaston says. His grip on my elbow tightens, constricting along with my throat.

I struggle to speak, to protest my innocence. But not very convincingly, I'm afraid. The croak that escapes my lips seems to be the voice of a stranger. "I don't understand—"

Lieutenant Gaston is speaking to me in a policeman's dreary monotone, reading my rights from a tiny card he's holding in his free hand. He informs me that, among other limited options, I have the right to remain silent.

I wish Dorie were alive to think of something clever I can do to pass the time in prison.

Dead Man

B eyond the eight-foot-high brick wall topped with jagged bits of broken glass embedded in cement, beyond
the towering cottonwood trees that swayed in dark
rhythm with the night wind, atop a gentle but long rise
of rain-slickened grass, sat the Masters house, its cupolas
and jutting dormers and gables seeming to lean defiantly
into the blasts of wind-driven rain. It seemed the perfect
night, the perfect setting, for the simple (therefore successful) murder that was to occur.

Adrian Masters was alone in the house, and eighteen
rooms on three floors was a lot of house in which to be
alone. Margaret, his elderly housekeeper-maid, had taken
her night off, and everyone else was away, one place or
another. Not that Masters was the sort who minded being
alone, except for the inconvenience of having to wait on
himself.

He'd had an early dinner out, and now he went from
the living room down the hall to the large and spotless
kitchen to prepare his own usual evening cup of tea. Margaret had thoughtfully left the kettle out on the counter
where Masters couldn't miss it, and he removed the lid,
placed the expensive and aromatic tea leaves into the
strainer, and ran water into the kettle. After placing it
on the stove to boil, he flipped out the light in the kitchen
and walked down the hall to his study.

As soon as the study door opened, a low growl came from a corner and, as the light went on, Major, Masters' hundred-pound German shepherd, cocked his head and erect but graying ears in recognition, then ambled back to lie near the bookcase and return to sleep.

Masters smiled at the dog as he crossed the room to his desk. He'd had the big shepherd since puppyhood, and for the past twelve years the dog had been completely loyal and devoted to Masters and no one else. Major dozed most of the time now, but he was still usually alert and served his purpose as companion and watchdog.

Animals were one thing, but Masters trusted few people. Along with Major's ominous presence and the protective high brick wall that surrounded the grounds, the locks on the outside doors of the house were of the highest, most pick-proof quality. Too, every night when Masters and his wife retired he threw the switches that activated an elaborate and sensitive burglar-alarm system. In his fifty-odd years, Masters had accumulated enviable wealth to go with an already substantial inheritance.

The wind gusted, blasting sheets of rain against the dark windowpane. It had been raining steadily all day, adding to Masters' boredom. As he went to close the draperies he observed his distinguished Roman features reflected in the window and with unconscious vanity subtly altered his carriage and expression to be more imposing. The heavy red draperies swept together in the center of the window and concealed Masters' reflection, like curtains closing out a scene for an actor.

Masters sat down at his wide desk in the oak-paneled study and toyed idly with a gold-handled letter opener. From another part of the house came a soft creaking sound, but no doubt it was the wind and he paid little attention to it. Deciding after a few minutes that he should make use of his time and get some work finished, he dropped the letter opener onto the desk, rose, and walked to the stained-oak panel by the bookcase.

The flat of Masters' hand pressed the panel inward about half an inch, then to the right so that it slid sideways on hidden tracks to reveal the gray steel door of a walk-in vault. After working the combination dial, Masters effortlessly swung out the heavy but thick counterbalanced door and stepped into the safe.

The inside of the vault was about six feet wide by eight feet deep, the walls lined with filing cabinets and shelves that contained strongboxes. Masters pulled open one of the file drawers on the right side of the vault, leafed through the folders thoughtfully for a few minutes, and was reaching for the Summers file when the teakettle came to a boil and began its shrill whistle.

Cursing, Masters removed the file folder, and in that split second a dread ran through him, brought about perhaps by the subtle altering of the piercing whistle. Masters turned, saw a slight shadowy movement outside in the study, realized that someone had cleverly used the whistle of the teakettle to cover the sound of his approach, and in horror watched the heavy vault door swing toward him. A black edge of darkness swept across the interior of the vault with the swinging of the door, encompassed and passed Masters, and, as the locks clicked firm, the inside of the vault was in total darkness, total silence.

Masters had never in his life panicked, but never in his life had he had a harder time fighting panic than now. No one was due in the house until tomorrow morning, when Margaret would arrive to prepare breakfast, and the vault was completely airtight and escape-proof. Add to that the fact that someone had obviously set out to imprison him in the vault until he suffocated, and his chances of breathing fresh air again were negligible. Always one to face things squarely and calculate instantly, accurately, and realistically where he stood, Masters arrived at the conclusion that he was a dead man.

A practical joke was the only alternative, and no one played practical jokes on Adrian Masters.

Now that the initial soul-chilling fear was over, he accepted his position fatalistically. He would last somewhere between two and six hours, he estimated, and then he would die of suffocation here in the darkness. He wished now he'd gone to the trouble of having a light fixture installed in the safe even though, when the door was open, the light from the study was adequate to find anything he sought.

Masters groped his way to a corner and slumped down to sit with his back against the shelves. He knew he should remain calm and keep his breathing regular to conserve oxygen.

An hour passed with surprising speed; then two hours. Masters' breath began to rasp.

There was only one great curiosity that remained in his mind now: Who had killed him?

Seizing on the question to avoid the impending horror, Masters' disciplined and precise brain began to work.

There were plenty of people with motive. He hadn't got where he was in the business world by being anything but ruthless, a characteristic he'd early discovered in himself in abundance. What dismayed Masters now was that the list of possible suspects in his murder was so long it would be virtually impossible for him to reason out who was guilty.

Then, surprising even himself, he smiled. There was one thing that narrowed the field to workable proportions. Whoever had entered the study and swung shut the vault door had to have got past Major, which meant that the murderer was one of the few people the dog was familiar enough with to tolerate without attack. Masters sorted this condensed list of suspects in his mind.

His wife Lynette; yes, she had motive—Masters' money, along with her freedom. Lynette was twenty

years younger than Masters, strikingly beautiful in a
cold long-legged sort of way, and for a long time he had
known of her extramarital escapades. Two days ago Masters had seen her off at the airport as she left for New
York to visit her sister, a moderately successful off-
Broadway actress. Lynette should be over a thousand
miles away.

Masters' younger brother Neville; he was an artist, the
unlikely combination of a welder of grotesqueries in
scrap steel and a painter of landscapes. Though successful in the ways of artists, his art brought him little monetary profit, and the monthly income from the trust fund
left by the aunt who had raised both Neville and Adrian
sustained him. Money was the motive here. Neville was
quite aware of his aunt's will, stipulating that in the
event of either brother's death the principal of the fund
would go to the surviving brother, on the condition that
the deceased brother's estate and regular monthly payments in the amount at the time of death would go to the
deceased's immediate family. Which meant that Lynette
would inherit Masters' possessions plus the monthly income from the trust fund, while Neville would be able to
lay his artistic hands on any principal in excess of the
amount needed to sustain those payments—fortune
enough to engender murder.

Of course Masters and his brother had always got
along well enough, at least on the surface—but who knew
what went on below a person's surface, even a brother's?
Masters was sure there were facets of himself that his
balding aesthetic brother could never suspect.

Masters had telephoned Neville just that morning to
see if he wanted to meet for lunch. He had apparently
awakened Neville, for the voice on the other end of the
line had sounded groggy and had not dispensed with any
of Neville's customarily dry wit. Neville had declined the
invitation, saying that he'd observed a field of sunflowers

off the highway yesterday afternoon and was determined to paint them that day before a construction crew nearby destroyed them. Neville was always seeing things he must paint on impulse. He told Masters that if anything happened to force a change in his plans, he would without fail telephone Masters and meet him someplace downtown. Neville hadn't phoned; his art had consumed him as usual.

The third suspect was Dwayne Rathman, Masters' business partner and the company vice-president. With Masters gone, he could gain complete control of the company riches. Rathman was supposed to be in Saint Louis working on a deal with a textile company, so, like Lynette, he was ostensibly out of town.

Masters was sure there was no one else, no other familiar enough member of the household or frequent visitor. There was, of course, his first wife Natalie, but she had remarried and stood to gain nothing but small satisfaction from Masters' death.

Which of the three? Masters could feel the stale air thickening, and he had to draw it into his lungs almost like liquid. He knew his capacity for reason was lessening, and he knew he had less time than he'd originally thought. Willing himself to be calm, he concentrated on the problem that helped keep his mind off the inevitable.

Lynette had telephoned long-distance that morning from her sister's in New York. There would have been time for her to take a flight here, accomplish her mission, and fly back before the body (his body!) was discovered.

If she really had gone to New York; the flight hadn't been nonstop.

Then Masters remembered that he'd talked on the phone that morning to Lynette's sister, Anne, as well as to Lynette. So Lynette really was in New York, and with her sister. Which meant that if she had planned Masters' murder, that brought about the unlikelihood of both women being in on it. Otherwise it would have been impossible for Lynette to disappear for a long enough period without running the very high risk of Anne finding out about it. Then, too, Lynette was the suspect with the weakest motive. Though she had much to gain by Masters' death, compared to her previous situation as a barmaid she was well-off.

Neville and Rathman were something of a toss-up. Neville's outwardly blasé attitude toward material wealth didn't fool Masters in the slightest. No one was that impervious to the temptation of great wealth within near reach, and Rathman, of course, was a businessman like Masters himself. That was why they were partners. Whatever was necessary, Rathman would do.

Then Masters recalled asking about the textile figures. Rathman had talked with him on the phone earlier, promised to get the figures, and was supposed to call and relate the information to Masters at exactly nine o'clock that evening. Masters stared at his luminous wristwatch dial: eight-fifty-two. Like Masters, Rathman was painstakingly punctual. If the telephone rang at exactly nine o'clock, it would almost undoubtedly be Rathman with the textile figures, which would mean he'd be calling long-distance from Saint Louis. He'd have no reason even to try to fake a long-distance call if he knew Masters was already in the vault and suffocating to death.

The question now was, could Masters hear the phone through the thick vault door. He should be able to, he decided, if, as in all probability, the murderer had left the oak panel pushed to the side so the murder would pass as an accident.

At exactly five minutes to nine, Masters felt his way through the darkness and lay with his ear pressed to the edge of the heavy steel door. If the phone didn't ring at nine, his murderer would probably be Rathman. If it did . . .

Then, softly, almost imperceptibly, the unmistakable, intermittent ring of the desk phone reached the black interior of the vault.

One minute to nine; it was like Rathman to be a minute early.

Masters backed away from the door, breathing more laboriously from either the tension or lack of oxygen. He didn't know which, tried not to think about it.

Was it possible he could pound on the end wall of the safe and cause someone on the outside of the house to hear? He crawled along the steel floor, reached the wall, and scooped papers and boxes from the shelves. He pressed his ear to the wall. No outside sound penetrated. Foolish of him to expect anyone to be there to hear his feeble efforts anyway, he told himself. There was not even a one-percent chance that someone—Margaret returning for something she'd forgotten?—would be able to hear. Even with his ear pressed to the steel, he couldn't detect the sound of the rain beating against the outer wall—if it was still raining.

Masters sat back with a start, not even noticing he'd bumped his head on a shelf in the darkness. He knew!

It had rained all day, from midmorning on, and Neville had told him he was going to paint sunflowers—outside! Impossible! Neville hadn't phoned, as agreed, to meet Masters downtown for lunch, and he certainly hadn't spent the day outside. Yet Masters had to admit that his brother might simply have been sleepy when he'd talked to him this morning, had simply not remembered what he'd said when he'd awakened later.

Yet Rathman was in Saint Louis and Lynette was in New York.

It had to be Neville.

Masters felt more satisfaction in having puzzled out the answer than anger at Neville. With the self-honesty of a man near death, he realized that he understood, even condoned Neville's actions. A lot of money was at stake.

Neville, however, would never enjoy that money. As all through their boyhood, Masters had played the game with him and beaten him. The thing now—the overriding thing—was to ensure that Neville would pay the full price.

Masters felt in his shirt pocket. He had his ball-point pen. For light he had his cigarette lighter—though he knew that burning it in the tiny cubicle would consume precious air and greatly shorten his life. Still, he knew what must be done. His breath came in violent rasps as he felt with trembling, eager fingers, opened a file drawer, and withdrew a folder. Then he readied the folder flat on the floor, clicked out the point of his pen, and with his left hand flicked the lever of his cigarette lighter.

It took only half a minute. In careful script he wrote out Neville's name on the blank face of the folder, the accusation, then below that the words, *I saw him close the door.* The state had recently reinstated the death penalty for premeditated murder for profit. Those last six words would make sure that Neville, like Masters, would die alone in a tiny cubicle, fighting uselessly for breath.

Even as Masters scrawled his signature, the dwindling flame of the lighter flickered wildly, hurling fantastic shadows about the vault, then died.

"You saw the oak panel in front of the vault door open, thought something was wrong, so you called us," Lieutenant Garr said patiently to Margaret.

Margaret nodded her gray head in affirmation. "But it wasn't only that, sir. Mr. Masters was always in his study when I came in the mornings to prepare breakfast. I'd always ask him what he wanted and he'd tell me so's I could have it prepared by eight o'clock. There was nobody ever more punctual than Mr. Masters."

The morning was gray, low-skyed, and rain still fell. The draperies were open now, as was the steel vault door, and the police photographers were just finishing photographing Masters' body, his dying message, and everything else inside the vault. The medical examiner had already pronounced Masters dead and left for his coffee and doughnuts.

Margaret cried silently as the police technicians finished and Masters' sheet-encased body was carried from the room. She walked hunched in sorrow behind the stretcher and watched as the attendants opened the front door and moved quickly through the rain to the waiting ambulance. As they slipped out of the house, so did Major, who had not had his usual morning exercise.

The big dog ran around the house and romped playfully as always on the huge back lawn, though not for as long a period as he had when he was younger. He favored his right leg, for he still ached from when he had leaped up and struck the heavy vault door as the sudden scream of the boiling teakettle had startled him awake.

Inside the house, Lieutenant Garr asked Margaret, "Who is Neville?"

Games for Adults

I t was seven P.M., and a fine, cool drizzle was settling outside the cozy Twelfth Avenue apartment building when the Darsts' telephone rang. Bill Darst got up from where he'd been half reclining on the sofa reading the paper and moved to answer it. His wife Della had been in the kitchenette preparing supper and he beat her to the phone in the hall by three steps. A medium-sized, pretty brunette, she smiled at her husband and stood gracefully with a serving fork in her hand, waiting to see if the call was for her.

Apparently it wasn't, but she stood listening anyway.

Bill watched her at a slightly sideways angle as he talked. "Oh, yes, sure I do. Yes," he said. ". . . Well, sort of short notice, but I'll see." He held the receiver away from his face and spoke to Della.

"Is supper so far along you can't hold it up? We have an invitation for this evening from the Tinkys."

"The what?"

"He's on the phone," Bill said impatiently. "Quick, yes or no." He smiled knowingly, aware that she hated to cook and seldom turned down an opportunity to escape the chore.

"Sure," she said, shrugging. "Why not?"

As Bill accepted the invitation and hung up, he

watched her walk back into the kitchen, untying the apron strings from around her slender waist. They had been married only two years, and he still sometimes experienced that feeling of possessive wonderment at what he considered his incomprehensible and undeserving luck.

"They'll pick us up here in about twenty minutes," he called after Della. "Said the directions were too complicated to understand over the phone."

"Fine." Her voice came from the bedroom now, where she was changing clothes.

Della appeared shortly, wearing the form-fitting but modest green dress that he liked on her. "Now, just where are we going?" she asked. "Who on earth are the Tinkys?"

Bill grinned at her. "Cal and Emma Tinky," he said. "Remember, we met them in that lounge on Fourteenth Street when we went there to escape the rain last week."

Recognition widened her eyes. "The toy manufacturer and his wife! I'd forgotten about them completely."

"Well, they didn't forget about us. Cal Tinky said something at the bar about inviting us for dinner and games some night, and I guess he meant it. I don't see any harm in us taking him up on a free meal."

"Games?" Della asked, raising an artistically penciled eyebrow.

"Tinky's the president and owner of Master Games, Incorporated," Bill reminded her, "and they're not toy manufacturers. They make games, mostly for adults. You know, three-dimensional checkers, word games, party games. They're the ones who make crossword roulette."

"We played that once," Della said, "at the Grahams'."

"Right," Bill said. "Anyway, the Tinkys live outside of town and Cal Tinky happened to be in this neighborhood, so he invited us out to his place."

"I hope his wife knows about it."

"He said she does." Bill picked up the paper again and began idly going over the football scores that he'd read before, but he didn't really concentrate on them. He thought back on the evening he and Della had met the Tinkys. Both couples had gone into the tiny lounge to escape the sudden deluge, and they had naturally fallen into an easy conversation that had lasted as long as the rain, well over an hour. Cal Tinky was a large-boned beefy man with a ruddy complexion and a wide, toothy smile. His wife, Emma, was a stout woman in her early forties. While friendly, she seemed to be rather withdrawn at times, the line of her mouth arcing downward beneath the suggestion of a fine mustache.

Only fifteen minutes had passed since the phone call when the doorbell rang and Bill went to answer it.

Cal Tinky stood in the hall, wearing an amiable grin and a tweed sportcoat and red tie that brought out the floridness of his complexion. "You folks ready? Emma's waiting down in the car."

"Sure," Bill said. "Come on in a minute and we can go."

"Evening, Mrs. Darst," Tinky said as he stepped inside.

Della said hello and they chatted while Bill went into the bedroom and put on a coat and tie. He could hear Della's laughter and Tinky's booming, enthusiastic voice as he stood before the mirror and ran a brush over his thick dark hair. He noted his regular-featured, commonplace appearance marred by a slightly large, slightly crooked nose and again counted his good fortune for having Della.

"We'll just take my car," Tinky said as Bill crossed the living room and got the coats from the hall closet. "You're apt to lose me in the fog, and it's not so far I can't drive you back later on."

"You don't have to go to all that trouble, Mr. Tinky,"

236

Della said, backing into the raincoat that Bill held for her.

"No trouble," Tinky said reassuringly. "And call me Cal—never did like that name Tinky."

Bill put on his topcoat, and they left and took the elevator to the lobby, then crossed the street to where Emma Tinky was waiting in a rain-glistening gray sedan.

The ride to the Tinkys' home took almost an hour through the misting, foggy night. They wound for miles on a series of smooth blacktop roads surrounded by woods, listening to the steady muffled rhythm of the sweeping wiper blades. Cal Tinky kept up an easy conversation of good-natured little stories as he drove, while Emma sat silently, gazing out the side window at the cold rain.

"I hope you won't go to too much trouble," Della said from the rear seat.

Bill watched Emma Tinky start from her silent thoughts and smile. "Oh, no, I put a roast in the oven before we came into the city. It's cooking now."

The big car took another turn, this time onto a steep gravel road. Bill caught a glimpse through the trees of the distant city lights far below them. He hadn't realized they'd driven so far into the hills.

"I don't suppose you have much in the way of neighbors," he said, "living way up here."

"You're right there, Bill," Cal Tinky said. "Nearest is over two miles. Folks up here value their privacy. You know how it is when you work hard half your life and manage to become moderately wealthy—always somebody wanting to take it away from you. Up here we're not pestered by people like that."

By the looks of the Tinkys' home they were more than moderately wealthy. As the car turned into the long driveway bordered by woods, Bill gazed through the rain-streaked windshield at a huge house that seemed in the dark to be built something like a horizontal wheel. Its rounded brick walls curved away into the night in perfect symmetry on either side of the ornate lighted entrance. Off to the left of the car Bill saw a small beach house beside a swimming pool.

"Like it?" Cal Tinky asked. "I can tell you it cost more than a pretty penny, but we sure enjoy it, Emma and I."

"What I can see of it looks great," Bill said.

"You shouldn't brag," Emma said to her husband.

"Just giving them the facts," Tinky said heartily as he neared the house and a basement garage door opened automatically.

For just a moment the sound of the car's engine was loud and echoing in the spacious garage, then Cal Tinky turned the key and they sat in silence. Bill saw a small red foreign convertible parked near some stacks of large cartons.

"No fun sitting here," Cal Tinky said. "Let's go upstairs."

They got out of the car and the Tinkys led them up some stairs to a large utility room of some sort. After passing through that room they entered a large room containing some chairs, a sofa, and a grand piano.

"Come on in here," Cal Tinky said, "into our recreation room."

Bill thought the recreation room was fantastic. It was a spacious room, about thirty feet square, with a red-and-white checkerboard tiled floor and walls hung with large decorative dominoes and ornate numerals. At strategic spots on the gleaming tile, four-foot-tall wood chessmen stood on some of the large red squares. Several tables were situated about the room, with various games spread out on them—chess, dominoes, and several complex games that were manufactured by Master Games, Incorporated. A smoldering fire glowed in the fireplace, over which hung a huge dart board.

"Let's sit down," Cal Tinky invited. "Dinner'll be ready soon."

Bill removed his coat and crossed an area rug designed to resemble the six-dotted plane of a huge die. He sat down next to Cal Tinky on a sofa embroidered with tic-tac-toe symbols.

"Is there anything I can do to help?" Della asked Emma Tinky as the heavy set woman took her coat.

"No, no," Emma said, "you are a guest."

Bill watched Emma remove her own bulky coat and saw that she was wearing slacks and a black sweater covered with a heavy corduroy vest. There was something that suggested hidden physical power in her walk as she left the recreation room to hang up the coats and prepare dinner.

Della sat opposite Bill and Cal on a chair that matched the sofa. "Quite a decorating job."

Cal Tinky beamed. "Thanks. Designed most of it ourselves. After we eat we can make use of it."

"A house this big," Bill said, "do you have any servants?"

Cal Tinky stood and walked to an L-shaped bar in a corner. "No," he said, "we mostly take care of it all ourselves, fifteen rooms. Had servants, but they stole on us. Now we have someone come in from the city twice a week to clean. Course, most of the rooms we don't even use." He reached for a top-brand bottle of Scotch and held it up. "Good enough?"

Bill nodded.

"Make mine with water," Della said.

Cal Tinky mixed the drinks expertly. When he'd given the Darsts their glasses he settled down on the couch and took a long sip of his straight Scotch.

Emma Tinky came back into the room then, picked up the drink that her husband had left for her on the bar, and sat in a chair near the sofa.

"You certainly must be fond of games," Bill said,

looking around him again in something like awe at the recreation room.

Cal Tinky smiled. "Games are our life. Life is a game."

"I agree with that last part," Bill said, raising the excellent Scotch to his lips.

"There are winners and losers," Emma said, smiling at Della.

They sat for a moment in that awkwardness of silence that sometimes descends on people who don't really know one another. Bill heard a faint clicking that he'd noticed in the car earlier. He saw that Emma was holding in her left hand one of those twisted metal two-part puzzles that separate and lock together only a certain way. With surprisingly nimble fingers she was absently separating and rejoining the two pieces expertly.

"Winners and losers," Della said to fill the void. "I suppose that's true."

"The basis of life," Cal Tinky said. "Have you folks ever stopped to think that our whole lives are spent trying to figure out bigger and better ways to amuse ourselves, bigger and better challenges? From the time we are infants we want to play the 'grown-up' games."

Bill didn't say anything. It was something about which he had never thought much.

"And business!" Cal Tinky laughed his booming laugh. "Why, business is nothing but a game!"

Now Bill laughed. "You appear to be a winner at that game." He motioned with his hand to take in the surroundings.

Emma joined in the laughter. She had a high, piercing laugh, long and lilting with a touch of . . . Of what? "Yes," she said then in a suddenly solemn voice, though a smile still played about her lips. "Material possessions are some of the prizes."

"Enough talk of games," Cal Tinky said. "I'm hungry."

Emma put the twisted pieces of shining metal into her vest pocket. "We can eat any time," she said, "unless you'd like another drink."

"No," Bill said, "not unless the food's so bad you don't want me to taste it."

Again came her high, lilting laugh, backgrounded by her husband's booming laughter.

At least she has a sense of humor, Bill thought, as they all rose and went into the large and well-furnished dining room.

The meal was simple but delicious; a well-done roast served with potatoes and carrots, a gelatin dessert with coffee, topped by an excellent brandy.

Throughout the meal they had kept up a running conversation, usually led by Cal Tinky, on the importance and celestial nature of games in general. Emma would join in now and then with a shrewd comment, a high and piercing laugh, and once, over the lime gelatin, Bill had seen her staring at Della with a strange intensity. Then she had looked away, spooning the quivering dessert into her mouth, and Bill heard again the soft, metallic, clicking sound.

After the brandy Cal Tinky suggested they go back into the recreation room for some drinks and relaxation. For a short time the Tinkys stayed in the dining room as Cal helped Emma put away some perishables, and Bill and Della were alone.

Della nudged Bill playfully in the ribs and moved close to him. "These people are weird," she whispered.

Bill grinned down at her. "Just a little eccentric, darling. Maybe we'd be, too, if we had their money."

"I hope we find out someday," Della said with a giggle. She quickly hushed as the Tinkys came into the room.

Cal Tinky was carrying a fresh bottle of Scotch. "The

241

first order is more drinks," he proclaimed in his loud voice.

He mixed the drinks at the bar and served them, then he looked around at the many games and entertainment devices. "Anything for your amusement," he said with his wide grin.

Bill smiled and shrugged his shoulders. "You're the game expert, Cal."

Cal Tinky looked thoughtful and rubbed his square jaw.

"Make it something simple, if you will," Della said. "I don't feel very clever tonight."

"How about Bank Vault?" Cal asked. "It's a simple game, but it's fun for four people."

He walked to a shelf and took down the game. Bill and Della followed him to a round shaggy rug, where he opened the box and spread out the gameboard. Emma spread four cushions for them to sit on.

When they were seated with fresh drinks, Cal Tinky proceeded to explain the rules.

It was an easy game to learn, uncomplicated, based like so many games on the advance of your marker according to the number you rolled on a pair of dice. The board was marked in a concentric series of squares, divided into boxes, some of which had lettering inside them: "Advance six squares," "Go back two," "Return to home area." Occasionally there were shortcuts marked on the board where you had your choice of direction while advancing. Each player had a small wooden marker of a different color, and if the number he rolled happened to land his block on the same square as an opponent, the opponent had to return to the home area and start over. Whoever reached the bank vault first was the winner.

They rolled the dice to determine in what order they'd play, then settled down on the soft cushions to enjoy themselves.

Cal and Emma Tinky played seriously and with complete absorption. Cal would roll his number and move his red block solemnly while his eyes measured the distance his opponents were behind him. Emma would move her yellow block in short firm steps, counting the number of squares as she moved it.

The game lasted through two drinks. Bill had rolled consecutive high numbers, and his green block was ahead until near the end of the game. Then he had landed on a "Go back ten" square and Cal had overtaken him to win. Emma was second, only three squares ahead of Bill, and Della's blue block brought up the rear after an unfortunate "Return to home area" roll.

"Say, I have another game similar to this only a little more interesting," Cal said, picking up the board. "Let's try it."

Bill reached to help him put the game away and found that his fingers missed the block he'd tried to pick up by half an inch. He decided to go easier on the Scotch.

Cal returned with the new game and spread it out on the soft rug to explain it to them. It was almost exactly like the first game. This time the board was laid out in a circle divided into compartments. The compartments were marked as rooms and the idea was to get back first to the room in which you started. This time the obstacles and detours were a little more numerous.

"Does your company manufacture this game?" Bill asked.

"Not yet," Cal Tinky said with his expansive grin, "but we're thinking about it. It's not the sort of game with mass appeal."

They rolled the dice in the same order. Bill rolled a twelve and moved well out ahead, but on his second roll he came up with a seven, landing him in the dining room, where the lettered message instructed him to skip his next turn for a snack. Della moved out ahead of him

243

then, landing in the den. Emma rolled a three but landed in the utility room, where she was instructed to advance ten squares. This brought her yellow block only two squares behind Della's and she emitted her high, strange laughter. Cal rolled snake eyes, allowing him a free roll, and he came up with a twelve. His red block landed on the den, and he placed it directly atop Della's blue block.

"Does that mean I go back to the entrance hall?" Della asked, smiling like a sport but feeling disappointed.

"In a manner of speaking," Cal Tinky said. He drew from beneath his sport jacket a large revolver and shot Della.

The slam of the large-caliber bullet smashing into her chest sounded almost before the shot. Della flopped backward, still smiling, her legs still crossed. A soft sigh escaped her body and her eyes rolled back.

"Della . . ." Bill whispered her name once, staring at her, wanting to help her, knowing she was dead, finally and forever. A joke, a mistake, a horrible, unbelievable mistake! He turned toward the Tinkys. Cal Tinky was smiling. They were both smiling.

Words welled up in Bill's throat that would not escape—anger that paralyzed him. He stood unsteadily, the room whirling at first, and began to move toward Cal Tinky. The long revolver raised and the hammer clicked back into place. Bill stood trembling, grief-stricken, enraged and afraid. Cal Tinky held the revolver and his smile steady as the fear grew, cold and pulsating, deep in the pit of Bill's stomach. The floor seemed to tilt and Bill screamed, a hoarse sobbing scream. He turned awkwardly and ran in panic from the room, from death.

He stumbled through the dining room, struggling to keep his balance. At the edge of his mind he was aware that Cal had put something in the drinks, something that had destroyed his perception, sapped his strength, and he tried to fight it off as he ran to a window. The window was small and high, and as he flung aside the curtains he saw that it was covered with a steel grill. With a moan, he ran awkwardly into the next room, to the next window. It, too, was barred. All the rooms that had windows were inescapable, and all the outside doors were locked. He ran, pounding against thick barred windows that wouldn't break or open, flinging himself against doors that wouldn't give, until finally, exhausted and broken, he found himself in the kitchen and dragged his heaving body into a small alcove lined with shelves of canned goods, where he tried to hide, to think, to think . . .

In the recreation room, Cal Tinky looked at his wife over the gameboard. "I think he's had enough time," he said. "It never takes them more than a few minutes to run to cover."

Emma Tinky nodded and picked up the dice. With a quick expert motion of her hand she rolled a nine.

Cal rolled a six. "Your shot," he said.

Emma rolled the dice again, a seven. She leaned over the board and, counting under her breath, moved her yellow block forward in short tapping jerks.

"The kitchen," she said. "Damn! They never hide in the kitchen."

"No need to get upset," Cal Tinky said. "You'll probably get another roll."

Emma drew a long revolver exactly like her husband's from beneath her corduroy vest and stood. Stepping over Della, she walked from the recreation room toward the kitchen. Her husband picked up the game and followed, careful to hold the board absolutely level so that the dice and the colored blocks wouldn't be disturbed.

The sound of the shot that came from the kitchen a few minutes later wasn't very loud, like the hard slap of an open hand on a solid tabletop—but Emma Tinky's high, long laugh might have been heard throughout the house.

The Butcher, the Baker

B e careful of that wristwatch, it cost a lot of money. I
know, I know, but I'm *willing* to talk. *Have* to talk.
You don't understand about Evelyn, how she always, *always* nagged me about not spending enough money on
her. Do you realize how a woman like that can get under
your skin? For your sake, Lieutenant, I hope not. She'd
be furious when I wouldn't buy her some frivolity. My
work as an artistic pastry chef doesn't pay that much,
even if I *do* have my own business. "I don't create the
kind of dough that buys things," I'd tell her, and that
would make Evelyn all the more furious, all the more
. . . well, *sadistic.*

So the time came—yesterday, to be precise—when I'd
had enough. *E*-nough! I made up my mind to kill her in
the morning, when she complained about her *cheap* one-
slice toaster. That doesn't sound like much to you, I'm
sure, but to me it was the straw that was *final.*

Of course I didn't *want* to get caught, so after a lot of
thought in my velvet recliner I decided to make Evelyn's
death appear as a suicide. Let the police suspect, I told
myself. If I kept the operation simple enough there could
be no *real* proof against me.

I simply went out to the hardware store and bought a

rope. Evelyn is—was—a trifle larger than the norm, so I purchased the quarter-inch clothesline that was on sale. I strung it over the iron beam in the basement and called Evelyn down.

How simple it was. "Garvin, what are you doing with that clothesline?" she asked in her nagging whine. And before she could say more I had the rope looped about her neck and was leaning my own weight and strength down on the opposite end.

When I saw that her feet were a few inches off the ground, I wrapped the rope about a nearby support and stood watching.

She kicked a lot at the empty air, and her body began to sway. Evelyn never *did* have a good complexion, and her face turned the strangest color. Her tongue protruded, and it was bigger, thicker than I thought, and it was a funny color, too. That's when the rope broke. It *should* have held, but it didn't.

Evelyn was as upset as I'd ever seen her, choking and cursing—language you wouldn't *believe* a woman would know. Then she began to chase me with the rope still around her neck. The suicide by hanging plan was *definitely* out.

I ran up the stairs in an absolute panic. In the kitchen I turned and started to throw a heavy teapot at her, but I saw at the last second that it belonged to our best and most expensive set of china. I ran into the living room.

The huge pressed-glass ashtray that we'd purchased at a garage sale brought her down neatly, without even a chip. I knelt and looked at Evelyn and saw she was still breathing.

Well, I didn't know *what* to do. So I used the length of rope around her neck to tie her up tightly, then I went into the bathroom and got a piece of adhesive tape and used it for a gag in case she came to. I had to have time to *think.*

Keep it simple, I told myself. Murderers always get caught when their plan gets too complicated and full of pitfalls. With the mark around Evelyn's neck, plus the head wound from the ashtray, the self-inflicted idea would never work. Necessarily, I had to kill her then and remove the body so that it could never be found.

First things first. *How* would I kill her? She'd regained consciousness now and was staring at me and writhing about angrily on the carpet. Her complexion was still florid.

I could go out to a sporting goods store and purchase a gun. It *was* hunting season; but to spend a small fortune for a firearm and use it only once would be not only excessive but might draw attention to myself in some future investigation. Then, too, there was the noise.

A knife was a reasonable solution. Stick to the classics. More strangling or battering was at that time a trifle distasteful to me, but one quick thrust . . . I went immediately to the kitchen.

I returned with the carving knife from a set I'd bought at a *fantastic* savings when Evelyn and I were in Mexico. I knew she must recognize the knife as she looked at it and her eyes widened. Without hesitation—I am a man of resolve—I knelt by her and my hand arced downward *to plunge* the blade into her breast.

It is *not* like in the movies or detective novels. Apparently I struck bone, and the blade snapped, giving my thumb a nasty gash.

Evelyn was *incensed.* They say in situations like that people get some sort of extra strength. That must be how Evelyn freed herself from the ropes I'd so tightly knotted.

In my *second* absolute panic of the hour, I ran, practically *flew,* into the kitchen and down the basement stairs.

I don't actually remember, but I must have had some idea of dashing out through the basement door. I knew I'd locked the rear door from the kitchen and would *never* have time to unlatch it.

Well, I'd just reached the bottom step and there was this *terrible* thumping behind me and I was struck in the back and bowled over to find myself lying partly beneath Evelyn. I saw immediately that she was *dead*. She must have tripped over the rope that still trailed from one of her ankles and struck her head in the fall down the stairs.

So here I was with this body with all kinds of wounds left by knife, ashtray, rope, and stairs. It brought me to the next step of my plan: how to get rid of the body. A fire came to mind, but it always seemed stupid to me to insure a house for any substantial amount against fire. I mean, when you *really* calculate the odds.

It occurred to me to drive Evelyn out to some peaceful country setting and bury her. But our car *is* a sub-compact, and a trifle-larger-than-the-norm woman like Evelyn would never fit in the trunk of a reasonably sized vehicle.

It came to me then that Evelyn would simply have to become haulable even if it were necessary for me to make *two* trips. The best thing about that plan was that I hadn't yet returned the power saw I'd received on a thirty-day free trial so I could cut down the diseased willow in the backyard. The only thing I really needed for my plan was—well, meaning no *disrespect*—trash bags, the large plastic kind.

I remembered an ad I'd seen in the *Neighborhood Journal* that's delivered free every Wednesday, and I leafed through the paper and found it almost at once in the food section. Jumbo-brand twenty-gallon plastic trash bags were on *sale* at Hrazdka's Speed Market—buy one box at the regular price and get the second box for *one* penny.

For a moment I debated buying our regular Econo-trash brand, also on sale, but then I decided that they might . . . well, *leak.* There was nothing in my plan that wouldn't keep for the moment, so I went immediately and got the car out of the garage. Hrazdka's Speed Market was just off the freeway exactly five miles down the road.

Well, that's when things started to go wrong. Hrazdka's was *completely* sold out of Jumbo trash bags— and no *wonder* at the price. That meant I would have to drive all the way across town to the only other Hrazdka's Speed Market, where I was sure the bags were also on sale. The thing to do, though, was to *phone* first, in case the other Hrazdka's was also sold out. Yes, it *was* possible.

As things turned out, however, I never did get a chance to ask. I drove across the parking lot to use the telephone booth, and that's when the whole day became an absolute *horror.* It's not as if I were actually *stealing.* Why, I've been doing it since I was a boy. You see, if you unscrew the mouthpiece of the telephone receiver, press a metal key to two metal points and also to a clean metal spot on the side of the booth, you get a dial tone without inserting your *dime.*

With other things on my mind, how was I to notice the policeman waiting to use the phone? When he opened the booth door to talk to me about stealing from the phone company—he should see the trouble I have with *my* bills from them—he spotted this blood on the front of my shirt. I hadn't even been *aware* of it. There was blood on my suede shoes, too, which weren't even two years old.

The officer began to question me and, like anybody else would, I'm *sure,* under the circumstances, I became flustered and blurted out some wrong answers. Of course, if he'd questioned me *fairly* . . . but it doesn't really matter now; the whole thing is ruined and here I sit.

Yes, I *know* it can be held against me, but I simply *must* talk. You can see I'm in an emotional *state!*

Life might depend on it? I'm aware of all that—but, Lieutenant, I don't create the kind of dough that buys things. I can't *afford* a lawyer!

No Small Problem

T he plain block lettering on the frosted glass read: WINKLER, M.D., PSYCHOANALYST. The frosted glass was in a door at the end of a hall on the seventh floor of the Preston Building, which was in one of the newer, wealthier areas of the city.

Winkler, a man of about thirty-five with a lean scholarly countenance, sat in the soft leather chair and glanced at his desk clock. It was past three o'clock. His next patient was already fifteen minutes late. Winkler was still recovering from his last patient, a nervous twittering dowager who started every interview with, "Doctor, the most revealing thing has happened!" Then she would proceed to tell him about some trivia that she expected to have deep psychic significance, and he played her game, right up to the final, shrill, "Until next week, Doctor." The underbrained, overmoneyed idiot, how was she to know that the M.D. on Winkler's door stood for Marion Dwayne, not medical doctor. Winkler would have been the last to correct her.

A buzzer sounded, and Winkler stood, buttoned his tweed sportcoat, and lit his pipe. His next patient, Virgil Sprang, had arrived. Since Winkler used a confidential answering service instead of a receptionist, he opened the door to the anteroom and greeted his patient.

"Mr. Sprang?" Winkler asked, for it was Sprang's first visit.

The short, rather plump man nodded nervously, and Winkler ushered him into the office. He motioned Sprang into the semi-reclined lounger alongside the desk and then sat in his leather swivel chair behind the desk, angled so that he could see Sprang much easier than Sprang could see him.

"Now, who was it who referred you to my services, Mr. Sprang?"

"I chose your name from the phone book," Sprang said in a high, nervous voice. "I, uh, didn't know any psychoanalysts, and you're located in a good section of town, so I knew you'd be reliable. . . ." His voice trailed off self-consciously.

"Well, that's not the usual way I obtain my patients," Winkler lied, "but under the circumstances it was probably a wise thing for you to do." He opened a notebook and pursed his lips professionally. "Now, what seems to be your specific problem, Mr. Sprang?"

"Midgets."

"Ah, midgets," Winkler said, making a note of that. He looked up to see that Virgil Sprang had twisted his neck awkwardly and was watching him. Sprang had amazingly fishlike blue eyes behind thick glasses, and Winkler could see that he was waiting for some incredulous reaction to his statement.

"Any particular type of midget?" Winkler asked.

"Small ones," Sprang said, turning and lying back again in the lounger, "and redheaded."

"And just how do these redheaded midgets concern you, Mr. Sprang?"

"Why, they concern me by turning up everywhere I go and pointing those tiny silver guns at me."

"Silver guns?"

Sprang nodded. "They carry them in shoulder holsters, and they're very quick on the draw."

Winkler's pen moved over the paper smoothly, drawing absentminded doodles of little fish. It really didn't matter because the tape recorder was spinning silently inside the desk.

"Just why do these midgets bother you in particular?" he asked Sprang. "Have you done anything to provoke them?"

Sprang thought and shook his head. "I haven't done anything to provoke anybody, but almost everybody is out to get me. Only the midgets are out to get me even harder. *They're* out to kill me, no matter what!"

A paranoiac, Winkler decided. He'd had a few before and found that he could sell their files quite easily at a good price. The various confidence men with whom he did business could think of a thousand ways to make money off a man like Sprang, just as Winkler was making thirty dollars an hour off of him. The difference was that Winkler wasn't taking any risks by doing anything illegal. Anybody could hang up a psychoanalyst's shingle in this state. No medical degree was necessary, as it was to be a psychiatrist, and it wasn't Winkler's fault that his name was Marion Dwayne.

"Tell me," Winkler asked, "have you ever seen two of these midgets at the same time?"

"Well . . . no," Sprang admitted. "But they don't look exactly alike. I think there are at least three of them."

"But it *is* possible, isn't it, Mr. Sprang, that there is only *one* redheaded midget?"

"Oh, sure, it's possible, but it isn't likely. I've seen them too frequently, and sometimes they're dressed differently."

"But why would they be after *you?*"

"Why is everybody after me?"

Momentarily stumped, Winkler puffed on his pipe and

turned to his notes. "That's what we intend to find out, Mr. Sprang," he said at last.

Sprang was remarkably at ease for a patient on his first visit, and Winkler had no trouble getting him to talk freely. While the patient was rambling on, Winkler thought of different things and doodled on his note paper, letting the tape recorder do its job.

"It's been very interesting, and possibly very informative," Winkler said when an hour was up. He closed the notebook with a quick little snap as Sprang stood.

"If you could just tell me what I'm doing that makes them want to get me," Sprang implored. "I went to the police but they laughed and said—"

"Yes, yes," Winkler cut him off gently. He handed Sprang some white forms and a pen. The forms requested information about Sprang's personal life, everything from his marital status to his bank account. "If you'll just fill these out at the table in the reception room on your way out . . ."

"Certainly, Doctor," Sprang said, and Winkler knew that he had his confidence.

He accompanied Sprang to the office door with a patronizing hand on his shoulder. "Is next week at this time agreeable to you as your next appointment?" he asked, puffing loudly on his smoldering pipe.

"Just fine," Sprang said, "and thank you, Dr. Winkler."

Winkler had examined Virgil Sprang's forms carefully before filing them. He was interested to find that Sprang was married, childless, and had no outstanding hobbies or weaknesses. He was even more interested to see that Sprang had some time ago inherited a good deal of very lucrative income property and was not wanting for money. Now, when he answered the waiting-room buzzer and the well-heeled blonde identified herself as Mrs. Virgil Sprang, Winkler saw where most of that money no doubt went.

"The purpose of my visit, Dr. Winkler, is to find out whether or not my husband is a patient of yours," Virginia Sprang said as she sat opposite Winkler on the other side of the wide desk.

"You mean he came to see me without confiding in you?" Winkler asked. "Highly unusual."

"Virgil is a highly unusual man," Mrs. Sprang said with a smile. She was a beautifully built woman, expensively groomed, but there was something vaguely predatory about her lipsticked mouth, with its fine, even teeth and the slightly underslung chin. When she smiled, Winkler was reminded of a shark about to turn for the fatal snap of its jaws.

"How long," Winkler asked, "has he been afraid of these midgets that he sees?"

"Then he *has* told you about that," Virginia Sprang said, crossing her long legs with a swish of nylon. She put a forefinger to the corner of her mouth and closed her eyes momentarily in thought. "He's been on the midget kick for a little over a month," she said after a pause, "but before that it was somebody else out to get him. He's got this idea that everyone's out to get him."

Winkler placed his pipe between his teeth. "A not uncommon ailment," he said professionally to Mrs. Sprang. "Tell me, has your husband sought treatment before?"

She nodded. "He's been to several doctors. He gets better for a while, then in a few months he's back to his old ways, like buying shutters and padlocks for all the windows in the house."

Winkler tore his eyes away from the expensive diamond on Mrs. Sprang's finger. "I assume the main purpose of your visit is to find out how you can help your husband in the psychoanalytic process."

"Sure," Virginia Sprang said. "But like I told you, it never does much good."

"I've studied your husband's case, Mrs. Sprang, and I'm sure that eventually he can be cured by professional help." Winkler smiled and stood. "Of course this will demand your cooperation also, occasional appointments for us to talk about your husband."

"Of course," Virginia Sprang said.

Winkler walked to the office door and opened it. "And now if you'll excuse me, Mrs. Sprang . . . I'd like to talk to you longer but I have an appointment with a patient in five minutes." He shrugged. "A friend of the mayor's who can't be kept waiting."

"I understand, Doctor." She walked to the door and gave him her slyly eager smile.

"I'll be in touch," Winkler said.

Virgil Sprang was obviously more upset than he'd been on his previous appointment. He almost fell into the lounger beside Winkler's desk, and even in the air-conditioned office he was perspiring heavily.

"You look as if you ran all the way here," Winkler observed.

"Ran for my life, Doctor!"

Winkler opened his notebook and tapped his pencil point lightly on the desk. "The, uh, midgets?"

Sprang nodded and rested his head against the back of the lounger. "One of them followed me all the way here in one of those little foreign cars. Every time I turned a corner he turned, too. It was terrible."

Winkler drew a smiling fish and said nothing.

"When I finally got rid of him I drove straight here," Sprang went on, "and there was one of them right there in the lobby, by the elevators. I ran all the way up the stairs."

"Have you had any other experiences with them during the past week?" Winkler asked.

"All the time. And once the one who makes nasty jokes even shot at me."

Winkler raised an eyebrow. "Shot at you?"

"In the garden behind our house," Sprang said. "He stepped out from behind a tree and grinned at me. Then he aimed and fired."

Winkler thought about that for a long time. "Did you look for the bullet, Mr. Sprang?"

Sprang sighed. "I thought you'd ask that. I looked in the side of the house but I couldn't find anything that looked like a bullet hole." His voice took on a hope. "But it might have hit a tree limb!"

"Might have," Winkler admitted. "You mentioned that one of these midgets cracks jokes?"

"Nasty jokes," Sprang said, shaking his head in disapproval. "He yells things at me you wouldn't believe, Dr. Winkler. Things I wouldn't repeat."

"I see no reason to repeat them," Winkler said. Not wanting to lose Sprang as a patient, he let Sprang rant on while he sat and pretended to take notes, waiting for the monotonous hour to come to an end.

Winkler thought no more about Sprang until three days later when he read in the morning paper that the poor man had leaped from the roof of a ten-story building. He had left no note but suicide was assumed. Winkler cursed at having lost such a promising patient and dismissed the matter from his mind.

Then a week or so later he chanced across Virgil Sprang's file and a thought occurred to him. Certainly the bereaved and now even wealthier Mrs. Sprang deserved consoling; and if Winkler was any judge, she would be a very consolable widow.

That afternoon he parked his car in front of the Sprang residence and walked up the winding sidewalk to the front door. Virginia Sprang herself answered his ring. She was very pale, and visibly surprised to see him.

He detected a certain reluctance as she invited him inside.

"I dropped by to say that I was sorry about Mr. Sprang," Winkler said. "I had no idea from our interviews that he was considering such a drastic thing."

"Virgil could get very depressed," she said, staring at the carpet. She seemed to have no intention of inviting Winkler to sit down, so he walked past her and helped himself to a chair.

"I suppose it was quite an ordeal for you too," he said.

She followed him into the living room but did not sit. Winkler noticed that her black dress fit her very snugly.

"I do appreciate your concern, Dr. Winkler," Virginia Sprang said, glancing at a sunburst clock over the stone fireplace, "but I really have to be somewhere in less than a half hour. . . ."

"Can I drive you?" Winkler asked.

"Oh, no, I've called a cab."

"Well, in that case . . ." Winkler stood and walked slowly to the front door, which she already had open for him. "I'll drop by some other time," he said with a smile. "That is, if you don't mind."

Her return smile was quick and apprehensive. "Not at all. But do call first to make sure I'm home."

Winkler patted her cool hand consolingly and left.

He was halfway to where his car was parked, his head bowed thoughtfully, when he became aware of someone walking toward him up the long winding sidewalk. He raised his head to look and his step faltered with surprise. Approaching him, strutting jauntily, was a redheaded midget.

"Afternoon," the midget said as he passed, and Winkler made it to his car fast.

He reasoned the whole thing out as he drove to his office. The midget and Virginia Sprang were obviously in cahoots for Virgil Sprang's money. They had taken advantage of his acute persecution complex and hounded him to death, turning up everywhere he went, firing blanks at him. It was no wonder the fool was so agitated the last time he'd been in Winkler's office.

Winkler parked in the Preston Building lot, stopped in the lobby cocktail lounge for a drink, then went up to his office to consider the possibility of blackmailing the midget and Virginia Sprang.

As soon as he opened his office door he gave himself a mental kick and recalled with certainty that he'd had only one drink downstairs in the lounge. Standing on the square-tiled floor like so many strategically placed chessmen were three redheaded midgets, all wearing identical well-pressed dark suits. As Winkler instinctively walked around behind his desk and sat down they moved in front of him to form a small barrier between him and the door.

"I assume you gentlemen are in the employ of Virginia Sprang," Winkler said, regaining some of his composure. He noticed that one of them had Virgil Sprang's file folder tucked beneath his arm.

"Virginia Jones," the midget in the middle corrected. "She's married to me now. I'm Stubby Jones."

Winkler cleared his throat of fear and swallowed. "Congratulations," he said, for lack of anything else to say.

The midget waved a short arm. "My brothers, Spike and Louis." They nodded. "We sort of stick together to get along in this world."

"Then all of you—"

"Oh, we didn't murder him," they said almost in unison. "He ran up on the roof and we just walked toward him and he jumped."

"Still"—the midget in the middle shrugged—"the police might not see it that way."

"And one of you *did* shoot at him in his garden."

Stubby Jones grinned. "Only blanks. We wanted him to be a suicide, not a murder victim."

Winkler looked at the small men and decided not to be cowed. He gathered his courage for a bold front. "I take it you want to buy my silence," he said.

"I don't think we can afford that," one of the midgets said, and three small hands darted inside three small dark suitcoats and three small-caliber chrome pistols were aimed at Winkler; tiny guns, to be concealed beneath tiny clothes and fit tiny fingers.

"These guns are untraceable," the midget on the left said. "We bought them in Europe when we were with a circus. From a tattooed lady who—"

"Now see here!" Winkler began.

"Now, now, Doctor," Stubby Jones said with a nasty leer, "there's no need to be a Freud." High-pitched laughter sounded through the office.

"But I'm not even a real doctor!" Winkler tried desperately to explain as he started to stand.

There was a soft staccato sound, like a miniature motorcycle engine turning over nine or ten times and failing to catch, and Winkler dropped back into his desk chair. Tiny holes appeared magically in his forehead and the tweed of his sportcoat, and he sat very still, his glazing eyes wide open in surprise.

Still smiling, one by one, the midgets left the office.

Deeper and Deeper

I 'm cold, and I'll never be warm again. Each wave is higher than the one before. And I was the daughter always unfairly referred to as vain, greedy, and "shallow." Mother was the first to tell me: "Maudie, it ain't your fault, but the piece of you that lets you know right from wrong is missing."

If that's true, that it *wasn't* my fault, then I don't deserve this. I mean, crime is mostly in the intent—that's where right and wrong come in—and I wasn't thinking about being right or wrong when I planned on killing Graham. I was thinking only about being rich. But here I am, in my Gucci velour bathing suit, wrapped up in a sheet tight as a mummy. I can't twitch so much as a muscle.

Larry did this to me—he tied me out of sight here, to the base of the pier at Graham's private boat dock. When the tide rises enough, I'll drown. By now Larry's in his car halfway to Miami. When the authorities determine the time of my death he'll have an alibi. He'll have been in another part of the state with friends. Tomorrow morning when the tide's out again he'll drive back here, untie and unwind me, and let me be discovered washed up on the beach, unmarked and dead, my hair a mess. Accidental drowning will be the verdict. Nobody'll connect Larry and me.

Larry doesn't know right from wrong, either. But he knows smart from dumb.

It doesn't do any good to scream. This is a private, desolate stretch of beach, and the roar of the surf is so loud if anyone did hear me they'd probably think it was a gull.

A particularly large wave swells in the moonlight and rolls toward me, rising higher and breaking out in white foam at its crest, fascinating and horrible. I hold my breath and close my eyes as it washes over me, then it recedes and I gasp precious air. The water is high above my waist now, and the next wave is roaring in like an oncoming train, swelling green-black and monstrous in the moonlight.

Sure, I married Graham for his money, but I wasn't the first to do that. His former wife was a two-timing gold digger. He hired detectives and managed to divorce her without giving her any of his multimillion-dollar real-estate holdings in Florida. She couldn't even get back into the house to get most of her clothes—

Another wave strikes me, colder and with more savage force than the last. I have to shake my head to clear my eyes and nose of water. I cough, choking and spitting. I can't believe I didn't die right there. Wouldn't that cross up Larry, if I died without water in my lungs!

Okay, I married Graham but I didn't want to live the rest of my life with him. And after hearing about how he cut off his first wife, I knew divorce wasn't my answer. So I started driving my Porsche down to the Overlook Lounge about five miles down the coast. That's where I met Freddie.

He was sort of an aging beachcomber, with broad shoulders, a big smile, and a beautiful tan. He asked if he could buy me a drink. I said yes and we sized each other up.

He was single, living alone, seeing life getting shorter while his unfulfilled ambitions kept their distance. We got along well enough. "There's no way we can keep this a secret forever," I told him one night. "Word's bound to get out."

"So?" he said, tilting back his gorgeous head to drink his piña colada.

"So you can't be the one to kill my husband," I said.

He lowered the glass and stared at me. I explained how it would be better if he hired someone to kill Graham—that way the murderer would be once removed from anybody with a motive. Freddie could have an ironclad alibi and so could I.

"You're crazy," he said. "You don't know right from wrong."

I told him how much my husband was worth. He thought about it. Then we got down to details. Freddie hired Burt, an old acquaintance of his who used to be in the marine salvage business but was down on his luck and needed money. Burt had served time in the Midwest for killing a man who deserved killing. He figured the government owed him a victim who *didn't* deserve killing but whose demise would profit Burt. Graham was made to order.

The three of us worked out a plan and it worked just as neat as can be, like when I cried and cried until my father bought me a convertible for my high school graduation. I was the first girl in my crowd to own a car—but then I was way ahead of everyone in school in most things, not excluding looks, if you'll pardon my bragging about what happens to be true.

Anyway, while Freddie was with his mom in Milwaukee and I was on a shopping spree in Orlando, Burt hit Graham on the head, put him in his Mercedes sedan,

264

and shoved the car and Graham over the cliff near the
coast road by the estate. Nobody saw it as anything but
an accident. I got lots of sympathy and really got to like
how I looked in black.

Freddie, Burt, and I kept our distance from each other.
That was supposed to last for six months, but about
month three I started thinking, and worrying. Besides
me, there were two other people who were aware that
Graham had been murdered. I couldn't feel safe knowing
that. Even if I married Freddie, we'd both have to worry
about Burt. Of course I could have Freddie kill Burt, or
vice versa, if you'll pardon the pun. But then I thought,
why not hire someone to kill them both, someone twice
removed from Graham's death? The police would never
make a connection.

So after spending a week in Orlando and sort of screen-
ing candidates, I chose Larry. He was a great-looking
guy, slender but strong, with sharp features, a neat little
moustache, and kind of cold gray eyes that gave me shiv-
ers I liked. —Oh, this is terrible! That last wave was really scary! Wait a second, let me catch my breath before
I go on.

It didn't take long to convince Larry he should do
away with both Freddie and Burt and then spend the
rest of his life with me and Graham's real-estate holdings.

Larry did a swell job, too. As far as the cops or newspapers knew, Freddie and Burt were just two guys who
barely knew each other who'd been killed in accidents in
different parts of the state. That Larry sure is resourceful.

Too resourceful, it turns out. He talked me into putting a big, big chunk of Graham's money in a safe-deposit box in his name—to protect it from inheritance
taxes, he said. He must have used the same mathematics
I did—if two people besides me knowing about Graham's

death was risky, *one* was risky. He figured I'd get rid of him after a while.

But he was wrong. I didn't plan on waiting a while. That's my single solace. Larry doesn't know about the dynamite from one of Graham's construction sites I wired to a timer under the front seat of his car. He'll never reach Miami. He'll die before I do.

And the state will get all of Graham's money! All of it! I ask you, is that right?

I suppose there's a moral here somewhere—the sort Mother always found. Like if you keep getting yourself involved in something deeper and deeper, you're bound to drow—

On Guard

I board the Seventh Street bus on my way to work on a gray and drizzly morning, pay my fare, and lurch to a seat by a curbside window as the bus accelerates. Block by block, we pick up passengers as the bus rumbles stop-and-go through traffic toward the downtown area. Every seat is taken now, and unobtrusively I survey my fellow passengers.

The growing suspicion, the creeping knowledge, is within me. Across the aisle a man in a plastic raincoat makes quick, seemingly thoughtful marks with a sharp pencil on his morning paper quarter-folded to the daily crossword puzzle. Two seats forward a well-dressed man holds a pencil poised over some papers atop the attaché case on his lap. Beyond him—no, that one is using a ball-point. But I hear the unmistakable scratching sound, twist my head slightly, and see behind me a woman moving a long yellow pencil over the same morning crossword puzzle that occupies the man across the aisle. Or that he pretends occupies him.

All these sharp-pointed pencils. It isn't just coincidence. Or if it is, might not be next time. I know what to do. Near the next bus stop is a small shopping center with a drugstore. At the last minute I rise and pull the cord that signals the driver to stop, then I step down off the bus, walk directly to the drugstore, and purchase two large rubber erasers.

Ridiculous? Hardly. A sharp pencil in skilled hands is as deadly a weapon as a stiletto. At the slightest inkling of an attack on my life, I will draw the large erasers from my pockets, warding off the blows so that the pencil points are embedded in the soft rubber instead of myself. And while my assailants are using precious seconds to remove the blunted points of their weapons, I will run to the authorities and take the necessary steps to see that the vicious homicidal animals who tried to write my obituary are penned where they belong.

I feel much safer now, with erasers in my pockets, and I flag down the next bus and continue my way to work.

My job is to help assemble components for General Conglom's Watchever portable television sets. Harvey Slater, a large man with small eyes who works at the bench on my left, wearily punches his time card and glances over at me without a change of expression.

"Mornin', Quayler," he says. "Hope you ain't as shot down as I feel and you look."

What does he mean by that?

No time to dwell on it. I take my place at my bench and begin to work. Slater ignores me as he deftly solders delicate wiring beside me. It's easy to modify an electric soldering iron so that at the touch of its tip a deadly jolt of electricity kills. It's easy with Slater's know-how. And I'm sure he'd like to, and maybe already has, altered some of his tools to implements of death.

Oh, he has motive enough. We've worked together side by side for six years, and we hate each other, grate on each other's nerves in our forced confinement. Slater pretends otherwise, but I know and pretend right along with him. I also know that every day people kill for less reason than he has to kill me. If you don't think so, read your newspaper.

268

What Slater doesn't know is that I've taken precautions. Around my waist runs a slender copper wire and attached to it is an even more flexible wire that runs down the outside of my right leg, into my shoe, and through a small hole I've drilled in the heel to a flat-headed copper nail in the bottom of my shoe. I am grounded. Here in the shop I am careful always to rest that shoe with its nail on some metal part of my workbench, which is itself grounded, but even outside I am grounded. Slater isn't the only one who knows about electricity. Whoever tries anything with me will be in for a shock, and attempted murder will be the charge.

After an interminably long day of work, I take a bus directly to the ballpark. Usually I sit in the bleachers, but this evening I have a box seat because my favorite baseball team, the Dodgers, is in town.

It's a warm night, still humid from the rain, and by the sixth inning the Dodgers are ahead five to one. When the pitcher doubles in two more Dodger runs, the crowd around me begins to get ugly. Most of the men and several of the women hold their scorecards or programs rolled up, gripped in white-knuckled fists like clubs or waved like spears. Can they know I'm a Dodger fan? In the right hands, used mainly as a jabbing weapon, a rolled up scorecard can be a surprisingly wicked and lethal instrument.

The Dodger shortstop walks on a disputed call. Around me the crowd roars, wielding tightly clenched weapons menacingly. I stand to leave, edging my way toward the main aisle.

"Watch't, you!" a perspiring man snarls as I step on his toe. I don't answer.

I begin to breath easier as I reach the concrete corridor beneath the grandstands and head for the Third Street exit. The crowd roars again, louder, with bloodthirsty overtones, the sort of sound that must have burst from Roman arenas of the past. I can imagine the rolled-up scorecards and programs being waved threateningly. Another roar. Is it possible they'll come after me? Thousands, tens of thousands of them, their weapons brandished above their heads like cavalry sabres as they charge.

Outside the stadium I see a small gift shop, and quickly I duck into it.

"A pair of scissors!" I tell the startled clerk. "The largest you have!"

He places six-inch blades on the counter before me.

"No, you fool, a pair! Two of them!"

He complies, and I don't even wait for my change before stepping cautiously back onto the street, scissors in each hand.

After a block or so I realize there is no need for caution. Let the base hordes come with their paper pikes and cardboard cudgels. They will be committing a fatal error. I will not balk at cutting them to ribbons. Confident now, I slip the scissors into my pockets and walk home.

By the time I get home I have torn my pockets and jabbed myself in the legs several times with the pointed tips of the scissors. It would be unwise to walk the streets without the scissors, but with the erasers I carry in my pockets there is little room for them.

Before I go to bed I fashion two lightweight imitation leather holsters with material from the underside of one of the sofa cushions. The holsters attach neatly to the copper wire about my waist and the scissors ride on my hips beneath my trousers quite comfortably and hardly visible.

It is difficult to get up the next morning after only a few hours sleep, and I struggle into my clothes, eat a quick breakfast (portions of which I have tested on the cat), and must hurry if I'm to get to work on time.

As I cross the street and walk briskly toward the bus stop, I glance over at Paloni's Fruit and Vegetable Market and see Paloni in person, a foreign dark-haired type with perverse eyes, standing just behind his display window tossing and catching a tomato easily with his right hand. He looks directly at me, smiles a white, sinister smile and hefts the tomato as if gauging its weight in ratio to the distance and velocity he can attain by throwing it.

I stop.

A tomato, while the favorite fictional missile of many a cartoonist, is actually quite a deadly object, especially a green one. In fact, Paloni stands amidst a veritable arsenal, and judging by the way he hefts the tomato he knows how to use the weapons at hand. I would hate to pit the thickness of my skull against an unripe peach, or have to dodge a skillfully thrown sharpened carrot or the unpredictable arcs of zucchini or sharp-edged eggplant. Even innocent-appearing lettuce can suffocate.

I cross to the other side of the street as if nothing is wrong and return to my apartment.

When I leave again my Miracle Whacker vegetable slicer hangs on a leather cord about my neck. Nothing to fear from Paloni now, or from some hurtling edible that can produce a fatal wound. Deftly I will use my Miracle Whacker to intercept the deadly projectiles in midair, and they will fall a salad of failure at my feet.

But to be safe I use the bus stop a block east. Paloni himself might be a plant to throw me off my guard.

I don't get off at my usual stop, but four blocks farther south down Twelfth Street. Then I cross two blocks over to Tenth and begin walking north. It's impossible to be too careful.

The morning is hot already, and I'm unused to walking. At Dover Avenue I stop and sit on a hard wooden bench in the shade of a tiny maple tree fighting for survival in its environment of concrete, glass, and exhaust fumes. Several passersby glance slyly at me. I know I'll have to move soon.

Sooner than I thought. The hard bench is uncomfortable and the points of one of the long-bladed scissors I carry are jabbing furiously at my right leg, causing me to squirm on the unyielding wood. Tonight I must improve on my secret holsters.

No sense in sitting here squirming uncomfortably any longer. I stand and walk on, the Miracle Whacker bouncing reassuringly against my chest beneath my shirt.

"You! Hey, mister! . . ."

My heart plunges to icy depths and I don't even turn, walking faster and trying to lose myself among the thronging pedestrians.

"Your wallet! Hey, you left your wallet on the bench!"

He hasn't fooled me there—one of the oldest tricks in the book.

Footsteps, behind me!

"Stop, Mr. . . . Mr. Quayler! Hey, Stop!"

He even knows my name! Can there be any doubt now that he's after me? I need help—where can I go for help?

"Stop that guy!"

The Government Building! Two blocks over is the Government Building! I'm running now, my heart a desperate hammer beating itself toward oblivion. Gasping foul air, I dash through a narrow alley, summoning speed before the brick walls can close in on me.

Tires scream, and a gray car, glowering at me with hooded menace, swerves and barely ticks the heel of my shoe as I spin away. They are after me with cars now! In the next block I can see the Government Building with its tinted glass panels, its decorative pond and towering fountain. I put my head down, brush someone aside who darts at me from a doorway. I know my only chance.

Cars cannot drive through water! Water that gushes into the carburetor, that shorts the ignition! Triumphantly I fling myself into the pond in front of the Government Building and struggle amid bright splashing toward its center.

The water is cold, and deep. Deeper than I thought. . . .

The bottom abruptly drops away and my momentum carries me farther toward the center of the pond. I cry out! My right arm is entangled in the cord that holds my Miracle Whacker and the points of each scissors jab painfully into my legs with every frantic movement.

How could they have known? How could they have ferreted out the fact that I never learned to swim? . . .

J. Dammerung, director of PROBE, Section 3, VITAL of the Central Intelligence Agency, gazes seriously across his bare desk at Bauman, one of his underlings.

"This man who drowned outside the building yesterday, what do you make of it?"

Bauman, a youngish man with intense gray eyes, frowns. "Possibly just a crackpot."

"But why the Government Building?"

"Coincidence?"

Dammerung shakes his head slowly. "With all that equipment on him? Outside the Government Building? Hardly. And if it was coincidence this time, it might not be the next time. Section Five has determined that what specialized uses the implements found on the dead man might have, other than the purposes for which they were manufactured, would have to do with sophisticated alarm bypass."

Bauman tactfully remains silent.

"And a crackpot, let me remind you, would hardly have taken the precaution of removing his identification before his attempt."

"Attempt at what, sir?"

Dammerung smiles a grim smile, taps a pencil on the bare desktop. "The dead man in all probability is the skilled and unidentifiable Agent Foursquare, and what he was no doubt attempting was the assassination of General Crane, one of the key links in Attack Command. If General Crane were to die at precisely the right instant, precious minutes, maybe hours, would be lost before we could launch our counterattack. Remember, too, the satellite reports of recent missile build-up in the Ukraine."

"But General Crane wasn't here yesterday."

"But did they know that? And we weren't subjected to missle attack yesterday, either. It could be, Bauman, that Someone is watching over us, but we must also help ourselves."

"Help ourselves how, sir?"

"By steeling ourselves to our duty. By initiating the Red Plan. Advising the president to strike first—now!"

Bauman's swallow is a muted explosion in the quiet room. "W-we must be careful, sir. . . ."

"What you're observing, Bauman," Dammerung says with rigid features, "is the ultimate, the final step, in being careful. If we're *not* careful, they'll attack first and destroy us!"

Dammerung pulls open a bottom desk drawer and very deliberately, almost reverently, lifts out a blood-red telephone. "The time for mere suspicion is over!"

Fractions

S ondra rolled over. "You know I love you," she said to
Judson Avery. "I could get someone to pay *all* my
rent."

Judson raised his hawk-nosed but handsome face from
where it was buried in the clean white pillow. He looked
around him at Sondra's small but very plush apartment.
Through the open door to the living room he could see the
thick carpeting, the stone fireplace (genuine), and a corner of the wide-screen color TV. He could be paying all
of her rent, easily—Sondra knew that—but how could he
explain to Margaret where that much more money was
going?

"I don't understand," Judson said. "Why are you this
way all of a sudden? Restless."

"All girls reach a point, Judson." Sondra fluffed her
pillow and scooted backward on the mattress to sit up
halfway. Long blond hair fell to cover her well-rounded
breasts. "I'm tired of waiting."

"So what do you want me to do?" Judson asked. "Kill
her?"

"What do you think I *am*, Judson!"

"Only joking, honey." Judson maneuvered his lean
frame so he was leaning back beside Sondra against the
headboard. He looked from the corner of his eye at her

275

sexily pout-lipped profile. "But Margaret won't consent to a divorce under any circumstances. She's made herself clear on that."

"Murder isn't necessary," Sondra said. They both knew that half of Margaret's money would be sufficient. Not a fortune, but enough to support Judson and the new Mrs. Avery in high style for a long time. Half was better than the electric chair.

"There is one circumstance that would make her consent to a divorce," Sondra said.

Judson snorted. "I've certainly given her all the grounds she needs. If you can think of anything else, let me know. Even if it doesn't work it should be fun."

"How about adultery?"

Judson, in the process of lighting a cigarette, started to laugh so suddenly that he choked on the smoke. "Oh, hell," he said as Sondra clapped him on the back, "she's even caught me with her half-sister."

"You don't understand," Sondra said as she stopped pounding and began a gentle massaging action at the base of Judson's neck. "I don't mean *you.*"

Now Judson did laugh. "You can't mean Margaret! Staid and steady Margaret! Why, she's as passionate as crushed ice!"

"Ice melts," Sondra said, and Judson was shocked to see that she was serious. He also knew that Sondra was no fool.

Suddenly serious himself, Judson arched an eyebrow and asked interestedly, "What do you have in mind?"

"I don't know exactly, but a girlfriend of mine told me she heard about a company that . . . arranges things."

"Arranges things how?"

"I don't know," Sondra said. "I don't even know if such a company really exists, but I did find the name in the phone book. I called six times, but there was no answer."

"So you want me to look into it," Judson said thoughtfully.

"You could go to the address and see what's there," Sondra said. She let herself slide down in the bed until her blond hair was spread over the pillow. "Why not?"

"Why not?" Judson agreed, smiling down at her. He'd been asking himself that question all his life.

The next afternoon found Judson riding a slow and spastic elevator to the top floor of one of the older office buildings in a decaying downtown section of the city. He stepped up off the elevator and explored the corridor. When he'd almost decided he'd come there for nothing he saw the door at the end of the hall. It was a narrow dark-stained door, more like the entrance to a broom closet than an office, and the plain black letters were almost unreadable against the dark wood: THE ASUNDER CO.

Inexplicably hesitant, Judson finally drew a deep breath and entered. He was in a small anteroom, very plain, with cheap plastic chairs lined evenly against opposing walls.

"Come in, please," a voice called from behind the frosted glass door to the main office. Judson obeyed.

The office, like the reception room, was plain. There were no pictures on the pale green walls, no artificial potted plants; there were only two chairs, a desk, a battered filing cabinet, and an ancient floor fan that turned its blades slowly and noisily. The wide desk was bare except for a nameplate that read "Mr. Polygus." The owner of that name, a dark, smiling, middle-aged man with luxuriant black hair, stood and extended his hand to Judson.

"A good afternoon to you, Mr. . . . ?"

"Avery. Judson Avery."

Mr. Polygus motioned to the chair before the desk and sat down himself. "What exactly is it you wish, Mr. Avery?"

"To know what the services of your company are," Judson said, sitting down uncomfortably.

"Ah, but you must have some idea or you wouldn't have come here." Even white teeth shone against dark skin.

"I have some idea," Judson said, "but not enough."

Mr. Polygus looked at him through friendly but careful dark eyes. "The service of our company," he said, "is the termination of marriages."

Judson felt his senses quicken. "And how is that brought about?"

"We arrange for the unwanted partner of our client to commit adultery," Mr. Polygus said, his smile broadening. "And of course we arrange to have proof of this adultery."

"But what if the unwanted partner . . . doesn't want to commit adultery?"

"Oh, no worry of that," Mr. Polygus said reassuringly. He reached into a desk drawer and removed some blank forms. "If you'll just carefully fill these in with all the personal information about the Unwanted One, we should anticipate no problem."

"You don't know Margaret," Judson said, taking the forms.

"That information will be fed into a computer," Mr. Polygus said. His smile fairly beamed. "We have in our employ the man for every job."

"I see," Judson said slowly.

"In the most difficult cases," Mr. Polygus said, "there are even mild drugs—harmless, but effective."

"But what about divorce proceedings?" Judson asked. "Won't this appear . . . contrived? Margaret's not stupid, only ugly."

Mr. Polygus raised a friendly palm, as if to catch Judson's question gently in midair. "We are, ah, affiliated with a detective agency. Usually our divorces are uncontested. However, when proof is obtained, a detective will testify in court, if necessary, that you had long suspected your wife and came to him and hired him to secure your peace of mind."

"Masterful," Judson said. "There are no loose ends."

Mr. Polygus acknowledged the compliment with a nod.

"And the price?" Judson asked.

"Merely five thousand dollars," Mr. Polygus said. "Actually no more expensive than a first-class funeral if your poor wife should pass away."

"Put that way," Judson said, "it sounds more than reasonable." He began to fill in the forms.

The Asunder Company must have worked subtly, ever so subtly. Judson watched Margaret closely for the next month, but there was no noticeable change in her. She would be a demanding job for someone, Judson realized. Though looked at bit by bit Margaret was not unattractive, there was about her bearing and personality that which was just the opposite of animal magnetism.

Then one day the package was delivered to Sondra's apartment, proof in glaring eight-by-ten glossy photographs of Margaret's infidelity.

"Good grief!" Judson said as he and Sondra thumbed through the photographs. "I would never have believed it of her. Great shots! Really great!"

Of course, when confronted with the photographs, Margaret agreed not to contest the divorce. It was, Judson was sure, her only indiscretion, and he almost felt a bit sorry for her.

As he'd promised, Judson married Sondra. They traveled, they lived, they loved. For six months it was freedom and bliss, and then one day Judson found that he was growing tired of Sondra. As his wife she was not nearly as appealing as she had been as his mistress.

It wasn't that Sondra would ever be *un*appealing; she was nothing like Margaret. It was just that Judson was getting back his old urge to explore. The same thing that had driven Hillary up Mount Everest, he often told himself. So, though married life with Sondra would always be better than bearable, Judson decided to roam.

It was about this time that he noticed the withdrawals from his and Sondra's joint bank account, and it was about this time that the unbelievably buxom redhead moved into the apartment above them. The redhead was adjusting her stockings one day while waiting for the elevator, and Judson was smiling and walking toward her to strike up a conversation, when the terrible suspicion hit him.

He went immediately to see Mr. Polygus.

"What I want to ask," Judson said to Mr. Polygus, as he sat before the bare desk, "is whether your company accepts woman clients."

Mr. Polygus smiled handsomely. "Of course, Mr. Avery. There are as many women who want to be rid of husbands under favorable circumstances as vice versa."

"Then you employ women to do . . . what was done to Margaret?"

"Certainly."

Judson leaned forward, earnest desperation in his voice. "Mr. Polygus, do you ever reveal your clients' names?"

Mr. Polygus looked appropriately shocked.

"My wife, Sondra . . . ?" Judson placed an imploring hand on the edge of the desk.

"But that would be unethical, Mr. Avery."

"Would money make it more ethical?"

"A bribe?"

Judson nodded.

Mr. Polygus shook his head. "I *am* sorry. We have our reputation to consider. We can be hired, but we cannot be bought."

Judson stood angrily. "Now see here, Polygus!"

Mr. Polygus merely shrugged and smiled politely.

As Judson stalked out of the office he slammed the door behind him with shattering force.

Judson went to a lounge he frequented and sat alone at the bar, drinking morosely. He hardly noticed the heavily made-up, attractive blonde four stools down until she smiled alluringly at him in the backbar mirror. She was wearing a low-cut pink dress, and her skirt was hiked up to show a wide expanse of pale thigh where her legs were crossed.

Judson forced himself to turn away from her, his fingers tightening about his glass. Keeping his eyes averted, he finished his drink as quickly as possible. It was, Judson was discovering anew, twice as tempting when it was forbidden.

Pure Rotten

May 25, 7:00 A.M. Telephone call to Clark Forthcue, Forthcue mansion, Long Island:

"Mr. Forthcue, don't talk, listen. Telephone calls can be traced easy, letters can't be. This will be the only telephone call and it will be short. We have your stepdaughter Imogene, who will be referred to in typed correspondence as Pure Rotten, a name that fits a ten-year-old spoiled rich brat like this one. For more information check the old rusty mailbox in front of the deserted Garver farm at the end of Wood Road near your property. Check it tonight. Check it every night. Tell the police or anyone else besides your wife about this and the kid dies. We'll know. We mean business."

Click.

Buzz.

Snatchers, Inc.

May 25

Dear Mr. Forthcue:

Re our previous discussion on Pure Rotten: It will cost you exactly one million dollars for the return of the merchandise unharmed. We have researched and we know this is well within your capabilities. End the agony you and your wife are going through. Give us

your answer by letter. We will check the Garver
mailbox sometime after ten tomorrow evening. Your
letter had better be there.

Sincerely,
A. Snatcher

Snatchers, Inc.
May 26

Mr. Snatcher:
Do not harm Pure Rotten. I have not contacted the
authorities and do not intend to do so. Mrs. Forthcue
and I will follow your instructions faithfully. But your
researchers have made an error. I do not know if one
million dollars is within my capabilities and it will take
me some time to find out. Be assured that you have my
complete cooperation in this matter. Of course if some
harm should come to Pure Rotten, this cooperation
would abruptly cease.

Anxiously,
Clark Forthcue

Dear Mr. Forthcue:
Come off it. We know you can come up with the
million. But in the interest of that cooperation you
mentioned we are willing to come down to $750,000 for
the return of Pure Rotten. It will be a pleasure to get
this item off our hands, *one way or the other.*

Determinedly,
A. Snatcher

Snatchers, Inc.
May 27

Dear Mr. Snatcher:
I write this letter in the quietude of my veranda,
where for the first time in years it is tranquil enough
for me to think clearly, so I trust I am dealing with

this matter correctly. By lowering your original figure by twenty-five percent you have shown yourselves to be reasonable men, with whom an equally reasonable man might negotiate. Three-quarters of a million is, as I am sure you are aware, a substantial sum of money. Even one in my position does not raise that much on short notice without also raising a few eyebrows and some suspicion. Might you consider a lower sum?

Reasonably,
Clark Forthcue

Dear Mr. Forthcue:

Pure Rotten is a perishable item and a great inconvenience to store. In fact, live explosives might be a more manageable commodity for our company to handle. In light of this we accede to your request for a lower figure by dropping our fee to $500,000 delivered immediately. This is our final figure. It would be easier, in fact a pleasure, for us to dispose of this commodity and do business elsewhere.

Still determinedly,
A. Snatcher

Snatchers, Inc.
May 29

Dear Mr. Snatcher:

This latest lowering of your company's demands is further proof that I am dealing with intelligent and realistic individuals.

Of course my wife has been grieving greatly over the loss, however temporary, of Pure Rotten, though with the aid of new furs and jewelry she has recovered from similar griefs. When one marries a woman, as in acquiring a company, one must accept the liabilities along with the assets. With my rapidly improving

nervous condition, and as my own initial grief and
anxiety subside somewhat, I find myself at odds with
my wife and of the opinion that your $500,000 figure is
outrageously high. Think more in terms of tens of
thousands.

Regards,
Clark Forthcue

Forthcue:

Ninety thousand is *it! Final!* By midnight tomorrow
in the Garver mailbox, or Pure Rotten will be disposed
of. You are keeping us in an uncomfortable position
and we don't like it. We are not killers, but we can be.

A. Snatcher

Snatchers, Inc.
May 30

Dear Mr. Snatcher:

Free after many years of the agonizing pain of my
ulcer, I can think quite objectively on this matter.
Though my wife demands that I pay some ransom,
$90,000 is out of the question. I suggest you dispose of
the commodity under discussion as you earlier
intimated you might. After proof of this action, $20,000
will accompany my next letter in the Garver mailbox.
Since I have been honest with you and have not
contacted the authorities, no one, including my wife,
need know the final arrangements of our transaction.

Cordially,
Clark Forthcue

Forthcue:

Are you crazy? This is a human life. We are not
killers. But you are right about one thing—no amount
of money is worth more than your health. Suppose we

return Pure Rotten unharmed tomorrow night? Five thousand dollars for our trouble and silence will be plenty.

A. Snatcher

Snatchers, Inc.
May 31

Dear Mr. Snatcher:

After due reflection I must unequivocally reject your last suggestion and repeat my own suggestion that you dispose of the matter at hand in your own fashion. I see no need for further correspondence in this matter.

Clark Forthcue

Snatchers, Inc.
June 1

Clark Forthcue:

There has been a take over of the bord of Snatchers, Inc. and my too vise presidents who haven't got a choice agree with me, the new president. I have all the carbon copys of Snatchers, Inc. letters to you and all your letters back to us. The law is very seveer with kidnappers and even more seveer with people who want to kill kids.

But the law is not so seveer with kids, in fact will forgive them for almost anything if it is there first ofense. If you don't want these letters given to the police you will leave $500,000 tomorrow night in Garvers old mailbox. I meen it. Small bils is what we want but some fiftys and hundreds will be o.k.

Sinseerly,
Pure Rotten

Autumn Madness

T hings were not going well between Blane and Willa
Winslow, and the same could be said about the situation between the Dixie Stompers and the Gulf Coast
Kings, two teams in the newly formed Southern Pro
Football Conference. Neither team had been able to drive
for a score, both had fumbled in the first quarter, and
several fistfights had broken out between opposing players. The Kings' big lineman, Dale Stover, had been forced
out of the game on the second play with a badly torn liga-
ment. As Blane leaned forward in his vinyl easy chair,
concentrating with all his being on the important third-
down play about to be run, a familiar and ominous form
partially blocked his view. It was his wife Willa.

"There are things to be done around here," she said.
"I think you've watched more than your share of football
tonight." With seeming nonchalance she shifted her
weight so that her ample hip completely blocked the TV
screen just as the ball was snapped.

"Weston gets the ball," the excited voice of Howdy
Curtiss, the network announcer, cried. *"He's hit at the
line, he struggles—oh, he's brought down by a vicious tackle
by Otis Keefer, the middle linebacker of the Stompers!"*

"That had to rearrange his old insides," Jeff "Granite"
Gratowski, the color man, said with a chuckle.

"Get up," Willa said. "I know you heard me."

Blane glared at her. There was no way to make her understand the importance of the game, the profound things it stood for. And this was the network's Terrific Tuesday game, the last one until Monday night's battle between the Colts and the Chargers. That one would be a classic.

"I'll get to the basement and help you during half-time," Blane said firmly. He knew it was wisest not to refuse flatly. Willa had always been intractable, but since she'd become interested in women's liberation she had become almost impossible to deal with. Her once pretty but stern features had molded into mere sternness, the prettiness overpowered by an aggressive glare beneath no longer plucked brows. And last week, after the first meeting she'd attended of FIGHT—the Female Institution for Generally Harder Tactics—she had come home, awakened him from his dozing on the sofa, and told him things were going to change. FIGHT, she explained, was working on the draft of an ultimatum.

Willa stared hard at him, decided this wasn't the time for a showdown, and stalked to the basement door to continue her cleaning. The way she dressed now, she no longer had to change to do heavy work. Her daily uniform was Levi's and a faded sweatshirt, sans bra, of course. Small matter, thought Blane. He noticed a cobweb clinging to the seat of her Levi's as she stamped angrily down the stairs.

"Oh, he's hit hard!" Howdy Curtiss' voice cried. *"He's slow getting up after that one!"* Blane settled back in his chair, feeling the vinyl warming his back.

The red-jerseyed Stompers had to punt from their own ten. Hill, their kicker, sent up a high, hanging punt, affording his team plenty of time to get downfield and avoid a long runback. The man the Kings had back deep to return the punt caught the football, broke one tackle, and was just beginning to hit his stride and pick up some blocking when he collided with two Stompers and was flipped completely into the air before being buried by red jerseys.

"A bone-crushing tackle!" Gratowski said. *"How he held onto that football I'll never know."*

"Sheer courage and determination," Howdy Curtiss observed in a reverent tone.

During an official time-out Blane went to the kitchen to open his fourth bottle of beer. The score was still nothing-nothing and he was nervous. He'd bet even money on the Stompers. Not that he'd bet that much, really. It was more than the money, just a feeling he'd always had that the Stompers were *his* team.

As he loosened the cap on the beer bottle he could hear Willa in the basement, sliding some heavy cardboard boxes over the cement floor. Let her work like a man, Blane thought. He stood behind a counter selling tires all day while she found new ways to antagonize him. It was her job to work on weekends and in the evenings, if she really wanted things to be fifty-fifty. He walked softly back to his chair so she wouldn't hear his footsteps.

"Aggressive as they come," Howdy Curtiss was saying. *"His coach at Western U. said he has the real killer instinct."*

They had to be talking about linebacker Otis Keefer, one of Blane's favorite sports figures. There was no more vicious tackler than Otis Keefer. Blane remembered the close-up on him before the game during the playing of the national anthem—a solemn gum-chewing individual, dark-haired, jut-jawed, not unlike Blane himself, though younger and larger, of course. Keefer had dwarfed the tiny cornerback next to him as they'd stood staring upward at the rippling flag. Pure dedication.

"I think that one put Cardwell out of the game," Gratowski was saying. *"I don't like to second-guess the doctors, but*

I wouldn't be surprised to hear Cardwell had some cracked ribs for his efforts."

Blane saw now what had happened. Keefer had come up fast and hit the Kings' running back Cardwell hard, forcing a fumble, and the Stompers had the ball now on the Kings' forty-eight-yard line.

"We certainly hope he isn't badly hurt," Howdy Curtiss said with concern. *"While we're waiting for Cardwell to be carried from the field there's a shot of the commissioner and his lovely wife to his left. The man on his right is Chuck Hogan, one of the innovators of the moving-zone defense, a fine upstanding American."*

"Blane!" Willa's voice suddenly barked from the basement. "Is it halftime yet?"

Blane pretended not to hear.

"Blane! You answer me!"

Some day he would divorce her. Oh, some day. "Just a time out," Blane called back. He stayed with Willa, he told himself, only for economic reasons. She and her divorce lawyers would milk him drier than a dead cow. There'd be no talk of women's independence then.

"Blane!"

Again he pretended not to hear.

"All right," Howdy Curtiss said in an expectant voice, *"first and ten for the Stompers, the quarterback Gregson calling the signals. He gives the ball to Green—he breaks through! Runs to the Kings' thirty-five where he's knocked out of bounds!"*

Vic Green, the powerful halfback, was another of Blane's favorites.

"You throw me the broom, Blane! It's hanging where you go down the steps!"

Without answering, Blane walked quickly to the basement door and absently tossed the broom down, hearing it hit the basement floor with a clatter.

"Damn you, you almost hit me in the eye!"

"Power running," Gratowski was saying. *"What a punishing runner that Green is!"*

The Stompers tried two passes that were incomplete, then Green plowed into the Kings' line again and picked up five yards. Time out. Fourth and five with seven seconds left in the half. The field goal kicker came onto the field and attempted a field goal into the wind. Blane held his breath.

Partially blocked! Off to the left, the official's signal indicated. Still nothing-nothing.

Blane cursed as the half ended with a gunshot and a drum and bugle corps strutted into camera range with waving flags and pounding drums, forming the outline of a large asparagus on the field as they saluted the canning industry.

Blane felt so bad about the missed field goal he decided to let the halftime intermission slip by without telling Willa, so he could watch the highlights of last week's games. She could do a good enough job cleaning the basement by herself. If she complained he'd ask her how she'd like to sell tires all week.

The game was almost over when Willa marched heavily up from below. A feeling of dread shot through Blane, and he wished she'd waited another few minutes before coming upstairs. The Kings were now ahead on a field goal, three to nothing, but his Stompers had driven down to within five yards of a touchdown on short sideline passes with only twenty-one seconds left in the game.

"Halftime was an hour ago," Willa said with quiet fury. "I heard the band playing."

Blane didn't answer; he stared straight ahead at the TV. He wished with total commitment that Willa would just drop dead.

"I'm talking to you!"

The Stompers were ready for their second-down play. Green ran straight ahead, picked up two yards, then was hauled down by the neck. The Stompers called time out with thirteen seconds left in the game.

"Wait until after the football game, Willa, please!"

"Murderous hitting in the line," Howdy Curtiss exclaimed. *"You can hear the popping up here."*

"I'm talking to you now, Blane!"

"The tight end Smathers was really creamed at the line of scrimmage," Gratowski said.

The Stompers lined up and tried a quick pass over the middle that was knocked down. But the play stopped the clock with nine seconds left. Third down—and three yards from a touchdown and victory.

"You chauvinistic crud!" Willa screamed. "I've had you and your football up to *here!*"

Green tried a running play and was smashed hard to the ground at the one-yard line. Another time out. Three seconds left.

"Do you hear me!"

Time for just one more play. The Stompers decided not to take the field goal and a tie. They'd go for the win!

"Shut up, Willa!"

"That front four just destroyed Green on that last play! Zynowski and Omar Bird brought him down, then Hoyle and Rogers smashed him for good measure."

"I won't shut up!"

The Stompers were lined up. They'd try a running play again with Green. Who else but Green?

"That Zynowski is one of the most hostile and vicious tacklers in the league. A fine football player and a credit to the game on and off the field."

"He almost snapped Green's neck on that last play. But here we go!"

Willa advanced on Blane so that he had to peer around her to see the TV screen. He leaned forward in his chair, his every muscle taut, straining, as the quarterback called the signals.

"Green gets the ball!"

"Blane!" Willa grabbed at his tense shoulder.

Blane saw Green's body lift into the air as it struck a solid line of defensive players and was hurled back and crushed to the ground.

"He doesn't make it!"

"Damn you, Blane!"

"He doesn't make it!"

Blane found himself on his feet, clutching at Willa's faded sweatshirt. "Shut up, Willa! Shut up!" He was shaking her violently. She kicked at his legs, sending a jolt of infuriating pain up one shinbone.

"Green didn't get over! He was thrown back and buried alive by that charging front four!"

"Blane, you're hurting my neck—"

"A bone-crushing tackle!"

The heavy ceramic ashtray in Blane's hand came down again and again on the back of Willa's head—

"A great play!"

Willa's body went limp and Blane stood over her, his lips drawn, his shirtfront and hands covered with blood. Trembling, he dropped the ashtray and stood rigidly with both arms extended straight upward.

Touchdown!

"It'll be a tough battle, but we can win it," Blane's lawyer was saying. "We'll attack their strength, and then when they prepare their defense for our maneuver we'll plead guilty with extenuating circumstances—the old end around."

With his arms folded on the plain wooden tabletop Blane sat staring quietly downward. "Willa was a violent woman. Everybody knew she was a violent woman."

"That's an extra point in our favor."

Slowly Blane lowered his head onto his arms and began to weep, feeling his tears spread into the coarse blue denim of his prison shirt. The lawyer didn't know what he was talking about; he didn't really understand the game. Blane knew the officials were determined that he should have the major penalty. And it was useless to argue with officials.

Understanding Electricity

G listening with chrome and tinted glass, the headquarters of the Powacky Valley Light and Power Company soared needle-like fifty stories heavenward, as if taunting the lightning. In the building's top floor were the spacious ultramodern offices of the company's top executives, and in a tasteful outer office sat the moderately attractive, though impeccably groomed, Miss Knickelsworth. She smiled with her impeccably white teeth, lighting up her whole mouth if not her face and unchanging wide brown eyes, and said, "Mr. Appleton from out of town is already in the conference room, Mr. Bolt."

B. Bainbridge Bolt, president of Powacky Valley Light and Power, revealed his own capped dentures, nodded, and strode briskly past her and through a tall doorway. He was the "human dynamo"-type executive in image and action, and was proud to think of himself as such.

Behind Bolt, Elleson of Public Relations entered the office with a PR smile for Miss Knickelsworth as he strode through the tall doorway.

Five minutes later young Ivers, regional vice president and renowned hard charger, went into the conference room. The smile he flashed on Miss Knickelsworth was his bachelor's best, but she responded with the blank expression that had earned her the company title of "Miss Resistor" two years running.

Grossner of Advertising followed Ivers in, then old Stabler of Customer Relations, who was something of a fixture with the company. The tall doors were silently closed on the outer office wherein sat Miss Knickelsworth, and after orderly hellos and introductions the immaculately attired, somehow similar men all sat down at a long tinted-glass conference table with gleaming chrome legs and trim. The table matched the glass-and-metallic decor of the large room. Everyone had his accustomed place at the long table but for Appleton from out of town, who remained where he'd been sitting at ease in his chrome-armed chair at the opposite end of the table from B. Bainbridge Bolt, who cleared his throat and drew a slip of paper from his attaché case.

With a nod to Appleton from out of town, Bolt said, "There is some business to be discussed before we get on to Mr. Appleton's investigation of yesterday's five o'clock power failure . . . if Mr. Appleton agrees."

"Surely," Appleton said, nodding ever so slightly his handsome head of flawlessly combed graying hair.

"We have something of a public relations problem," Bolt went on, "concerning our last raise in the rates for electricity. Let me read you this note that arrived in the morning mail."

He placed gold-rimmed reading glasses on the narrow bridge of his nose and glanced commandingly at each man. The note read:

> *Gentlemen:*
>
> *I was shocked by your letter stating that my monthly bill was ten days past due. At your current rates, I'm afraid that you find me a little short. However, I do believe ten days is rather a brief period of neglect and that it does not behoove a com-*

*pany of your stature to conduct yourself in such a
negative manner. In farewell, I regretfully must
fuse and refuse to send your requested remittance,
and as another futile outlet for my frustration I
have wired my congressman direct.*

Tired of plugging away,
A. C. McCord

Bolt lowered the slip of paper, sat back, and sipped on
a glass of juice from the silver tray Miss Knickelsworth
had left on the table.

After a pause, Stabler of Customer Relations said,
"The work of a madman in its phrasing, but other than
that it seems the usual sort of letter we receive."

"There's one other difference," Bolt said dramatically.
"This is a suicide note."

"That should solve part of our problem right there,"
young Ivers said. "Especially since this McCord was obviously unbalanced when he wrote such a letter."

"How did he commit suicide?" Stabler asked.

"He wrote and mailed this note yesterday," Bolt said,
resting his large clean palms on the metal table trim. "He
left a carbon copy in his home; then, during our Karl and
Karla Killowatt commercial before the five o'clock news
yesterday afternoon, he pulled his radio into the water in
his bathtub with him."

Grossner of Advertising looked concerned.

Bolt sat unnaturally still, as if waiting for something.

"Wait a minute!" young Ivers said. "Is this McCord—"

"Still alive." Bolt finished the sentence without a question mark.

"Of course!" Elleson said. "The power failure at five
yesterday! It must have coincided with his pulling the
radio into the tub with him."

"Almost," Bolt said. "McCord was found stunned, in a
state of shock, but still alive. He'd also left a message for

a reporter friend, explaining what he was going to do, and his story was written up in the papers for tonight's late edition."

"But the man's obviously a maniac," Ivers said.

"Remember," Grossner cautioned, "our last rate increase was legal but not what an uneducated public would call ethical."

"They were notified of the public hearings," Ivers said, referring to the public notices in the newspapers that Elleson and Grossner had cleverly worded for maximum confusion.

"There were the necessary three people at the meeting," Elleson said. "The vote constituted a majority."

"No one is arguing the legality of the last increase," Bolt said sharply, to stop that area of discussion. "That and the subject of this meeting are poles apart. What we have here is a problem in maintaining some rapport with the public, and I've taken some steps to insulate us from any critical comment."

"If the story will be printed showing us in an unfavorable light," Ivers said, "it seems that the cat is already out of the bag."

"What I have done," B. Bainbridge Bolt said, "is change the nature of the cat."

Elleson the PR man nodded approvingly, though he resented not being consulted on the matter. Appleton from out of town chuckled softly.

"We have taken space in both daily newspapers to remark on the silver-lining-in-every-cloud aspect of a power failure saving a life." Bolt paused.

"There's a switch," Ives said brightly.

"Excellent," Elleson said admiringly, but he wondered if it was.

"Agreed," Grossner said, "but won't it also draw further attention to the incident?"

"To continue," Bolt cut them off reprovingly, having

successfully sprung one of his little conversational traps, "we will then explain how Powacky Valley Light and Power is generously paying for the would-be suicide victim's complete recovery."

"Great!" Grossner said. "Really sock it to 'em!"

"I believe we will have gone full circuit," Bolt said smugly, "transformed a lemon into lemonade."

Everyone laughed as always at the familiar lemon analogy.

"But how do we know he *will* recover?" Ivers asked. "People who unsuccessfully attempt suicide usually try again."

Bolt shrugged. "Doesn't matter. The whole thing will be out of the public's collective mind in a week or so. This McCord ought to stay alive that long. Right now he's confined in the psychiatric ward at State Hospital at our expense, undergoing electrotherapy treatment."

"Can you be sure of that?" Appleton from out of town said.

"Of course," B. Bainbridge Bolt said.

Appleton smiled indulgently. "I mean, what if he escaped? What if he somehow made his way here, to Powacky Valley Headquarters?"

"I get it," Grossner said. "He could do something drastic—generate some tremendous adverse publicity."

"Not only drastic," Appleton said, "but fantastically daring and grand."

Bolt squinted at Appleton. Several throats were cleared.

"Security isn't very tight here," Appleton said. "An imaginative man could find out things, make his way to the top."

Bolt leaned forward in his chair and cocked his head. "You're not—"

"Correct," Appleton from out of town said. "A. C. McCord, at your service."

Ivers' eyes widened. "But . . . where's Appleton?"

"Tangled up in some high-voltage lines, actually," McCord said, placing a small black box on the table. He smiled. "I took the liberty of attaching some wires to the table and chairs," he said, "so together you can all experience with me, one of your many customers, the unpleasant sensation of being overcharged," and he pressed a button on the box.

"Watt now?" Miss Knickelsworth asked herself in the outer office, as her electric typewriter suddenly went dead.

Discount Fare

Milner hurried through the bustling terminal building, clutching his scuffed brown two-suiter suitcase. Around him fellow travelers were striding purposefully in the same direction, some of them carrying attaché cases or carry-on garment bags. A nasal voice on the airport's public-address system droned on in the background announcing departing and arriving flights.

As Milner approached the Small World Airways reservation counter, he was glad to see that there was only a short line. The trip to New York on business had come up unexpectedly, and his secretary had phoned for his reservation. He had only to pick up his boarding pass, check his luggage, and walk to the departure gate on the lower concourse.

The line moved quickly, and when Milner reached the counter a blue-vested SWA reservations clerk smiled prettily at him. He smiled back and told her his name and that he had a reservation.

After punching some buttons and scanning the screen of a small gray computer, the girl glanced up at him, no longer smiling.

"This line is for full-fare passengers, sir. I'm afraid you'll have to join that line." She pointed to a long line at the other end of the counter.

"Don't I have a full-fare ticket? My secretary made the reservation."

"You have our Small World Airways Cheap-Chargers Six-City discount ticket, sir."

"Well, couldn't I—"

"I'm sorry, sir, it's too late to change your reservation. The flight leaves in twenty minutes."

A small man with a sharply receding hairline and mild blue eyes, Milner knew from experience that he wasn't the persuasive type. Besides, there was no time to argue. He nodded to the girl and joined the longer line.

Milner found himself standing behind a heavyset woman carrying a child of about three. The child—Milner couldn't be sure of its sex—glared over the woman's shoulder at him with absolute hostility.

Ten minutes later, when Milner was halfway to the counter, the child spat at him. Milner backed up a step and looked around to see if anyone else had witnessed this extraordinary breach of etiquette. When he turned back he found that a large man carrying a black sample case had crowded into line ahead of him. Milner cursed silently but said nothing.

Finally, he reached the counter. A squat woman with acne and a huge nose soberly filled out his boarding pass.

"I have one suitcase to check," Milner told her.

"Discount-fare passengers must carry on luggage under twenty-four by seven by twenty inches," she informed him, squinting over the counter at his suitcase.

"I've never measured—"

"You'll have to carry that one on with you, sir." She handed him his boarding pass.

"But I've always checked this suitcase."

"Gate twenty-nine," she said.

An elbow jabbed into Milner's ribs and he was forced aside. He lifted his suitcase and began walking toward the gate.

302

When he reached the departure gate, he was surprised to see that there were few people in line waiting to board the plane. He handed his boarding pass to the attendant to process. He was not asked for a seat preference. Careful to avoid the fat woman with the hateful child, he joined the line several passengers behind her.

When they boarded the plane, Milner saw that the first-class and full-fare passengers had already boarded and were drinking complimentary cocktails. The plane was going to be full. A sign proclaimed that the rear of the plane was where discount-fare passengers were to sit. There was a mild scramble for seats. Milner found himself beside the fat woman with the malevolent child.

"I'm sorry," she said as the child kicked Milner. "He's a problem, Damon is. Probably always will be."

"I hope not," Milner told her, and fastened his seatbelt.

His suitcase wouldn't quite fit beneath the seat, and when he pointed this out to a stewardess she informed him that he would have to hold it on his lap.

"I thought that was against safety regulations," Milner said.

"The regulations have been waived for discount-fare passengers, sir," she said, hurrying off.

It would only be for a few hours, Milner assured himself, squeezing the heavy suitcase onto his lap, then he would be off the plane and in the comparatively courteous atmosphere of a New York taxi. The plane took off smoothly. A small clenched fist began to beat on Milner's suitcase as if it were a drum.

Shortly after they reached cruising altitude, the stewardesses began rolling their service tray along the aisle as they handed out SWA lunches and beverages. Milner watched the two attractive women bend gracefully and smile, not once spilling a drop of coffee or soda.

By the time they reached the tail section, the plane was

flying through rough air. Milner could feel every bump against the firm upholstery, his body compressed by the heavy suitcase. A stewardess handed him a watercress sandwich and a bag of cheese snacks. This didn't look at all like the food served to the full-fare passengers.

"I'll have a cup of coffee," Milner told the stewardess. She poured it dutifully and handed Milner the scalding paper cup. "That will be one dollar."

Milner looked up at her in surprise, balancing the lunch and the hot cup on his suitcase. "I thought meals were complimentary."

"They are, sir, but not the beverages—for discount-fare passengers."

Milner contorted himself beneath his burden and extracted a dollar from his wallet.

When the stewardess had gone, he looked at his meal. At least the lettuce in the sandwich was fresh. He'd skipped lunch, so he was hungry enough to settle for anything. He peered closely. There was a small bear-shaped cookie floating in his coffee. As he watched, the hot liquid disintegrated it.

Milner ate the sandwich and cheese snacks but skipped the coffee. Next to him a tiny voice began to complain about the missing cookie.

When they'd been airborne for over an hour, the captain's voice came over the speaker system announcing that they would soon put down in Pittsburgh and that the weather there was fine.

Pittsburgh? Milner was going to New York! He began signaling frantically for the stewardess, who was adjusting the seat of a full-fare passenger. Pinned as he was in his own seat, Milner waved both arms and a leg violently until the stewardess glanced in his direction. A mustached man across the aisle shook his head and pretended to read a paperback novel, obviously disdainful of Milner.

When the petite blond stewardess arrived, Milner asked why they were landing in Pittsburgh.

She arched her elongated, penciled eyebrows. "Why, it's our destination, sir."

"But I'm going to New York. My ticket says New York!"

She produced an SWA smile. "Yes, sir. But there's a two-hour layover in Pittsburgh."

"My ticket doesn't say that!"

"It must, sir."

Shifting the weight of his suitcase, Milner withdrew his ticket and examined it. The stewardess was right.

"Full-fare passengers are booked on the through flight to New York, sir. All discount-fare passengers change planes at Pittsburgh."

"But I don't *want* to stop at Pittsburgh!"

She looked at him oddly—"I'm sorry, sir"—and moved smartly up the aisle.

"I have to be in New York before three o'clock," Milner said to the woman beside him. "On business."

She nodded unconcernedly. The child in her lap glared at Milner.

The plane flew through a sharp downdraft and the tail section lurched crazily, its motion exaggerated by its distance from the wings. Milner had forgotten about his coffee. The now-icy liquid spilled over his suitcase and down onto his pants. He was wearing a new suit, and the coffee would stain unless he could dilute it with water. Milner reached beneath the sopping suitcase and worked to unbuckle his seatbelt. He attempted to smile at the woman but couldn't. "Pardon me," he said, "I have to go to the rest room."

She stared ahead as if he'd suggested something vulgar.

When his seatbelt was unbuckled, he tried to swivel in his seat so he could stand and in the process drove a corner of the suitcase into Damon's chubby side. Finally upright in the aisle, Milner bent forward to apologize. That was when Damon grabbed a ball-point pen from Milner's pocket and plunged it into Milner's left ear.

Milner retrieved his pen and, his hand clamped to his wounded ear, teetered to the rear of the plane.

Inside the cold confining rest room, he forgot about toweling the stain from his pants. The ringing in his horribly aching ear was maddening, causing him occasionally to shudder.

Pittsburgh! He didn't want to go to Pittsburgh!

Methodically, hardly conscious of what he was doing, he unwrapped several of the small bars of soap and held them under the water until they'd soaked and welded into one another. Then, with fingers possessed, he began to mold them into the shape of a gun.

When the gun was finished he let it dry to firmness, then slipped it into his suitcoat pocket. If he covered it with a handkerchief it would seem real enough.

He left the rest room and made his way toward the blond stewardess, who was standing near the door to the pilot's compartment. A few of the full-fare passengers glanced at him as he went by.

"This is a gun," he said softly to the stewardess. He saw her eyes widen, fooled by the carefully molded contour beneath the white handkerchief. "Into the pilot's compartment," he commanded.

"What is this?" the pilot asked as they entered. He'd been reading a news magazine while occasionally checking the automatic pilot. "Regulations forbid anyone unauthorized in the cockpit."

"He's got a gun," the stewardess whispered.

The co-pilot, who had been idly toying with an unlighted cigarette, glanced around quickly and began to stand.

"Steady, Harry," the pilot said. Harry settled back down in his seat. "What do you want?" the pilot asked.

The ringing in Milner's ear was almost gone now but it was of higher pitch. "We're going where I say."

"Cuba?"

"New York. And not Newark Airport. LaGuardia. It costs a fortune to take a cab from Newark."

"But you have a connecting flight to New York from Pittsburgh," the stewardess said impatiently.

"Change course," Milner told the pilot, who nodded resignedly.

The plane banked sharply and began its turn.

The stewardess stumbled into Milner and the co-pilot stood up and grabbed at the gun. As the two men struggled, the soap flew out from between them onto the floor beneath the co-pilot's seat. The stewardess and the pilot scrambled for it. The stewardess found it, straightened, and tried to point it at Milner, but it slipped from her grasp.

"It's not a real gun!" the pilot cried, and, standing, he struck Milner with his fist. Milner sank to the cockpit floor and pretended to be unconscious.

"The controls!" the co-pilot said in alarm. "We're losing altitude!"

"There's no cause for concern," the pilot said. "I can set us down."

There was a hurried conference between the pilot, co-pilot, and stewardess, and Milner could hear the passengers in a turmoil on the other side of the closed door. The stewardess went out to calm them.

"We're having mechanical difficulties," she said in an almost-cheerful voice, "but don't worry. Our captain is going to land the plane on the Monongahela River."

"I'll put her down so gently you'll hardly know it," the pilot broke in over the speaker system.

There was near-panic among the passengers as they felt the plane descend. Seizing the moment, Milner crept from the pilot's compartment and lost himself among the frightened passengers. Then suddenly, as smoothly as the pilot had promised, the plane was down. There had been only an unexpected series of jolts.

"Don't be alarmed," the pilot advised the passengers. "The aircraft will float long enough for everyone to disembark through the emergency exits." Indeed, passengers were already disembarking as Milner felt the cold waters of the Monongahela lap at his shins.

Making himself as inconspicuous as possible, he stood and got into line for what was so far a remarkably calm and orderly deplaning. Once away from the plane, he would make his escape and somehow try to make amends for his temporary madness.

The blond stewardess was standing alongside the nearest emergency door, directing people as they left the plane. The cold water was now above Milner's knees.

He reached the door. The stewardess had a bump on her forehead and her eyes were slightly glazed. She was in mild shock, Milner imagined, and didn't recognize him when she moved him aside with her arm and said, "Full-fare passengers deplane first in emergency procedures, sir." As the water rose, people rushed quickly past Milner and out the door.

"Full-fare passengers deplane first," the stewardess repeated as the water rose faster.

When the water was nearly to Milner's neck, the stewardess announced "Full-fare passengers first" for the final time, and she swam out the door with a flick of her shapely ankles.

Milner tried to protest, but the icy water reached his mouth, his nose, and swirled over his head.

As the aircraft settled nose up on the bottom of the Monongahela River, Milner's body sank slowly to the rear of the plane.

Close Calls

S he wasn't supposed to die. She had no life insurance, no liquid assets to speak of, no really solid reason to be dead. Yet there she lay, looking, Graham Hopper thought, rather smug about the whole thing. It was so like her.

And here was Graham, now a widower—middle-aged and getting older by the minute—with little cash, very dim prospects, and a voracious mortgage payment. The future seemed an abyss.

His wife Adelle had done this to him—Adelle, along with Martin Marwood. It was their fault that Graham was about to attend a funeral that should never be taking place.

It was one of the most miserable affairs Graham had ever endured. The preacher was garrulous. A chilling light rain fell throughout and the mourners were forced to stand about the grave in a virtual swamp. It took Graham hours to shake his depression.

Then he went directly to see Martin Marwood at Close Calls, Incorporated.

Close Calls was on the sixteenth floor of the Belmont Building downtown. Ostensibly it was a telephone-solicitation company that did seasonal work, but Graham knew better. Close Calls had been very discreetly recommended to him three months ago by a very close friend. Some friend!

At the sixteenth floor, Graham stepped from the nervous elevator and walked down a long gray hall lined with office doors. From behind some of the doors came the rhythmic clatter of electric typewriters. Near the end of the hall Graham saw the wood door with its frosted glass panel on which was lettered CLOSE CALLS, INC. WE COMMUNICATE. Graham cursed under his breath as he entered.

There was no one in the small plainly furnished anteroom. Graham pressed a button as directed by a hand-printed sign, a buzzer sounded, and after a moment Marwood himself opened the door to his inner office and peered out.

Marwood was a small man, neatly if flashily dressed in a muted plaid blue suit that must have been tailor-made. He had a professionally cheerful blunt-featured face, a receding hairline, and deep-set electric dark eyes. "Hey," he said, grinning as if nothing were wrong, "Mr. Hopper."

"You bet your business," Graham said.

Marwood appeared puzzled. "I don't follow."

"You muffed it," Graham said with controlled anger. "You killed my wife as dead as the Edsel."

"Oh, that," Marwood said. "Come into the office and we'll talk about it."

He led the way into his large office, plainly furnished as if for efficiency like the anteroom. No high overhead here, the office seemed to say—more for your dollar. Marwood sat behind a cluttered steel desk and motioned Graham toward a high-backed padded chair nearby. Graham shook his head and remained standing. The faded green walls of the office were restful, their framed dime-store prints perfectly aligned. A window air-conditioner emitted a soothing hum. Graham refused to be soothed.

"Now what's this about your wife?" Marwood asked, making a neat pink tent with his fingers.

"My wife is dead."

Marwood appeared perplexed, and then his potatoish features expressed comprehension. "Say, that's right, Graham—may I call you Graham?—I remember reading the operative's report yesterday. Your wife stepped directly into the path of a speeding car. A hit-and-run, I'm afraid."

Graham felt the room becoming warmer. "But the car was supposed to barely miss her," he said in exasperation. "That's the service Close Calls is supposed to render. Adelle was to be badly shaken so she'd think hard about dying and transfer some of her assets into my name and take out a large life insurance policy. As it stands, I can't touch the business, and Adelle had no insurance. You've reduced me to poverty."

"Hey, Graham, I'm sorry." Marwood began to doodle with a gold pen on a small writing pad. Graham saw that he was sketching intricate little mazes. "But you're not exactly poverty-stricken," Marwood said. "In cases like these, Close Calls does refund half the fee."

"Half?"

"That's five-thousand dollars, Graham. Nothing to scorn."

"But nothing to what I've lost!" Graham almost shouted. "Lost because of your incompetence!"

"Don't say incompetence," Marwood implored in a hurt tone. "Ninety-nine percent of our clients are more than satisfied. You are unfortunately one of the other one percent. Hey, nothing is perfect. I assure you I feel as badly about your wife as you do."

"But you profited from her death. I lost."

"Consider the squirrel," Marwood said.

Graham was dumbfounded. "Squirrel?"

"Yes. Have you ever noticed what happens when a

squirrel runs out into the street and finds itself in the path of an oncoming car? The squirrel freezes, Graham, then usually it runs away from the car. But occasionally it darts directly beneath the car's wheels. It's a reflex action, a sort of death wish. Well, people are sometimes like squirrels. People are unpredictable. That's what happened, Graham. Your wife froze, then ran the wrong way, directly into the path of the car that was supposed to barely miss her. There are off days in this business when things like that happen, which is the reason we have certain built-in safeguards."

"Safeguards?"

"Sure, Graham. Like recordings of all conversations that take place in this office. I mean, hey, let's be candid, guy, you can't very well go to the police. You're implicated, guilty of second-degree murder." Marwood was sketching rows of barred windows on the pad.

Graham sighed deeply, and stood in the center of the office with his hands in his pockets. "I'm not a stupid man, Marwood. I've taken all this into consideration."

Marwood touched the point of the gold pen to his chin. "Have you?"

"We're both guilty of murder. And you have a profitable business to lose. I'd say the police are out of this entirely."

Marwood smiled and began to doodle again, crossing out the bars on the windows. "I'm glad you realize that, Graham."

"And I understand what you mean about one accident occurring out of a hundred successful close calls. That's inevitable."

Marwood's smile stretched even wider. "It's nice to know you've been listening to me."

"And you can keep my entire fee, for all I care. In my position—which is bankruptcy—the money would simply be devoured by my creditors anyway."

"Vultures," Marwood agreed, but a glint of uneasiness had kindled in his dark eyes.

"All that's left for me, really," Graham said, "is revenge. Or, to be more specific, poetic justice."

Marwood had stopped smiling, but he was still confident. "You should know, Graham, that upon my death certain records will immediately be brought to light. It's another necessary safeguard."

Graham shrugged. "Oh, I'm prepared to place my fate in the hands of chance—both of our fates, in fact."

Marwood began to doodle frantically. "I don't follow."

"One time out of a hundred," Graham reiterated, "something goes wrong. But is it going to be the first time, or the hundredth?"

"There's no way to know," Marwood said, deftly marking out a neat pattern of question marks.

Graham removed the gun from his pocket.

Marwood glanced up just in time to see the flash of the muzzle. He was too stunned to scream as the gun roared and the bullet went snapping past his right ear with a sound like a cracking whip. He lifted a hand to his head incredulously, turned, and stared, horrified at the ugly bullet hole in the green plaster behind his desk. If he had happened to incline his head to the right a fraction of an inch at the moment of the shot . . .

"One," Graham said simply, replacing the gun in his pocket. "Think about the next ninety-nine. Consider the squirrel."

He walked to the door and opened it, then, before leaving, he turned.

"Take care," he said to Marwood.

One Man's Manual

There are experiences that change men's lives, and David Blout was sure that he'd undergone such an experience when he turned the last page of *Triumph Through Toughness*. He'd begun the book after dinner, lying on the sofa with his shoes off, his stereo turned to high so that the sound of his popular-music tapes permeated the small tenth-floor apartment.

But within five minutes Blout became oblivious to the pulsating music, so engrossed was he in *Triumph Through Toughness*, advertised as "the indispensable manual for the realistic rising businessman." Here was a book Blout could sink his teeth into, chew, and digest. The author, Sternn Moxie, a successful real-estate broker, was a man much like Blout wanted to become—moneyed, hard-driving, pragmatic, a man on top, on the very apex. And in straightforward language Sternn Moxie through his book was telling Blout how to emulate that success. And Blout was listening.

Five loud evenly spaced knocks on the apartment door broke through Blout's reverie like muffled gunshots. Blout placed the book on the coffee table and went to the door.

His neighbor in 10-D, Sam Milquist, was standing in

the hall preparing to knock again. As the door swung inward, Milquist's upraised fist opened like a rose and he lowered his arm. He was about Blout's age, thirty-six, but shorter, with defeated blue eyes. He was balding and apparently putting up no struggle against middle-aged fat.

"Your stereo," he said to Blout, his round tentatively smiling face gleaming with beads of perspiration. "I'd appreciate it if you'd turn it down. It's late and I have to get up early tomorrow for work. . . ."

"Sure," Blout said curtly, and shut the door. He didn't want trouble with his neighbors, but he was tired of Milquist's complaints about his music.

But when he stood before the stereo, Blout's hand stopped a few inches from the volume-control knob. Did Milquist think he was in charge of the tenth floor? Blout paid his rent. He had as much right to live as he pleased as Milquist. More, maybe, considering he'd been a tenant longer.

Turning his back on the still-blaring stereo, Blout went back to the sofa and picked up his book. He thumbed through the pages to Section Three, "Victory Through Intimidation—The Art of Instilling Fear."

Blout read it over again to the rhythmic blasting of the stereo. There were no more knocks on the door. His faith in Sternn Moxie's book expanded.

When he finally went to bed, Blout marveled at how fate was favoring him. *Triumph Through Toughness* couldn't have entered his life at a more advantageous time. He was in the running for the new southeast district manager's job at Colfarr Container. The company's higher-ups were observing both Blout and Will Tremain, trying to determine which of the two men would be best for the managerial job. The incline to success was slippery, with room for only a select few. It was rumored that the man not chosen for the job would get the ax, with the economy what it was. But Blout was suddenly confident now that the job would be his.

"Morning," Will Tremain said to Blout the next day on the elevator.

Blout didn't answer him. Let him stew. Let him begin to wonder just how important he really was.

When the two men left the elevator, Blout was pleased to notice the faintly puzzled expression on Tremain's blandly pleasant features. Sternn Moxie had described that expression (Chap. 2) as the first sign that a rival had been knocked off balance.

At lunchtime that day Blout waited until it was almost time for Tremain to return before leaving himself. He went to the restaurant where Tremain usually ate, walked past his rival's table with a casual wave of his hand, and took a table in the more expensive dining room beyond, where Tremain could see him. Blout ordered a martini and sat sipping it, glancing now and then at his watch as if waiting for someone. He knew Tremain had a 1:30 appointment and would soon have to leave, not knowing for whom Blout was waiting. And when Tremain was gone, Blout would cross back to the lower-rate dining room and order a sandwich.

But apparently Tremain hadn't read Sternn Moxie's best-seller. He rose from his chair and walked toward Blout, smiling. Blout was careful not to return the smile.

"David," Tremain said through his widening smile, "who are you waiting for?"

"Oh. A friend . . ."

"Listen, you didn't speak to me in the elevator this morning. I hope nothing's wrong."

"No, Will, I guess I just didn't hear you."

This wouldn't do! Tremain was standing and Blout was sitting. Blout stood up, holding his drink.

316

"You leaving?"

"Afraid so."

Blout made a point of staring at Tremain's tie, on which there was a gravy spot. Tremain seemed not to notice, or not to care.

"What about your friend?"

"He'll have to make it some other time," Blout said, finishing his drink. "See you back at the office."

Blout left the restaurant ahead of Tremain, and they walked to where Blout had been careful to park next to Tremain's car. Blout's was a newer car, recently waxed. Without a word to Tremain, Blout got into his shining sedan and drove from the parking lot. He was glad his car was royal blue—a power color.

When Blout reached his apartment door that evening, tired and not in the best humor, Sam Milquist stepped from his adjoining apartment, buttoning his wrinkled suitcoat. He gave Blout a self-conscious sideways glance and hurried toward the elevator.

"Milquist," Blout said, so softly that he might not have spoken.

By the time Milquist had turned, Blout was stepping inside his apartment and shutting the door, feeling better.

That night Blout again studied Section Three of *Triumph Through Toughness,* marveling anew at its simplicity and practicality. Eventually Tremain would have to be affected by the techniques Blout was applying. Sternn Moxie was careful to point out (Chap. 6) that certain types sometimes took longer to break.

But in the meantime the situation annoyed Blout. When he heard the muted sounds of Sam Milquist's return, he turned up the volume on his stereo. A doormat like Milquist was living proof (if you wanted to call that living) that the book's techniques worked. Basically, Tremain was a sensitive, quiet sort like Milquist. Deep inside they were all the same (Chap. 4). Blout went to sleep that night confident that time was all he needed to accomplish his goal.

He got the opportunity to try more of Section Three's techniques the next day in Tremain's office, where the regional general manager was going to give the two candidates instructions for a dual research project. Ostensibly the assignment was to reduce by half the possibility of human error, but Blout knew that the man who turned in the most impressive report would in all likelihood secure the new Southeast Division managerial position.

The regional manager was late for the meeting, and Blout politely refused Tremain's invitation to sit down. Instead he paced slowly, almost absently, glancing down at a sharp angle from time to time at the seated Tremain.

Tremain seemed unconcerned, completely at ease. "I understand," he said, "we're to examine ways to increase the bursting test strength of the new heavy-duty container without adding to production costs."

"I can think of several possibilities offhand," Blout said—so softly that Tremain would have to strain to hear.

"Speak up, will you, Dave?" Tremain said amiably.

The man was maddening! Blout felt a cold rage—he wanted Tremain to hate him, to be afraid of him!

When the regional general manager, an imposing gray-haired man named Rogers, came into the office, Blout treated him with respect but at the same time in a manner that made it plain that he, Blout, felt that he was Rogers' equal (Chap. 9). Rogers seemed not to notice.

The bursting test reports were what was required. All through Rogers' instructions Blout kept his "dominant glare" trained on Tremain, whose bland features registered more puzzlement than submissiveness.

318

"Blout," Rogers said suddenly, "are you listening?"

"Yes, sir! Certainly!" Blout countered. It was difficult to concentrate on both the dominant glare and what Rogers was saying. Just as he'd feared. Not enough practice before the mirror. And Tremain was smiling—at least he seemed to be smiling. Frustration grabbed like a claw at Blout's stomach. He took work home that night.

Most of the evening his thoughts were concentrated on cardboard thicknesses, corrugation patterns, cubic inches, and stress factors. Finally, he decided that the answer was to reduce the size of the side cardboard flaps while increasing that of the end flaps. According to Engineering, that was possible.

When his eyes began to ache from studying fine print and his head throbbed with a dull but persistent pain, Blout set aside his work and lay down to relax to his favorite music. But he kept thinking of Tremain, the imperturbable, infuriatingly unconcerned Tremain.

The knocking on the door couldn't overpower the beating bass rhythm that pulsed like a mad heartbeat through the apartment. Blout ignored the knocking with a certain pleasure.

But he couldn't ignore the telephone. Cursing, he rose from the sofa on the sixth ring and plucked the receiver from its cradle, disgusted with himself when he heard Sam Milquist's diffident voice on the line.

"Mr. Blout, you didn't answer my knock. Please, you've got to turn down the music. I have to sleep . . . I'm under a great strain . . . My entire family isn't well. My brother's in the hospital . . ."

Blout became encouraged by the cringing quality in Milquist's voice. Sternn Moxie's methods certainly worked on him. Milquist seemed not only respectful but in petrified fear of Blout.

"I'm not interested in your family problems or in who's in the hospital," Blout said testily.

"I don't expect you to be. But the noise . . ."

"Oh, all right, Milquist, I'll turn it down." This was the "agree and anger" ploy (Chap. 7). Blout replaced the receiver without saying good-bye and returned to stretch out again on the sofa, the stereo volume unchanged. The apartment manager was on vacation, and Milquist didn't have the nerve to phone the police.

Blout fell asleep on the sofa.

He awoke at four A.M. with the stereo still blaring; it had automatically replayed dozens of times the last cassette he'd inserted, "Drummers Wild." Milquist hadn't phoned again—or if he had, Blout hadn't heard him.

By chance, Blout and Milquist were alone in the descending elevator in the morning. Milquist appeared unhealthy, with dark circles under his sad eyes and a waxy pallor to his face. He refused to look at Blout, who never averted his gaze from him. Blout knew there was nothing to fear from Milquist physically; the Milquists, the Tremains, of this world were simply not the sort capable of physical violence except in their fantasies (Chap. 8). The real world belonged to the fearless, the takers, and Blout was one of those.

Milquist was an interesting and therapeutic exercise for Blout, but it was Tremain who was important—and he somehow refused to become intimidated by Blout's techniques.

Later that week, the evening before the bursting test reports were due, Blout worked late at Colfarr Container, and when everyone else on his floor had left he used a plastic credit card to let himself into Tremain's office. His breathing was loud, like escaping steam, and his heart pounded with an exhilarating rhythm as he searched Tremain's desk. This was "reasonable reconnaissance" (Chap. 5), and Blout knew that Tremain would have surreptitiously entered his, Blout's, office if he had had the nerve. Crime paid, and the clever and audacious collected.

Blout found the bursting test report in a middle drawer. He scanned it quickly. Tremain's solution to the container problem was the use of a different type of glue on the flaps and a rougher-textured cardboard. It was a more economical solution than Blout's—costs would actually be cut.

After only a second's hesitation, Blout carried the lengthy, complex report to his own office, altered a few figures, then returned it to Tremain's desk drawer.

Blout returned home in a cheerful frame of mind that night. He practiced his dominant glare before the medicine-cabinet mirror for a while, then decided to have dinner out. After a shower, he changed into casual clothes and left the apartment, leaving his stereo playing to discourage burglars.

The next day Rogers informed Blout that the Southeast District manager's job was his. Rogers shook Blout's hand. He treated him as an equal. Section Three had proved prophetic.

Tremain seemed philosophical about the selection, his disappointment held in careful check. Blout didn't feel sorry for him; the weak were unworthy of pity. Sometime in their lives they had made a conscious or unconscious choice to be as they were. They were the necessary casualties over which men like Blout climbed to eminence.

Blout seldom drank to excess, but that night he had cause for celebration. Near his apartment there was a dim but respectable lounge where he'd stopped a few times with friends. Tonight he drank there alone, and not until he made his unsteady way home did he realize he'd drunk too much.

There was something brittle—broken glass?—on the

321

hall carpet outside his apartment door, Blout noticed, when he inserted his key in the lock on the third try.

Once inside, Blout was startled out of his alcoholic daze. The handworked cabinet of his expensive stereo system was splintered, smashed. Cracked tape cassettes were strewn about the floor. The imported turntable lay bent like a junkyard tin-can lid. Blout swayed, clenched his fists, stared unbelievingly.

"It was the only way I had left," an apologetic voice said behind him.

Blout turned away from the wreckage of his stereo to see Sam Milquist sitting rigidly on the edge of the sofa, his hands folded in his lap.

"I didn't want this," Milquist continued. "I'm not a violent person . . . but I'm not well. Schizophrenia runs in my family. You made me afraid of you, made me hate you, forced me to resort to this. . . ."

The alcohol Blout had drunk suddenly turned sour in his stomach, and the black bile of anger rose, choking him. He took a heavy, deliberate step toward the seated Milquist. "You little marshmallow, you'll pay for this!" he cried. "By God, you'll pay!"

"I'm afraid *you'll* pay," Milquist corrected him politely in a firm voice not at all like his own. Smiling jauntily, he stood and raised the emergency fire ax he'd taken from the shattered glass case in the hall.

Blout stood gaping at his set intense face, at the long-handled ax as it descended, parting the air with the dread whisper of impending death. And in that instant of incredible calm, he remembered the layman's term for schizophrenia—split personality—and he wondered what Sternn Moxie would have to say about this.

Mail Order

Angela lay quite still. I watched her sleep. About her blond-streaked locks wound the black lace contraption that was supposed to protect her hairdo as she slept. An elastic chin strap was relentlessly working to keep her double chin from growing. Dark eyeshades covered the upper part of her face to keep the morning sun from waking her prematurely. I knew that beneath the special Thermo-weave blanket was an intricately designed sleeping bra the purpose of which was to preserve her bosomy uplift. At the foot of the bed a wire framework beneath the covers lifted them tentlike eighteen inches above the mattress to prevent them from causing pressure on the toes that would lead to ingrown toenails and later serious foot problems. Lying open across Angela's softly heaving chest was the latest Happy House mail-order catalog, its colorful pages riffling gently in the soft breeze from the air-conditioning vent near the bed.

Angela was a mail-order maniac. Almost every day some item featured in one of dozens of catalogs we regularly received would find its way into our mailbox or onto our front porch, while the checking account struggled for survival.

I had talked to her, explained to her, argued violently with her. What was the use? Like many other women, her mail-order addiction was too strong for her. The miniature watermelon plants, the inflatable picnic plates, the battery-heated ice cream scoops, and countless similar mail-order items continued to pour into our household. Angela was incurable and I was slowly being driven mad.

The electric scent dispenser that emitted a pleasant-smelling antiseptic spray every fifteen minutes hissed at me from my dresser as I bent down to lift the Happy House catalog from Angela's sleeping form. Through some cross-up in the mail due to our having moved three times during the past two and a half years, this Happy House catalog that had arrived two weeks ago was the only one we'd received during that time.

I don't know if you've ever seen what happens when you haven't ordered from one of these catalogs for a long time, but they become quite adamant that you should continue to buy from them. This one contained a particularly strong through typical warning printed on the back cover with our family name typed in to make it seem more personal—or more ominous.

"Final warning:" it was very officially headed. *"It comes to our attention,* Mr. and Mrs. Crane, *that you haven't ordered from our catalog for the past two years. This is to warn you that we must have an order of at least five dollars from the* Crane *family NOW in order to maintain your account. Remember,* Mr. and Mrs. Crane, *this is your last chance—it's up to you!"*

As I was lifting the catalog lightly, the doorbell rang, and I lowered the open pages again onto Angela and crossed the room to climb into my pants. Almost midnight, I noticed with a glance at the imported family-crest clock as I tried to locate my slippers. I didn't know who could be on the porch, but I hoped they'd refrain from punching the doorbell again before I could reach the door. Even through her special sleep-aid earplugs the sound of the loud bell might wake Angela. As I straightened and buckled my belt I almost struck my head on the portable TV aerial attachment that allowed clear, free reception in any weather, then I hurried from the bedroom and down the hall to the front door, my slipper soles padding noisily across the carpet.

Just as I reached the foyer the bell clanged again, and I angrily flipped the night latch and opened the door.

They were in uniform. One of them carried a flashlight that he shone onto a little notepad as if double-checking the address.

"Mr. Harold Crane?" the tall one asked. He was trim and broad-shouldered, with clean anonymous features and short-cropped hair. His partner with the flashlight was much shorter, heavyset, with a blank moon face and long blond hair that stuck out from beneath his high-peaked black uniform cap. In fact, their uniforms were completely black; they wore gloves and black leather jackets with insignia on the shoulders.

"I'm he," I said, rubbing my eyes. I'd been sleeping on the sofa before going into the bedroom and my mind was still sluggish.

"Come with us, please," the taller man said in a clipped but pleasant voice.

In the moonlight I saw the initials P.D. on the short man's shoulder patch. "Are you police . . . ? Come with you . . . ?"

Both men took me gently by the upper arms and I was led toward a small dark-colored van parked at the curb in front of my lawn.

"Just cooperate, please," the round-faced blond one said, lagging behind for a moment to close the front door softly behind us.

"Now, wait a minute . . . !" But the van doors were open and I was pushed gently inside. The two men climbed in behind me and closed the doors. The tall one tapped on a partition with his gloved knuckles and the van pulled away.

"I'm not even dressed!" I objected. I was wearing only my pants, slippers, and pajama top.

Neither man answered me, or even looked directly at me, only sat on either side of me on the low bench as the van sped through the dark streets.

We drove for almost an hour, and gradually my eyes became accustomed to the dim light in the van. I studied the uniform of the man on my left. He wore two shoulder patches on his black leather jacket, one of them a red circle with the yellow P.D. initials that I'd noticed earlier, and below the circle a blue triangular patch containing a white cloud and the initials H.H. I studied the black square-toed boots, the brass studwork designs on their glossy outer sides. I didn't have to be told that the P.D. on the patches didn't stand for "Police Department" as had originally run through my sleep-filled mind. I wasn't sleepy now.

"A kidnapping?" I asked incredulously. "You must have the wrong victim."

No answer.

"You'll find out," I said. "It's a mistake. . . ."

"No mistake, Mr. Crane," the tall one said without looking at me.

The van suddenly braked to a smooth halt. I could hear the crunching of footsteps on gravel as the driver got out and walked to the rear of the van. The van was opened and I was led quickly into what looked like a motel room, though in the darkness it was hard to tell. The closing of the room's door cut short the high trilling of crickets. The van driver, whose features I had never clearly seen, stayed outside.

The inside of the room was neat and impersonal, clean and modern with a small kitchenette. I was led to the kitchenette table and both men forced me down into a chair. The tall one sat opposite me across the small table while the pudgy blond one remained standing uncomfortably close to me.

"I'm Walter," the tall man said. "My partner's name is Martin."

"And you're not police," I said, braving it out despite my fear. "Just who the hell are you?"

"Police . . . ?" Walter arched an eyebrow quizzically at me from across the table. "Oh, yes, the P.D. on our shoulder patches. That stands for 'Persuasion Department,' Mr. Crane. We're from Happy House."

"Happy House? The mail-order company?"

Walter nodded with a smile. There would have been a suavity about him but for the muscularity that lurked beneath the shoulders of his leather uniform jacket. "We're one of the biggest in the country."

"In the world," Martin corrected beside me.

"This is absurd!" I said with a nervous laugh that sounded forced.

Martin pulled a large suitcase from beneath the table and opened it on the floor.

"Our records show it's been almost two years since your last order, Mr. Crane," Walter said solemnly.

"Actually it's my wife . . ."

Walter raised a large silencing hand. "Didn't you receive our final warning notice?"

"Warning . . . ?"

"Concerning the infrequency of your orders."

"He knows what you're talking about," Martin said impatiently.

"Yes," Walter agreed, "I think he does. What's been the problem, Mr. Crane?"

"No problem, really . . ."

"But a problem to Happy House, Mr. Crane," Walter politely pointed out. "You see, our object is for our organization and our customers to be happy with our merchandise. And if we don't sell to our customers that's not possible, is it?"

"Put that way, no . . ."

"Put simply," Walter said, "since Happy House has to make a profit through volume to be able to keep on offering quality merchandise at bargain prices, in a way each customer's happiness is directly related to each other customer's continuing willingness to order from us."

"In a sense, I suppose that's true. . . ."

"Here, Mr. Crane." Walter placed a long sheet of finely typed white paper on the table before me.

I stared at him. "What's that?"

"An order blank," he answered.

"Since you've been hesitant to order from our catalog," Martin said, "we thought you might be more enthusiastic if we showed you the actual merchandise." From the suitcase on the floor he drew a flat red plaster plaque and set it on the table.

"What is it?" I asked, looking at the black sticklike symbols on the plaque.

"Why, it's your name, Mr. Crane. Your name in Japanese. A real conversation piece."

"Perhaps you missed it in our catalog," Walter said. "Only nine ninety-nine."

"No, thanks," I said, and I didn't even see Walter's gloved hand until the backs of the knuckles struck me on the jaw. I rose half out of my chair in rage only to be forced back down by the unbelievable pain of Martin digging his fingers skillfully into jangling nerve endings in the side of my neck.

"Of course, you don't *have* to order the plaque," Walter said, smiling and laying a ball-point pen before me.

I picked up the pen and checked the tiny box alongside the plaque's description on the order form. Martin's paralyzing grip on my neck was immediately loosened.

Martin bent again over the large suitcase and came up with a coiled red wire with tiny brass clips on each end. "Everyone needs one of these," he said.

"I bought the plaque with my name in Japanese," I pleaded.

Walter smiled at me and began to pound his right fist into the palm of his left hand.

"I'll take it," I said, "whatever it is."

"It's a Recepto-booster," Martin explained. "You hook one clamp onto the aerial of your transistor radio, the other end you clamp onto your ear. Your entire body becomes a huge antenna for your portable radio."

"Only five ninety-nine," Walter said. "Two for ten dollars."

"I'll take two," I said, checking the appropriate box on the order form—but not any too happily.

"I thought you'd be receptive to that." Walter smiled.

A gigantic red-handled scissors with one saw-toothed blade was placed on the table next. "Our Jumbo Magi-Coated Lifetime All-Purpose Garden Shears," Martin said. "The deluxe chrome-plated model. You can cut or saw, trim grass or hedges, snip through inch-thick branches. Never needs sharpening. Twenty-nine ninety-nine."

"Twenty-nine ninety-nine!"

Walter appeared hurt. "It's made of quality steel, Mr. Crane." The back of his hand lashed across my cheek and I was the one who was hurt. This time I did not try to rise. I checked the order form.

The gigantic scissors was followed by inflatable rubber shoes over three feet long for walking on lake surfaces, an electric sinus mask, a urinal-shaped stein bearing the words "For The World's Biggest Beer Drinker," tiny battery-operated windshield wipers for eyeglasses, finger-tip hot pads for eating toast . . . I decided I needed them all.

"Excellent," Walter said, smiling beneath his black uniform cap. "This will make the organization happy, and since we're part of the organization we'll be happy. And you, Mr. Crane, as one of our regular customers back in the fold, you'll be happier, too."

I didn't feel happy at all, and indignation again began to seep through my fear.

"He doesn't look happy," Martin said, but Walter ignored him.

"Mr. Crane, I'm sure you'll feel better after you sign to make the order legal and binding," Walter said, motioning with a curt nod toward the ball-point pen.

"Better than if he doesn't sign," Martin remarked.

"But he will sign," Walter said firmly.

The sureness in his voice brought up the anger in me. "I won't sign anything," I said. "This is preposterous!"

"What about this?" Walter said, and with the flash of a silver blade severed the tip of the little finger of my left hand.

I stared down with disbelief and remoteness, as if it were someone else's hand on the table.

"This is our imported Hunter's Hatcha-Knife," Walter was saying, holding up the broad-bladed gleaming instrument. "It can be used for anything from scaling fish to cutting firewood." He wiped the blade with a white handkerchief, slipped the Hatcha-Knife back beneath his jacket, and tossed the handkerchief over my finger. Martin picked up the fingertip itself and dropped it into a small plastic bag as if it were something precious to him. He poked it into a zippered jacket pocket.

I held the wadded handkerchief about my left hand, feeling the dull throb that surprisingly took the place of pain. There was also surprisingly little blood.

"I'm sure Mr. Crane will sign the order form now," Walter said, picking up the pen and holding it toward me.

I signed.

"Now, how much money do you propose to put down?" Walter asked, and I felt Martin remove my wallet from my hip pocket. I only sat staring at Walter, trying to believe what had happened.

"Twenty-seven dollars," Martin said, returning my empty wallet to my pocket.

Walter turned the signed order form toward him and entered the $27 against the $210.90 that I owed.

Martin gathered all the merchandise I'd purchased and dumped it back into the suitcase.

"So you can carry everything, we'll throw in as a bonus our Traveler's Pal crushproof suitcase," Walter said.

As I stared at him blankly I heard myself thank him— I actually thanked him!

"I'm sure Mr. Crane will be a satisfied regular customer we can count on," Walter said. "I'm sure we can expect an order from him . . . oh, let's say at least three times a year."

"At the very least," Martin agreed, helping me to my feet.

The ride home in the van was a replay of the first ride, and it seemed like only seconds had passed when I was left standing before my house with my heavily laden Traveler's Pal suitcase. Gripping the wadded handkerchief in place tightly with the fingers of my left hand, I watched the twin taillights of the van draw together and disappear as they turned a distant dark corner.

As I walked up the sidewalk past the trimmed hedges toward my front door I tried to absorb what had happened, to turn it some way in my mind so I could understand it. Had it really happened? Had it been a dream, or somebody's idea of a bloody, macabre joke? Or had it been just what it seemed—the unprovable, ultimate hard sell?

331

I knew I'd never find out for sure, and that whether or not Walter and Martin had really been from Happy House, the mail-order company could expect my regular orders for the rest of my life.

The Traveler's Pal suitcase heavy in my right hand, I entered the house and trudged into the bedroom, a deep ache beginning to throb up my left arm.

There was Angela, still sleeping in blissful unawareness with her eyeshades and sleep-aid earplugs. The Happy House catalog was lying on her chest where I'd left it, the pages riffling gently in the soft breeze from the air-conditioning vent.

Angela didn't stir as I dropped the suitcase on the floor and the latches sprang open to reveal the assortment of inane merchandise I'd bought. The loud sob that broke from my throat startled me as I stared down at the contents of the suitcase. It was all so useless—all of it!

Except for the Jumbo Magi-Coated Lifetime All-Purpose Garden Shears. Oh, I had a use for them!

JOHN LUTZ: A CHECKLIST

COMPILED BY FRANCIS M. NEVINS, JR.

I. NOVELS

The Truth of the Matter. Pocket Books pb #75654, 1971; no British edition.

Buyer Beware. Putnam, 1976; Robert Hale, 1977. First paperback: Paperjacks pb #0398, 1986. Nudger.

Bonegrinder. Putnam, 1977; Robert Hale, 1979. First paperback: Berkley pb #04606, 1980. Sheriff Billy Wintone.

Lazarus Man. Morrow, 1979; New English Library, 1980. First paperback: Berkley pb #04544, 1980.

Jericho Man. Morrow, 1980; no British edition. First paperback: Berkley pb #05003, 1981.

The Shadow Man. Morrow, 1981; no British edition. First paperback: Berkley pb #05399, 1982.

Exiled! (as Steven Greene). Fawcett Popular Library pb #07400, 1982; no British edition.

The Eye (by Bill Pronzini and John Lutz). Mysterious Press, 1984; no British edition. First paperback: Mysterious Press pb #40294, 1986.

Nightlines. St. Martin's Press, 1984; Macmillan (London), 1986. First paperback: Tor pb #50648, 1987. Nudger.

The Right to Sing the Blues. St. Martin's Press, 1986; no
British edition. First paperback: Tor, 1987. Nudger.
Tropical Heat. Henry Holt, 1986; Macmillan (London),
1987. First paperback: Avon pb #70309, 1987. Fred
Carver.
Ride the Lightning. St. Martin's Press, 1987; no British
edition. First paperback: Tor, 1988. Nudger.
Scorcher. Henry Holt, 1987. Fred Carver.

II. SHORT STORIES IN MAGAZINES

Alfred Hitchcock's Mystery Magazine

12/66   THIEVES' HONOR. (*Coffin Corner,* ed. Alfred
Hitchcock, 1969.)

8/67   A RARE BIRD. (*Let It All Bleed Out,* ed.
Alfred Hitchcock, 1973.)

9/67   *THE EXPLOSIVES EXPERT. *Rolling
Gravestones,* ed. Alfred Hitchcock, 1971;
*Alfred Hitchcock's Anthology #3: Tales to
Make Your Blood Run Cold,* ed. Eleanor
Sullivan, 1978; *The Arbor House Treasury of
Horror and the Supernatural,* ed. Bill
Pronzini, Barry N. Malzberg, and Martin
H. Greenberg, 1981.)

1/68   DEAD, YOU KNOW. (*Alfred Hitchcock's
Anthology #16: A Choice of Evils,* ed. Elana
Lore, 1983.)

3/68   THE MIDNIGHT TRAIN. *Coffin Break,* ed.
Alfred Hitchcock, 1974.)

4/68   FAIR SHAKE. (*This One Will Kill You,* ed.
Alfred Hitchcock, 1971.)

7/68   THE CREATOR OF SPUD MORAN.

*Note: Starred stories are included in this collection

9/68	*NO SMALL PROBLEM. (*Alfred Hitchcock's Anthology #18: Crimewatch,* ed. Cathleen Jordan, 1984.)
2/69	OBEDIENCE SCHOOL. (*Happy Deathday!,* ed. Alfred Hitchcock, 1972.)
3/69	ONE WAY. (*I Am Curious (Bloody),* ed. Alfred Hitchcock, 1971.)
5/69	THE WEAPON. (*Alfred Hitchcock's Anthology #19: Grave Suspicions,* ed. Cathleen Jordan, 1984.)
7/69	*HAND OF FATE.
11/69	DOOM SIGNAL. (*Behind the Death Ball,* ed. Alfred Hitchcock, 1974.)
11/70	TWO BY TWO.
5/71	THE FINAL REEL. (*Bleeding Hearts,* ed. Alfred Hitchcock, 1974.)
6/71	GARDEN OF DREAMS.
7/71	PROSPECTUS ON DEATH.
8/71	MURDER MALIGNANT.
9/71	THEFT IS MY PROFESSION.
10/71	*THE DAY OF THE PICNIC. (*Murder-Go-Round,* ed. Alfred Hitchcock, 1978.)
11/71	FRIENDLY HAL.
12/71	*GAMES FOR ADULTS. (*Alfred Hitchcock's Anthology #4: Tales to Scare You Stiff,* ed. Eleanor Sullivan, 1978; *The Best of Mystery,* ed. Alfred Hitchcock, 1980.)
1/72	*IN MEMORY OF . . .
3/72	THE VERY BEST. (*Alfred Hitchcock's Anthology #17: Mortal Errors,* ed. Cathleen Jordan, 1983.)
4/72	WITHIN THE LAW. (*Alfred Hitchcock's Anthology #6: Tales To Be Read With Caution,* ed. Eleanor Sullivan, 1979.)

5/72   LIVING ALL ALONE. (*Alfred Hitchcock's Anthology #10: Tales To Make You Weak in the Knees,* ed. Eleanor Sullivan, 1981.)

6/72   *FRACTIONS.

6/73   SHADOWS EVERYWHERE.

7/73   OBJECTIVE MIRROR.

8/73   KING OF THE WORLD. (*Alfred Hitchcock's Anthology #9: Tales to Make Your Hair Stand on End,* ed. Eleanor Sullivan, 1981.)

2/74   THE LEMON DRINK QUEEN.

3/74   *DEAD MAN. (*Alfred Hitchcock's Anthology #21: Words of Prey,* ed. Lois Adams & Gail Hayden, 1986.)

5/74   GREEN DEATH.

7/74   *THE BUTCHER, THE BAKER.

8/74   ALL OF A SUDDEN. (*Alfred Hitchcock's Anthology #8: Tales To Make Your Teeth Chatter,* ed. Eleanor Sullivan, 1980.)

10/74   ARM OF THE LAW.

3/75   IT COULD HAPPEN TO YOU. (*Miniature Mysteries,* ed. Isaac Asimov, Martin H. Greenberg, and Joseph D. Olander, 1981.)

4/75   *MAIL ORDER. (*Best Detective Stories of the Year,* ed. Edward D. Hoch, 1976.)

6/75   YOU AND THE MUSIC. (*Death on Arrival,* ed. Alfred Hitchcock, 1979.)

9/75   *UNDERSTANDING ELECTRICITY. (*Alfred Hitchcock's Anthology #22: A Mystery by the Tale,* ed. Cathleen Jordan, 1986.)

1/76   WONDER WORLD.

8/76   HAVE YOU EVER SEEN THIS WOMAN? (*Alfred Hitchcock's Anthology #2: Tales To Take Your Breath Away,* ed. Eleanor Sullivan, 1976; *Rogues' Gallery,* ed. Alfred Hitchcock, 1978; *Alfred Hitchcock's Tales of Terror,* ed. Eleanor Sullivan, 1986.)

9/76	NOT A HOME.
3/77	*ONE MAN'S MANUAL.
6/77	MISSING PERSONNEL.
10/77	EXPLOSIVE CARGO.
11/77	*SOMETHING FOR THE DARK.
2/78	THE MAN IN THE MORGUE. (Nudger.)
4/78	WHERE IS, AS IS.
7/78	MARKED DOWN.
10/78	CHEESEBURGER. (By Bill Pronzini, John Lutz, and Barry N. Malzberg, as John Barry Williams.)
11/78	*CLOSE CALLS.
12/78	PAST PERFECT.
2/79	DANGEROUS GAME.
3/79	*THE MUSIC FROM DOWNSTAIRS.
4/79	*DISCOUNT FARE.
8/79	WHERE IS HARRY BEAL? (Nudger.)
10/79	FRANTICMAN.
1/30/80	*UNTIL YOU ARE DEAD.
3/26/80	A GLIMPSE OF EVIL.
7/16/80	THAT KIND OF WORLD. (Sheriff Billy Wintone.)
12/15/80	WHEN OPPORTUNITY KNOCKS.
1/7/81	DOUBLE MURDER.
9/16/81	*DEAR DORIE.
3/3/82	THE CASE OF THE CANINE ACCOMPLICE.
6/82	TIME EXPOSURE. (Nudger.)
8/82	*BURIED TREASURE.
11/82	WHAT YOU DON'T KNOW CAN HURT YOU. (Nudger.)
5/83	THE RIGHT TO SING THE BLUES. (Nudger.) (Later expanded into the novel *The Right to Sing the Blues.*)
10/83	ONLY ONE WAY TO LAND. (Nudger.)
1/85	RIDE THE LIGHTNING. (Nudger.) (*The Year's Best Mystery and Suspense Stories,* ed.

Edward D. Hoch, 1986.) (Later expanded
into the novel *Ride the Lightning.*)

10/85   *TRICKLE DOWN.

CAVALIER

1972?   IN THE BLOOD. (Note: Lutz sold this story to
Cavalier late in 1971 but we have not been
able to determine whether it was published
under this or any other title.)

CHARLIE CHAN MYSTERY MAGAZINE

2/74   FIGURE IN FLIGHT.
5/74   A VERDICT OF DEATH.

87TH PRECINCT MYSTERY MAGAZINE

5/75   MOON CHILDREN.
6/75   LEASE ON LIFE.
6/75   PERSONALIZED COPY. (As Elwin Strange.)
8/75   LIFE SENTENCE.
8/75   MEN WITH MOTIVES.

ELLERY QUEEN'S MYSTERY MAGAZINE

8/67   QUID PRO QUO.
9/68   *THE INSOMNIACS CLUB. (*Ellery Queen's
Anthology #24,* 1972; *Cops and Capers,* ed.
Ellery Queen, 1977; *Ellery Queen's Mystery
Stories #1,* 1979.)
6/71   *THE REAL SHAPE OF THE COAST. (*Ellery
Queen's Mystery Bag,* ed. Ellery Queen,
1972; *Masterpieces of Mystery, Vol. 17: The
Seventies,* ed. Ellery Queen, 1979; *The Arbor
House Treasury of Mystery and Suspense,* ed.

Bill Pronzini, Barry N. Malzberg, and
Martin H. Greenberg, 1981; *Top Fantasy,*
ed. Josh Pachter, 1985.)

11/72 *AUTUMN MADNESS.

8/73 *THE SHOOTING OF CURLY DAN. (*Ellery Queen's
Murdercade,* ed. Ellery Queen, 1975;
Midnight Specials, ed. Bill Pronzini, 1977.)

1/78 *SOMETHING LIKE MURDER. (*Ellery Queen's
Anthology #45: Eyewitnesses,* 1982.)

5/78 IN BY THE TENTH.

10/78 *THE OTHER RUNNER. (*Circumstantial
Evidence,* ed. Ellery Queen, 1980.)

1/1/81 *MORTAL COMBAT.

3/24/82 *THE LANDSCAPE OF DREAMS. (*Child's Play,* ed.
Marcia Muller and Bill Pronzini, 1984.)

9/82 *DEEPER AND DEEPER.

9/84 *THE SECOND SHOT.

9/85 HEAT.

ESPIONAGE

12/84 WINDS OF CHANGE.

2/85 TWICE REMOVED.

8/85 ON JUDGMENT DAY.

THE EXECUTIONER MYSTERY MAGAZINE

4/75 GOING, GOING.

6/75 THE LEDGE WALKER.

6/75 NEXT TO THE WOMAN FROM DES MOINES. (As
Paul Shepptarton.)

6/75 THE ORGANIZATION MAN. (As Elwin Strange.)

6/75 ROOM 33. (As Van McCloud.)

6/75 DAY OF EVIL. (As John Bennett.)

8/75 HIS HONOR THE MAYOR.

GALAXY

6/68   BOOTH 13. (*Dark Sins, Dark Dreams,* ed. Barry N. Malzberg and Bill Pronzini, 1978.)

KNIGHT

?   ONE FOR ALL. (Note: Lutz sold this story to *Knight* in the early 1970s but we have not been able to determine whether it was published under this or any other title.)

THE MAN FROM U.N.C.L.E. MYSTERY MAGAZINE

11/67   THE CROOKED PICTURE. (*Mike Shayne's 1973 Annual; Tricks and Treats,* ed. Joe Gores and Bill Pronzini, 1976; *101 Mystery Stories,* ed. Bill Pronzini and Martin H. Greenberg, 1986.)

MIKE SHAYNE MYSTERY MAGAZINE

4/68	DEATH ON THE SILVER SCREEN.
10/68	ABRIDGED.
11/68	KING OF THE KENNEL.
11/72	A KILLER FOILED.
3/73	SO YOUNG, SO FAIR, SO DEAD.
10/73	THE BASEMENT ROOM.
5/74	A PRIVATE, RESTFUL PLACE.
6/74	DAY SHIFT.
9/74	A HANDGUN FOR PROTECTION.
12/74	THE OTHER SIDE OF REASON.
2/75	REST ASSURED.
7/75	THE CLARION CALL.

7/76   NOT JUST A NUMBER.
8/77   *PURE ROTTEN. (*Miniature Mysteries,* ed. Isaac Asimov, Martin H. Greenberg and Joseph D. Olander, 1981.)
11–12/77   DEATH BY THE NUMBERS.
11/80   TOUGH.
7/81   THE BEAR COTTAGE.
12/82   THE RETURN OF D.B. COOPER.
2/84   SPLIT PERSONALITIES.
6/85   THE LAST TO KNOW.
8/85   HECTOR GOMEZ PROVIDES.

MYSTERY

9/81   TIGER, TIGER. (By Bill Pronzini and John Lutz.)

MYSTERY SCENE

9/86   *ON GUARD.

NEW BLACK MASK

#8(1987)   FLOTSAM AND JETSAM.

THE SAINT MYSTERY MAGAZINE

6/84   *HIGH STAKES. (*The Year's Best Mystery and Suspense Stories,* ed. Edward D. Hoch, 1985.)

SIGNATURE

8/67   *BIG GAME.
11/67   *THE WOUNDED TIGER. (*Alfred Hitchcock's Mystery Magazine,* 5/21/80.)

SWANK

1968?   SPORTING BLOOD. (Note: Lutz sold this story
to *Swank* late in 1967 but we have not been
able to determine whether it was published
under this or any other title.)

1971?   DEATH FOR SALE. (Note: Lutz sold this story
to *Swank* in 1970 but we have been unable
to determine whether it was published
under this or any other title.)

TV FACT

9–10/71   CASE OF THE DEAD GOSSIP. (As Tom Collins.)
(Serialized in four parts, from the issue of
Sept. 26–Oct. 2 to the issue of Oct. 17–23.)

WOMAN'S WORLD

10/28/86   SHORT SHRIFT.

III. SHORT STORIES PUBLISHED ORIGINALLY IN ANTHOLOGIES

1981   WRIGGLE. (In *Creature!,* ed. Bill Pronzini.)
1984   ALL BUSINESS. (In *Ellery Queen's Prime
Crimes 2,* ed. Eleanor Sullivan and Karen
A. Prince.)
1984   TYPOGRAPHICAL ERROR. (Nudger.) (In *The
Eyes Have It,* ed. Robert J. Randisi.)
1986   THE THUNDER OF GUILT. (Nudger.) (In *Mean
Streets,* ed. Robert J. Randisi.)

IV. ARTICLES

THE WRITER

104064

(Credits continued from page iv.)

Mystery Magazine, September 1981); DEAD MAN (*Alfred Hitchcock's Mystery Magazine,* March 1974); GAMES FOR ADULTS (*Alfred Hitchcock's Mystery Magazine,* December 1971); THE BUTCHER, THE BAKER (*Alfred Hitchcock's Mystery Magazine,* July 1974); NO SMALL PROBLEM (*Alfred Hitchcock's Mystery Magazine,* September 1968); DEEPER AND DEEPER (*Ellery Queen's Mystery Magazine,* September 1982); ON GUARD (*Mystery Scene,* September 1986); FRACTIONS (*Alfred Hitchcock's Mystery Magazine,* June 1972); PURE ROTTEN (*Mike Shayne Mystery Magazine,* August 1977); AUTUMN MADNESS (*Ellery Queen's Mystery Magazine,* November 1972); UNDERSTANDING ELECTRICITY (*Alfred Hitchcock's Mystery Magazine,* September 1975); DISCOUNT FARE (*Alfred Hitchcock's Mystery Magazine,* April 1979); CLOSE CALLS (*Alfred Hitchcock's Mystery Magazine,* November 1978); ONE MAN'S MANUAL (*Alfred Hitchcock's Mystery Magazine,* March 1977); MAIL ORDER (*Alfred Hitchcock's Mystery Magazine,* April 1975); JOHN LUTZ: A CHECKLIST (by Francis M. Nevins, Jr.).

347